STRENGTH

To Natalie

AMY DAWS

Copyright © 2018 Amy Daws

All rights reserved.

Published by: Amy Daws, LLC

ISBN-13: 978-1-944565-22-0
ISBN-10: 1-944565-22-1

Editing: Stephanie Rose
Formatting: Champagne Book Design
Cover Design: Amy Daws

This book is licensed for personal enjoyment only. No part of this book may be reproduced in any form, or by any electronic or mechanical means, including information storage and retrieval systems, without written permission from the author. The only exception is by quoting short excerpts in a review. If you're reading this book and did not purchase it, please go to www.amydawsauthor.com to find where you can purchase a copy. Thank you for respecting the hard work of this author.

This book is a work of fiction. Names, characters, places, and incidents are products of the author's imagination or are used fictitiously. Any resemblance to actual persons, living or dead, events, or locales is entirely coincidental.

Author's Note

This book was originally entitled *That One Moment*. It was featured as book five in my London Lovers Series and inspired The Harris Brothers Series spinoff. I received many messages from readers saying they didn't realise the Harris Brothers' sister had a book already. So, after much consideration, I rebranded *That One Moment* to fit with the Harris Brothers look and feel.

Strength is the original story, *That One Moment*, with new, never before published scenes and epilogues. I hope you enjoy the story of Vi Harris and Hayden Clarke.

Dedicated to my readers who love to go where I take them.

PROLOGUE

Hayden

EVERY MOMENT IN LIFE HAS A RIPPLE.

Every day has twenty-four hours.

That's one thousand, four hundred forty different chances per day that can affect the course of your life.

Watching a ripple that you caused and immediately wishing you could take it back is a devastatingly powerless feeling. You have to sit there and witness it grow and spread, like an infection.

And once it starts, there's not much you can do to change its path or pattern of movement.

Unless, of course, you decide to make a splash.

Challenger

Hayden

"**H**AYDEN CLARKE. GOOD TO SEE YOU AGAIN." DOC RISES FROM behind his desk and extends his hand to me. He's a tall, robust man with a grey beard. Dressed in khaki trousers and a navy jumper, he is the perfect cliché shrink.

I give him a firm, confident shake, trying to portray my entire state of mind with one simple gesture. "Hiya, Doc."

"Please sit. I've been looking forward to this appointment for weeks." He gestures to one of the maroon leather armchairs and takes the one seated directly across from it.

I drop down onto the familiar seat and rest my ankle on my knee. "You probably say that to all your patients."

"I wish I could, Hayden. I wish I could." Instead of grabbing his notepad like he normally does, he crosses his arms over his chest and eyes me speculatively. "Tell me, how are you feeling with your one-year anniversary approaching?"

He dives right in. Every time. "I'm feeling fine. I'm focusing on preparing my speech for the charity gala, as you well know."

"Yes, that's right. Are you still confident about speaking? It's a sensitive subject matter." He cocks his head to the side like he can see the answer if he looks at me hard enough.

Glimpses of the night I wish like hell I could forget flash through my mind. I straighten my posture and mindlessly touch my brown leather cuffs on each of my wrists. "Definitely confident. I can handle it," I answer pragmatically.

A look of fondness lights up his features. "I think it will be a big turning point for you, Hayden. I really do."

"That's sort of the point." I release the cuffs and rub my hands down my denim-clad thighs. "I'm ready to get on with my life. The last few days, I can't seem to stop thinking about the days leading up to that night."

He nods thoughtfully. "That is expected given that the anniversary is only days away. What are you doing to continue progressing in your recovery beyond the charity gala? Who are you spending your days with?"

I shrug my shoulders and frown. "Leslie, Theo, and Baby Marisa mostly."

His brows arch. "Anyone outside of your family?"

I clench my jaw because he's asking a question he already knows the answer to and it irks me. "Not really. I help out with the baby a lot, and I'm back working with my brother again. We're busy." The truth is I don't have many friends left after spending the last four years drinking my life away. *And eventually trying to take my life.*

"Any word from Reyna?"

My eyes cloud over at the mention of her name. "She texts occasionally. I don't really engage much with her."

He simply nods and I let out an exasperated laugh. "We've already established that she's not a good friend for me to lean on. Now you want me to go out and make new friends? How am I supposed to know what kind of friends are safe?" I challenge him.

"Hayden, it's not about making friends. It's about putting yourself out there. There are lots of people you can converse with who wouldn't be anything like what Reyna was to you. I'm just noticing a pattern here. You've lived with your brother, his fiancée, and their new baby for three months now. You don't appear to be showing an effort to intermingle with people outside of your family, to become a part of society once again."

"I disagree with you," I jeer, slicing my hand through my hair. "I'm getting up in front of hundreds of people to tell my entire bloody story. That seems like the definition of putting myself out there."

Doc smirks and nods again, which only further frustrates me. I stand up and stride over to the window to gaze down at the busy west end London traffic. A red double-decker bus full of tourists passes by. I'd give anything to be out there as a foreigner on holiday and oblivious to the shit that goes on in here.

"So, what then? You don't think my speech will be much of a challenge?" I snap, looking over my shoulder at him.

"I didn't say that." He sighs heavily and narrows his eyes at me, obviously gauging my temper.

"I'm reading between the lines." I like Doc because he doesn't bullshit me, but I get tired of having to find all the answers myself. Him questioning my recovery makes me feel insecure at a time when I'm desperate to prove to everyone that I'm not the same person. "Come on now. Out with it, Doc. Tell me one thing that would be more challenging."

"Look, Hayden. You've done the twelve steps. You've told your story in group therapy. You're staying clean. These are all good things, so let's focus on them."

I walk back to my seat. "Don't hold back on me now, Doc. Come on! Challenge me," I dare, tossing my hands out wide as I sit down. I always did love a challenge.

He shrugs his shoulders like he expected my reaction. "What if I asked you to tell your story to a single person? Not a room full of others in therapy. Not a ballroom full of people. Not a family member or close friend. Rather, an acquaintance. Telling your story to an audience full of strangers is one thing. But finding someone whom you can sit down with, look in the eyes, and tell your story to is another completely. The point is you would not just be talking at them. You'd be engaging with them. They'd likely have questions and comments, and you'd have to field them all with an open mind."

"And you think that's the ultimate challenge," I scoff arrogantly but feel a churning in my abdomen over the idea.

Doc shrugs. "You said you've been recalling the days leading up to your attempt?"

"Yeah," I reply, grimacing at where he's going with this.

"All right. Let's try this. Find one person and tell them about the five days you experienced leading up to your attempt. Be honest. Be open. Be vulnerable. It will be difficult and it will pull you back to that time, but getting it out will be the ultimate test to your recovery. We'll call it the Countdown Challenge."

"Bloody hell," I snap. "I thought that's why I am doing my big gala speech. To test myself. To push my recovery."

"You're doing that speech for many reasons, Hayden—one of which is for your family. It is a benefit they began for you after all. But both of these challenges will push you in different ways." He pauses, scratching his beard as he attempts to collect his thoughts. "Let me ask you this. Do you remember how important Leslie felt to you the day she found you?"

I nod, wincing at the flashback that blasts through my mind's eye.

"She was important because you didn't know her well. She wasn't someone close to you, so you believed her intentions. Sharing your truth with someone new to you would be a very similar experience. It could be incredibly enlightening."

I huff, "And how will I find someone?"

Doc grins. "You're a charming bloke. I'm sure you'll find someone."

The Brothers Harris

Vi

"**O**I, VI! GET YOUR ARSE DOWN HERE, WENCH! WE ARE IN *desperate need of libations!*"

I stop dead in my tracks on the sidewalk near my flat and crane my neck toward the faint sound of shouting coming from down the alley.

"Don't you ignore us, Vi! We know you're up there!" a deep, booming voice bellows.

I'd know those voices anywhere.

"I think I can climb this wall. Quick, Booker, give us a lift."

My eyes fly wide when I hear a faint groan and a scuffle. I rush around the corner and peer down the narrow alley that leads into the private entrance of my flat. "Oi! Tell me I'm hallucinating!" I shout, pushing my stray blonde strands away from my face to get a better look.

My four brothers freeze like the cat that got the cream. Tanner—who's all of twenty-three, but acts like he's twelve—is sitting on the shoulders of his twin, Camden, while our baby brother, Booker, is bracing his hands low in preparation for Cam's foot.

"What the bloody hell are you all doing?" I ask. My gaze swerves accusingly at our older brother, Gareth, who's leaning against the

5

brick wall of my building looking thoroughly entertained.

Gareth shrugs his broad shoulders. "Just trying to determine who's going to break a bone this time."

"Get down, the lot of you. Dad will string you up if someone gets injured! What were you planning to achieve there?" I glance up to the fire escape ladder that's a good fifteen feet above our heads.

Tanner drops lithely off Camden's shoulders and says, "I figured you were up in your garden with your ear buds in and couldn't hear us. I thought we could grab hold of the fire escape if Booker gave us a boost." He scratches the back of his shaggy blonde hair as his blue eyes squint up toward the roof. He stares off into the distance speculatively and admits, "It didn't seem so high a minute ago."

"I live on the eleventh floor! You were going to climb the entire way up?"

"Of course! I'm made of stronger stuff than most, Vi!" Tanner says, puffing his chest out.

"And Booker?" I snap, ignoring Tanner's cocky demeanour. "You think putting the smallest one on the bottom of this death trap was a good idea?"

"We asked Gareth, but the bastard wouldn't—" Camden starts but is cut off.

"I'm not that small anymore! I've been doing two-a-days." Booker frowns and rubs his triceps defensively while maintaining his proud posture.

Truthfully, not one of them is small. They are all over six foot and athletically built. Gareth, Camden, and Tanner are more heavily muscled than Booker, but none of them have an ounce of fat on them.

I grin and rustle Booker's brown hair affectionately. "You need a cut again."

"Come home and give me one." He grins sheepishly and my heart lurches at the tenderness in his eyes. I've only lived in my new flat for a year now, and Booker makes it no secret that he misses me living at home. I miss him, too. The adorable, cheeky bugger.

"So, what are you guys doing here, shouting up my neighbour-hood?" I ask, placing my hands on my hips in a motherly, scolding type of way that is all too natural for me when I'm around them.

"You think you can get away with celebrating your birthday without us?" Camden replies, strolling over to me with a devilish smile. He's such a man-whore that I can hardly look at him without rolling my eyes. He has twinkling blue eyes set in the darkest of lashes that have a way of sucking you right into his games. And of course he wears his blonde hair like all the other slutty footballers, having just enough length on top to sweep off to the side. The prat knows women can't resist him. I quit moaning at him about his conquests a long time ago. He'll never change.

He throws his huge arm around my narrow shoulders and musses my hair. "Come on, Vi. Off we go."

I planned to spend the afternoon on my balcony, soaking up some sun with my dog, Bruce, but it's useless to say no to my brothers. The five of us walk through the top end of Brick Lane Market toward Welly's Pub—the spot my brothers quickly dubbed their hangout in my neighbourhood.

It's finally starting to feel like *my* home area at last. A few years ago, I got a proper job as a designer for Nikon working on high fashion camera bags. Their headquarters is located in a big converted warehouse in Shoreditch, East London, not far from our dad's home in Chigwell. I turned into a commuter bee every day, until last year when I saw a brilliant penthouse flat open up within walking distance from work. Living in proper East London feels like a fun adventure compared to Chigwell. This part of the city has a gritty, urban edge to it that I find thrilling. It's chock-full of eclectic independent shops, street vendors, and shabby chic pubs. The graffiti-covered warehouses have a quintessential East London vibe that can't be replicated.

"How's Bruce?" Gareth asks, pulling a cap out of his trousers and securing it low on his head to conceal his face from on-lookers.

He suddenly turns to walk backwards so he can eye a pretty brunette we just passed. She shoots him shamelessly obvious bedroom eyes.

"A monster as usual," I say.

"As long as he's protecting you, that's all I care about."

Several more heads turn as we walk, many people likely recognising Gareth since he's a defender at Manchester United Football Club. He signed at twenty-one and became a starter straight away. He gets noticed everywhere on this side of town, as do my other brothers.

We stroll into the dimly lit pub and, as it's not even four o'clock yet, it's practically empty aside from the few day drunks holding the bar up. Gareth heads to the bar to get us our drinks while the rest of us grab the large, round corner booth that always feels as if it is here just for us. I slide in and eventually end up sandwiched between Booker and Tanner. Camden strides over to help Gareth carry the round of Guinnesses.

One extra Guinness sits ominously in the centre of the table. Gareth looks down and yanks his hat off, smoothing his hand over his dark hair in preparation. With a quick exhale, he raises his glass. "To Vilma on her birthday," he begins, his hazel eyes glossing over as he looks at me. "You share a lot more than a name and a birthday with our mum, but you'll always be Our Vi to us."

My chin wobbles as the others murmur, "Happy birthday, Vi. Happy birthday, Mum." We clink our glasses with the spare drink in the centre, then tip the liquid into our mouths, remaining silent for a moment.

This is the first birthday I've spent away from home and, if I'm being honest, I've felt a bit emotional about it all day. I'm just newly twenty-five, but I fully admit that I lived at home for longer than I should have. However, when you grow up as the only female in a house full of men, you can't help but become attached to the feeling of being needed.

Our mother, Vilma Harris, died of cancer when Booker was

only one year old. Tanner and Camden had just turned three, and I was four. Gareth was eight, so he remembers a lot more about her than the rest of us, but he rarely speaks of her.

What I do know is that in only a few short months, our father, Vaughn Harris, went from being a professional footballer with a large, happy family, to a single parent of five kids, four of which were under the age of five. It was certainly a game changer for all of us. Dad was a star striker for Manchester United and one of the best they'd ever seen. He was in the prime of his career in the 80s when they won the FA Cup in '83 and '85. About ten years later, he was still a starter when our mother got the diagnosis of stage four ovarian cancer. It had spread to other organs before she even had a chance to start treatment.

She passed away in our family home sometime after her diagnosis. Dad retired from the sport just before then. Both our maternal and paternal grandparents passed away before I was even born, so there were no other family members to help him take care of us. Although, I'm not sure it would have mattered since he refused all offers of help from friends. He was determined to raise us on his own. Truthfully, I think he just didn't want anyone around to witness his immense grief.

It was…painful.

After Mum's death, Dad moved us permanently into the mansion he and Mum owned in the posh neighbourhood of Chigwell. They had a smaller flat in Manchester during football season so Dad could be closer to his team, but I don't remember much about living there. Our dad's career was very successful and had set us all up for life. Materially, we wanted for nothing. But it still wasn't an easy childhood. He loved us fiercely, but being both a mother and a father is too much for any one person to handle. I think the stress of it would have killed him had he not been offered a managing position for Bethnal Green Football Club.

Once football came back into his life, he was a new man. Happier and more alive than I'd ever remembered him being. I was so delight-ed to see this newfound light in him that I was all too willing to help pick up the slack with my brothers. And when your dad manages a team and your brothers all play, you pretty much have no choice but to submerge yourself in the lifestyle.

Football was my life. Without question. I didn't play a lick of it, though. Honestly, I had no desire. Booker was a killer goalie, and Camden and Tanner argued over who was the better striker between the two of them. Me? I was just happy to mother-hen them and know the ins and outs and needs of a footballing athlete.

Last year, I finally reached my breaking point when Gareth got in a massive row with my boyfriend at the time. Rumours had been circulating that Pierce was cheating on me. He showed up when we were all at a pub, and Gareth grabbed him around the throat. He looked positively homicidal as he slammed Pierce against a wall. Paparazzi got hold of pictures, and the whole scene almost ruined his football career. It wouldn't have been that big of an issue for me if it was the first time Gareth did something like that, but it wasn't. My relationship track record is meagre to say the least. Regardless, every one of my breakups involved one of my brothers turning into a crazy, neurotic, bruiser of a brother. Maybe if I had been the one to do the dumping, things would have been easier for them to accept. However, I am cursed with constantly being the dumpee.

But Pierce was the straw that broke the camel's back. After that incident, I knew I had to get out of my dad's house or I'd never have a life without my brothers interfering. And I am doing a proper job of it if I may say so myself. Of course I'm still very close to my family and I see them every week, but having my own space to go to has been extremely liberating.

"How was China, Vi?" Gareth asks after some idle football chat-ter. They're *always* talking football.

"Fine, fine. Nothing too exciting. I'm just finally starting to feel human again. It's always so exhausting over there. Those factories work intense hours."

"I want to go with you sometime," Booker says, propping his head on his hand. "I imagine it's beautiful there."

"You see plenty of the world with the team, Book," Camden admonishes.

"Yeah, but it'd be quite different if I didn't have to think about the game the whole time."

"Oh, stuff it. We live a life other sorry bastards only dream about. You'd do well to remember that." Camden scowls into his glass as he takes a sip.

"There's more to life than football," I snap defensively on behalf of Booker. He's the littlest and even though he stands six inches taller than me, I can't help but see him that way. I'm protective over him the way all of my brothers are protective over me. And I sometimes get the impression he doesn't even like playing football but is too scared to ever say.

"Not in the Harris house." Camden takes another long drink of his beer.

"You doing anything special for your birthday, Vi?" Tanner asks, oblivious to Camden's owly mood toward Booker. Tanner doesn't take anything too seriously, including girls. He and Camden aren't identical but they look very similar, which is probably why Tanner wears his blonde hair shaggy around his ears. It matches his playful personality perfectly.

"Not really. I mean...I have...well, a date I suppose." I look down and cringe.

"Who the fuck—" Tanner barks and Camden finishes his sentence.

"What's his name? I better not bloody well know him."

"Why don't you just spend it with us?" Booker asks quietly beside me.

"He better not be a prat like the last one," Gareth's voice booms loudly over all of them. "I won't tolerate another wanker like him stepping inside our home. I'll fucking lose it, Vi. You better not bring him around."

I turn my wide, accusing eyes on him. He's the oldest one! He should be more mature about this! "Do you hear yourself right now? You're nearly thirty, Gareth! I expect more from you. All of you! Christ, I'm twenty-five years old, and you lot are going mental over your sister having a date! I'm going to date! This is why I moved out. This, right here. You guys can't just let me figure things out on my own. Do you want me to end up alone forever?"

"Stop being dramatic. You'd hardly be alone," Tanner bellows. "You'd have us!"

"Are you fucking dense? You lot are going to find nice girls to settle down with someday, and I'm not going to be the lonely sister tagging along with you on romantic holidays."

"Oh, Christ, be serious. We're not going to settle down," Camden mumbles into his glass.

Gareth at least has the cheek to look contemplative.

"You know what's worse?" I groan. "I don't even have a date. I made it up as a test, and you buggers all failed miserably."

I see Camden exhale with relief as Gareth murmurs, "Thank fuck for that."

Booker turns his quizzical brow to me. "This is good then? You don't have a date?"

"No, I don't have a date!" I shriek. "Let me out." I shove against Tanner to move over. He eyes me sternly and doesn't budge an inch. "You know what? I'm going to start throwing punches if you all don't let me out of this booth right now."

Tanner bursts out into a hearty laugh. "I love when you throw punches. You get that weird vein in your forehead that looks like Harry Potter."

That sets Camden off, too. "Fuck, you're right! She does! It's like a little bitty lightning bolt of ineffectual fury!"

When I see Gareth start chortling, too, it makes me see red.

"You know what? It's my birthday and you guys are ruining it. I don't have a date. I have nothing. I just wanted a quiet day at home and the opportunity to move on with my life. There's nothing bloody wrong with that." I'm surprised when I feel the sting of tears pricking at my eyes.

Tanner's face drops instantly. "What's this? No tears! Christ, Vi, we are only messing about." I fight his huge embrace as he pulls me under his arm and rubs my shoulder.

"Bugger, I didn't think you'd get emotional over it," Camden says, reaching out and gripping my hand in an apologetic gesture.

"Vi, I'm sorry. I didn't mean it," Booker says, which only makes me laugh.

"Book, you really need to stop apologising for these prats," I giggle and sit up, dabbing the corners of my eyes.

"Camden's the prat," Tanner mutters. "He's the one who always makes you cry."

I hold my hand out to stop Camden from unleashing on Tanner. "Stop. I'm fine. I'm just feeling a bit emotional today. It's probably my period."

I look up and see all their faces frozen in horror and disgust. "I thought you boys are supposed to be tough footballers!" I exclaim, erupting into a fit of giggles.

They all shake their heads and, in unison, pick up their glasses to take long gulps of their beers. They even set their drinks down at the same time. Now my eyes are wet from tears of laughter instead of sadness. These brothers of mine are a pain in the arse, but they're mine. And the truth is it isn't just them that upset me today.

They have no clue how incredibly hard it is to share a birthday with a ghost.

The next day, I'm decked out in green and white as I hop into a cab and head to the Bethnal Green F.C. stadium, Tower Park. Normally, summertime is the off-season when my brothers are gifted some very rare downtime. However, tonight is a friendly match against Arsenal.

These matches are a big draw in London, so I arrive extra early before the crowds really begin to roll in. Although, there aren't many sights that beat a packed Tower Park. Loud and bustling. Electric and inspiring. It has a magic about it that I wish I could bottle up and sprinkle all over London.

Tower Park is a second home to the Harris family in many ways. When our father started managing here, things in our home really improved. The biggest difference was that it pulled Dad out of his grief over losing Mum. He had a sense of purpose again. Something to get up for every day that didn't remind him of her. And when the boys began showing interest in the sport, it helped him reconnect with them in ways I didn't know were possible. It was a joy to witness because they needed it. Dad has always been harder on the boys than me, but football brought the five of them together.

For that reason alone, I fell in love with football as well.

I spot Gareth standing at the player's entrance, posing with a couple of young boys as their dad snaps a photo with his mobile. I lean against the brick wall and watch him with pride as he offers an easy smile to the dad and signs the kids' jerseys. He's always been great with fans, especially children. He even started a youth football program in Manchester a few years ago, called Kid Kickers, and it's going brilliantly.

I know he'd make a wonderful father, but he never seems to give women the time of day enough for that to happen. Of course I've seen him flirt loads, but I always get the sense he does it for show more than genuine interest. And the women he does give any attention to seem to disappear just as quickly as they come.

Gareth's eyes find mine as he waves goodbye to the kids. I walk over to him, and he throws his arm over my shoulders to pull me down into a playful headlock. "Let's get inside before anyone else sees me."

We are permitted through the gated entrance that's reserved for players because the entire staff knows us. However, it's quite rare for Gareth to attend Bethnal Green matches because of his own football schedule, so it's a fun treat to have him by my side.

We make our way to our seats that are midfield, first row. I've never sat in the upper box seats where the wives and girlfriends sit. It's much too far away, and I need my brothers to hear me from their positions on the pitch. Not to mention I get the distinct impression the WAGs aren't nearly as into the manoeuvres of the game as I am.

I sit back in my seat and watch Camden, Tanner, and Booker warm up just as a girl plops down in the open seat on the other side of Gareth. She's tall and lanky with blonde hair that she's endlessly flipping as she giggles at her own daft jokes. Gareth doesn't seem the least bit interested, but she doesn't notice.

Finally, an older man stands in front of her and shows her his ticket to grumpily inform her that she's in his seat. The blonde gets a big pouty lip and leans over Gareth to address me. "Want to trade seats with me, lovey?"

My brows arch. "Excuse me?"

"I'm only a few rows back. Swap me." She winks like she's speaking some secret girl code I should know.

I open my mouth to reply, but Gareth leans forward and states with a deep warning tone, "You can go. I'd rather watch this game with my sister."

She huffs out a laugh. "Surely you're joking. She can't possibly be more fun than me."

"She is ten times more fun, and I'm serious. You should go," Gareth deadpans.

The corner of my mouth curves up into a smile as the girl's eyes flick from Gareth's to mine. With a frustrated little growl, she turns her head and whips Gareth in the face with her hair as she stomps off.

Gareth sits back and shakes his head, his jaw ticking with annoyance. "Ignore her. She's just a Harris Ho."

My nose wrinkles. "I hate that term you guys have coined."

His brows lift. "It's just another term for groupie. If you played football, I'm sure you'd have some male Harris Hoes yourself."

"Hardly." I roll my eyes so far back, I swear I can see the pouting blonde behind me. "They wouldn't get past the Harris Shakedown you lot would put them through. That is a large reason why no one is breaking down my door."

"Well, they would be if you knew how to pick good ones," Gareth says, looking at me with warning eyes. "That ex of yours was a wanker."

"Can we please not talk about him?" I groan, crossing my arms. "He was the first bloke in ages who didn't care about you four, so I had blinders on to his other annoying qualities."

"I'd say," Gareth replies through clenched teeth.

"You don't get it," I snap back at his tone. "It's really bloody hard to date anyone with the headlines you guys carry around with you. Plus, all four of you are constantly trying to call the plays in my life!"

Gareth's face contorts with frustration. "If you dated a man who was worth anything, we wouldn't have to because he would know that you are the superior Harris in all ways."

I roll my eyes, hating the way Gareth gets when he puts me on a pedestal like I'm God's gift to the world. The truth is I'm painfully ordinary in a family full of extraordinary.

Gareth leans in closer to me, his eyes intense and pinning me to my seat. "Plus, you deserve a man who's not afraid to stand up to us, Vi. The minute you bring someone around who has some balls for himself, I promise, I'll back off and let you live your life."

Part of me wants to stay cross at him, but the other part hopes a man like that exists for me. I need someone in my life that will worship me and put the insecurities I have inside of me to rest. A man like that would be worth the anxiety my lack of a love life currently gives me.

The match begins, and it's a belter to the very end. A high-scoring match is never good for the keeper. Booker looks angry and frustrated in the net as he claps his goalie gloves together and yells at his defenders for not doing their jobs. He's yelling everything that I'm hoarse from yelling as well. Gareth shakes his head every time I stand up and scream at the ref for not calling some very obvious tackles.

Thankfully, Camden is on fire, already earning a hat trick with over ten minutes left in the match. Tanner has scored one goal, but the opposing defender is all over him, yanking on his kit and throwing legs out for some seriously cheap shots. Tanner is doing all he can to draw a foul, but the ref must still be on a fucking holiday.

With only minutes left, Tanner goes down hard. The dirty wanker of a defender went in for a high tackle, popping Tan right in the face with his elbow. It was a red card move by any standards, but the game continues. Tanner struggles to see as he moves to stand up, yet the ref still calls nothing.

Gareth—my normally silent brother—is on his feet in seconds, yelling louder than I've ever heard him yell before. He's nearly climbing over the barriers as a slew of expletives not suitable for children stream from his mouth. I join him, even more fired up now and plotting ways to slash the ref's tires before he leaves tonight.

Our father turns to look at us from his position on the sideline. His eyes are steely on us as he shakes his head and silently tries to shut us up.

But neither of us care because nothing comes above our beloved Harris Brothers.

3
The Baby Whisperer

Hayden

S PRAWLED OUT ON THE LONG GREY COUCH IN MY BROTHER'S FLAT, I flick mindlessly through the channels on the telly, trying to stop myself from going upstairs to help my brother's fiancée, Leslie. The baby has been crying for fifteen minutes straight, but Leslie made me promise to back off and stop helping so much.

"You're not going to live here forever, Hayden. Theo and I have to figure this out on our own. She's fine crying for a few minutes."

My jaw clenches as I stare at the clock, watching each passing second that I'm forced to sit here and listen to my niece's desperate cries. I unsnap and re-snap the leather cuffs on my wrists to try to distract myself. She wants me. I know it. I can feel it for Christ's sake. She's the most gorgeous and the most colicky baby you'd ever meet, and she likes me for some reason.

"Colicky," I huff. What an odd word for a single, twenty-six-year-old male to know, but fuck. I couldn't *not* read the baby books Leslie and Theo have laying around. Especially when I bloody well live with them and hear the poor child wailing every single night. The five *S*'s are like the Bible around here. Swaddle, side, shush, swing, and suck. No five tips have ever helped a family more, I assure you.

I glance down at my watch for the fourth time in the last three minutes and see it tick over to 11:11. I pinch my eyes shut and exhale a wish for luck. A wish for a time machine. A wish for change.

Finally, as if Leslie could hear my silent pleas, her head pops up over the cast iron railing that looks down on the sunken living room. Her face looks flushed and she is near tears. Without hesitation, I spring up and take the steps two at a time all the way to her and my brother's loft bedroom.

"She doesn't even like the football hold right now. I've rubbed her tummy, but she's not gassy. I thought if I strapped her to me while I got ready, she'd settle down, but she won't. She's tired. I know she is. She just won't fall asleep." Leslie's voice cracks at the end.

"I wish you'd stop fighting my help," I say, scooping up a besotted three-month-old Baby Marisa off the bed. I tuck her into that perfect place between my shoulder and neck where my voice can tunnel right into her ear. Then I begin shushing her loudly while I swoosh from side to side in short, fast spurts. Her tiny, rigid frame instantly relaxes. A few more loud puffs of air later and her wails morph from battle cries into the cry that sounds more like she's saying, *It's about bloody time you got here, Uncle Hayden. Mum's been messing about with me for ages.*

Her cries continue to calm as I swing. She doesn't like to be bounced. Everybody wants to bounce her, but it just pisses her off more. I peek at our reflection in the long horizontal mirror on the side wall between the bedroom and the large en suite bathroom. Marisa's eyes look dazed and heavy. She's seconds away from falling asleep.

"Hayden, you freaking baby whisperer," Leslie gripes in her distinct American accent.

"She was going to crash any second. You almost had her. This is just luck."

She drops down onto the bed and pushes her auburn hair back from her face. "It's not luck, Hay. You have the touch. Jeez, I don't know what we'd do without you here."

I huff out an incredulous laugh at the preposterous notion. She's got no clue how much they help me a thousand times more than I could ever help them. She saved my fucking life for Christ's sake. Yet I know that Doc is right. There is more to the world outside this flat.

I pause when I hear a soft snore coming from beside my ear and glance at the mirror to find Marisa out cold. I smile triumphantly and turn her to show Leslie.

Her face splits into a grin as she thrusts her hands into the air and does a hilarious silent scream with a little wiggly butt dance. My chest rumbles with laughter as she flops herself back onto the bed and lets out a huge sigh.

After a minute, she sits up and has a serious look on her face. "Hayden, I know tonight is your big night and you probably have like a trillion things on your mind, but is there any way you can hold her for a while so I can make some calls and take a shower?"

"It's a tough job, but I think I might just be man enough to do it," I say with a wink. "Don't tell my brother, though. He'll thump me if he knows he missed out on cuddle time again."

Leslie smiles in a quiet way she only ever does when she thinks of my brother. "He's hauling the last furniture pieces for the auction over to the ballroom now. He should be back any second and you shall be relieved."

"No worries. There's an old football game on downstairs. I got this," I say, lifting my eyebrows and glancing down at the limp, pink, perfect bundle against my chest.

Leslie smiles affectionately at Marisa before she turns her twinkling green eyes on me. "Thank you, Hayden."

I head downstairs, thinking about how lucky my brother is to have a woman like Leslie. I'll be proud to call her my sister after their wedding. Resuming my place on the couch, I allow the slow, rhythmic breaths of Marisa to calm my nerves over what I'm about to do this evening.

The truth is I've wanted to hold Marisa all day. She is my moment in reality that reminds me there are bigger struggles happening in this world than my own, and that there are people who need me, even if they are only thirteen pounds. This perfect, fussy baby has become my safety net. My anchor. Holding her against my heart reminds me exactly why I need to always keep it beating.

Easy Favour 4

Vi

"**V**ILMA, I NEED YOU!" LESLIE'S VOICE PEELS LOUDLY THROUGH the phone line.

I shoot up out of my wheelie office chair, clutching the phone tightly to my ear. "What? What is it? Is something wrong with the baby?"

"Oh no, no. Marisa is fine. I mean, colicky as always and killing me with the no sleep thing, but healthy as a fussy foal."

My face scrunches in confusion. "A what?"

"Healthy as a horse? Do the Brits not use that reference? Never mind. I have something serious to ask you, Vilma."

I sigh. "Leslie, why do you insist on calling me by my full name? You're seriously the only one. You haven't been in the office for a couple of months, so I rather got used to being called Vi again."

"I love Vilma! It reminds me of Scooby-Doo." She giggles and I realise how much I've missed that sound around here.

I drop back down on my chair and begin spinning around in slow circles. "I still have no idea what you're going on about," I reply. I never watched telly much growing up, and Leslie can't seem to wrap her brain around that notion.

"Scooby-Doo and the gang! You seriously need to catch up on

22

your American cartoons. I know they play them in England—Hey! Did you get my happy birthday text? You never replied."

"Oh, crap. Yes, I did. Sorry. My brothers showed up, so I got distracted."

"Sexy soccer brothers?" she asks with a provocative purr.

Groaning in disgust, I answer, "It's football over here, mate. You've been in London long enough now to use the proper term. Now, did you call for a reason, or just to distract me from my very serious work to educate me on animated American telly and tell me I have hot brothers?"

"Uptight British—" Leslie grumbles, but I cut her off.

"Oi, darling, don't you have a go at me! You left me stranded here at the office because you had to go and have a cute, perfect baby with that sinfully sexy fiancé of yours. I'm not to be trifled with right now. I've had to deal with Benji, Hector, and Roger all on my own. Plus two trips to China since you left."

"Fine, fine…Viiiii." She drawls out the *I* in an exaggerated, smug British accent.

Leslie and I have been working side by side for several years. She was in charge of working directly with the Chinese factories that make our camera bag designs until her recent maternity leave. I've had to pick up the slack ever since. Leslie, Hector, and I are the three designers. We work on various satchels, wallets, clutches, and totes that are technology and photography friendly. There are a handful of other clerical people we work alongside, as well as our boss, Roger.

"Thank you for taking care of the fort while I am away. You know I love you." She makes obnoxious kissy noises into the receiver. "Okay, stop distracting me. I don't want to talk about work. I have a very serious question. Are you ready?"

"Ready," I answer.

"Are you sure?"

"Sure."

"Are you prepared?"

"Primed and poised," I quip.

"Do you have a formal evening gown?" she rushes out in one breath.

My brow furrows at her query. Leslie excels at random, but this still surprises me. "This seems like an incredibly peculiar question."

"Well, do you?"

Sighing heavily, I recall the white floor-length evening gown I bought last year for New Year's Eve. Normally, I despise wearing white with my blonde hair because I feel washed-out. But this dress is a diamond white that has just enough glimmer to make my alabaster skin look positively luminous.

"I do happen to have a dress," I reply sadly at the fact that I have never worn it anywhere. It's tragic, really. Pierce was a DJ who worked at a posh nightclub in Chigwell, and they were hosting a huge formal party. Then the cheating rumours began and the whole Gareth blowout happened the day before New Year's Eve. Leslie tried to strong-arm me into going just to spite him. Instead, I had a cosy night in with my main man, Bruce.

"Perfect! I have a proposition for you."

Leslie goes on to explain that Theo's family hosts a formal charity gala every year in London, and two of her former roommates who were going to attend had to back out last minute.

"Theo's family is throwing the event?" I ask cautiously. "So they'll *all* be there I assume."

"Yes, yes. Of course," she replies dismissively. "You'll be at a table with some of my old roommates. Frank, Finley, and Brody. Then Reyna and Liam will be at your table as well. You met them all at The White Swan Pub soft opening a couple of weeks ago."

I exhale when I realise she hasn't mentioned the one I'm most curious about. Recalling my less than stellar first impression with Theo's brother, Hayden, I can't tell if I'm relieved or disappointed to hear he won't be sitting at my table.

Hayden Clarke is memorable, to say the least. He had a sexy

soulful look about him that lured me right in.

"That sounds quite fun," I reply, clearing the frog in my throat.

"Do you think you can secure a plus one?" Leslie asks. "The plates are three hundred quid a piece and are already paid in full. Oooh, maybe one of your brothers?" Her voice rises with excitement.

I exhale sharply while rolling my eyes. My gaze happens to land on our coworker, Benji. I catch him picking dirt out from beneath his fingernails with an opened paperclip and my nose crinkles. "What would you say to me bringing Benji instead?" I whisper quietly into the phone. "I really think the bloke needs a nice night out."

Leslie groans. "Your brothers would be much more thrilling, but dammit, you're probably right about Benji. Do you think you can keep him occupied, though? I can't trust that Theo won't get twitchy if he starts following me around all night."

I purse my lips to conceal my giggle. Benji is our personal assistant, and he's hopelessly in love with Leslie. It's quite cute, really. He's twenty-three, small bodied with mousy brown hair, and has an awkward, nerdy way about him. He's not unattractive, but he is the polar opposite of Theo. Theo is large and heavily muscled with trimmed dark blonde hair. He's brooding and intense with a confidence that can't be faked. And the passion that radiates from him when he's around Leslie gives me butterflies, and I'm not even on the receiving end of those looks. Not to mention he pulls off smart glasses like no bloke I've ever seen.

"He'll be fine," I appease. "Maybe he'll meet a nice girl?"

"Aw, I'd love that for Benji," Leslie sings hopefully into the phone. "So you'll do it then. Yay! Thank you, my love. It means a lot. I gotta run, though. Marisa is stirring and I still have to get in the shower. It takes hours to do anything when you have a colicky baby. I'll email you the details."

"Great," I reply.

"Okay, bye-bye, Vi. Oh look, I made a rhyme! I'm a poet and I didn't know it!" She snickers like a loon, and I can't help but laugh pathetically in response. Her voice grows serious again. "I'm sorry. Mommyhood has murdered my brain cells. Talk later!"

I shake my head as I hang up thinking about how much Leslie's life has changed since she came to London. At twenty-seven, she's only a couple of years older than me. I can't even imagine being where she is currently in her life. I'm still getting dumped by douchey DJs for goodness sake.

"Hey, Benji," I sing merrily as I saunter over to his desk which is situated behind the designer cubbies.

He looks up, dropping his paperclip on the desk and clumsily tries to cover it up. "Hiya, Vi. What can I get for you?"

Shooting him a cheeky grin, I ask, "Have you got plans tonight?"

His brow furrows as he blinks in confusion. "Not particularly."

"Leslie called and wondered if you and I would be keen to go to a fundraiser tonight. It's a formal do I'm afraid."

Benji shoots up out of his chair. "Leslie called? Are you serious? Did she ask for me specifically?" His voice rises to a high-pitched squeal.

"Benji," I chastise like a proper mum. "If you're going to act this excited around her tonight, it's probably not a good idea for you to go. She's got a lot going on right now with a new baby and all her wedding planning. She really needs a nice evening out."

His face drops. "No, I just…Oh, bugger. I didn't mean to…It wasn't that—"

"I know you're fond of her. Leslie's a great mate. Just promise to be cool and we'll go together and have a fab time, all right?" Benji adamantly promises to be calm, and I know I can trust him. He's harmless, really. Just overeager.

Since Roger is not in the office today, we both decide to scoot out early to prepare for our big night. Benji has to go rent a tux and I need extra time to do my hair. A formal affair requires a bit more effort than my daily long and straight do.

"I'll pick you up in a cab outside your building at seven," I say as we clamber out of the large swing-open window of our building.

"Sounds lovely," he replies, his voice rising at the end as we descend down the wrought iron fire escape stairs.

There's a call centre located on the first level of our two-floor warehouse, and we look at those employees like zombies who could infect us with a case of "dull and painfully boring." It was Leslie's idea to start using the fire escape steps to enter and exit so the drab lower-level office doesn't mess with our creative mojo.

Just as we reach the bottom of the steps, my dad's name pops up on my phone screen. I wave Benji off and answer as I make my way down the sidewalk. "Hiya, Dad!"

"Hello, my darling. You sound rather chipper." His warm voice is always a welcome sound.

"Well, I just got invited to a formal do tonight. I was going to call you, actually. I'm afraid Bruce and I won't be around for tea."

"What's the event for?"

"Oh, erm, crap." I was so excited by the prospect of who might be in attendance that I completely forgot to ask Leslie what the charity was even for. "I suppose I don't know. It's sort of a favour for a friend."

"Well, have fun. I'll try to ward off your brothers for you."

I let out a huff of laughter. "As if that's even possible."

"They mean well, darling. It's off-season, so they have too much time on their hands to worry about you."

Rolling my eyes, I reply, "I know, I know."

"You will be by Sunday, right?" he asks.

"Of course, Dad. You needn't even ask."

"All right, just making sure. Be safe and text me when you're home tonight."

"Will do! Bye, Dad."

"Bye."

I stride down the street with an extra bounce in my step from the prospect of a big night out. This is what I envisioned when I moved.

Doing fun, spur-of-the-moment things with friends that don't involve going over match footage. And now that Leslie lives with Theo full-time, she's only a ten-minute walk from my flat. Maybe now that she lives closer we'll see each other more often? I know she's got a baby, but surely mummies need a break here and there.

I walk through the narrow alley between the two shops that my flat sits above, shaking my head at the image of my idiot brothers trying to make a three-man-tower. They demanded a key from me, but I refused. I love my flat too much to give those animals access to it.

I have the penthouse above a large period building that hosts a Hookah Lounge and a gift shop on the ground level. I didn't need the penthouse, but my dad insisted and, damn, it is bloody perfect. As soon as you walk in, you're greeted with an entire wall of exposed natural brick which compliments the floor-to-ceiling windows that overlook a huge balcony. The balcony opens from the living room, and the master suite is concealed by French doors on the left. On the right is a modern kitchen with glossy black cabinets and pale wooden worktops.

As if all that isn't gorgeous enough, there's a ladder up to a private rooftop terrace with a huge flowery oasis. My own personal secret garden. I wish I could say I tend to the flowers myself, but I do not have a green thumb. I pay someone to maintain it, and it's the best money I spend every single week. I lose hours up there reading and people-watching down over my quaint neighbourhood. It's dreamy.

I let myself into the side entrance where the private lift to my flat is located. I pop my key into the panel and push the only button labelled eleven. Just as the doors open into my flat, I'm socked right in the belly by none other than Bruce.

"Bruce! You vile monster. Get back," I shout, pushing him away from me. "Now just look at the state of me." I glance down at my soaked jeans. The cheeky bastard has the nerve to drop down on his butt and cock his head at me in that cute puppy-dog way he still has about him.

"You think you're cute, don't you?" I glare at him angrily. Bruce is an enormous Saint Bernard that I ended up with when one of my neighbours passed away six months ago. It was quite sad, really. Mrs. Renack lived below me. Her children bought her Bruce as a puppy when she was diagnosed with cancer. She used to drop him off at my flat whenever she went for treatments and we always had the loveliest chats. Unfortunately, Bruce isn't a miracle worker. When I showed up at the funeral, her kids spoke of sending him to a shelter and I couldn't stomach the thought.

The horrid animal weighs nearly one hundred forty pounds, and his big head reaches my waist. He's got a half white face with a mahogany brindle covering his right eye. The rest of his body is spotted with various shades of black, brown, red, and tan amongst his white fur.

"I'm going to get you into classes one of these days, Bruce. You mark my words." His enormous tongue flicks out and licks his nose as he continues to stare at me expectantly. Two streams of drool hang from his chops as he awaits my command.

"All right, all right," I groan. "Let's go have a walkies." He leaps up and rushes into the kitchen to grab his lead, dragging it across the white slate flooring. He may not be well-trained in greetings, but he sure as shit knows how to get a walk. I clip the lead onto his collar and head out to let him relieve himself. It's a lot like leading a small horse rather than walking a dog. The looks I get are rather comical considering the bugger weighs more than I do.

This area of town is quite busy with tourists and shoppers, but anywhere you live in London you'll always find a quiet, green oasis amongst all the hustle and bustle. These tiny parks are my favourite part of London. And the park where I take Bruce is extra special because it has an entire area for dogs.

Once we return to my flat, I lead him into the kitchen to refresh his water and feed him. Then I pop into my en suite bathroom to get ready for the evening. Bruce eventually resumes his post at the bathroom doorway, watching me the entire time with his sad puppy-dog eyes that say, *"You look like you're going out for the night. I hope that means you're taking me. And, oh, can you scratch my back while you're at it, pretty please?"*

"Not this time, mongrel," I say, patting his head before applying one last layer of mascara.

I give myself a final once-over in the mirror. I've always been the thinner, ganglier, awkward type, like a young girl who still hasn't hit puberty. Leslie used to say I had a runway model's body, but I'd much rather have a bit more meat and some curves than the spindly frame I inherited from my mother. It's easy to develop a complex over thin legs when you have footballers with massive muscular thighs for brothers.

Still, my dress makes me feel like I actually have curves. It's a diamond white, sweetheart strapless, fit-to-flare cut dress. I curl my platinum blonde locks into loose, soft waves and pin them off to one side so they trail down the front of my exposed shoulder. My minimal makeup allows my bright blue eyes to carry the show. Add a layer of peach gloss and I think I've actually achieved the perfect sun-kissed look I was going for.

Tonight, I feel different. Tonight, I feel ready for anything.

Hear 5 Now

Hayden

MY EYES BLINK SLOWLY AGAINST THE SPOTLIGHTS, SEARCHING for the clock on the far wall of the ballroom that I saw when I came in from the back. I know I have a watch on my wrist because I never go anywhere without it. But for some reason, I feel the need to confirm the time on another clock every place I go.

To ensure that the time continuum hasn't failed.

To ensure that where I'm standing right now is real life.

To ensure that I am still alive.

And to ensure the fact that my incessant wish to erase moments from my past still hasn't come true.

I know it was crap for me to skip the mingling portion of the fundraising event, but I am too fucking nervous to sit with everyone and visit like it is a normal Friday night. This night is anything but normal. I'll talk to everyone afterwards. Lord knows I'll have to. They've all been texting me to make sure I'm okay. My mum, my younger sister, Daphney, my brother, Theo, and Leslie. I shoot a quick text back to Leslie to let her know that Marisa was fast asleep when I left her with the sitter at their flat. I ignore all the others.

Touching the inside of my wrist concealed beneath my dark brown leather cuff, the texture of the ridged scar sends a churning through my stomach. Before I have a chance to close my eyes and slip back to that moment, I hear the master of ceremonies announce my name.

"And now, a word from one of our generous benefactors, Mr. Hayden Clarke." The woman's voice cracks on the end of my name, and I bite back the growing urge to roll my eyes. This woman knows I'm not one of the actual benefactors—my parents are the ones mostly involved. This woman also knows that I'm considered the tragic, wayward son whom everyone watches like a ticking time bomb. They're all bloody terrified of what I'm about to say.

Maybe they should be.

I stride across the shiny wooden stage, adjusting my black Windsor tie and fastening the button on my navy tuxedo jacket. I left it undone on purpose to give my hands something to do. It's a small attempt at feigning a level of confidence. Power. Intimidation.

Don't let them see you shake. Don't let them see you falter. Don't let them see you weak. You're not weak anymore. You're different. You're healed.

The woman's plump cheeks widen, making me cringe at the fake warmth she's radiating. She offers me a curt British smile. The British are always polite. Always controlled. And always on guard. Maybe that's why I always feel oddly around them, like I don't belong.

I've always hated surface shit.

That fact alone is probably why last year I fell hopelessly in love with the dark and ominous American dust storm that is Reyna Miracle Miller. Reyna whited out everything around me. She kept me in a dark vortex where I could see nothing but her, and us, and the misery that we lived in every time our bodies connected. The desolation in which I lived in with Rey felt real and right at the time. It felt like home. I was exhausted by the superficial airs that were so common in my family. Reyna was anything but surface. Reyna was dark, and twisted, and sad, and just as fucked-up as me. I was drawn to her like a moth to a flame.

Ignoring the painful slice I feel in my heart every time I think about Rey, I nod pleasantly at the woman as she steps away from the podium and I fill her space. I squint against the spotlights and see that the ballroom is covered in white linens, low-hanging chandeliers, and splashes of dark purple floral centrepieces on each table. My eyes settle on the table front and centre and land on my mother. Even from up here, I can see how nervous she is. My father is doing a proper job at appearing strong and regal. Next to my mum is Daphney, Theo, and, of course, Leslie. I avoid looking at the table next to them because I know exactly who's sitting there.

I know her face better than I should. I used to watch Rey sleep. I could even tell when she was dreaming. Her eyeballs would flicker rapidly behind her lids, and she'd let out gut-wrenching cries that made me beg the universe for some magical power that would grant me a look inside her head. I was desperate to know more than just her physical beauty. She has long dark hair and a curvy bombshell figure, plus an entire sleeve of tattoos on one arm and three black roses on her shoulder and collarbone. I had my suspicions about the meaning behind all her ink, but we never discussed them. We never discussed much. Her grey eyes held millions of secrets that she never shared with me. Our relationship was much more carnal, and I was too frozen in my own misery to ever push for more.

By the time I was able to admit to myself that I was in love with her, it was too late. Now she's engaged to my brother's best mate, Liam Darby, and I'm at a suicide gala giving a bloody survivor speech.

Fuck me.

Clearing my throat, I stare into the spotlights and begin the speech I've been reciting in my head for months now. "One year ago today, as my watch struck the hour of 11:11, I dragged a blade across both of my wrists."

A soft gasp emits from somewhere in the room, and I pause to let my amplified words settle in over the audience. I glance sideways at the announcer standing off stage. Her eyes flare nervously and I clench my jaw to conceal the smirk threatening my lips.

"It's quite a laugh, really…Well, not the trying to kill myself part. That was the opposite of comedy. But what's funny is that when I volunteered to be the keynote speaker for this evening, the charity gave me a list of trigger words. Taboo phrases they advised me not to say. They gave me suitable alternatives for things like *kill myself, slitting my wrists*, and even *blood*."

My eyes ache to look over at Rey to see her reaction, but I resist. She's not a part of my life anymore. Her approval isn't what I need to be healthy. It's not why I'm doing this.

"But since I'm a Clarke and this is our benefit, I'm doing this speech my way. So if any of you are afraid of a trigger or whatever sod all word they give for things that are uncomfortable, this is your chance to exit."

Chairs shift in the audience as the ballroom full of British tight-arses begin to squirm in their seats. I can just hear the old birds saying silently, *"Oh heavens, I want to go, but that might appear rude!"*

"If Madge is staying, I'm bloody well staying, too!"

"Blimey, Victoria knew I was wearing blue. How could she wear it, too?"

When I see no one attempting to leave, I continue. "It was this exact night a year ago—this same charity, this same ballroom—that I walked out of, stumbled into a cab pissed out of my mind, and headed through the streets of London. The entire ride, I looked at the driver and thought to myself, 'He's got no idea he's driving a dead man.'

"I arrived at my brother's furniture shop, grabbed a small, circular saw blade he used for trim work, and drug it across each one of my wrists." A faint cough echoes in the distance, and I sigh heavily at the ridiculousness that normal things like coughing still happen while I'm up here revealing the incredible fucking darkness in my soul. "You see, I was at the end of a dark and depressing tunnel that I had been living in for several years." I pause momentarily to collect myself for my big moment of truth. The most painful truth that I still struggle with to this day.

"Four years ago, I was part of a horrific accident that took my sister's life." My voice cracks and I frown at the annoying emotions that overcome me. I let my chin hit my chest and suck the insides of my cheeks in between my teeth and bite down. The spongy bounce on my inner cheeks smarts and distracts me enough to continue.

"I still have difficulty labelling what happened to my sister as an accident. It truly *was* an accident, but that's a tough pill to swallow when you were the one behind the wheel. Why did it have to be her? Why did I have to be driving by just as she came around the house? So many ripple effects from all the choices we both made that resulted in that one moment. That's an incredibly hard result to live with, which is likely why I spiralled out of control for so many years.

"Booze and pills became my best mates, even landing me in the hospital for several weeks at one point. So when shit really hit the fan in my personal life, slitting my wrists seemed like the answer."

I pause again as I recall that one dark night with Reyna when I could feel her slipping away from me. I could feel her leaving me, and I knew I wasn't good enough to make her stay. I knew her heart wasn't mine to care for because I was nothing. I wasn't important enough for her to love fully. That was my breaking point. I had hated myself for so long because of what I did to my sister that when I finally accepted the fact that I couldn't be loved by even someone as dark and twisted as Rey, it truly was the end.

"The pain was minimal at first. Just a wincing sort of ache. Then it spread like wildfire to a burning, sweltering rage. I remember this strange twinge in my shoulders as the blood flooded out of my body and hit the concrete floor beneath me. When I looked down at the sea of red around my shiny dress shoes, I forgot about the pain. I forgot about the cause. I forgot about everything leading up to this one incredibly profound moment. This one moment that I chose was permanent. In that one moment, I had finally erased my life forever."

Out of the corner of my eye, I see my mum clap her hand over her mouth. Her eyes strain against the tears flowing out of them. She's heard this story before, but I imagine hearing it without any interruption from my therapist is probably a great deal different.

"But dying that night was all right by me. That was the point, right? The gruesome blade had provided its service. It had yielded my death in a dramatic and manly fashion. I wasn't sure how long it took to die, though. This was my first proper go at it. My watch still said 11:11 when my blinking started to feel sticky. It felt as though I was one second closer to not opening them ever again. One second closer to my requested death."

I clear my throat and push back every shred of emotion attempting to erupt inside of me. *Christ, not now, Hayden! Get your shit together.* I grip my leather cuffed wrists and touch the face of my watch. "Just when I thought I was about to die, *she* arrived." My eyes drift down the stage and land on Leslie. Her auburn hair lies softly around her shoulders, framing her face and accentuating her perfectly sincere smile. Leslie doesn't smile like the British. She smiles like the beautiful, vulnerable, and quirky American that she is.

She gives me the tiniest nod, and it's like I'm transported back to that night all over again. "She wasn't the woman occupying my thoughts in that moment," I continue, staring straight into Leslie's watery green gaze. "She was simply…reality."

I break eye contact and look down at my hand that's now gripping the edge of the podium like I could break it. "You see, I knew I had loads of people who cared about me, but I couldn't believe any of them. Not one. I was too entrenched in my emotional world of misery and horror. I felt alone, and pointless, and utterly wasted here on this earth. I felt like I didn't belong anywhere. I wanted nothingness. I wanted fucking oblivion."

I snap out of my private reverie when I realise my very blatant curse. My mother shoots me a proper scowl, and I purse my lips to reel myself back in. "Having someone walk in on you just as you've thrashed your wrists to ribbons is ten times worse than having someone walk in on you in the loo. It's horrifying and you curse yourself for not locking the bloody door. Why didn't I lock the door? Why did she come in at that time?

"Regardless of the whys, the way she looked at me—the way her terrified gaze met mine—made me realise far too late that I was living in the wrong world. Seeing myself through her eyes made me desperate to take it all back. I wanted to save this poor woman from the absolute pain that my choice was causing her."

Leslie shakes her head at me incredulously as we have a silent conversation amongst the several hundred people in the audience. My brother, Theo, moves to wrap a protective arm around her shoulder. He pulls her to him and I see a small tear slip out from beneath his glasses. My heart lurches at the sight. There's something utterly raw and humbling about witnessing your strong, older brother break down. His love for me after everything that's happened still floors me. It crushes me in the most vulnerable and real way. The honesty of it is almost too much for me to take.

Leslie's eyes don't flicker to Theo's, though. They stay locked on mine in a silent chastisement. I quickly continue before she marches on stage and curses me out for apologising for what I put her through, because Leslie Lincoln is just the type to do that.

"This woman who walked in on me skidded to the floor in an evening gown and scooped me up. She held my head in her lap and my life in her hands as her *real*, wet tears dripped onto my face."

I close my eyes and recall her shaky hands holding my wrists tightly to help stop the flow of blood. Her frantic fumbling to call 999 on her phone. Her crying. Her questioning. Her pain. I laid there lifelessly watching this nearly perfect stranger desperate to save my life.

"I realised in that moment that reality and emotions can live in entirely different worlds." I frown, desperate for the audience to understand exactly what I feel so strongly in my heart. "And nothing was more real than what I had just done to this poor innocent person. Watching her cry as she stood above me was more painful than the slits I had carved into my wrists. It was more painful than the pain I felt in my heart leading up to that moment. Living in the world of my misery and wanting to leave it was unrealistic. I was running away. And looking into the eyes of just one person who gave a damn—especially someone who didn't know me all that well at the time—was such a beautiful reality that I didn't even know existed."

I clench my jaw to stop the tears that like to surface every time I picture Leslie in that one horrendous moment. The agony I put her through is soul-crushing. But it's also exactly what makes my decision to continue living so incredibly easy. I never want to put that hurt on her face again, or anyone else's for that matter.

"I can't take away the pain that I've caused everyone close to me, but I can continue to fight the darkness that I nearly let swallow me whole. And I'm not just doing it for myself. I'm doing it for the person who saved my life…and for the person who lost hers."

Flashes of my older sister, Marisa, and her wild blonde hair blast through my thoughts, and my chest does the strange shuddering thing it does every time I think about her.

"I couldn't even say my sister's name a year ago," I croak and reach down to touch my cuffs again. "But now I'm able to say her name every single day." I smile, picturing Baby Marisa and her red, peach-fuzzed head and huge round cheeks. "And saying her name feels a hell of a lot better than that blade did across my wrists."

I look up and the audience seems completely frozen. *No stopping now, Hayden. You're nearly finished.* "Most people would assume I wear these cuffs to hide my scars," I say, holding both my wrists up. "But the truth is I wear them to band my reality to me. And my new reality…is to live everyday…for Marisa."

I pause as an awkward silence stretches across the room. I'm faced with the emotional and uncomfortable looks of an audience unsure whether to applaud or stay silent. They stay silent, which I'm grateful for. This isn't something to applaud. Not everything needs a pretty fucking bow at the end.

I walk off the stage without another glance at anyone, willing myself to hold my head high. As soon as I'm concealed behind the curtain, I bend over and take in huge gulps of air. I did it. I fucking did it. I said I could and I did. No one thought I should. Not my mother or my doctor. Not even Leslie. But I proved to them what I was desperate to prove to myself.

I'm not weak anymore.

Pummelled Fantasy

Vi

BLOODY HELL.

Bloody, bleeding, blimey hell.

I quickly swipe over my cheeks and realise that my face is drenched with tears.

That's Hayden Clarke.

The Hayden Clarke who is Theo's brother.

The Hayden Clarke whom I've been fantasising about ever since I ran into him two weeks ago. How the bloody hell did I not know anything about his backstory? Leslie never mentioned a thing about what happened to him. She did mention them becoming closer over the last year, but I thought that seemed normal since she is engaged to his brother. I had no idea what was going on in their family.

Why the hell didn't I ask what the event was raising money for? Not that it would have changed anything. I was desperate to see Hayden again to know if that initial spark I felt before was real or a figment of my imagination. I never would have suspected that he— Lord, I can't even finish the thought.

"Did you know any of that?" Benji leans over and hiccups loudly. The scent of alcohol permeates heavily from his breath.

I look away and murmur, "Not a drop."

Benji better cool it on the booze. The night is still young.

"Blimey," he slurs and looks back attentively toward the announcer who's resumed her post. She informs everyone there will be a small break before the auction portion of the evening begins.

I look around the table where we're seated. The dim chandeliers cast a warm glow, doing a proper job of concealing everyone's emotional distress. Regardless, it's obvious the entire ballroom is visibly shaken by Hayden's speech. Reyna suddenly stands up from our table and turns for the exit, her body moving lithely past the occupied seats. Her fiancé, Liam, watches her with a sad look in his eyes.

"I'll be back," Liam says, looking a bit morose and follows in her wake.

Frank gets up next—his large fluff of bright red hair makes him impossible not to notice. I've met Frank several times with Leslie and have always got on well with him. He's got an uncanny way of making me feel fabulous in my own skin.

"Right then. If ever there was a time for a bloody drink." He buttons his denim blazer and straightens his bowtie, then turns to his date. "I think this party needs a bit of Ginger Sparkle. Lionel? Join me, love."

Lionel nods woodenly and the two men saunter off toward the bar. Leslie's friend Finley shifts in her seat next to me and grabs her cloth napkin off the table to dab around her eyes. Her husband, Brody, embraces her, then looks over at me. "You okay, Vi? Glad you came?" he asks, catching my anxious expression. Finley turns her vibrant blue eyes to me.

"Oh yes. I'm, erm, fine," I stammer, nervously tugging up on the bust of my white gown.

The truth is Finley and Brody kind of intimidate me. They're both American and I've met them a couple of times before, but it never gets easier. She's tall, brunette, and drop-dead gorgeous. He's even more of a conundrum on my verbal skills. He's got to be at least six-two, and his mussed, curly, dark hair makes him look sexy in that

"I didn't even try" type of way. They look like a celebrity couple.

Finley and Brody moved here sometime last year and live with Frank. From what little Leslie has told me, I believe Finley and Liam had a fling at one point. But it must have been rather minor for them all to be sitting at a table together tonight.

Mustering a shred of my confidence, I ask, "Did you guys know all of that about Hayden?"

"Most of it, yeah. You didn't?" Finley asks, her eyes looking sympathetic.

I shake my head. "No, Leslie's never said a thing. Baby Marisa... Is she—"

"Named after Theo and Hayden's sister? Yeah," Finley finishes for me.

"Wow. When did she—"

"She died—" Finley begins to answer, but Brody interrupts her.

"I'm not sure it's our place to say, Fin. Sorry, Vi. Nothing personal, but maybe Leslie would be better to tell you. Or, better yet, Theo or Hayden," he adds sympathetically.

Nerves over seeing Hayden up close again take flight in my belly. He could be coming out any minute. Excusing myself to go freshen up, I make my way to the loo in an attempt to collect my thoughts. Once inside, I wait for a couple of older ladies to exit before bracing my hands on the counter and staring at myself in the mirror.

"Bloody hell, Vi. That's him, all right," I whisper under my breath. Preparing myself for our inevitable encounter, I stand up straight and smooth down my shimmery gown. I grab a tissue and dab the slightly smudged makeup beneath my eyes as I recall the first time we met.

Two weeks ago, I had just returned from a work trip to China when Leslie rang to invite me to the soft opening of a pub called The White Swan. Reyna and Liam are the new owners and had implemented several changes, so they wanted to do a dry run with some close friends. I hadn't seen Leslie since she had the baby, but I'd been away from Bruce for too long and couldn't bear to leave him alone my first night back. When she said I could bring him along, I sort of lost my excuse to say no.

On my way there, I happened to be rounding the corner at the same time as Hayden, and we slammed into each other like two freight trains. Bruce's lead went flying, and the three of us twisted together like a fishing lure around a tree branch. It was a mess. I certainly did not inherit my brothers' athletic agility. Bruce was lapping all over Hayden's face. I didn't even get a proper look at him until Reyna came outside and found us all tangled up.

As soon as we broke apart, we locked eyes and…it was weird.

Like, mega weird.

Like I knew him from somewhere kind of weird.

Hayden is tall and fit without being overly muscled. He has coppery blonde hair that is cut with a bit of length left on the top, which was stylishly gelled every which way. The angles on his face are chiselled and masculine; the tautness of his jaw is very stern; and his eyes…Bloody hell, his eyes. They are an intense grey that make him look both mysterious and dangerous.

He looked like he could see right through my clothes…and he liked what he saw.

When he introduced himself as Hayden, it didn't ring any bells at first. It wasn't until later when I was inside the pub that Frank told me Hayden was Theo's younger brother. Then it all clicked. Of course he was Theo's brother. They both have the same intimidating, brooding way about them. Aside from their eye colour—and Hayden being a bit taller and leaner—they really do look a lot alike.

The rest of the night, our gazes kept finding each other like magnets. And every time we locked eyes, he looked almost angry. I swear he even scoffed once, like he was annoyed by how often I kept looking at him. Me! The cheek of him considering he was molesting me with his eyes as well! I felt like a young girl on a playground who got sand thrown on her by a mean boy, only making her want to play with him more. I think the fact that we were communicating all this angry, sexual tension without uttering a word to each other was what made it so thrilling. It was like a silent, sexy game of cat and mouse. But I wasn't sure it was two-sided. Watching him with everyone there, I could tell he was uncomfortable, like he was dying to leave.

Later, we both happened to be leaving the pub at the exact same time…

…Okay, I'm full of shit. I saw him getting ready to leave and I wanted to talk to him, so I decided to say my goodbyes then as well. What can I say? I'm glutton for punishment and the bugger was drawing me in with his sexy, half-mast, grey eyes. We stepped outside and I was just mustering up the courage to ask him if he wanted to grab a drink. Suddenly, Bruce stopped dead in his tracks right in front of me and off I went. Hayden caught me mid-fall in a close embrace, and I blurted out my awkward invitation. His bemused eyes turned icy cold. He quickly let me go and stuffed his hands in his pockets, muttering some unintelligible excuse. Without another word, he turned on his heel and took off, leaving me standing there like an absolute prat with my cock-blocking animal, Bruce.

The past couple of weeks, I sort of wrote him off. I assumed I was mental and had manufactured the odd chemistry between us. Now, after hearing him speak tonight, I realise I hardly knew a thing about him. He's obviously got a lot on his plate, so I'm sure he's not at all interested. Best to let sleeping dogs lie.

But, bloody hell, he's still hot as sin and the darkness of him only adds to the mysterious attraction. I shake my head confidently at myself in the mirror. "Just a normal night, Vi. Let's get on with it."

I stride out of the ladies' room with my head held high, and Leslie bustles past me in the dark hallway with a large tote thrown over her shoulder.

"What are you doing, Leslie? What's that?"

"Oh, jeez. This is my freaking breast pump. My boobs are engorged to the point of blowing up right now! Look at them. Theo calls them my porn star tits."

The corners of my mouth turn down as I glance at her cleavage that is spilling out the top of her red corset dress. "Wow, you aren't joking. They're massive!" I have to prevent myself from reaching out and poking the luscious mounds.

"Freaking nuts, isn't it? I produce more milk than a Holstein. Anyway, are you having a nice time?" she asks, her eyes wide with curiosity.

"Erm, yes, I suppose. Leslie, I feel a bit odd. You never mentioned any of what happened to Theo's family. I'm feeling like a bad friend."

"Oh, Vi, don't ever think that. When Theo and I got together, there was so much drama right off the bat. And just when things settled down for us, I got pregnant. I hardly even had time to confide in Finley."

I nod solemnly knowing that Finley and Leslie have been best friends since childhood, so things must have been tense for her. "Okay, well, if you ever need anything, I'm always here for you. And I'm coming over to meet Marisa tomorrow. I won't take no for an answer."

Leslie grins at me with a weird panic around her eyes.

"What is it?" My smile drops at the peculiar look on her face.

"I can feel my milk coming down," she whispers in a choked tone.

My eyes drop down to her breasts in confusion. "Coming down where? What the bugger does that mean?"

"It means that I love you, Vi, but get the hell out of my way before I spray milk all over your pretty dress!"

I quickly step aside as she clambers into the loo. Just as I begin to walk away, the door pops back open. "Benji is at the bar. You might want to check on him. Oh, and remind me when I come back to work that I want to talk to Roger about us designing a fashionable breast pump tote, okay? I'm serious! Boob juice machines need to look fierce as well!"

Lady in White

Hayden

Afterwards STEELING MYSELF TO BE COOL, CALM, AND COLLECTED again, I stride out into the ballroom where everyone is up and mingling about, refilling drinks and probably gossiping about everything I just said. It doesn't surprise me. People are inclined to discuss whatever guest speakers had to say. My mission for speaking tonight wasn't only to help bring awareness to suicide, but to prove to myself and everyone else that I am moving forward with my life. I'm fucking tired of being looked at like a ticking time bomb.

Theo sees me approaching and meets me halfway. "You all right?" he asks, his serious brow beneath his glasses even more de-fined than usual.

"Of course! I'm right as rain. Told you I could do it," I sing with a hearty air of confidence to my voice.

He eyes me seriously. "I know, Hayden, but it's just me you're talking to."

I pat his shoulder playfully and give him the smallest of nods. In one quick glance, we have our silent brotherly conversation that says he knows how hard that was for me and he's proud of me for do-ing it anyway. My relationship with Theo has done a complete one-eighty in the last year. After the quad accident that took our sister's life, we became somewhat estranged. I assumed it was because he blamed me for Marisa's death, but the truth is Theo blamed himself for the incident. He claimed that if he wouldn't have distracted me, I wouldn't have looked away. We were a sorry pair of Clarke brothers for many years.

Theo is thirty-one now, which is five years older than me. Marisa was between us in age. Then there is our baby sister, Daphney, who's nearing her twenty-first birthday. Our entire family was in a dark pit of despair for three years after Marisa's death—me taking it the hardest, of course. I learned in therapy that some people are inclined to slip into the deepest holes of depression more than others. And I let my survivor's guilt eat me alive and push away anyone who wanted to help me. My suicide attempt was the turning point for me, though.

Leslie was the turning point for Theo. She entered his life and that's when everything started to change. I saw glimpses of Theo being happy again, and I felt sick over the fact that it made me feel even more alone than before. It was Leslie who brought him back to life. It is just a crazy coincidence that she happened to be the one to save mine as well.

"Come on. You need to give Mum and Dad some bloody attention. They've been twitching ninnies all night." Theo claps his hand across my back and I sigh heavily as we make our way over to my slightly dishevelled-looking parents.

My mum trembles when she hugs me, clutching me tight against her robust figure. She always did give the best squishy hugs. My dad's hand holds tight to my shoulder as Mum pulls away and looks into my eyes with the matching brown hue of Theo's. "I'm incredibly proud of you, Hayden. So...so—" Her voice cracks and she covers her mouth to hide her cry.

I look away, trying my hardest to not roll my eyes. Daphney catches my gaze and offers me a meek smile from the other side of the table. Daph is the quiet type, but she's got her own ways of showing me she cares, which often involves loads of texts.

"You all should go and get a drink. Try to relax. The scary part is over." My mother looks at me and I shake my head. "I'm fine, Mum. I'm not going to break my sobriety just because you all are having a glass of wine. I haven't slipped in a year. I'm not going to falter now."

They eventually shuffle off toward the bar and Theo says he's going to go check on Leslie. I decide to man up and brace myself for the table next to me. I approach to find Brody, Finley, and Frank and his date seated at the table. I briefly wonder if Reyna and Liam ended up leaving early.

I visit with them for a bit, and Frank does a proper job of lightening the mood. "Did you know that leather cuffs are a trending fashion in the lesbian community?"

"Frank!" Finley admonishes.

I huff out a genuine laugh and it feels fantastic.

"You know, Hayden," Frank says, shuffling across the two empty seats to perch on the one beside me. He reaches into his breast pocket and hands me a business card. "I've been dabbling as a life coach for the past year now. I'd be happy to give you a free consultation if you'd like. Friends and family discount and all that."

I look down at the card in my hand. It's solid red with thick block lettering that reads: SAVIOUR IN RED. I smirk when I flip it over and read on the back: EVERYTHING LOOKS BRIGHTER WITH A TOUCH OF RED.

I glance up to ask if Frank is serious or not, but my eyes land on Reyna and Liam as they approach behind him.

"Hiya, Rey Rey," I say with a lazy half-smile.

"Hey, Hay," she huffs out a laugh and leans against Frank's chair.

"Oxford! You smell divine!" Frank exclaims while glancing up at her. "What is that scent? Unfinished Business? Or, Bone to Pick? I can't quite tell."

She rolls her eyes and looks at me apologetically. "Got a minute?"

I nod and rise, buttoning my jacket as I follow her out of the ballroom. I glimpse back at Liam. He doesn't look angry. He doesn't look sad. He looks respectful.

"Do you mind if we go outside?" Rey asks nervously. "I could use some fresh air."

"Sure…Everything okay?" I ask cautiously as we walk through the vestibule.

"Yes. I just…want to talk. Just the two of us without fucking Frank there making jokes the whole time."

We step out onto the dark London sidewalk, illuminated by several golden landscaping lanterns. My eyes drift from the bright lights and peer down at Rey's sunflower-sleeved arm—a tribute to Marisa she eventually told me about after everything that happened between us. We were best friends for years, yet there is so much we don't know about each other.

She tugs at the thin straps of her black dress, securing them back over her inked shoulders. Her dark hair is pinned up in a formal do. She looks good. She always looks good. But right now, she also looks healthy, albeit nervous.

"Your speech tonight, Hayden—" she starts and I cut her off.

"Look, I'm sorry if there was anything I said that felt too personal. I honestly didn't have it all written down. A lot of it was off the cuff."

"No, it was great. It was real, and raw, and honest. I'm sure it was incredibly enlightening to so many people who are affected by similar things. Honestly, it was enlightening to me! I feel like I finally got a glimpse inside your head. I'm happy that you're so open now and obviously doing so well."

"Thanks?" I say, skeptically. "I'm sensing a 'but' coming."

"But…I just…I can't help but feel responsible for pushing you to your breaking point, Hayden. It feels like I pushed you to do what you did. That 'shit hitting the fan' was me, wasn't it?" Her grey eyes blink nervously, the glow of the streetlight reflecting off her pupils.

I shake my head. "No offence, Rey, but don't flatter yourself." Her head jerks back quickly. "I don't mean anything by that, really.

Just that there were so many moments in time that led up to that night. You were only one."

She purses her lips and nods, her brow crinkled seriously. "I wish I could have done more. Said something to change it all."

"I wouldn't have believed you," I say, leaning forward and shoving my hands in my pockets.

She looks like she wants to say something more. She hesitates for an instant before asking, "But you believed Leslie?"

I huff out a sad laugh and shake my head. "Rey, you don't understand. It took a stranger caring for me to get a fucking wake-up call. I was bloody drowning in guilt and depression over Marisa. I wasn't letting anybody throw me a life raft. Including you. Even though I cared about you—loved you even—it didn't matter. Nothing you could have said would have stopped me. Lust and recovery do not mix."

She nods her head and looks down, picking at the cuticle on her nail. Her expression is troubled, but she doesn't tell me why, and I'm not going to ask. Truly, we are two completely different people than we were back then. We have so many dark and complicated memories together, being mates would only remind us of all of that. Distance is best for Rey and me. That was glaringly obvious when I saw her at her pub opening a couple of weeks ago with Liam. Her finding Liam was the best thing for both of us. I'm done with the sorry bastard I was with her.

"So, no love on the horizon for Hayden Clarke then?" she asks playfully.

I laugh. "No, I'm putting myself at number one for quite some time. This is something I'm always going to have to work at. But I feel good. I feel at peace. Tonight felt like a graduation ceremony for me. Made me feel like I can be a normal bloke again someday."

"I can see that." She smiles and steps closer to me, grabbing the lapels of my jacket and pulling me down for a hug. She giggles softly at my awkward hunch and whispers, "I'm always here if you need me."

I tuck my face into her and inhale deeply. It brings me immense relief when her familiar scent puts me at ease rather than making me feel love-sick. "I've always known that, Rey." Despite how bad we were for each other, I've never doubted that.

We head back inside and join everyone at the table, which is now filled with Theo, Leslie, Liam, Brody, and Finley.

"So, Lez, when are we going to have a hen night?" Finley asks as I take a seat next to my brother. "Your wedding is in five weeks and we have to get this planned."

"Oh, God, I haven't a clue," Leslie groans. "I still have a million things to do."

"Well if you guys wouldn't have rushed the wedding—"

"Rushed?" I interrupt Finley with a laugh. "Theo's been cross at Leslie for ages for making him wait this long. If she'd put him off even another day, he would have gone completely mental."

Theo eyes me sternly through his glasses as everybody gawks at him. "Hayden, my dear brother," he starts. "You watch the love of your life give birth to the second love of your life, then tell me that you could wait a second longer to make your family completely yours in every way possible."

His devoted proclamation stuns me. It stuns the whole table as we all stare at him completely gobsmacked. A sniffle from Leslie diverts my eyes.

"Damn, Theo. You can't say that shit in public. I'm still a postnatal emotional mess." Leslie wipes fresh tears from her eyes and grabs his face. She plants a fierce kiss on his lips, completely oblivious to the audience around them. She breaks their kiss, and her eyes are swimming with emotion. "I love you."

Theo rests his forehead against hers and closes his eyes and breathes a deep, contented breath. It's as if he's drinking in the words from her mouth, pulling them into his lungs, and pushing them out through his bloodstream straight to his heart. It's such a tender moment, I can't look away.

The announcer breaks the mood, informing everyone to take their seats for the auction portion of the fundraiser to begin. Leslie, Theo, and I stand to head over to my parents' table, but my heart stutters as I catch sight of a familiar woman in a white dress.

"Vi," I say on a quiet exhale without even thinking. I look around nervously, and I'm grateful no one seems to have heard me. I didn't even mean to say her name out loud, but her name has been on repeat in my mind since two weeks ago. This mess of long blonde hair and long, spindly limbs literally knocked me flat on my back, and I've been seeing stars ever since.

What the hell is she doing here?

My eyes do a double take to confirm they aren't tricking me. My view is distracted by some guy in a baggy tuxedo who has his hands wrapped tightly around her waist. He's standing behind her and whispering into her ear as she giggles halfheartedly. Or at least I think it's halfheartedly. Just then, she gives him a coy "come hither" look that immediately makes me feel annoyed.

Without permission, my gaze takes a walk down her body, absorbing how her snug dress hugs every line of her slim frame. The dim chandelier light bounces off the shimmering fabric and creates a glowing effect all around her.

Christ, she's still gorgeous.

She appears to be guiding the man-boy in our direction.

Leslie's voice snaps me out of my daze when she calls out, "Vi? Benji? You guys okay?"

Curiosity keeps my feet planted. Vi glances up, her brow puckering in the middle as she looks pleadingly at Leslie. When this Benji fellow sees Leslie, he releases Vi and steps around her. His droopy eyes grow wide in shock.

"My sexy lady in red," he bellows and stumbles toward Leslie with his arms outstretched.

Before I have a chance to react, Theo moves in front of Leslie with his chest puffed out protectively. Now the two men are eye-to-eye, or chin-to-eye I guess you'd say since Benji is on the smallish side. Vi's face turns from uncomfortable to nervous, so I take two steps closer and place a calming hand on Theo's shoulder.

Vi's wide blue eyes peer past the small space between Benji and Theo and land right on me. Her round cheeks flush a rosy hue. She instantly looks away, then right back at me again. I can't help but stare back. It's that same fucking strange pull that I felt at The White Swan Pub. Frustrated, I look away, clenching my jaw.

"I think you've had a bit too much to drink, mate." Theo's voice is low and controlled but has an obvious edge to it. He adjusts his glasses like he always does when he's feeling cagey. I swear it's a defence mechanism that he developed growing up. Whenever we tussled as kids, he'd get so barking mad at me if I'd gone at him when he was wearing his glasses.

"I think you might be spot-on, good sir," Benji slurs and pokes his finger into Theo's chest. "Good Lord, are you wearing protective armour under your dress shirt?"

"No," Theo replies without a shred of amusement.

"Someone needs to get control of him," I grumble.

Vi moves in and grabs Benji around the arm. "Come on, Benji Boy. Here are our seats."

Her eyes flash coolly to me as she pulls him down onto a chair. She looks away and pours a glass of water, then shoves it against his chest. Her eyes find mine again, and I can't help but frown at the whole situation. If he is her boyfriend, she should have better control over him. Wanker.

Leslie catches me scowling at Vi and steps in between my line of sight. "Hayden, you remember my coworker Vi, right? And Benji?"

I nod dismissively, then quietly excuse myself. I'm confused by how I feel about having the woman who sparked something I thought was dormant inside of me be here to witness the speech I just gave about my innermost secrets. Definitely not the first impression

I would have wanted with her. And now she's eyeing me like I'm the prat here.

I stroll over to my parents and take my seat. The further I stay away from Vi tonight, the better. Perhaps I don't affect her the same way she affects me. The way she was eyeing me at The White Swan Pub led me to believe otherwise. Regardless, something about her makes me feel out of control, and I don't like it. It doesn't help that every time I look over at her, she looks over at me. God, it's so maddeningly juvenile I could laugh.

"You were rather rude to my coworker," Leslie chastises as she settles down beside me, followed closely behind by Theo.

"Why is she even here?" I whisper as the announcer begins the bidding on a custom dining room set built by Theo.

"Good question," Theo drawls. "Fucking Benji wears on my last nerve."

"Oh, shut up! He's harmless. Vi and Benji took Mitch and Julie's tickets. What's the big deal?"

"It's kind of inappropriate for her boyfriend to get pissed at a charity if you ask me," I sneer.

Leslie's green eyes widen in disbelief. "Pot! Meet kettle!"

My face goes white as I realise what I just said. "That was different," I bite out between clenched teeth. Christ, I walked right into that one.

Leslie's face softens. "Don't be hard on my coworkers. They're good people. Really, you'd get on with Vi, I'm sure."

That's exactly what I'm afraid of.

Turkey's Done

Vi

*B*URR. *FEELS FUCKING GLACIAL IN HERE NOW*, I THINK TO MYSELF after my less than warm and fuzzy greeting from Hayden. Not that I had much to expect I suppose. It's not like we really know anything about one another. But, bloody hell, he could have at least acknowledged my presence without a moody glower.

Benji sucks down the glass of water I handed him. He begins hiccupping and giggling to himself. "I've never drank wine before."

I roll my eyes and shake my head. "You're drinking water." The bugger can't handle his liquor, that's quite apparent. I just hope I'm able to pour him into a cab after this.

As the auction begins, I find myself impressed by the furniture pieces being displayed for bidding. Leslie told me about Theo's talent, but I've never made it over to his shop to see for myself. Their flat rests above his business, so hopefully I can see more when I pop around tomorrow.

The announcer continues rattling off numbers as a suited man carries several small wooden boxes out and places them on every few tables. He drops one on ours and Finley reaches for it first, smoothing her fingers over the glossy, nearly black wood. The announcer explains there's a silent auction sheet inside each box. As soon as Finley places the box back in the centre of the table, I grab it to get a look.

It would seem we're bidding on something inside the box, but I'm less concerned about the contents and more interested in the keepsake box. Based on the explanation sheet, the box comes with the winning bid. I instantly have to have it. I write down my name and fill in an exorbitant pound figure, hoping it's enough to secure the beautifully intricate box.

I get a funny sensation and look up to see Hayden practically glaring at me, his brow furrowed in the most frustrated manner. *What the hell is this guy's problem?* If I was trying to forget about the sexual chemistry I felt before, this is a right proper way of achieving it.

"I think I'm gonna be sick," Benji croaks, then burps and slaps his hand over his mouth.

"Oh, fuck," I whisper as he shoots up out of his seat and makes a mad dash for the exit. "Where the hell is he going?" I say out loud to myself. Christ, I did not intend to be someone's babysitter tonight!

I follow Benji out of the ballroom—a bit more gracefully than him—and stroll outside to find him hunched over a waste bin, retching his guts out. "Benjiiiiii," I groan, looking away so I won't make myself sick as well. *Mustn't smell it, Vi. Mustn't smell it!*

"You guys okay?" Leslie asks, hurrying after us.

I shake my head and gesture silently to the scene because it truly does speak for itself. I think I might even hear Benji weeping. Theo comes out next and assesses the situation.

"You can't get him in a cab like that. The driver will take one look at him and tell you to get stuffed," he says, removing his glasses and rubbing the bridge of his nose.

Damn, he really looks like his brother without his glasses on.

"He lives in Notting Hill," I say, placing my hands on my hips. "It's not terribly far. Maybe I can lump him onto the Tube?"

"The hell you can!" Leslie admonishes. "Theo, go get Hayden. He's sober. He can take them."

"No!" I exclaim and then rein in my reaction since Theo and Leslie gawk at me in shock. "No…Thank you, but that's completely unnecessary. Really, I'll figure something out."

"Stop, Vi. It's no trouble. Theo, go."

Theo doesn't hesitate before he takes off back into the ballroom. Oh, God, this is going to be awkward. "I really wish you'd just let me figure this out, Leslie. I'm a big girl."

"I know you are, but that's what friends are for!" she says, gazing over at Benji apologetically. "Poor bastard. Your heart was in the right place."

"Yeah, well, don't feel too sorry for him. It was self-inflicted."

A moment later, Hayden and Theo are outside and Hayden does not look pleased. Annoyance is written all over his features as our eyes connect.

"Thanks, Hayden. Our hero with a chariot!" Leslie sings with glee.

Hayden's eyes narrow on me. "I hope he doesn't vomit in the car." He hands the keys to the valet, who hurries off to bring the car around.

"See! This is a bad idea, Leslie. We can't have him mucking up anybody's car. I'll get him on the Tube. It's only one stop. I can manage."

"How are you going to get him on the Tube?" Hayden huffs, his eyes roving down my entire body.

Crossing my arms over my chest self-consciously, I reply, "Don't worry about me, mate. I'm stronger than I look."

"Wearing that? I have a hard time believing you." He rolls his eyes and saunters away, raking his hand through his hair.

"Hayden's right, Vi. Let him help. Here's a bag just in case." Leslie hands me a clear plastic baggie that I pray Benji doesn't end up needing because he won't be the only one needing a bag in the car if that's the case.

"I gotta get back in, babe," Theo says. "Mum wants me to say something when they finish auctioning my pieces."

"I'm coming, I'm coming." She looks at me. "You good?"

I glance over at Hayden who's propped himself against the brick wall with his arms crossed in a moody stance. "I'm great," I reply with a fake smile.

"I'll talk to you later," Leslie says, waving me off as she rushes to follow Theo back inside.

I turn to face away from Hayden with a bit of an attitude as we wait for his car. I don't know what the hell his problem is with me, but I'm certain I did nothing to deserve it.

When a black BMW comes around the bend, I hear Hayden push off the wall and walk over to Benji. I breathe a sigh of relief because I want nothing to do with that bin.

"In you go," he says, folding Benji into the backseat.

I get a cutting glare from Hayden when I walk around to the other backseat door. "What are you doing?"

"I'm going to ride in the back with him."

"What on earth for?"

"In case he gets sick! You don't want him puking in your car. I won't be much help to him from the front seat."

"I'm not a fucking chauffer. Ride in the front." Hayden stands back, holding the passenger door open for me like it's the end of the discussion. I do my best to stomp the whole way over and then slide in. I reach down to grab the extra bit of my dress to tuck inside the car, but Hayden beats me to it.

"Bloody helpful, rude bastard," I mumble as he walks around the car.

He slides into the driver's seat. "Where am I going?" His voice is flat as he stares straight forward.

"Notting Hill. On Portobello Road."

We sit in silence as he navigates the streets to the neighbourhood where Benji lives with his aunt. I hear some faint groans from Benji and look back nervously for fear of another rupture.

"Did I do something to offend you?" I ask after a bit of silent tension.

"Of course not," he replies dismissively.

"It's just that this is the first time you've spoken more than one word to me and you haven't been super friendly."

"You didn't do anything," he mumbles and offers nothing more on the subject.

When we arrive at Benji's flat, Hayden pulls up to the curb behind a black cab.

"Benji, we're here," I say as I get out to open the back door nearest him.

Hayden beats me to it as he opens his side first. He grips Benji's arm that's now completely limp.

Benji moans out, "Can't walk. Two whole floors. Too far. I'll die."

Hayden rolls his eyes and grabs Benji by the arm to throw him over his shoulder.

"You don't honestly mean to carry him up two flights of stairs," I scoff as Benji groans in weak protest.

"Just point the way to your boyfriend's flat, would you?" he snaps, rolling his eyes.

His impertinence angers me like crazy, so I storm off without looking back to see if he's struggling. I wrench open the entry door and the doorman gawks at me in confusion.

"Benji Abernathy." I point to the doorway as Hayden emerges.

"Second level, second door on the right," the doorman replies, looking rather taken aback. "There's no lift."

Ignoring his warning, I storm up the steps as quickly as possible. Aside from tonight, I've been to Benji's flat one other time to pick him up for a work do, but I've never been inside. He lives with his Aunt Agitha, whom Benji is always telling stories about in the office. Apparently she's a psychic, or a clairvoyant, or something. For that reason, she doesn't get on with a lot of the family who are heavily religious. Leave it to Benji to connect with a fellow outsider.

I knock on the door. When it swings open, I am met by a heavy-set woman wearing a giant floral print moo moo and hair rollers and who's looking at me in shock.

"Aunt Agitha, I presume?"

"Yes." She eyes my dress briefly. "Are you Benji's mate?"

Just then, Hayden catches up. I can feel him looming over my shoulder, his breathing a bit heavier than before. Ignoring the prickling sensation his hot breath on my neck causes, I silently point backward with my thumb.

Agitha's eyes grow wide in acknowledgement and she tsks, "Foolish child."

Hayden drops Benji to his feet and he wavers, holding onto Hayden's shoulders for support. Benji then wraps both hands around Hayden's back and gives him a mighty bear hug. "Thanks for the lift," he mumbles against Hayden's chest. Then he stuns us all when he steps back and drops a kiss right on Hayden's mouth!

It wasn't a proper snog. Just a quick peck on the lips. But Hayden's shocked expression is priceless. I bite my lip to conceal the growing urge I have to laugh. When Benji turns around, his eyes are completely closed. His aunt steps past me and grabs him by the arm. "Come on, Benji. Off to beddy-bye you go."

"Top night!" Benji shouts and then stumbles into me. Hayden reaches forward, grabbing me firmly around my waist to prevent me from falling.

Agitha's eyes fly wide as if she's been stung. Standing only a foot away from my face now as she clasps Benji's arm, she looks back and forth between Hayden and me. I swear her pupils dilate, so I look down briefly to ensure she isn't hurt anywhere.

"You two," she gasps, her voice tight and high-pitched. "Are you together?"

"No," I jeer, a bit overly defensive as she continues looking back and forth between us. Perhaps Hayden's charms are affecting her as well.

"I just thought. No, no. Never mind." She shakes her head as if trying to snap herself out of a daze. Then Benji moans loudly that he thinks he's going to be sick. She scurries him into the flat and shuts the door, offering us a quick thank you.

"You sure your boyfriend is into girls?" Hayden grumbles, wiping his lips as we make our way back toward the stairs.

I snicker, "I couldn't care less who he's into." Benji kissing Hayden was the perfect end to an already weird evening. Serves Hayden right for being a brooding, cranky wanker.

He glances over at me, allowing me to pass him on the steps. "I just assumed."

I pause and look up at him. "He's a coworker I thought could do with a night out."

Hayden's brow furrows. "I think he'll need a morning in after this."

I laugh softly and continue our descent. Hayden opens the car door for me again, and his crabby expression from before seems slightly lifted.

"Benji's snog soften you up a bit?" I ask as he starts the car and pulls away.

"What do you mean?"

"You seemed rather moody earlier. It seems Benji's affection warmed you up."

As if compliments crush him, his eyes turn back into slits. "Where do you live?"

"Oh, you don't have to take me home. Just take me back to the ballroom. I'll grab a cab there."

"Where…do…you…live?" he repeats slower and with more force.

"You are awfully bossy for someone who's only spoken one word to me before tonight."

"You're awfully sassy for someone whose dog has licked my balls."

61

"What?" I exclaim and start laughing. "Is that what all this fuss is about? Are you mad at Bruce?"

"Of course not." Hayden scowls, looking out the side window. "But I really need to know where I'm going."

Sighing heavily, I tell him I live by Brick Lane Market and he gives me a shocked look.

"What?" I ask.

"Nothing."

He's back to the silent treatment for several more miles. This man's temperature changes are making me feel like I have the flu. Finally desperate to break the silence, I say the first thing that pops in my head.

"You...did well up there tonight." I fidget with the outer layer of fabric on my dress, pinching it and rolling the smooth material between my fingers. "It was a very moving speech."

I'm dying to look at his face to gauge his reaction, but I'm too scared. Instead, I do something really smart. I continue babbling.

"I was always crap at speeches. I'd clam up and lose my words. Then I'd look down at my notes and everything would suddenly look backwards. One time I belched right in the middle of the speech. I think the class thought I was going to puke like poor Benji." I laugh awkwardly and look out the widow, slamming my eyes shut tightly. *Shut up, Vi. Shut up!*

Thankfully, he chuckles and says, "Thanks. It wasn't easy." I can't help but glance back at him. His hands are gripping the wheel so hard his knuckles are white. "Just trying to bring awareness and help raise funds to support others in need. It's more common than you'd think."

His demeanour transforms from an agitated, cagey alpha to a cool, suave business man. It seems like an act.

"I know. I mean, I can imagine...I mean...Bugger..." My voice trails off and I look away, feeling my cheeks heat with embarrassment. Clearing my throat, I decide to pry further. "Have you done a speech like that before?"

He shakes his head slowly.

"So this was kind of a big night then." He continues to squint against the city lights, appearing deep in thought. Feeling brazen, I add, "I, erm, actually have questions…if you ever want to answer them. I mean, of course you don't have to. But if you do want to, I'd be interested to learn more."

Questions? Christ, Vi, why didn't you just tell him you're a morbid freak who sleeps with porcelain dolls?

Silence stretches out between us again and he looks confused.

"Do you mean questions about the charity?" he asks, his voice low.

"That and other things," I answer. I'm curious about many things regarding Hayden. I'm not sure I've been this intrigued by a male in my entire life. His speech did nothing to deter that curiosity.

"Are you a suicide survivor?" he asks.

"No," I reply, frowning.

"Do you know someone who is?"

"No."

"Then what on earth do you care to know more about?"

"You," I blurt out.

He doesn't seem to like my answer. His jaw clenches as we drive around the familiar streets to my neighbourhood. I exhale and look out the window, feeling like an absolute prat. I went from loathing him to wanting to pick his brain. Now I just want out of this tense car of emotion.

"This is me," I say, pointing to the curb in front of my alley.

He pulls up in front of the Hookah Lounge that's illuminating the entire sidewalk with its glowing neon purple and green sign. The doors are drizzling with people wafting in and out with big puffs of smoke billowing out each time they open.

Just as I begin to thank him, he hops out of the car and walks around to open my door. "Thanks for the ride," I say, clambering out.

"Which is yours?"

"I'm just down this alley. I'll be fine. Thanks again," I say, waving and attempting to scurry away from him with my tail tucked between my legs.

He ignores my dismissal and begins walking toward the dimly lit alley. I remain still on the sidewalk and say, "Mr. Bossy is back again, I see."

He stops and turns on his heel to glare at me. The purple light is shinning through his dishevelled spiky hair and gives him a tasty glow. I glance down to see the green light is reflecting on my dress. I try crossing my arms over my chest to look more intimidating now that I'm the colour of the Hulk.

"I'm not about to let a beautiful woman in an evening gown walk down an alley at night by herself." His voice has an edge of annoyance to it. "Some people would call it gentlemanly."

Beautiful. He said beautiful. My nerves sizzle beneath my skin as that one word uttered from his perfectly shaped mouth instantly made him hot to me again. Okay, fine. He never stopped being hot. But with the way he's been behaving, I was trying my hardest to be put off by him.

"I'm not some people."

With a huff of a laugh, he replies, "I've gathered."

He unbuttons his suit coat and opens it just enough to slide his hands into his trouser pockets. My eyes follow the action and land right on his crotch. I look up and the cheeky bugger is smirking at me. I look away, feeling mortified once again. So much for a Hulk smash.

"Look, I'm sorry, but I'm not quite going home yet."

His scowl returns as his jaw shifts back and forth in obvious annoyance. "What do you mean?"

"I mean, I have an errand to run."

"An errand. At nearly"—he looks at his watch—"eleven o'clock at night. What on earth—"

"It was my birthday on Wednesday, and I still haven't had my cake. There's a bakery around the corner that closes in five minutes. If you don't shut up and leave, I'm not going to get my birthday cake and I bloody well love cake." I think I stamp my foot, but I'm too busy thinking about cake to notice.

"Cake. You want cake?"

I nod earnestly.

"Well then, let's get some cake."

Let Her Eat Cake

Hayden

*F*UCKING CAKE, I THINK TO MYSELF AS I FOLLOW VI PAST THE Hookah Lounge. She smiles at some of the eclectic-looking patrons, and my gaze simmers down her bare shoulders, all the way to the curve of her back that leads to her pert arse.

Fucking hell, she really is gorgeous.

Aside from her lithe and feminine body, it's her face that captures me. She's got round, rosy cheeks that make her look sweet and innocent, but her eyes portray something entirely different. They slant upward in a way that makes her look sexy as hell in a feline sort of way. Her long blonde hair contrasts with her dark brows and thick lashes. The combination of all her features is sexy as fuck.

Why are you doing this, Hayden? You should have let her go get her own bloody cake. The last thing you should be doing is distracting yourself.

But fuck if I didn't get an immense sense of satisfaction when her eyes glimpsed down at my package and her pupils dilated ever so slightly. She feels it. She feels whatever this strange, magnetic pull is between us. It's moments like this that I would give anything to close my eyes and wish away the dark choices I've made in my life and have it come true. Meeting a gorgeous, luminous girl who seems like she's got her life together is not something that happens every day. If this were five years ago, before Marisa died, I'd turn on my cocky boyish charm, grab her by the waist, and tell her to fuck the dessert…That we could make our own.

"Here we are," she says softly, snapping me out of my reverie. "You want one?"

I nod and notice her rubbing her slender arms as if she's cold.

"Any allergies?"

I shake my head and she orders two cakes from the small to-go window of the brick building. There's a glass door with BOLT FROM THE BLUE CAKES scrawled on it and there appears to be a darkened seating area inside.

I shrug out of my suit coat and drape it over her shoulders. She turns her head and our eyes connect again, like they have been all night. But this time, instead of feeling annoyance, I only feel attraction. Carnal, chemical attraction. Damn if it doesn't feel good, too.

The employee comes back to the window with two brown boxes. I quickly grab a tenner out of my pocket and hand it over.

"I can buy my own cake," she says, leaning her back against the brick wall. She watches me take my change with a coquettish look that makes it hard for me not to smile.

"You can't buy your own birthday cake. That's bad luck or something."

"Superstitious much?" she asks, grabbing one of the boxes from my hands.

Instead of answering her question, I change the subject. "So why didn't you get your birthday cake on your birthday?"

Her blue gaze casts downward and a look of discomfort mars her pretty features.

"Did I hit a button?" I ask, frowning.

She swallows and shakes off my query. "It's nothing. I just never really enjoy celebrating on my actual birthday. It's like…a thing with me. There's always so much expectation for the day to be perfect and for you to hear from all the right people. The anxiety, and the pressure, and the specialness of that one day a year annoys me. Life isn't like that. It's not perfect. It's unexpected. Birthdays aren't always a great day. Sometimes they are sad. And now I'm rambling." She gestures over to a small metal patio table and chairs nearby and adds, "Enough of that! I hope you like surprises!"

As we sit down, my curiosity about her is only piqued more. She's definitely got some strange hang up about her birthday. I know asking questions will only make things extra personal, so I decide to shift my focus to the box in my hand. When I open it, I find a chocolate frosted cupcake with a white sprinkled dusting on top. Before I remove the wrapper, I peek over to watch Vi open hers.

She's got a soft smile on her face like she's sharing some private memory with herself as she peels back the wax paper. She chews on her lip excitedly before opening her mouth and sinking her teeth into the white frosted cupcake. Her eyes close in ecstasy.

"I win," she groans, the streetlight casting a warm glow on her platinum blonde hair.

"Win what?" I ask, attempting to conceal my look of amusement.

"Life," she beams, then licks the bit of frosting stuck to the arch of her lip.

I huff and take a bite. "Okay, I might see what you mean now." I have to physically restrain myself from closing my eyes and moaning.

"Told you," she says, extending her cupcake to me. "Let me try yours."

"No!" I exclaim defensively.

Her blue eyes turn to saucers. "Are you joking? Why ever not?"

"It's mine. You're winning life. I'm winning the afterlife. This cake is life-changing. I've died and gone to Heaven, and they serve cake." I turn back to my coveted dessert, but secretly smirk at her exasperated huff.

"I can't believe you!"

I shoot her a dangerous glower. "I'm *not* a sharer…of many

things." I slide my eyes down to her bust in a possessive stare before sinking my teeth into another bite.

Her amused face falls in response to my serious expression, and her eyes lock on my mouth as I chew. She draws her lush lower lip into her mouth and bites down on the pink flesh. My gaze drifts to her lip and then shoots back up to her stunning blue eyes.

Christ, this is so wrong.

"But it's my birthday." Her voice is husky as she shifts to the edge of her seat and rolls her shoulders forward, extending her line of cleavage.

That, coupled with her flirtatious smile, makes me feel things in all areas south of my neck. Suddenly, I am desperate to kiss her. "You said Wednesday was your birthday."

She shrugs her small shoulders that are nestled inside my large jacket. "Close enough."

Just then, my eyes widen as I realise I've lost track of time. I glance down at my watch the second 11:11 ticks over to 11:12.

"Fuck," I growl.

"What's wrong?"

I shake my head, my previous mood evaporating instantly. "Nothing. Here." I hand her my cupcake and refuse the offer of hers.

She looks hurt and confused, her eyes full of questions, but I don't have time to worry about that. I lean over and alternate gripping the cuffs on my wrists and curse myself for losing track of time, tonight of all nights.

"Are you about done?" I ask, my tone clipped.

"Quite," she snaps and slips out of my jacket, depositing it on the table in front of me. She chucks the barely eaten cupcakes into the nearby bin and begins walking toward her flat.

Fuck. Now what? I snatch my jacket up and hustle to catch up to her, tossing it back over her goose-pimpled shoulders. "Will you please keep this on? It's brass monkeys out here."

"I don't need it!" she snaps and turns to face me. "Look, Hayden. Thank you for walking me to get cake, but I can't keep up with your mood swings. I'd just like to say goodnight."

I exhale and slice my hand through my hair. I've hurt her feelings. That wasn't what I was going for. I just got caught up. "I just—" I start but stop because I don't know how to say that without sharing every sordid detail.

"You just what?" She stamps her foot. I idly make a mental note that that's the second time she's stamped her foot at me, and it's cute as fuck. But I shouldn't be noticing how anything she does is cute.

"I just have a lot going through my mind, Vi. You heard my speech tonight. It's no bloody secret. 11:11 is kind of an important time on my radar and I missed it."

"What do you mean you missed it? What would you have done?"

I shake my head knowing that there's no way I'm going to unload all of that on her. I haven't unloaded all of that on anyone. Not even Doc.

"Fine, Hayden. I told you I have questions and that I'm curious, but you're obviously not able or interested in sharing yet. So, like I said, probably just best we say goodnight."

I nod my head and follow her lead as she turns to continue our journey back to her flat. As we walk, Doc's Countdown Challenge keeps churning over and over in my mind. He's fucking spot-on. Telling my story to a ballroom full of blank faces was miles easier than telling even one shred of my truth to Vi.

When we round the corner to her alleyway entrance, she says, "Thanks for the ride...and for the cake." She slides my jacket off and hands it to me, looking a little sad. "I wish you luck with all things."

As I grab my jacket, our fingers graze and the spark that I felt earlier is back. I swear her chest rises with a gasp as our eyes connect. Then she narrows her baby blues with a renewed sense of determination. Just like that, I'm no longer concerned about 11:11. I'm concerned about all things Vi.

Desperate not to say goodbye to her, I say the first thing that comes to mind. "Would you want to help me with something?"

Her brow furrows. "Depends what it is."

I rustle my jacket in my hands and look down at it as I reply, "Look, I know I've been a bit of a prat tonight, but I have this challenge I'm supposed to complete. I'm thinking if it is you who helps me, maybe you will get why I'm being like this toward you."

She swallows. "What kind of challenge?"

Christ, she looks terrified of you, Hayden! "Well, you said you are curious about my story. If that's true, then hopefully it wouldn't bother you too much. Basically, I have to tell you about the days leading up to my, erm, attempt."

She nods seriously without uttering a word. God, I feel like a fucking fool. This is awkward and horrible. I hate Doc. He's a fucking wanker. "It's not pretty…and it's not easy. It's dark and it's fucked. I was in a bad place."

"I'll do it."

"This is a bad idea. I'll find somebody else," I continue nervously, hardly recognising her reply.

"I'll do it."

"Or I'll tell my doctor to get stuffed. He's a little unconventional, so—"

"I said I'll do it!" she exclaims, swatting me on the arm and snapping me out of my internal chastisement.

"Could have just said so," I mumble, secretively grinning at her. I rub my arm where she whacked me, feeling somewhat shocked by her strength. I look into her eyes and I'm surprised to see a look of confidence that wasn't there before. "Okay then," I reluctantly agree, noting the determined set of her jaw.

"I would like to hear your story, Hayden Clarke," she adds. Her breaths come deeply as if she knows what she's agreed to and is invigorated by the challenge. The pain. The anguish of it all.

My chest feels heavy from the intensity behind her blue eyes. The willingness and complete trust she's got in me to share this with her is a lot. "Then I have a very serious question to ask you."

"Go on," she says, curiously arching one brow.

"May I have your phone number?" Fuck if I'm not anxious asking for her bloody digits. I've been out of the game too long.

She shoots me a saucy smirk and it relieves me. I give her my phone and she punches her digits in. When I reach to take it back, she pulls it out of my grasp just before handing it over. Her brazen playfulness is a huge fucking turn-on. It's like someone who laughs instead of screams when they sky jump out of an airplane. And the fact that it's coming from this willowy sexy blonde is mind-boggling.

I tuck the phone back into my pocket and step closer to her. My eyes lock on her chest as she backs up against the aged, brown brick building beside her door. I love that her self-possessed poise drops when I am closer. I love witnessing the effect I have on her.

She looks taken aback. "What are you doing?" she asks, her eyes dancing around my face nervously. A spark of excitement glimmers in her baby blues.

"Things between us are about to get very heavy, Vi," I start, flicking my eyes back and forth between hers. "And before all of that happens—before I drag you down the rabbit hole with me—I have something very serious I'd like to do."

"What?" she croaks, her voice husky and trembling.

"Tonight I just want to be a man who walks a gorgeous woman to her doorstep and kisses her senseless."

She nods her permission slowly, her eyes sparkling with shocked excitement. Without pause, I drop my jacket on the ground and slip my hands around her face. I stare down at her luscious, peach lips. She grips my dress shirt just above my hips, and I devilishly grin at the tickling sensation of her tiny hands on my sides.

"I haven't kissed a woman in a while. I want to be sure I do this properly," I say, my voice gravellier than I intended it to be.

She nods slowly and lifts her chin. I pause a mere centimetre away from her lips and change course to her cheek. I drop a feather-light kiss on that cheek, breathing in her blissful womanly scent. What is it that makes women smell so incredibly divine? And Vi better than any other I've ever smelled before? It's like a combination of expensive shampoo and sweet, sugary fruit. I quickly move over and kiss her other cheek, allowing my lips to trickle down to the curve of her jaw and to her chin. I flick my tongue out on her chin and trail it slowly upward, grazing the tip of her lower lip. Her mouth drops with a throaty gasp, inviting me in. But I hold back. I am savouring every delicious second of this. I won't be rushed. I press my lips to her forehead before placing another soft drop on her perfect button nose. Finally, I pull back to appreciate her sexy awed expression.

"Is that all—" she starts, but I crush my mouth to hers before she can finish her smartarse remark.

Swallowing the sweet taste of her sugary lips sends shivers up the back of my neck. I plunge my tongue in, desperate for a more satisfying sample. Her tongue responds to my request, pulsing and kneading in a perfect rhythm of ecstasy.

Fuck, she tastes as good as she smells. If that cupcake earlier is the afterlife, then Vi's lips are eternity. Her grip tightens on the belt of my trousers and she pulls my hips flush against hers. If she didn't know how much this kiss was affecting me, she sure does now. I press her up against the wall with my groin and she moans into my mouth.

Blast it all.

Her hands roam up my sides to my shoulders. Then they slide down to my triceps, to my forearms, to—

I pull back, jerking my cuff-covered wrists from her grasp. She's panting heavily. Her mouth looks raw and swollen. Her hair is mussed and wild, doing nothing to tamper my needful desire for her.

In short, she's the most beautiful woman I've seen in my entire life.

I bend over and pick my jacket up off the ground, covering the evidence of our encounter. "Thank you," I say and turn on my heel, striding down the dark alley and cursing myself a thousand times over for every moment that lead up to that one.

Winner Winner Chicken Diiner

Vi

"I'M NOT KIDDING, BRUCE. YOU SHOULD HAVE SEEN HIS FACE. HE looked like I slapped him. I have no bloody clue what I did wrong, or what he was thinking. Maybe I'm a crap kisser?" I groan and cover my face with my thin afghan as I stretch my legs out to prop on the top rail of my balcony.

After a fitful night's sleep and thinking about Hayden Clarke the entire time, it's a new day at last. Bruce and I have been out for our morning stroll, stopped over to the dog shop for a new chew, and now we're lounging on the balcony, soaking up some rare London sunlight. Anything I could think of to keep myself busy. Brick Lane Market is noisy and bustling with Saturday morning shoppers, street vendors, and traffic. It was a good distraction while it lasted.

Bruce pauses on his chew and licks his lips, looking at me curiously. "Do you think I'm a crap kisser, Bruce?" I drop down off my patio lounger and grab his wet muzzle to kiss him right on his nose.

He takes this as an invitation to "Bruce Hug" me. Bruce Hugs consist of him walking into me until I'm forced to lie down. Then he flops his entire body on top of me. He's heavy as hell and he'll Bruce Hug me for ages if I let him. I think lying on top of me gives him a sense of security by enabling him to keep me right where he can see me.

"All right, Bruce, off you go. I have to get a move on. Leslie is expecting me." He sneezes in protest.

A bit later, I step out of my flat, freshly showered and wearing a pair of denim skinny shorts, brown braided leather flats, and a jewelled print crop top. It's a beautiful day outside and Leslie's flat is only a ten-minute walk, so I'm able to enjoy my stroll through our neighbourhood. My father wanted me to have a vehicle, but with a Tube stop just around the corner, I talked him out of it. It really doesn't make sense when there's only street parking here and my office is so close.

I arrive at the large warehouse that houses Theo's custom furniture on the lower level and his and Leslie's flat up above. There are large windows looking into his workshop, and I press my face against the glass to get a good look. It's filled with various elements of his process and some partially completed projects. Around the corner is a window that looks into a small showroom with an attached office. Leslie has said it's an appointment only type of studio, and I immediately see why. From everything I can see, his work is exquisite. He has somehow captured the beauty of a rustic country style with a fresh and modern design. I imagine his work is coveted and high-priced.

I enter the side door by the garage that Leslie told me would be open. I'm greeted by steps to the left and the shop entrance straight ahead. She said the steps would lead right up to their flat door, so I reach the top and knock, shifting a gift bag in my hand as I wait.

When the door opens, my face is eye level with the most adorable red-haired baby I've ever seen. I presume the masculine blond-dusted forearms wrapped around her are Theo's until I catch sight of familiar brown leather cuffs. I'm stunned when my gaze lifts to find Hayden's grey eyes peering down at me.

"Hayden!" I exclaim in surprise.

"Vi...What are you doing here?" His face appears just as

confused as mine.

I look around for a moment like I'm in the wrong place. "I'm here to meet Marisa."

"I didn't know you were coming around. You never mentioned."

"I didn't know you were visiting as well," I state, grabbing my hair, twisting it around my hand, and releasing it nervously.

He adjusts Marisa, who's facing out in his arms, and she makes an adorable growly sound. She grabs hold of Hayden's leather wrist cuff with her chubby digits and awkwardly tries to get it to her mouth.

"I'm not visiting. I live here."

This shocks me. "Since when? I thought this was Leslie and Theo's flat."

"It is. I, erm, live with them." He looks rather embarrassed.

"Oh." I glance back down at Marisa and touch her hand. She instantly wraps her fingers around mine and tries to pull them to her mouth. "Had I known, I wouldn't have—"

"Wouldn't have come?" he asks, a peculiar frown marring his face.

I stare up at his fallen expression. "No, I just mean. I don't know what I mean." My cheeks heat. I know exactly what I mean, but I don't have the nerve to say it. This feels awkward, especially given that all I care about right now are the reasons for his abrupt exit last night.

"Vi!" Leslie sings from inside the flat and rushes over to greet me. She moves past Hayden and brings me in for a hug. She's dressed in yellow and black polka dot leggings with a long, billowy, green tank. She makes mummyhood look fun and fashionable with her ever-present eclectic style. She beams proudly. "You made it! I'm so pumped. This is Marisa, as you can tell. And your timing is perfect. She's actually having a great morning, isn't she, Hayden?"

He nods in agreement as Leslie drags me from the steps and into their flat. It's all wide open with super high ceilings and tons of natural light pouring in from the sweeping industrial windows. It's very modern and bright with white walls and several familiar-look-ing grey wooden furniture pieces taking place of pride throughout the flat. An open staircase leads up to what looks like a loft bedroom. At the same time I peruse, Theo bounds down the steps in joggers and a white T-shirt, putting his glasses on and looking a bit groggy.

"Hiya, Vi. How are you?" he asks, coming in and dropping a friendly kiss on my cheek. Then he strides over to Hayden and takes Marisa in his arms. He kisses her over and over on the side of her chubby cheek, and she makes a cute gurgled squeal. "Morning, beau-tiful. You miss me?"

"Theo was up most of the night with her," Leslie explains. "She wouldn't sleep. Hayden kept him company for a good bit of it."

Hayden looks at me sheepishly, like he's uncomfortable that I'm learning so much about his life in one meeting.

"Well, she's gorgeous, Leslie. I'm only sorry I didn't get here sooner. Can I hold her?"

"Yes, but don't feel bad if she starts crying," Leslie adds. "She hates everybody."

"Not me," Hayden grumbles.

"Yes, Hayden, you're special. Marisa loves Uncle Hayden," Leslie says in a cooing tone.

"She loves Daddy, too." Theo gives Marisa one final smooch be-fore he passes her off to me. He turns to approach Leslie for a hug while murmuring good mornings to her next. I hear Leslie make a smart remark about how she's number two now, and the two of them playfully quarrel while I cradle Marisa in the crook of my arm. She instantly starts fussing and I struggle to find the right way to hold her so she relaxes.

"Try facing her out," Hayden helpfully offers, his grey eyes watching me thoughtfully.

I turn her around so she's facing Hayden and he smiles proudly as she settles.

"You know her rather well," I say, mildly impressed.

He shrugs. "Comes with the territory. It was sort of survival one-o'-one to live here."

"Where do you sleep?"

"There's a guestroom down that hall." He points behind himself toward an area just off the sunken living room. "I'd ask if you want to sit, but that's when the fussing usually commences."

"I'm fine standing," I say. "So how are you?"

His eyes turn a cold grey as he nods dismissively. "Just fine, thanks. You?"

Well that told me absolutely nothing. "Good."

"Vi! Oh my God, I completely forgot!" Leslie exclaims, snapping mine and Hayden's pensive eyeballing away from each other. She rushes over to the large dining room table covered in several floral centrepieces and other various items left over from last night's event. She searches around for a moment before she finds what she's looking for and turns to me. "You won!"

She's holding the trinket box I bid on last night.

My eyes alight. "Seriously?"

Leslie smiles broadly. "I know, you lucky duck. You get to go on an amazing holiday!"

"What?" I ask, confused.

"The holiday you bid on. It's a weekend in Barcelona. I'm so jealous I'm not even happy for you."

I frown. "Oh, crap. I didn't even realise. I was just bidding on the box."

"What do you mean?" Theo asks, eyeing me sternly as Leslie resumes her position in his arms.

I shift Marisa in my grasp before replying, "I really only wanted the box. I have a gift idea in mind for my dad and the box…I don't know. It called to me. Do you guys know where they came from? I'm hoping to find four more."

They all stare at me, completely gobsmacked. Leslie speaks first, "Vi, you bid six hundred pounds for a box?"

I immediately flush with embarrassment. "I just saw it as a donation," I reply meekly. *Christ, Leslie, did you have to blurt it out like that?*

Hayden's stare is piercing through me so hard I can barely look at anyone else.

Leslie laughs. "Vi, you do know that Hay—"

"Congratulations," Hayden interrupts her. "I hope you enjoy the trip, regardless. It is donated and paid in full already."

Theo adds, "We can find you more boxes, I'm sure." He and Hayden exchange a look like they are having a silent conversation, making me feel more confused than ever.

Leslie eventually ushers me into the kitchen area to make us some tea. Hayden and Theo respectfully retreat to the living room and turn on the telly. We chat for over an hour about work drama, China nonsense, and all things baby. We have a good laugh at Benji's expense I'm afraid. When you get pissed out of your mind and kiss Hayden on the lips, you're setting yourself up to be laughed at. Beyond all that, I give her the little outfit I picked up for Marisa from a street vendor near our office. It's very colourful, just like Leslie. I miss having that colour of hers with me at work every day.

By the time I get ready to leave, my arms feel like they are about to fall off. I can't believe how holding a tiny baby can feel like such a workout. Leslie grabs Marisa from me and hands me the keepsake box. Now holding my prized box, I know just how perfect it will be for what I have in mind.

As she begins to show me out, Hayden hops up from the couch and jogs over. "I'll walk you home," he says and Leslie eyes him with a frown.

"Do help yourself, Hayden," she states sarcastically. "Maybe ask Vi if she'd like to be walked home by you first, you cocky bugger."

"May I walk you home?" He flashes me a sheepish half-smile and stuffs his hands in his jean pockets.

This is a different man than the one I saw last night. He's not moody and defensive. He's not sexual and prowling. He's…shy.

I arch a curious brow. "By all means."

I giggle at Leslie's goofy expression and give her and Marisa a big hug goodbye. Then I wave to Theo before I follow Hayden down the steps.

We make our way out into the unseasonably warm summer day. We walk wordlessly for a couple of blocks and I force myself to not be the first to break our silence. It's hard because he's even hotter in his casual wear. A pair of perfectly fitted jeans with a big brown belt and a short-sleeved, black, V-neck T-shirt. Coupled with his leather cuffs, his layered watch, and leather sandals, he's got me reliving the kiss we shared in distinct detail despite his multiple personalities.

"You're quiet today," he finally says after a couple of minutes. "That's…different."

"I'm unsure what to think right now," I state.

He nods thoughtfully. "I'm sorry. I just got spooked. That kiss was—"

"Intense?" I blurt out and turn to watch his reaction.

His Adam's apple bobs as he swallows and licks his lips in agreement. His fiery grey eyes are showing me prowling Hayden again. But it's as if he's holding back, like he's putting that lion in its cage. "I just…I didn't want you to get the wrong idea."

"What wrong idea do you mean?"

"I'm not in a good enough place to be with anyone right now. I've worked my arse off to get here and can't have anything messing about my recovery." He pauses as his eyes cloud over. "I also have a very nasty track record of friends with benefits. I won't go down that road again, Vi."

The friends with benefits line was a jab right in my stomach. That's not once what I ever hoped for between us. To be honest, I'm not sure what I hoped for. And after he said "thank you" and took off last night, I suspected he simply didn't feel the kiss the same way I did.

"So I would be a distraction?" I ask, trying to figure him out. He smiles and runs his hands over his messy blonde hair. It's dishevelled in that perfect way that my hands itch to tangle through.

"Yes, Vi. That is exactly what you'd be. A beautiful, bright, bubbly, blonde distraction."

"That's a lot of *B*'s." I grimace at his characterisation of me. Is that really all he sees in me? My heart continues to sink further and further.

"I know I asked you to help me with my Countdown Challenge, but I think it's a bad idea," he says before I have more time to consider what he said about me.

"What do you mean?" I stop walking and cross my arms over my chest to look him in the eyes.

He gazes at me like it's harder to speak now. "After last night…I just…I can't go through with it. Not with you. I'll find someone else."

"No!" I exclaim, feeling a bit brassed off over his description of me. I'm determined to change his opinion. I'm a great deal more than those *B* words he used to describe me. "I don't want you to find anybody else. I want to be the person."

He shakes his head and looks away. "You don't know what you're asking."

"Let me be the judge of that." I reach for his arm so he looks at me. "Hayden, I'm not some meek little ditz. I may look like it, but I'm not. I was raised by my father and I'm surrounded by four football-playing brothers. They are all bossy, obnoxious men who like to butt their noses in my life whenever the mood strikes them. Believe me when I tell you, if I'm strong enough to handle the lot of them, I'm strong enough to handle this."

He looks somewhat intrigued. "Should I be afraid these brothers are going to hunt me down?"

"Yes." I nod truthfully. *Especially if you never kiss me like that again*, I want to say. "Seriously, are you quite strong? You might want to start doing more cardio. Running specifically."

His chest rumbles with laughter. "You have to promise me that if it ever gets to be too much, you'll tell me. We end it, straight away. No hurt feelings. I don't want to hurt you, Vi."

"Piece of cake," I reply with a simple shrug.

Full Circle Moment

Hayden

WHAT DID I JUST COMMIT TO? DOING THE COUNTDOWN Challenge with Vi is going to be bloody painful, but shit do I want to prove to myself that I can do it. Maybe there's even a part of me that wants to prove it to Vi as well. Either that or I'm thinking if I dump all my issues on her it'll help prevent me from wanting to pursue her. Or, better yet, her wanting to pursue me.

I don't need a love interest right now. I just need to stay clean and focused. Yes, that kiss was fucking memorable to say the least. Yes, I spent most of the night thinking that in another life I would have drug her upstairs, peeled her dress off her slim body, and made sure every bare curve and flat surface was touched by my lips.

Deep breaths, Hayden. Deep breaths.

But I stayed strong. I stayed the course. Because I'm not weak anymore, and I'm doing the Countdown Challenge one way or another.

I'm relieved when we decide there's no time like the present to dive in. Delaying our visits would only make it easier for me to find excuses to get out of it. She suggests we run back to her place first to grab Bruce so we can go sit at a nearby dog park to talk. I'm both dreading and ready for my first countdown confession. It will be very telling what kind of person Vi is and how strong I am in my recovery to openly discuss this with a new acquaintance.

As we approach her flat, a younger Italian-looking bloke with a backpack stands waiting at her alley entrance.

"Hiya, Vincent! Sorry I'm late," Vi calls, speeding up her pace toward the door.

"No problem, Miss Harris," he says as I watch his eyes linger on her exposed torso and drift down her legs.

I glare at him and he looks at me as if to say, "Hey man, I'm only human." Cheeky fucking wanker.

"Come on up. I'm going to pop out and take Bruce for a walk, so I'll just leave you to it."

The three of us slip into the small lift. Vi sticks a metal key into the slot, and my eyes widen in shock when I see the number eleven displayed as the only button on the control panel.

Without noticing my reaction, she looks at me and says, "Vincent tends the garden on my roof."

My brows arch. "You have a garden on your roof?"

She looks down in embarrassment. "It's only flowers and plants. Not like produce or anything."

"It's incredible. You should see it," Vincent says, nodding earnestly. "The roses are beginning to bloom."

"I can show it to you some other time." She shrugs her shoulders nonchalantly.

When the lift doors open to the eleventh floor, I'm surprised to see we're walking straight into her flat. Since I'm the first one out, my crotch is instantly pummelled by a wet mouth.

"Oi, Bruce!" Vi shrieks and stumbles over to grab him by the collar. She struggles to pull him back. "You disgusting creature. Go on and head up, Vincent."

I don't even attempt to help her with Bruce as I take in the stunning eleventh-floor penthouse. Vincent walks through her airy living room, out the large balcony door, and begins climbing a ladder on the building that evidently leads up to the roof. A huge flat-screen is mounted on one wall in the sitting area, and a quick glance through a pair of French doors to the left reveals a huge ornately, gothically decorated bedroom. The bed alone is a jaw-dropping piece of art.

Vi has a gardener, her flat is decorated immaculately, she was willing to spend six hundred pounds on a keepsake box, and she lives on the entire top floor of this building.

"Who are you, Vi Harris?" I ask, my gaze crashing on hers in accusatory curiosity.

She blows a puff of hair out of her face, still holding onto Bruce. "What do you mean?"

"You said your brothers are footballers," I start, beginning to put two and two together.

"I did."

My jaw drops. "Like professional footballers?"

She sighs heavily.

I inhale sharply. "Is your brother Gareth Harris? As in Manchester United's starting defender?" My face is deathly serious.

She purses her lips. "Are you a fan?"

My eyes widen as she confirms my suspicions. "That means your dad is Vaughn Harris, the manager of Bethnal Green."

"You're a fan," she murmurs.

"You could say that." I blink my eyes slowly and run my hands through my hair. "Christ. Now I'm afraid."

"Afraid of what?"

"Your brothers!"

She giggles and releases Bruce to pounce me. "Too late to back out now, mate." Just as Bruce nearly reaches me, she says, "Come on, Bruce. Time for a walkies," and he diverts his path toward a small basket in her kitchen to grab his own lead.

Still slightly star-struck by this very new information, Vi and I head out with Bruce in tow. Christ. I never would have guessed any of this about timid, quirky, and somewhat awkward Vi! I do my best not to fire a million questions at her because I assume she gets that a lot. And frankly, I'm more intrigued by watching her walk her enormous animal through the busy streets of Brick Lane.

She looks rather confident and at ease in her own skin. Bruce is actually quite manageable on a lead, which I'm grateful to see. One strong tug from him and he'd take Vi out and seriously injure her.

She leads us into a quiet little park oasis where a pair of poodles are prancing around proudly. They take one look at Bruce and freeze. Vi unclips his lead and he bounds over to them, immediately rolling over on his back to allow the two canines to sniff all of his wobbly bits until their hearts are content. One of his paws is the size of the pair of them put together. It's comical, really. The three begin chasing each other and yipping playfully as Vi and I find a secluded bench beneath a magnolia tree.

Pink flowers cascade down all around us. I grow ill as I take in the stark contrast of the surrounding beauty and the horror within me.

"So where do you have to start?" Vi asks, breaking the silence, her eyes wide with interest.

"Day five," I croak, shrugging. "Or at least that's what Doc said." I lean forward and rest my elbows on my legs, looking straight ahead as nerves shudder beneath my rib cage.

"What happened on day five?" she asks, her voice soft and probing. "Hayden, stop looking so terrified. I told you I am curious, remember? This is your challenge. I'm your helper. Don't worry about me. I get what I'm in for. Out with it."

I tsk my teeth and begin. "Day five was the first time in my life I had ever considered methods." Getting it all out in one sentence is an immense relief. I had spoken about many of my days leading up to my attempt in rehab during group therapy. But here, out in a dog park, is an entirely different situation.

I turn my head to watch her reaction.

"Methods?" she asks confused. Then her eyes alight with

realisation. "Oh."

I clench my jaw and nod, looking away. Watching the dogs as I speak my entire truth seems a great deal easier than staring at her innocent face. "I actually Googled the best ways to kill myself. I'd never done anything like that before. Never even considered it. Not properly. But on day five, I had reached my breaking point in my personal life, and researching methods felt like the ultimate fuck you to the universe."

"What caused you to reach your breaking point?" she asks quietly.

Frowning, I recall the intense night I had with Reyna in her flat. The one that resulted in me getting socked in the face by Liam. I close my eyes and reply, "Things were changing all around me. My best friend at the time was Rey and she was changing. Pulling away from me. I took it badly. That on top of everything else I had been dealing with was suffocating me.

"So I started Googling options. A great deal different than Googling a nice holiday, let me tell you. Once I got past all the self-help numbers that popped up like mad, I discovered that a gun is the quickest and most popular method, but I didn't have one of those. Carbon monoxide poisoning from running a car inside a closed garage could have been an option, but I didn't have a car either. Pills and booze could work, but I had seriously abused pills and booze in my past, so obtaining a prescription was and still is damn near impossible since my medical chart is flagged. And I'm not too keen on drug dealers." I laugh self-deprecatingly and shake my head. "I had lots of access to sharp, circular saw blades, though…So—"

"You slit your wrists," she finishes.

I nod woodenly, unsnapping and re-snapping one of my leather cuffs that conceals a horrid scar beneath. My throat constricts with anxiety. "I think I wanted to feel the pain. To watch the end. I wanted to choose the exact time it occurred. I couldn't stomach the idea of hanging myself, but I considered it."

I look over at Vi to gauge her reaction. Her face is frozen in a serious, sombre expression.

"You okay?" I ask, touching my finger to her cheek. Her eyes close at my caress, and the warmth of her skin reminds me that I'm not alone. That's she's right here. Heart beating, breathing, listening, absorbing, and enduring beside me.

She nods, her chin trembling. "It's sad."

No two words could better define such raw truth.

I nod in confirmation. "It is sad." I look away again and my eyes zero in on an elderly woman sitting on a bus bench. Her tiny hands are peeling away at an orange, and something about the simplicity of that act—the beauty of her eating a piece of fresh fruit that this world offered—gives me the strength to continue.

"I felt relief once I decided how to do it. I had a plan. I could see the end of the tunnel that seemed so utterly painful and horrid. I hated my life. I hated everything happening around me. I had no control in any aspect. I was fucking up at work. I was fucking up with my mates. With my family. Every turn was another opportunity for me to fuck up. So day five was the first day that I thought, 'All right. Now you've manned-up and have finally done something for yourself.' It's strange, but I felt brave. And I felt peace."

"You seem so different from the man you're describing," Vi says as I pinch the bridge of my nose to stave off the tears I can feel pricking my eyes. "I can't imagine that guy. So ready to give up. I know we don't know that much about each other, but you seem so confident. Strong."

"I was confident in my choice then. It didn't feel like giving up in my mind. It felt like a solution. A permanent mute button to silence all the noise in my head."

A thoughtful quietness stretches between us while we both absorb everything I just said. As if sensing our tense state, Bruce trots over, panting happily, and noses Vi's crossed legs. She remains still, so he moves on from her and shoves his face into my hands and through to my face. I half smile and give him a hearty pat.

"Bruce, go on and run! Leave us be," Vi reprimands.

"He's fine," I say. Then a man and his Dalmatian enter the closed gate and, without hesitation, Bruce trots off anyway to greet the newcomers.

Vi breaks the silence. "May I ask you about your sister?"

I lift my brows. "It's funny you ask because that's a lot of what day four was about."

"Go on then," she smiles sadly. "Was she pretty special?"

"She was the greatest," I laugh. "She was loud, and opinionated, and passionate about everything. A proper know it all. She was vivacious—" My voice falters and I stop, suddenly overcome by emotions I can no longer hide as easily.

Closing my eyes, I envision Marisa's body flinging backward the same way I had so many times before. I wish more than anything that I could block that image out, but it is forever on repeat in my mind's eye.

"On day four, I couldn't stop thinking about what happened to her. I went on a bender, drinking heavily and reliving the scene over, and over, and over." I swirl my finger near my temple.

"What did happen?"

"A tragic, freak fucking accident. That's what they taught me to call it in rehab. Maybe not the fucking part. I embellished there." I swallow hard and exhale sharply to prepare myself for the painful retelling of Marisa's death that is so poignant in my head.

"My parents live in the rural part of Essex. They have a large estate, and my siblings and I grew up riding quads all over the surrounding pastures. Even as we grew older, we did things like that together. It was always a good laugh when Theo, Daph, Marisa, and I went out on our adventures. My family had always been extremely close for as long as I could remember. The worst row I ever had with my parents was back when I told them I wasn't going to attend University. It was an issue because my dad expected me to take over his furniture distribution plant. His policy was that his children couldn't be management without proper education and experience. But I didn't want to take over the plant. That was the thing." I swallow hard, knowing that I'm stalling with ramblings about my childhood. But that's not what Vi's asking about.

I suck in a big gulp of air and continue. "Anyway, we were out on the quads and Marisa had to go inside to use the loo…She was riding with me." My voice cracks at the memory of her gripping me around my waist and laughing. "Marisa was always laughing. Always happy." I take a deep breath and place my head between my hands.

Vi's hand touches my shoulder, and it feels like a warm blanket of comfort. I turn my watery gaze to hers and see such sincere compassion it gives me the strength to continue.

"I dropped her at the door and was doing laps around the house while I waited for her. She stepped right in front of me. Just like that. I was looking away and never even saw her." A painful cough erupts from my throat and I turn my head. "It wasn't the impact of the quad that did it. It was the impact of her neck striking a bloody landscaping paver." My voice is pained and guttural. "My entire family was there to witness it. Theo. Daphney. Mum came running out of the house screaming. It was a fucking crime scene right where we grew up as kids. Right where we learned how to fucking walk. One piece of landscape fucked my family up for the rest of our lives."

I hear a sniffle and look over to see Vi crying. Her face is pinched like she's trying to hide her emotions but is failing miserably. Her blue eyes are rimmed red and tears are flooding her eyes, streaming down her face. Without pause, I open my arms and her face softens as she tucks in tightly to my side.

"I'm sorry," she croaks, her shoulders shaking from her soft sobs.

"Christ, what do you have to be sorry for? I'm the bastard torturing your heart and making you cry," I groan in frustration. This isn't what she deserves. She deserves to be taken care of. "I told you this was a bad idea, Vi. I should have listened to my instincts."

She sniffs loudly and pulls away. Then she shifts to face me on the bench, crisscrossing her legs. "No, Hayden. I want to be your person. The one to help you with your countdown. But, bloody hell, I'm going to be emotional. It doesn't mean I want you to stop. It just means I have feelings. You need to be okay with me feeling sad about this."

I frown at her and shake my head. "I don't like doing this to you. It goes against everything inside of me."

"Stop, all right. Come on. Tell me something happy. Tell me something sweet about Marisa. Or funny. Did you guys get on? Or did you fight a lot?"

I grin. "A bit of both. She and Theo were like the mummy and daddy of Daph and me. They always tried to boss us around and force us to do our chores because they were older, so I would try to manipulate Daphney to be on my side. We did things just to get up their noses." Chuckling to myself, I add, "One time when we were kids, I got Daphney to hide in the barn with me because I knew Marisa was taking her boyfriend out there to snog. We had water balloons and waited until they were nearly half-naked before launching a water storm at them."

Vi bursts into a full-on belly laugh, and it pleases me to see her smile push away her tears. It's a gorgeous sight.

"That's awful!" she exclaims.

I chuckle. "Daph couldn't have been more than ten. She was so confused over what they were doing to each other and had all these awkward questions for me. I told her to ask Mum and that just got Marisa in more trouble."

"You were a little sod, weren't you?" Vi asks, swatting at my shoulder playfully.

I nod and my chest puffs out with pride. "I really was. Still am, mostly." My hand finds its way to Vi's face to wipe at some stray tears still lingering. "This feels good."

She nods, obviously pleased. "I'm glad."

"I didn't think it would feel this good to talk about it with someone like you."

"What do you mean someone like me?" She looks mock offended and a flicker of confusion streaks across her face.

"I just mean someone I don't know all that well. It feels enlightening to see a stranger's reaction to my story I guess. It's all... surprising."

Her brows lift. "A stranger?"

I shrug, feeling a bit disconcerted. "Mostly."

Seemingly unaffected, she throws me a smile. "So, what's your next day? What was day three?"

I shake my head. "I'll get to it. But frankly, I'm shattered. Maybe we can get together another time?"

"You sure you want to hang out with me again, Hayden Clarke?" She wiggles her eyebrows, then quickly drops all playfulness and watches me warily. Affection and warmth radiate from her in a way that draws me in so acutely that it takes all the strength in my body to not cup her face in my hands and take her mouth with mine.

Her voice and smile are soft. "I have revealed my truth that I am an emotional ninny after all."

My eyes twinkle at her confession. "It might be my new favourite thing about you."

Birthday Swedish Pancakes

Vi

SUNDAY NIGHTS ARE SET ASIDE FOR FAMILY DINNERS AT THE Harris' during the off-season. Since our father's home is so large and close to Tower Park, Booker, Tanner, and Camden still live with him full-time, though the twins have been murmuring about flat-hunting for a few months now. Gareth has some swanky place in Manchester he lives in during the season since he plays for Manchester United, but he's back at Dad's in the off-season, too. Such is this, Sunday dinner has become a sacred tradition. Should anyone try to mess with it, my brothers would thump them into submission.

Fortunately, the cooking for said tea rests on my shoulders and not theirs. If we relied on them, we'd probably be eating day-old take-away fish n' chips every week.

Growing up, I learned how to cook rather quickly once we realised all our father could properly prepare was beans and toast. It became a bit of an obsession for me in my teens after I found a box full of our mother's old cookbooks. I was determined to make my way through every single recipe as some adolescent tribute to her memory. As a result of my obsessive hobby, our kitchen became the hub for all things Harris. It's where I spent loads of time. Consequently, it's where my dad and brothers would talk football, watch games, go over plays, and squeak in schoolwork as time allowed. The only time playbooks and condiments serving as footballers in various positions weren't spread out over our high-top table was when the cleaning people had just been in.

Bruce and I cab it out to Chigwell, along with all the groceries I picked up for today's meal. To rely on Dad's grocery supply is a fate I shall never attempt.

I let myself and Bruce into the cast iron gate by punching in the code. Striding down the long wraparound driveway, I sigh when our home comes into view. It's considered a mansion by many people's standards. But the way it's nestled back amongst a sea of Japanese cherry trees makes it feel idyllic and in no way imposing. The large brown brick home is anchored by two grand, white pillars and a welcoming yellow double entry door. Having it painted yellow was my idea when I was eight, and Dad didn't have the heart to tell me no. Some days I truly do miss living here.

Upon entering the house, a striking pale, wooden staircase curves up to the second floor where there are two wings of bedrooms. It's a six-bed with en suite facilities attached to every room. The community rooms are sparsely furnished as most of our mother's design choices were boxed up shortly after her death. Since my dad and brothers do so much travelling for football, I suppose furnishings were never a bother.

I wish I could remember what it looked like here when our mother was alive. How it smelled, what kind of music she listened to. I often wonder what her style was like, both in clothing and in home décor. Am I like her in more ways than just my first name and birthday?

Our mother's maiden name was Nyström. She was a full-blooded Swede whom our father met at a pub while playing champion league football, just before he signed with Manchester United. She was attending University in London and, from what little I've heard, it sounded like a pretty exciting love affair that resulted in Gareth.

I remember bits and pieces of Mum, but it feels more like I'm remembering photographs rather than actual times. Gareth is really the only one who remembers Mum and the immediate years following her death. He's never been very forthcoming about those times, and he's not one to push for answers. He's got a short fuse, and we all learned quickly that Gareth gets his way and that's that.

I unclip Bruce's lead. His paws clack loudly on the white marble as we walk down the hallway and turn left through the double doors into the kitchen.

"My sous-chef, ready and waiting!" I proudly announce, finding Booker reading a hardcover at the large wooden island that sits parallel to the galley style kitchen. "Where is everybody else?"

"They left this morning to check out a university player. They rang and are twenty minutes out." He shoots up from his stool and rushes over to grab the supermarket bags from my hands.

"Always a gentleman," I tease as Bruce noses Booker in the leg, excitedly begging for some affection. "Where did you learn that anyway? It surely wasn't from Camden and Tanner."

Booker places the bags on the island before squatting down to give Bruce a hearty cuddle. "Probably all those girlie films you made me watch growing up," he laughs. Then he strides over to the large patio door and lets Bruce out for a coveted romp around the fenced-in grounds. It's Bruce's favourite thing about coming here.

I prop my hands on my hips. "I never made you watch them!"

"Well, it was either that or get my arse kicked by Cam. I took my chances with you. And look at me now," he beams proudly, stretching out his sculpted arms and shooting me his boyish grin. "I'm a proper gentleman. Did you bring stuff for Swedish pancakes?"

"Of course."

Booker's smile grows as he ducks into the walk-in pantry to plug his phone into the overhead sound system. The notes of U2 fill the kitchen as we wash our hands and make quick work of prepping today's meal.

For several years, it has been tradition that the Sunday meal following mine and Mum's birthday include Swedish pancakes. The recipe is one I stumbled upon during my cooking quest. It had special Swedish notes in Mum's handwriting that I couldn't even read. The box of cookbooks ended up having a lot more than old recipes inside, that's for sure.

Swedish pancakes have become a favourite amongst my brothers. They're served extremely thin—similar to a French crepe—with homemade cream and berries or lingonberry jam if it can be found. And I have just the place I go to in Shoreditch for the jam.

After a while of quiet companionable prepping, Booker breaks the silence. "So, what's new, Vi?" He's eyeing me hopefully as he whisks the cream vigorously by hand.

"Oi! I forgot to tell you! I won a weekend getaway to Barcelona at a charity gala I attended Friday night. It's a trip for two, and I was going to see if you want to come along. It's in like nine weeks' time. Think you can manage?"

Booker's eyes alight. "Timing should be all right. Training will have started, but I think I can get away for the weekend."

"Brilliant!"

"Are you doing all right otherwise?" he asks.

"Of course I am." I frown as I pour oil onto the griddle. "Why wouldn't I be?"

Shrugging, he replies, "It's just that you seemed a bit emotional on your birthday. I wanted to talk to you about it before everybody gets here."

I stop what I'm doing to look at him. "I was only trying to make a daft point. Don't read too much into it."

"Well, you haven't dated anyone since Pricky Pierce, so I was wondering if you are okay. You aren't still holding candles for the prat, are you?"

Pricky Pierce. I'd laugh if I didn't think it'd only encourage him. "No candles I assure you."

"If you ever did, you can talk to me about it, you know. I'm not as stupid as the rest of them. I won't go completely mental."

I shoot him a sardonic smile because I'm not sure I fully trust that. However, Booker always did have a special fondness for me that superseded my other brothers. They always seem to put protection above affection. But with Booker, it's more often affection first. It's why he's got a special place in my heart.

Hayden's face flashes in my mind as I consider whether talking about my situation with him is a good idea or not. "Booker, how would you…describe me?" I grab the prepared pancake batter and pour it onto the hot griddle.

He moves over and props himself against the worktop next to me and frowns. "What do you mean?"

Poking mindlessly at the pancake bubbles with a spatula, I reply, "Like, if you were to tell me my most obvious traits, what would pop into your head?"

He grins dopily. "A great cook."

"Anything else?" I'm trying not to be too pushy, but I'm feeling a titchy bit anxious.

He nods earnestly. "Of course! You're fun. Upbeat."

"Like, bubbly?" I ask, my smile dropping.

"Maybe a bit, but it's more than that." He looks away like he's trying to form his words. "You're funny, but not in a joking way. More like you laugh really easily, which makes you a great time to be around."

I nod. "That doesn't sound so bad."

"It's brill." He turns and opens the double fridge, placing the cream inside and grabbing the fresh berries. He walks them to the sink for rinsing. "You're a bit soft, though, which I don't know how the bloody hell that happened since you grew up around all men."

I eye him seriously. "More like a pack of wolves. I'm probably emotionally scarred."

He chuckles. "I don't mean the soft thing in a bad way. You just feel everything very deeply. You're protective like Gareth, but in a different way. You take shit personally on behalf of the people you care most about, you know? Like, remember that red card I got in Liverpool last season. The one when—"

"God, don't speak another word about it! I swear that call was complete fucking shit," I seethe with a scathing glance over my shoulder. "I could spit just thinking about it! I very nearly got that referee sacked."

"Don't spit! We're making pancakes!" Booker laughs. "You did get the bloke suspended, though."

"Well, he was rubbish!" I exclaim as I toss the spatula into the sink.

"See what I mean? You're passionate about something that happened to me, and you're not even a coach or a teammate. You don't even play football. You're just my sister."

I nod thoughtfully. He makes a pretty good point. "Maybe I just don't make good first impressions."

Cutting his eyes at me speculatively, he asks, "Are you going to tell me what happened?"

I shrug. "I just…I met this bloke who's sort of a friend of a friend and…I don't know. I thought we hit it off, but then he got all awkward and his description of me left me feeling a bit…poorly."

"What did he say?" Booker's brow furrows.

I squint and look up at the ceiling, hoping I'm quoting him right. "A beautiful, bright, bubbly, blonde distraction."

Booker's face freezes, as do his hands on the berries. "I want his fucking name."

"Stop, Book. You're supposed to be different."

"I'm not messing about, Vi. He needs to be talked to. Only two of those adjectives are relevant. The other two are utter codswallop. You are so much more than those things."

"I know. Calm down. I think we're just friends anyway." Or at least that's what I'm trying to decide. I'm not sure I could handle being with Hayden.

Booker shakes his head. "I don't think it's a great idea to be mates with the bloke, Vi. Especially since he obviously has his head up his arse."

I hear voices in the hall and quickly shush Booker just as Camden, Tanner, Gareth, and our dad come strolling in, laughing heartily about something.

"My Vi," Dad says loudly, coming around the counter and scooping me up into a big bear hug while rubbing his scruffy chin on my cheek.

Vaughn Harris is legendary status in the world of English football. But to me, he's just the guy who sneaks a sausage before it's time to eat. He's wearing his usual Bethnal Green polo with cream trousers, looking the picture of a man who lives his passion. His salt and pepper whiskers cover his chin and match his greying hair perfectly.

"Happy birthday again, my darling. I can't wait for your birthday pancakes."

"Oi! Let go of me, Dad," I giggle and squirm out of his embrace, rubbing the area that he purposefully whisker-burned.

"Oh, happy birthday, my darling," Tanner coos in a high-pitched voice mimicking the Queen.

"Do just look at her, Tanner," Camden starts in a high, nasally tone and claps his hands together in adoration. "She's got her boobies. Our little girl has gone and got her boobies now that she's all grown up."

Gareth roars with laughter as Tanner picks up where Cam left off. He grabs two lemons out of the bowl on the table and holds them to his chest saying, "Oh, fiddle fettle, she won't fit in the beach ball jumper I got her for her birthday. She'll look like a proper tart!"

"Shut it, you prats!" I exclaim, rushing over and shoving them hard while giving Gareth a swift kick for laughing. Camden grabs my wrists and restrains me as I continue throwing kicks at Tanner, who's wresting to grab my ankles.

"Enough," Dad says, his husky voice booming. "The pancakes are going to burn."

Shaking my head, I eye him like a petulant child. "You raised them," I jokingly accuse.

"That's debatable," he replies, grinning proudly. "I could smell the sausage from outside. It looks great, darling." He dips his finger into the batter and licks it, closing his eyes appreciatively.

"It's almost ready," I reply. "Cam…Tan…Why don't you two stop being little sods and make yourselves useful by setting the table."

In no time, we're sitting down at the high-top table and devouring the feast of pancakes, sausages, fresh fruit, and jam. I am certain we are all probably internally musing over what they would taste like if our mum actually made them for us…just once.

Box of Secrets

Hayden

HUNCHED OVER THE WORKSHOP COUNTER, I RUB THE SANDING block against the dark Philippine mahogany, smoothing the surface and wiping away the excess sawdust. With every touch, I grow more and more excited about the fact that I'm nearly finished with the final one. It feels good to work with my hands. It's therapeutic. In the past, I only worked on the books and the appointment side of Theo's business, C. Designs. Theo's talents cannot be disputed, but I've since found that I also have some abilities I wasn't even aware of.

Theo strolls into the workshop. "Hey. Marisa just went down, so I think Leslie and I are going to turn in early. She's knackered from all the wedding shit. Are you making more?" he asks, gesturing to the keepsake box in my hands.

"Uh, yeah." I look down awkwardly, rubbing my hands down my navy T-shirt covered in sawdust. My tattered work jeans don't look much better. It's been three days since I last saw Vi and instead of calling her like I want to, I've been keeping myself preoccupied.

"Are these for Vi, perhaps?" he asks knowingly and adjusts his glasses while inspecting the three I've already completed. After I finish sanding the one I'm currently working on, they all just need to be stained and varnished. I shrug and his brows rise knowingly. "Want to talk about it?"

Shaking my head dismissively, I reply, "There's not much to talk about. Well, except for the fact that I sort of agreed to do this ridiculous Countdown Challenge for Doc, but it's a horrid idea."

"Why is that?" Theo grabs one of the metal stools. He drags it up to the counter and sits down.

I pause what I am doing and reply, "It just is, all right." I glare at him, annoyance dripping from my features as I grab my leather cuff and nervously unsnap and re-snap the clasp.

"Easy, sport. No need to get testy. If it's a bad idea, why are you working on more boxes?"

"I don't bloody know." I stand up straight and toss the sanding block on the counter in a huff. Leaning back on the opposite counter with my arms crossed, I continue. "Maybe I'm just trying to be a nice bloke for a change."

Chuckling, Theo replies, "That doesn't sound like you."

"No, it doesn't." I slice my hands through my hair and then scrub them down over my face. "I'm confused by her. She's so good, you know?"

Theo baulks. "How do you know she's good? What do you actually even know about her?"

My eyes find his. Christ, he's right. I hardly know her. We sort of went from cake to suicide in two seconds flat. I know sod all about her, and I feel like a proper jerk for just now realising.

"I guess I don't know that much, but that's part of the stipulation of the challenge."

Theo rises. "Well, I don't think it'd hurt you to get to know the girl a bit if it helps you finish your mission. You've never been one to back down from a challenge, mate." He touches the box closest to him and smirks. "And look, you went to all this trouble."

I eye the four keepsake boxes wistfully as Theo makes his way back up to the flat, insinuating in no uncertain terms that it would be wise if I stayed down here for a bit longer. Living with Theo and

Leslie has been good for me, but it's not ideal. I basically bear witness to them falling even more in love with each other every day as they tackle happy family life, fussy baby and all. It's a lot of fighting and making up and me taking long walks to give them space. I definitely need to find a place of my own and soon. But I'll feel a lot more confident with myself if I can get through Doc's challenge first. His approval means so much to me.

Seizing hold of my brief moment of bravery, I decide to shoot Vi a text.

Hayden: How do you feel about getting your hands a little dirty?

Vi: If it's illegal, I'll have to pass. I am a good girl after all. ;)

I chuckle at her cheekiness.

Hayden: It's perfectly legal, but you'd have to drop everything and come over to Theo and Leslie's right now. What do you say?

Vi: I'd say sure, why not?

With a pleased smile, I type back.

Hayden: Brilliant. See you soon.

I quickly get all my supplies ready and wait on bated breath for her arrival.

Thirty minutes later, I'm standing outside the shop thinking about how nice a cigarette would taste right now when Vi strides up. Her blonde hair is tied up on top of her head in an adorable messy bun. She's wearing black leggings, ballet flats, and a deep V-neck, black shirt that reveals a colourful neon yellow tank beneath it. She looks cosy, like she had been planning on a quiet night in.

"Where's Bruce?" I ask, pushing myself away from the side of the building.

"Left him at the flat," she says, eyeing me like she's trying to figure out my motive. "I don't have to lug him everywhere, you know."

I eye her seriously. "Probably safer if you do."

She frowns at my protective suggestion and says, "So, what are we doing? Your text was rather cryptic."

I grin and hold the door open for her to walk past me. My hand brushes the small of her back as I guide her through the shop entry. The urge to touch her more is heady, but I push it away as quickly as it arrived. She steps in and looks back at me in confusion. I gesture to the large wooden workshop counter and her eyes alight with realisation.

"Are these the same boxes?" She hustles over and picks one up. I take a mental snapshot of the surprised smile on her face as she opens the box.

"They just need to be finished," I offer.

"Where did you get them?"

I give her a sheepish look. "I made them."

Her jaw drops. "You made them? But you never said anything before!"

Shrugging, I reply, "I thought maybe you can help me finish them and we can talk."

"Oh yes, I'd love to!" She begins tugging at her top, attempting to knot it around her waist. "We can continue with your countdown while we work."

"Actually, I prefer we skip the countdown tonight." I grab a pair of rubber gloves off the counter. "I just thought…I don't know. I feel like a wanker for not knowing much about you, so I thought maybe we could spend the night talking like I'm not some complete fuck-up with a dark and twisted past."

I glance up just as her bright blue eyes darken. "Hayden, I've never looked at you like that. Not once."

Her severe expression winds me up. I nod awkwardly and hand her the gloves. "All right. Tonight I'm going to teach you how to stain. Think you're man enough for the job?"

She watches me for a moment, evidently letting my self-deprecation slide. "Manlier than most bubbly blondes I'd say."

I frown at her strange reply. Not entirely sure of how to respond,

I make quick work of showing her how we dip the cloth into the stain, rub it on heavily, and then wipe it off. I've already applied a thin strip of painter's tape across the top of each box for the design element I'll add later.

I set her up with her own supplies, and she sits down on the stainless steel stool next to me. Her loose shirt keeps getting in her way, so she stops what she's doing and peels off the offensive material.

I try to look away, but out of the corner of my eye, I'm transfixed. Now wearing only her small tank, her creamy alabaster skin is on full display and her cleavage is drawing me to her. My body reacts reflexively to the lush softness of her skin.

She catches me eyeing her. "So, what do you need these extra boxes for?" I ask, dragging my possessive gaze away from her and back to the box in my hands.

"My brothers," she replies, applying the first stroke of stain. "The one I got Sunday will be for my dad."

"What are you putting inside them, if you don't mind me asking?"

She looks over at me with a fleeting look of embarrassment. "Erm, it's just something I stumbled upon earlier this year. It took me a while to get it all sorted. Now that I have, I want to make it a special gift."

My brows lift as I angle toward her. "Do I get to know what the gift is?"

She shrugs. "It's not so much a gift I suppose. Just…I found a series of poems my mum wrote and some other trinkets. I think they'd make the best surprise gifts."

"That's a lovely idea. How does she feel about you giving away her poems?"

She looks back at her project and murmurs, "She died when I was young."

My heart clenches. "Vi, I'm so sorry to hear that."

"I was only four. I don't really remember much. But we shared a birthday, so I've always felt a connection to her on some level."

I look at her thoughtfully. "What are the poems about?"

"They were written in Swedish, so it took me a while to find a translator. But they're quite cool. They're all about motherhood. It's odd, but I felt like I got a glimpse inside her heart when I finally got them translated into English. Some of them are really beautiful, some tragic, some funny. It was surreal. I really connected to them… To her. My dad and brothers don't even know they exist. The book was tucked away with all of her cookbooks, so it's no wonder they never saw it."

"It's going to be incredible when you give them their gifts." I give her a smile and ask, "So, what about you? Do you like to cook?" I can easily picture her in the kitchen looking just as she does now with a towel tossed over her shoulder. The image elicits a tiny smirk.

Her brow furrows as she catches my playful expression. "I do. I love it. I did all the cooking growing up and my brothers can eat, let me tell you."

"I'm sure," I chuckle good-naturedly. "What was it like living with a bunch of athletes?" My curiosity about her lifestyle is definitely piqued. I grew up watching football on the telly, and my entire family is Manchester United fans through and through.

She shrugs. "I don't know any different."

"You played for fun, too, I assume?"

She scrunches her nose and shakes her head. "No, I didn't. I travelled with my dad and brothers instead." Suddenly, she stops what she's doing and looks up at the ceiling as if she's having an epiphany. "I loved being a mini-mummy to my brothers, but I submerged myself in their world and their schedules so much that I didn't have time to do much of anything just for fun."

I frown. "Surely there were some things you did for yourself."

She looks at me seriously as if she's just been whacked in the face by a sad truth. "Not a lot. I didn't even have many mates. Really, the first proper thing I've done was get my own flat last year. That's pathetic." She shakes her head in frustration.

"It's not pathetic to be close to your family. Growing up travelling with them sounds amazing. I'm sure being in a house with your brothers and dad was a life experience all in its own."

"You have no idea," she chuckles in a secretive, knowing way. "Are you, Theo, and Daphney close?"

I pause and try to determine the best way to answer without turning the conversation around on me again. "We used to be. Then we weren't. Now we are again."

Her face screws up in confusion. "Mind embellishing a bit?"

"Tonight isn't supposed to be about me. It's supposed to be about you, and you're treading into day three material." I squint at her speculatively.

She laughs and her smile lights up her eyes. "It's a give and take, Hayden. It's called conversation for a reason. This isn't an interview. Go on then, we'll get to day three eventually anyway."

She turns back to her box and swipes the cloth over the excess stain, her tongue flicking out as she applies more effort to a particular seam.

"Day three was a rather painful experience that Theo and I discussed in great detail during my stint in rehab. Theo has a tendency to blame himself for everything, from Marisa's death, to my attempt, to all the darkness in the cracks. Perhaps it's an older brother thing. Regardless, it took a great deal of opening up for him to relieve himself of that lot."

"Why would he blame himself for your attempt?"

"A few days before the charity gala last year, he and I…Well, we exchanged some very painful words right here in this shop. I was completely pissed out of my mind and had caught wind that he was bringing Leslie to the event. It just set me off."

"Why is that?" she asks, her brow quizzical.

"I felt he didn't have the right to be happy because no one else in our family was. It had been three years since Marisa's death and I was in no way moving on from my guilt. So Theo bringing a date to the gala felt like a slap in the face. Like he didn't care. About Marisa. About our family. About me. I took it all wrong, which I know now was ludicrous."

Vi frowns and shakes her head. "I don't think any feelings you had back then were ludicrous. You guys were all living in the wake of a very tragic accident. There's no way to know how long it takes you to get over something like that. I'm sure everyone processes at their own pace."

I half smile at her comment. "You sound like Doc, my therapist. I was so rat-arsed that I shoved Theo into one of his works in progress and it busted all to pieces. He exploded on me, telling me what a royal fuck-up I was and that I was going to end up dead in a ditch. He even took a swing at me with a two-by-four. It was bloody awful."

"God, were you hurt?"

Shaking my head, I answer, "No. I don't think he was really trying to hit me. I think he was just trying to snap me out of my stupor, but I was too pissed and too depressed. No one could get through to me. After that, I spiralled further downward.

"I showed up to the charity gala two days later for the sole purpose of fucking with him and the life he was starting with Leslie. Based on the couple of times I had spoken to Leslie, I knew he hadn't told her about Marisa. I even flat out asked her when I was really pissed one night. The secretiveness of it struck a nerve with me. Like what I did was some horrid, dark tale that couldn't be spoken. I felt so incredibly insignificant to my family, it was in that moment I decided everyone would be better off without me.

"It's crazy to think about now...because Leslie ended up being the one who saved my life. She's the one who found me and called the paramedics. After all of my horridness toward Theo—toward her— she was the one to walk in and pull me up from rock bottom." I pause as my eyes tear up over the affection I feel for Leslie. "I have an intense connection with Leslie because of all of that. It's something I think only her and I fully understand, but it's special. It's…meaningful."

Vi closes her mouth and nods in agreement. "I can't even imagine. Leslie's never mentioned a word of any of that to me."

"She won't. She's loyal and loving in ways that I never knew before I met her. She will always be an important part of my life, which is why I'm so grateful she's marrying my brother. Calling her family will put a nice label on what I feel for her." I pause and laugh quietly to myself. "My affection for her is only a fraction of what Theo feels for her. It's why he's rushed her into getting married so fast after they had Marisa."

"They are pretty disgusting to watch, aren't they?" Vi giggles, but her face drops just as quickly. "I'm glad she was there, Hayden."

I nod and frown, attempting to blink away my impending emotions. Then I turn back to the box I'm working on. "He's found his happy ending, and I'm grateful I get to be here to witness it. It took a lot of therapy with Theo to make him believe that I had made up my mind about killing myself prior to our row. But we've overcome our differences. Now he's like a proper mate."

She huffs out a laugh and I turn to catch her smiling.

"What?" I ask, curious where her mind just drifted off to.

"I think Booker is my best friend. He's my youngest brother and…I don't know. He's the only one I can talk to openly without pause, you know?"

I nod because I do understand, but I am curious. "You don't have any close girlfriends?"

She shakes her head. "Not really. The few I had in school were only interested in my brothers. Plus, I always felt uncomfortable around other girls. Except Leslie, surprisingly. I've always got on with her."

"Leslie's not the typical girlie girl," I confirm.

"No. She's the opposite of a bubbly blonde," she laughs awkwardly, peeling off her gloves and brushing back the few blonde wisps cascading around her face.

I stop what I'm doing and turn more fully to face her. "All right, that's the second time you've mentioned that. What's going on?"

She frowns and reaches over for a new box. "You tell me." Her brow arches at me in challenge.

"What do you mean?" I'm honestly completely in the dark, having no idea what she's going on about.

She looks at me out of the corner of her eye. "That's how you described me on Saturday when we were walking back to my flat. It kind of stuck with me I suppose."

Frowning, I attempt to recall what I said.

"'A blonde, bubbly distraction' were your exact words, I believe," she provides for me.

My features turn grave as realisation dawns on me. "I think you're missing a couple words."

She shakes her head and, for the first time, I see a look of distress on her face. This bothers me immensely because my characterisation of her was simply a defence mechanism. At that point in time, I was trying to get her out of my mind.

Fuck me, I'm a bloody prat.

Her stiff posture causes an ache in my chest. Without thinking, I stand up, strip my gloves off, and stride right over to her. She doesn't turn to look at me, so I wrench her stool around to face me. When her eyes remain cast downward, I tilt her chin up in an attempt to make her see my sincerity.

"I believe I said bright and beautiful if I'm not mistaken."

She rolls her eyes and purses her lips, still refusing to make eye contact with me. I hate how she's shutting down because of something daft I said in the moment. I clasp her face, forcing her blues to meet my greys.

"Vi—" I start, attempting to find the perfect words to relay how completely breathtaking she is in so many ways.

The wounded vulnerability in her gaze knocks all sense out of my head. When words refuse to come, I lean down and kiss her, willing my lips to do the apologising for me. She groans into my mouth in protest at first. But then she grabs me, holding me tight against her. Her fingers bite into my forearms as her mouth opens, permitting my tongue access to hers.

Actions always did speak louder than words.

Her legs spread and I tuck into the warmth of her, hunching over further to deepen our kiss. My thumbs push back the stray strands of her hair and relish in the suppleness of her round cheeks beneath my touch. Christ, everything about her is so soft. Her lips are smooth and responsive. Plump, pliable, and welcoming me to take every ounce of control I want. Her submission only excites me more. I press into her knowing that if I wanted to, I could take her. Right here, right now. I could yank the straps of her tank down and feast my eyes on the bare beauty of Vi before letting my mouth do the devouring.

But that's not what this kiss is about. That's not what she is to me. Vi Harris is so much more than a potentially soul-altering shag.

Pulling away, I rest my forehead against hers. "Please know there aren't enough words for me to describe how utterly intriguing I find you."

I watch her chest heave at my raw and exposing words. With a sigh, a sweet giggle escapes her moist lips. "Why didn't you just say so?"

Amused, I drop one final gentle kiss on her lips and then pinch her nose, smirking at how she's got such an uncanny ability to make my smile grow. I release her and position myself back on my stool. Once I turn away from her, we manage to get back to our task at hand with a charged, heavy silence. My beguilement fades as I realise my grave error. I was so blindly concerned about hurting Vi's feelings and fixing her misinterpretation that I let my body do the talking instead of my head. She attempts to fill the quietness with mind-less chatter, but the entire time, all I can do is chew on my lip and curse myself for being everything I promised I wouldn't be. When

I delivered that speech at the gala, I did it to prove one thing. One universal truth that I wanted to put on public record.

I'm not weak.

I am strong.

Vi Harris has somehow managed to rattle that truth.

Fear seeps into my soul again. If I'm weak with her, what else can get me? Can the darkness swallow me whole again without warning? Can I fall down the tunnel that is my depression? Can I be sucked back into that place I swore I would never return?

As I walk Vi back to her flat, I feel distracted and distant. I'm not being a complete arse like I was the night of the gala, but I'm definitely different. She looks at me curiously as she stands facing me in the darkened alley. Her eyes are wide and probing. Inviting. She wants me to kiss her again and, Christ, do I want to do nothing more. This would be the perfect time to make up for the last kiss I gave her in this very spot, when I left her abruptly with nothing more than a sodding thank you.

But I refrain. I withhold. I find some pittance of restraint and I move back. By the time she steps into the lift, my body is roaring for the bloody doors to close before I crash through them and capture her with my entire body.

Just as she disappears behind the steel, I glance down at my watch and catch it ticking over to 11:11. I exhale a shaky breath and turn to lean against the brick wall. Slamming my eyes shut, I clench my jaw and wish the same wish that I wish I knew how to stop wishing.

Dear John

Vi

THE NEXT DAY AT WORK, I'M SHOCKED WHEN I RECEIVE A TEXT from Hayden. I kind of assumed after his rather sudden brush-off last night on my doorstep that he'd go silent on me again. Instead, he asks if we can get together tonight to continue his countdown. I suggest a coffee shop, but he explained that he'd prefer somewhere more private for what we'll be discussing.

We settle on meeting at my flat. Wondering what day two of his countdown entails leaves me feeling anxious the entire day at work. He's obviously keen to get it all out, and I'm quite amazed at his tenacity. To relive, in great detail, the days leading up to an attempted suicide has to be intense for even the most healed survivors. But one thing I've learned about Hayden is he doesn't back down from a challenge.

I would have assumed that learning all of this about him would have tempered my attraction. A cold dose of reality is a sure-fire way to snuff out any sparks. But the truth is, it's only adding to the magnetic pull he's got on me. He's rich, and deep, and complicated. So many mysterious layers reside within Hayden Clarke, and I'm desperate to reach the centre. The fear of rejection is beginning to consume me, though.

Last night, his demeanour shifted back to that ice-cold way again. It was the same way he acted toward me when we were dealing with drunken Benji. He's sharing so much with me, but there always seems to be something about me that doesn't make men climb mountains for me. I remember Leslie sharing Finley and Brody's love story with me. He flew over a bloody ocean to chase her down after she crushed his heart with no clear explanation. Why can't I find even a fraction of that type of devotion?

Regardless, I must be a glutton for punishment when it comes to Hayden because I rush home early to tidy up my flat. Not that it needs it much. I definitely have a minimalist style, so there's not much tidying to be done. But my bedroom is an entirely different story than the rest of my flat. It is the one room where I let my personality play. Leslie calls the décor gothic glamour. It's basically like the Addam's Family meets Beverly Hills glamour. When I moved in, I covered the wall adjacent to my bed with a lilac and dark purple damask print wallpaper, adding to the drama of the room. My bed itself is a large king with a striking black baroque-carved headboard. The duvet is a decadent dark plum, crushed velvet material that Leslie found for me at some quaint fabric store in Brixton. Toss in the millions of upscale plush throw pillows and you have yourself a bed fit for a queen.

The room feels like a tribute to my upbringing, really. I fell in love with this style as a child when our dad took us on an incredible haunted house tour around London. The Jack the Ripper Ghost Tours inside old Victorian mansions sucked me in. I knew that when I grew up, I was going to have a room that looked just like those places. And with Leslie's help, I more than achieved my goal.

Hayden said he'll stop by after tea, so I take Bruce out for a nice long walk to tire him out. When I return, I take a quick shower and dress in a pair of soft black skinny jeans with holes in the knees and a white button-down blouse. I leave my hair loose and straight and try not to put too much effort into my makeup.

Just after eight, Hayden buzzes and I type in the code to allow him access to the eleventh floor. When the doors open, I'm awkwardly tugging at the buttons of my shirt, feeling like a kid on a platform at a tailor shop. Thankfully, Bruce pounces and distracts him enough for me to gain control of my fluttering heart.

After paying Bruce proper attention, Hayden strides toward me in a pair of sexily faded jeans that are snug around his muscled thighs. He's wearing a dark green fitted T-shirt that's tucked into the front of his jeans, revealing a masculine brown belt that matches the sexy leather cuffs on his wrists.

"Hiya," I say, swallowing nervously as I take note of his glowing grey eyes.

He nods. "How are you?" His gaze is wide and thoughtful, like he knows he's asking a lot from me by doing this and he appreciates it.

"I'm well. Are you thirsty? Shall I put the kettle on?"

"I'm okay, thanks." He clears his throat.

"I thought we could pop up to my garden to talk. It's really pretty up there this time of night with the sun setting. Does that work for you?" God, why does this feel so bloody formal? *Oh, maybe because he snogged you senseless, then looked at you like you grew two heads.*

He nods and sucks the sides of his cheeks between his teeth, chewing anxiously. I head to the kitchen to grab Bruce a new meaty chew and set it on his large pillow in the corner of the living room.

"Consolation prize?" Hayden asks, smiling at Bruce.

I nod. "There's no way to bring him up, so I always give him something special before I go."

Hayden follows me through the glass patio door. I flip on the light switch for the roof. Then I grab hold of the ladder and climb. Feeling his eyes on me the entire time, I do my best to make it up without stumbling. I turn to watch his reaction when he reaches the top and takes in the area that brings me the most joy in my home.

The sun is just beginning to disappear and a romantic orange dusk casts a hazy glow on everything, making the greens look even greener. A large, slatted, four-poster overhang resides right in the centre of the small roof, and hanging from that are climbing flowers and Chinese lanterns. Below the lanterns, an enormous, round, wicker sunbed rests on the fake moss flooring. A mess of colourful throw cushions match the various bushes and pots spread out all around the lush vegetation.

"Vincent wasn't exaggerating," Hayden says, inspecting the climbing ivy and roses alongside a small wrought iron archway.

"I don't know what most of them are," I admit. "I think those are azaleas, but they could be dandelions for all I know."

He huffs out a laugh. "More than I know."

"I love it up here, but I can't even call gardening a proper hobby if all I do is sit back and enjoy the flowers."

"A garden enthusiast, perhaps?" The corner of his mouth turns up and the set of his sexy, whiskered jaw sends pulse through my body.

"I'll accept that generous label." Laughing, I flip on my small Bluetooth speaker, grab my phone, and lie down on my belly on the sunbed, kicking my legs up behind me. Scrolling through the music on my phone, I ask, "What kind of music do you like, Hayden?"

"Oh, this sounds like dangerous territory." He strides over and lies down beside me on his side, glowering at me through hooded lashes. I close my eyes briefly, drinking in the heady musk of sawdust and soap that smells like his own perfect brand of cologne.

Suddenly, he snatches my phone from my hands.

"Hey!" I exclaim and reach over to grab it back. He holds it out of reach and I clamber over him to grab it. "Give it back!"

His chest rumbles with laughter. "Vi, this will be so much easier if we get this over with quickly."

"Get what over quickly?" I ask, looking down at him and realising with a burst of excitement that my chest is pressed snugly against his.

He looks down as if recognising the same thing. Rolling his

tongue against the inside of his cheek, his eyes twinkle with mirth as he returns his gaze to mine. "I'm going to go through your playlist, Vi." His voice is husky and ominous. "We can do this the easy way or the hard way."

I arch one challenging brow at him. "Which way means you don't get to go through my playlist?" I ask, propping my cheek on my hand and resting my elbow on his chest in mock indignation.

His face screws up in contemplation as he stares into the lanterns. "Neither," he teases while shooting out from beneath me and dashing away just as I make a swipe for my phone again.

"Oh, Christ," he moans, scrolling through the list.

"What?" I ask, certain I know the answer to my question but needing confirmation before I start defending myself.

The tone of his voice rises into a comedic shrill panic. "Oh, Christ! Vi, Vi, Vi. This is worse than I expected."

"Just tell me, you cheeky bugger!" I exclaim, resting my head on one of the pillows and preparing myself for the definite mockery coming my way.

"You have One Direction on here." He walks over to me with a pained look on his face and falls backward onto the cushion beside me. He wields my phone as a knife and acts as though he is piercing it through his chest. "And Bieber. And…Christ, I can't even say it." He covers his eyes with his arm. "Miley Cyrus. Fuuuuuck, Vi."

Without warning, and before he uncovers his eyes, I sock him hard in the stomach. He explodes a breath of warm air and curls up into the foetal position, laughing and groaning in unison.

"I didn't give you permission to look through it," I chastise, laughing at his ridiculous face. "Judge all you want, but their tunes are bloody catchy."

He sits up and looks at me pensively. His long leg is bent with one elbow resting on it in the most relaxed way I've ever seen him. "How did your tough footballer brothers ever let you get away with this?"

I bite my lip and it does nothing to conceal my huge shit-eating grin.

His knowing eyes turn wide. "They like them all, too," he guesses.

I nod, bursting into a fit of giggles. "You should see Gareth's pre-match playlist. He's got Taylor Swift!" My laughs really take off as Hayden sighs heavily and falls onto his back in complete defeat.

"I feel like a kid who's just been told there's no Santa," he whines.

"Oi, it's all right, love," I say in a proper mother hen voice while leaning over him so he can see into my eyes. "Father Christmas still lives in our Beiber-loving hearts."

The crinkles around Hayden's eyes as he laughs are enchanting. Every individual line is an expression of his heart. As if he sees something similar in me, his hand moves to touch my face. He drags the backs of his fingers down my cheek and then brushes my nose affectionately.

"I think I'll find a way to forgive you," he whispers.

My heart swells and I bite my lip, battling away the incredible urge I have to kiss him. He's right there…He's right fucking there! But it's him who needs to guide this ship. Not me.

I swallow hard and sit up, moving off his chest and into a more proper sitting position. "Day two, right?" I ask, attempting to shake off the heady desire rushing through me.

He sits up and I catch sight of his happy eyes draining into pools of anxiety. He clenches his jaw and nods stoically. I'm unsure if his mood shift is because of my abrupt change of subject or because of what we're about to discuss. Either way, he begins informing me that day two was the day he wrote his suicide note.

Suicide. Note.

Those two words alone cause my heart to thunder beneath my chest. I find myself nodding repetitively.

Hayden touches my hand. "I have it here with me, and I want you to read it…But only if you think you can handle it." His grey eyes are wide and haunting as he waits on bated breath for my answer.

The severity of his request is not lost on me. I'll never be able to unread something like this. But I can't say no. I need to read it as much as he wants me to read it. For whatever reason, Hayden Clarke has chosen me to walk this journey with him, and I can't turn off his path now. I nod again as he pulls out a tattered piece of yellow legal paper and hands it over to me.

My hands tremble as I unfold the note. Watching me must be too painful because he stands up and strides over to the edge of the rooftop. The city lights pop on one-by-one as the London skyline turns more and more black.

To My Family,

People write letters like this to tell you why, right? Why did I do this? Well, I hope I'm clear because the last thing I want to do is leave you all with any shred of doubt. I need you all to know that what I did to myself was something I chose to do on my own. It wasn't something that anyone pushed me into, and I don't want any of you worrying over the idea that you could have done anything to prevent this.

The truth is my heart has been aching and deteriorating every single day since Marisa's death. Scraps were all that was remaining. And now, at last, those scraps have also crumbled.

No matter what I do, I can't find a way to forgive myself. I can't let it go. In the wake of her death, I am drowning and I can no longer see the shore. I'm stuck here in the depths with the weight of her dead body pulling me further and further into the darkness. So much so, the darkness has become my only way of life. It's where I'm at while I'm living, and it's why I yearn for the nothingness of death.

Death feels like a break. Like a relief. Like a blessing. Like the only place I can find peace.

I don't know why I'm taking Marisa's passing harder than everyone else. Maybe because I was driving. Maybe because I felt the force of the quad against her body. Maybe because I loved her so much and I'm not sure I ever properly told her. How could I have never told her I loved her? She was the best sister anyone could ever ask for and I was oblivious. Ridiculous. Foolish.

It seems everybody but me is moving on with their lives. I refuse to continue to be the sad son, angry brother, disappointing friend, or jilted lover who holds everyone back. I despise being the charity case. When living hurts this much, what kind of life is it? So, instead of wishing every day that it was me who died in that accident instead of her, I'm going to do something about it.

My one final request from all of you, my only request, is to be happy.

I'm only sorry that I can't be.
Love always, -H

Tears stream down my face and onto the paper. Shaking, I quickly turn it over on the cushion to pat it dry. A huge knot aches in my throat, so I attempt a painful cough to relieve the pressure. I let out a frustrated and somewhat garbled cry. Then I feel Hayden's firm arms wrap around me. I curl up into a protective ball, failing miserably to stop my tears.

"Shhhhh," Hayden whispers against my hair and presses his lips to the top of my ear. "Shhhhh. I'm sorry, Vi. I'm so, so sorry."

"I'm sor—I'm sorry," I choke out painfully around the lump and bite down on my kneecap to stave off my cries. I shake my head. "I'm sorry for not being stronger right now. I just want to wish that time away for you, Hayden. I want to wish it away with everything inside of me." I wipe the tears from beneath my eyes and sniff loudly.

I turn my head and watch him exhale a shaky breath. His expression is grave as he taps the face of his watch mindlessly and replies, "You have no idea how many times I've wished the same thing. Still to this day."

"That's not you anymore, is it, Hayden? Is that man still inside of you?"

Terror courses through me from the absolute fear I have of

that darkness returning inside him. The Hayden I've been getting to know for the past week is nothing like the man in that letter. That man was a broken, shattered, semblance of a person who truly just wanted out.

"That darkness will always be inside me I think. But as you can see, I'm changed now. I told you before that deciding to kill myself felt brave, but deciding to live feels braver now."

I exhale at his important and meaningful proclamation. "I'm glad, but…wow. I can't imagine how your family reacted after reading that." I shudder at the thought. If I was his mum…If that was a note Booker had written…

"I've never shown that note to anybody, Vi."

My eyes fly to his just as he pierces me with a gravity in his gaze that scares me.

"How?" I clench the note in my hand as if the reality of it is somehow different now. "Surely your family found it."

"I never set it out. I never even told my doctor I wrote it." He shakes his head, his eyes looking downward as if he's embarrassed by his admission. "I've never told anybody. Not even Theo or Leslie."

I shake my head in disbelief. "Why me? Why did you choose to share this with me?" My voice cracks at the end in a panicky fear that the meaning behind all this is more than I can handle.

His grey eyes lift and stare into mine with an unspoken answer that strikes straight through my heart. The vulnerability and connection in this one look blossoms beneath my chest and brings tears to my eyes.

"Why me, Hayden?" I ask again. My body moves closer to him as if operating with a mind of its own.

His jaw clenches as he leans toward me as well, inching himself further and further into my space. His warm breath brushes my shoulder, and I delicately touch the leather cuff on his left wrist. He hisses softly and his eyes fixate on my hand, but he does not pull away.

Hayden Clarke has entrusted me with the deepest, darkest part of his soul. In that moment…In that second…In that briefest flicker of time ticking away on the watch around his wrist, I do exactly what my soul is screaming in agony for me to do. What my heart is pounding beneath my chest in anticipation for.

I kiss him.

God, do I kiss him.

I clutch his coarse jaw in my hands and press my lips to his in a fierce, passionate encounter. My mouth moves against his, coaxing and pleading. And, like the sway of a pendulum, his lips return my movement. It's in that second that everything inside of me clicks into place. Emotion rips through me as we rock back and forth, and I allow myself to believe that he feels the intense bind between us just as I do. His hands wrap firmly around my waist and push me back onto the cushion. The weight of him on top of me is intoxicating and heady. My body is screaming to take him inside of me with every passing second. I move to wrap my legs around him, but he suddenly rips himself away from me.

"Vi, no. Fuck!" he exclaims, sitting back on his knees. A look of agony casts over his face as he shakes his head at me accusingly.

"What?" I ask, sitting up and looking at him in complete shock.

"We can't do this! You don't get it. You read the note and you still don't get it!" He stands up and scrubs his hands over his hair and face. He begins pacing aggressively back and forth in front of me, the backdrop of the London night sky doing nothing to distract me from his charged demeanour. "Look, when I wrote that note, I truly felt like leaving would be a gift. A relief. I don't feel that way anymore. That is why we can't do this."

"I don't understand." I fold my knees to my chest, feeling like I need to grip something against me for protection.

"I've only been out of rehab for a year, Vi. I need to focus one hundred percent on myself. I called you a distraction for a reason. I'm sorry if that hurts you to hear, but it's the truth. When you told me last night how much that bothered you, I instantly put you first. I kissed you in the shop because I wanted to kiss the pain from you."

"And that's a bad thing?" I baulk defensively.

"Yes, because I can't put you first. I can't put anyone else first... Ever. Or that fucking darkness could return."

He snatches the note up off the ground where it fell and tosses it haphazardly beside me. My eyes fly wide. Does he seriously think that my presence in his life could cause him to become suicidal again?

Hurt. Deep. Painful. *Hurt.* Strikes me right in my back. It's happening again.

I stand up on shaky legs and cross my arms, turning away from him but keeping my shoulders held high. "I need you to leave, Hayden," I demand, my voice low and menacing. I refuse to let him see how much this is affecting me. How much this is shaking me to the core.

He exhales heavily and I hear his steps approach. "Vi, you are incredible. I still want to be mates. You've helped me through a lot." I recoil from the close proximity of his tremulous voice in my ear. "You'll find better than me, and whatever we are will shift into a brief and forgettable moment in time."

I let out a bark of a laugh as my face screws up in pain at his dismissal.

Once again, rejection fucking stings...Even in the dark.

15
Stag Night

Hayden

"**H**AYDEN, CAN YOU TAKE MARISA FOR A BIT? I HAVE A MILLION wedding calls to make and I'm near tears right now."

I close my laptop and frown at Leslie as she barrels down the stairs with a fussy Marisa in tow. I'm in the middle of reconciling the previous month's bank statements for C. Designs, but it's nothing that can't keep and a Marisa distraction sounds perfect. I am desperate to escape my roaring internal thoughts about what happened between Vi and me last night.

"Of course I'll take her. Don't cry, Leslie." I take in Leslie's haphazard auburn ponytail, sweat pants, and tank top. She looks frazzled and completely exhausted. "Is there anything else I can do?"

"No, but thanks," she says, passing Marisa over. I tuck her up by my face and shush her in soft puffs while doing my quick swinging bit. "Honestly, if you could just keep her so I can go down and talk to Theo, it would be ridiculously amazing."

"Say no more." I pull Marisa back to get a good look at her, which only causes her to start wailing more. After a pleading look back at Marisa, I wave Leslie off for her to go downstairs to Theo's shop.

"Hey now, pretty girl. Sounds like someone is ready for a nap," I coo as I find a swaddle blanket and make quick work of turning

Fussy Marisa into Baby Burrito Marisa. "Why are you so hard on your mummy some days? Did you just miss your Uncle Hayden?"

I drop a kiss on her soft head. Then I lay her across my thighs on her side. I stick a dummy in her mouth and shush her while swinging her back and forth with my legs. After a few minutes of fighting it, she passes out. Happiest baby on the block indeed.

Just as I reposition her sleeping body in the crook of my arm, my phone rings. An unfamiliar number illuminates the screen and, thinking it could be an appointment rescheduling, I answer.

"C. Designs. Hayden speaking."

"Hey, Hayden, it's Liam Darby," he says with a certain level of edge to his tone.

"Liam?" My brows lift in surprise.

My last meaningful memory of Liam and I replays in my head. I'm certain I was pissed. It involved a lot of puffed-up chests and me making a crass remark about being inside of Reyna. The bastard actually had the gall to hit me.

Okay, I probably deserved it.

Still, we are far from matey blokes who call each other.

"Listen, sorry to bother you, but Finley called me. She is putting together a last minute hen night for Leslie tomorrow night, and I'd like to throw Theo's stag party on the same night. I'm calling to see if you have any objection to that, or if you want to be a part of the coordinating and such."

I pause, trying to determine how to tactfully answer. "Look, I'm not really into the party scene anymore. I mean, I can attend. But as far as planning, I'd rather you handle things if that's all right."

"Sure, sure. But you will still be there?" His voice is hopeful.

"Of course I'll be there." *As long as I can manage it.*

"Good. It would be really important to Theo to have you there. And look, Hayden"—he sighs heavily—"I know we don't have the best history, but Theo's my best mate and I'd like to think that eventually you and I can be mates, too."

I stifle a disbelieving chuckle. I can't help but think that Liam's olive branch has more to do with keeping his enemies closer. Shortly after rehab, Reyna essentially ripped my heart out and threw it in the River Thames after I told her I was in love with her. I knew deep down she was with Liam, but it was still fucking painful. If I would have had that conversation with her prior to my attempt, I'm not sure how I would have reacted. But seeing the two of them together, engaged and happy at The White Swan Pub a couple of weeks ago, wasn't as bad as I feared it would be.

Although, it probably had a hell of a lot more to do with the fact that Vi literally swept me off my feet just before I walked inside. Or Bruce did, I should say.

"Sure, Liam," I reply stiffly, not able to bring myself to be overly kind to him. He did wallop me in the face after all. "Regardless, I appreciate you taking the lead on all this for my brother."

"No worries. All right, I'll text you the details for tomorrow. Cheers, Hayden."

"Cheers." I hang up and hope that a night out with a bunch of blokes will be just what the doctor ordered to get me over my Vi fixation.

Sending Out an SOS
16

Vi

"HEY, VI, IT'S FINLEY!" AN EXCITED AMERICAN VOICE TRILLS through the phone line as I sit at my desk at Nikon.

At the same time, Benji stumbles over with a tray of Starbucks and hands me my latte. He's been a bit quiet and sheepish around me since his drunken evening. I wonder if he remembers kissing Hayden, but I can't bring myself to ask. I lift my eyebrows and nod a silent thank you before he shuffles over to Hector next.

"Hiya, Finley. Nice to hear from you." I close out the leather satchel design I've been messing with all week, grateful for a break. "How are you?"

"I'm great, thanks! I'm calling because we've decided to throw together a last minute bachelorette party for Leslie tomorrow night. Or hen party I guess is what you Brits call it, isn't it? I'm really hoping that works for you because I know Leslie would love it if you came. She is so crazy stressed with wedding business. Theo thinks she needs a night out, so it feels like now or never."

"Oh, sure, I totally understand. I'm sorry to hear Leslie is so stressed. Being a new mummy is a lot of work I'm sure."

"Exactly. I've been trying to help her with the wedding stuff, but I've been travelling for work a lot, so ugh. It's just been hard.

And Leslie's family is pretty much not in her life anymore, so we're doing our best to fill those shoes and not let Leslie dwell on that too much. Frank has been popping over there a lot. Anyway, it'll be fine. We'll catch up and get everything done for the wedding one way or another."

"Blimey," I reply, stupidly unhelpful.

"Oh my God, I'm sorry. I just unloaded on you! We have four weeks. Plenty of time to plan a wedding," she laughs maniacally.

Swallowing, I add, "Well, I'm free tomorrow. I'd love to go. Can you let me know what I can do to help? With the wedding or the hen do?" I ask, praying that whatever she might have me help with doesn't involve coming face-to-face with Hayden again.

I close my eyes and wish away the annoying sting of rejection that's been niggling at me. After all we shared—after all I know about him in such a short amount of time—he still only saw me as a distraction. Hearing him say that having a relationship with me could make him unhealthy again is a real kick in the teeth. Christ, do I have bad luck with men. Ever since the altercation with Gareth over Pierce cheating on me last year, I've been wondering what kind of bloke I'll ever find who's right for me.

If my fear of rejection was a slow simmer before, it's at a proper boil now. Perhaps I need to stop seeking anything serious for a while and have a bit of fun for once. Not give anyone a chance to dump me. I never got to have my slutty university days that so many other girls my age experienced. I had brothers watching my every move. I am beginning to think a hen do is just what the doctor ordered.

"I'm so glad you can make it!" Finley says, pulling me away from my thoughts. "We have everything sorted for the hen party, so just show up and wear something fabulous and red. The party is starting at Frank's around eight o'clock. I'll text you the details. Just look red hot, all right?"

"Sounds great. I look forward to it!" I reply cheerily.

We say our goodbyes and, as soon as I hang up, a gift idea for Leslie comes to mind. It's an unconventional gift for a hen do. Nothing like lingerie, but I think it will be perfect.

Jaci no K

Hayden

Marisa wails as I set her on the couch just long enough for me to strap the BABY BJÖRN carrier on my chest. She grunts as I awkwardly shimmy her down the front of the makeshift baby front-pack.

"There you go," I sing proudly, glancing at the entryway mirror. I'm dressed in a pair of my favourite jeans and one of my go-to white V-neck T-shirts. Marisa is decked head-to-toe in red polka dots. Outfit number two for the day for both of us since she crapped through the last one, making a mess all over herself and me.

Her chubby arms and legs flail as she readjusts to her new outlook on life now that she's strapped to my chest. I slide on my Aviators before adjusting Marisa's matching mini-Aviators I got her last week. Then I give her two hearty thumbs-up. "We look top-notch, pretty girl."

Theo and Leslie's voices trail down the stairs from the master loft bedroom, and my brows rise knowingly. They are on their way to a proper row. That is Uncle Hayden's cue to take Baby Marisa for a neighbourhood stroll. Theo is attempting to convince Leslie that she's got to go out for her hen party tonight. He's already arranged for our parents to keep Marisa overnight so he can go to his drunken stag party as well.

Being around alcohol won't be a ton of fun for me. After my stint in rehab, drinking was the first thing I gave up. It was painful for a long time, but not nearly as bad as when I quit smoking. I didn't realise how much I had grown dependent on both fags and booze as part of my everyday survival.

Frankly, the cravings became a great deal easier when I moved out of my parents' house and back to London. After rehab, I wanted to earn my parents' trust back, and having a strong support system is key to recovery. So I moved back to rural Essex and lived at home with my mum, dad, and Daphney. They did everything they could to keep my spirits up, but working at my dad's furniture distribution company felt like a slow and painful death. When Theo and Leslie asked me if I'd want to live with them in their flat in London for a while, I thought they were having a laugh. They were due to have a baby any day. Why would they want a suicidal, post-rehab, recovering alcoholic roommate around their new baby?

But fuck me, here I am. I think Leslie had a lot to do with the offer, though. My bond with Leslie is so acute that I don't think either of us wants to be too far from one another for a while if we can help it. When someone finds you haemorrhaging from your wrists and you suddenly find the will to live again, it's not a connection that can be easily forgotten. From the second she found me and every moment since, Leslie has felt like my anchor, keeping my feet planted firmly on the ground. Or at least that was until Marisa was born. The first time I soothed Marisa's cries with my bare hands, life suddenly looked hopeful.

Despite Leslie's protests about going out, I tend to agree with Theo. She could use a bit of fresh air. Her mate Frank has been over all week, trying to help her with wedding stuff, but she's too distracted by Marisa to fully put him to good use. Putting on a dress and some heels might do her mental state a world of good, but it's not my place to say. I'd never gang up on Leslie with my brother. Maybe the other way around, though. My brother can be a moody sod sometimes.

"We best make hay so Mummy and Daddy can scream until their hearts are content," I coo to Marisa's soft head as I shift the diaper bag on my shoulder. "We definitely don't want to be around for the making up part."

A knock on the door sounds just as I'm about to grab the knob. I open it to find a robust woman in a cream pantsuit with a tight chignon of black hair pulled back. Her eyes are narrow and severe.

"Are you Theo Clarke?" she asks, eyeing me up and down, barely registering the baby strapped to my chest.

"No, I'm his brother, Hayden. Can I help you?" I drag my sunglasses down to get a proper look at this bird.

"I'm here for Leslie Lincoln." Her tone is clipped and formal. She thrusts a business card into my hand and on the front in large, swirly letters is "Jaci...no K."

"Regarding?" I ask as I flip it over and hear Theo and Leslie approaching behind me.

"Ah, Miss Lincoln I presume." The woman moves past me, completely oblivious to Baby Marisa, and sticks her hand out to an equally perplexed Leslie. "I'm Jaci Baxter, pronounced like *Jackie* but without the *K*. It's short for Jaclyn, which is French, of course. You may call me Jaci. I'm your new wedding coordinator."

Leslie shakes the woman's hand and looks at Theo. "Did you do this?"

Theo adjusts his eyeglasses. "I haven't a clue what this is about."

"I've been hired by a friend who wishes to remain anonymous," Jaci states pragmatically while handing a business card to each of us. "And I'll have you know, I'm fully qualified, licensed, and insured. Most importantly, already paid in full with a rush bonus for the next few weeks. And I assure you, Miss Lincoln and Mr. Clarke, I am not cheap. So if you turn me away, you're only hurting yourselves and your extremely generous friend."

All of our jaws drop. "Who in the bloody hell?" Theo asks first.

"It doesn't matter," Jaci snaps, her mouth pinched in a way that makes me wonder if she's sucking on a lemon drop. "Do you have a diary, Miss Lincoln?"

"A what?" Leslie asks, her agog expression firmly in place.

"A wedding diary. Something with your to-do list. I work seven days a week, so I'd rather get started now, if it's all the same to you."

Leslie shakes off her stupor and strides over to the table to grab a huge three-ring binder. "This probably won't even make sense to you. It's a bit of a mess."

"I'll manage. We'll discuss more in the car. I have one waiting out front."

"Waiting for what?" Leslie asks, looking frightened like a naughty child being sent to the chancellor's office.

Jaci's nostrils flare. "I have a hair, nail, and makeup session booked for you with the prestigious Trevor Sorbe, hairdresser to the stars."

Leslie scratches her messy auburn topknot and tugs down on her milk-stained, button-down, plaid shirt of Theo's. "How on earth did you get me in there?"

"I am well-connected, Miss Lincoln, and I have a standing Saturday appointment for all of my A-list clients." Jaci puckers her lips with a chuffed with herself expression.

"A-list clients? This sounds like I'm getting Punk'd," Leslie scoffs. "How do we know you're not some loony toon off the street?"

Jaci sighs in frustration. "Open any British bridal magazine and you'll see my name next to the celebrity spreads." She turns to me and snaps her fingers. I straighten my posture for fear of being sent to the naughty corner as well. "You...You're the brother?"

I cup Marisa's head protectively and warily reply, "I am."

"I shall tell you who the friend is so you can confirm the identity and that will be that. Then we can all get on with our work. But you will maintain your discretion."

Her eyes blaze with an unspoken threat. I nod nervously.

Marisa and I follow Jaci into the kitchen. She opens up her binder, shuffling through her notes. "Here it is."

She opens it to me, and my eyes land on the name assigned to the bill. Vilma Harris. Jaci's hand conceals the pound amount that's marked with a large stamp: PAID IN FULL.

"Vi?" I whisper in astonishment. Fuck. Just when I was doing a proper job of not thinking about her, she goes and does something like this.

"Discretion," Jaci seethes through clenched teeth. "Now, can you please go and inform Miss Lincoln that I am who I say I am so we can get on with our day? We haven't a moment to waste."

I nod, my eyes still wide with shock, and follow Jaci to inform Leslie that everything is legitimate. I can't imagine what Vi must have paid for this woman to assist for a month, but Leslie's green eyes alight with a level of excitement that just goes to show how truly in over her head she's been all week. She kisses Theo and Marisa goodbye. Then she smiles at me as I sway Marisa soothingly from side to side.

"I'll see you guys later!" she beams before scurrying out the door with hardly a second look.

"Blimey, she was a scary bird," Theo huffs, and I nod in agreement.

Girlfriends

Vi

I ARRIVE AT FRANK'S BRIXTON VICTORIAN MANSION JUST AFTER eight o'clock. It's a large imposing house right on the corner of a busy street with a skate park sitting kitty-corner from the lot.

Brixton is a diverse neighbourhood that was labelled "up and coming" quite some years ago. It definitely has a similar eclectic, artistic vibe as Shoreditch. A crew of young skater-types begin catcalling as I hop out of the cab.

"Oi, you tossers. Go shag yourselves and get a bloody life!" Frank bellows, stepping out of the purple front door that's framed in crawling ivy. He's dressed in red trousers with a black strip down each leg and a red dress shirt with a denim bow tie firmly in place.

"Vi, my dear girl. Fuck me sideways, you look like a proper lady of the night." He bounds down the steps to greet me, his eyes scrolling down my body appreciatively. "Designer, too, I can tell. Cheeky girl."

I'm wearing a two-piece, red, Valentino dress that reveals a couple inches of bare midriff. It has a scoop neckline and three-quarter sleeves. The skirt sits just below my knees, but the entire ensemble fits like a second skin. It's very Victoria Beckham posh. Paired with my black Monolo Blahniks, I feel like a proper footballer's wife to be sure. I'm not ashamed to say I put forth a bit more effort tonight. After hearing nothing from Hayden for the past few days, I knew I was in need of a proper night on the town to help move on.

"Thanks, Frank. A lady of the night is just the look I was going for," I reply sardonically.

"Get in here before those man-boys descend. You're the last one we were waiting on." He puts his slender arm around my shoulders and guides me up the front steps. A lascivious grin spreads across his face. "I hope you're ready to get your knickers wet."

"Am I what?" I ask. Before he can explain, I'm thrust into a full swing party.

Music booms loudly as Frank guides me through the large foyer and into the enormous formal dining room on the right. The large table is covered in a red sheet. Before I have a chance to inquire about it, Finley and Leslie both cheer loudly as they waltz out of the attached kitchen.

Leslie leaps toward me first. "Vilma, you're here! All my favourite London Lovers!" she sings merrily, throwing her arms around me and Finley, hugging us to her sides.

I turn my head to fully appreciate Leslie's dress. It's a red tutu skirt with sheer polka dots layered on top. The bodice is black and strapless with a high fashion, asymmetrical, red, feather sprout on one side. Her long auburn hair is pulled back into a high, bouncy ponytail, and her makeup looks stunning if not a bit pissed.

"You're just in time," Finley giggles, tugging up her strapless mini, red dress and sipping her drink.

Frank reappears beside me with a red cocktail in a martini glass. "Drink up! You're three behind these lushes."

He ushers me away from Leslie's grasp just as I take a sip and says, "Okay, introductions. You know the Lezbo. The bitch can't hold her booze since my beautiful goddaughter was born. Then we've got smartarse Fin Bin, who lives here with her sex monster of a husband. And there's Jiggly Jules, who also lives here."

"What makes me jiggly?" Julie asks, narrowing her Asian eyes at Frank. It's a good question because she is petite by any standards, and dressed in a red miniskirt and red tank, there's not much I can see jiggling on her.

Before Frank replies, a Prince song kicks on. Julie screams and runs into the living room to dance, dragging Finley and Leslie with her.

"See what I mean?" Frank asks, circling his finger by his temple. "I'd avoid her if I were you. Her boyfriend, Mitch, moved out last week and she's a ticking time bomb, that one. You remember Oxford," he says, gesturing to Reyna, who's striding over from the other side of the table. "You can call her Rey or Bitch Face. She answers to both. I've checked."

"Rey works," she replies flatly, glaring at Frank and then smiles sincerely at me. She looks fierce in a pair of red leather pants and a red sleeveless tee, revealing her extensively inked arms. Her dark hair is loose and wild down her back, making me feel slightly over-dressed as I smooth my low ponytail.

I eye Rey curiously as I consider what kind of relationship Hayden had with her, but then internally kick myself for even thinking about him again.

"And I am Ameerah, child," a large dark-skinned woman peels as she strolls into the dining room from the kitchen. She's wearing a head wrap and holding a cocktail, looking perfectly at ease with herself in a red and white print moo moo.

"Ame brings the cocks," Frank crows.

"The what?" I nearly choke on my drink.

"Let us begin, Frank," Ameerah says in a thick Caribbean accent.

Frank releases me to gather everyone around the table and props us in our assigned chairs. Ameerah makes a grand gesture of pulling back the red cloth to reveal a table full of...

Cocks.

Loads and loads of scary-looking cocks.

Bugger, that one has three heads.

"A new hot dog!" Leslie crows. "Frank, you shouldn't have!"

I look around confused as Ameerah begins her speech. Apparently she owns a sex toy boutique in Brixton and I have found myself smack dab in the middle of a sex toy hen party.

"I'm definitely going to need one of these." Julie hiccups in my ear and grabs a pink thing in front of me. It's shaped like the letter C, and I'm not even sure how it would work. "Since I'm newly single and all."

"Brody would go gaga for these, Finny!" Leslie laughs and chucks a sack of cock rings at her.

"Um, these are to make the guy last longer, and Brody has zero problem there, thanks." Finley tosses them over to me.

I eye the toys nervously as Ameerah begins describing the uses for each item. I wouldn't say I'm sexually prude, but I definitely don't have a drawer of sex toys. I've only had two partners, and neither of them seemed too keen on experimenting with BOBs. And I certainly don't need anything to help pleasure myself.

"See anything you like, Vi?" Frank asks from the other side of me.

I grab a small garment box with a pair of hot pink lace knickers sitting inside.

"That's French silk," Ameerah purrs, sauntering over to me. "I own a fabric store next to my husband's sex store. I commission all the lingerie from a designer I know."

"And it's not me!" Leslie whines. "I don't have time to sew anything anymore. I had to buy my own wedding dress for Pete's sake."

I smile fondly at Leslie. She always did have a great eye for technique. It's a big reason why she did all the China trips before she had Marisa. I'm better at digital design, but I'm becoming more well-rounded in her absence.

"Your dress is beautiful, Lez," Finley rebuffs and rubs Leslie's arms affectionately.

"I know, but it's not an original." Suddenly, her eyes alight with a renewed sense of purpose. "However! I might have some time to do some tweaking to it now that Jaci's on the scene! That's Jaci…no K!"

I try to school my features to look surprised as Leslie tells the group about Jaci being her new wedding coordinator. Apparently she tackled nine things off the list while Leslie got her hair done today.

"Guys, I think I might have a lady boner for Jaci. She's scary and reminds me a bit of that mean British chef, Gordon Ramsey, but it's kind of a turn-on! Maybe I should get her a present." She giggles and begins riffling through the products.

I'm relieved to see Leslie embracing the coordinator. That's exactly what I wanted her to do. However, if she knew it was me who paid for Jaci's assistance, she most certainly would refuse the help. But when I turned twenty-one, I received a large trust from my dad. I have never done a lot with the money except purchase the lease on my flat, so it felt good to spend it this way.

I knock back a couple more cocktails and relish in the fact that none of these women are like the women I went to school with. Perhaps it's because most of them are happily coupled off? Or perhaps it's because they don't have a clue or care in the world about who my family is, which is usually the deal-breaker for me and my new girlfriends. Regardless, this group feels so down-to-earth and completely unaffected by trivial London society troubles. It's refreshing.

The night takes a wicked turn when Leslie disappears into the bathroom to try some warming lube on her wobbly bits. I've never laughed as hard as when she waltzed out in her beautiful dress like she had just stepped off a horse. You'd think that would scare everyone away, but Finley ran in to try the same product!

These girls are so pleasantly original.

In the end, I don't buy any freaky sex toys, but I do purchase several of the sexy lingerie pieces. I have a little thing for sexy underwear ever since I moved out of my dad's house. I think I was always too scared to buy it before, fearing that my brothers might see it in the laundry and go ballistic. Now I have a proper collection of filmy goodies that make me feel girlie and sexy when I go to bed every night.

"The cabs are here!" Frank roars. "To Club Shay we go!"

We hustle into a couple of black cabs and buzz through the intoxicating city lights of London all the while musing over the last time I was at Club Shay. I haven't been back since before Leslie and Theo became a couple. Leslie was in the middle of some sort of insane love cleanse that Frank had put together for her. The night we were all there, she was challenged by Frank to do a girl kiss, and she ended up shocking all of us when she smacked Finley right on the lips. It was a right proper snog, too, which Theo was there to bear witness to.

I laugh at the fact that all of that was part of their unconventional love story. Now they are getting married soon with their own beautiful daughter as their flower girl. Will I ever find anyone who loves me enough to chase me through an entire love cleanse? Or am I destined to only be a motherly figure to my brothers for the rest of their lives?

"Why so glum?" Julie asks, sitting directly across from me and watching me through hooded eyes. She's possibly the drunkest of everyone here. I'm actually a bit worried for her.

I shrug my shoulders and smile. "I'm just really happy for Leslie. She's really got it all, you know?"

"It's not that easy for all of us," she drawls menacingly and stares out the window. "No sense getting your hopes up to find something similar because, just when you think you have your happily ever after sorted, you get the rug ripped straight out from under you. You think you know someone? You don't. You never really do." She sighs heavily and her eyes narrow further. "I'm just looking for a bloke to shag tonight. Someone to wet my whistle and walk away from. That's. It."

My brows lift as Julie speaks to the voice in my head that's trying its hardest to shout at me to stop obsessing over Hayden and wanting to turn him into something more. He pulled back because he's not interested, and I know I'd do right to avoid him full stop from now on. Tonight isn't about men anyway. It's about having fun with some friends.

When we pull up to Club Shay, I'm feeling on top of the world and ready to make tonight about me and nobody else. I'm not as pissed as the rest of the party, but I'm feeling relaxed and ready for anything.

Anything but a dizzyingly sexy Hayden Clarke standing at the entrance of the club.

Seeing Red

Hayden

A BLACK CAB PULLS UP TO THE CURB AT CLUB SHAY JUST AS MY watch clicks over to 11:11. I lean against the wall, ball my fists, and do my usual ritual. When I open my eyes, I see Leslie stumble out of the cab with Frank and Finley doing their best to steady her.

"Hayden!" Leslie bellows, running toward me with her arms open. I feel a bit twitchy from the coincidental timing of their arrival, but get over it quickly as she heaves me down for a drunken hug. Her breath reeks of alcohol as she asks, "Does this mean my Theo is here?" The tone of her voice hitches to a high-pitched squeal at the end with her undiluted excitement.

I shake my head knowingly and gesture that he's inside. "He's here just for you, Lez."

"Fuck!" she screeches. "I'm super glad I wore panties tonight!" I blanch as she suddenly stops and twirls around, halting Frank and Finley in their tracks. "Hands off bitches. His thigh is mine," she cackles and drags a crying-with-laughter Finley and Frank toward the entrance.

I shake my head in utter confusion and see Rey step out of a second cab.

"Hey, Hay," she says, nudging me with her shoulder.

"Hey, Rey," I chuckle. "How are you doing?"

"Good…Not as good as Leslie, but good. You clean up well." She wiggles her eyebrows playfully at me, attempting to be matey.

Matey and Rey just don't quite mix for me yet.

"They're all inside," I offer, trying not to roll my eyes.

She nods sheepishly and makes her way toward the door.

Once upon a time, I was completely sickened by jealousy over what Liam was able to get from Rey that I never could, and it's still not the most comfortable thing in the world to be around him. But I'm glad Rey has someone looking out for her. He's also Theo's best mate. I owe a lot to Theo and Leslie, so I'll be the bigger person and look past everything. And, truthfully, I have evolved enough in my recovery to know that I was being a complete twat and deserved the knock to my face. Still, I can only stomach so much grinning and bearing.

"Vi?" I say in surprise as my eyes catch sight of her walking from the other side of the cab arm in arm with Frank's roommate, Julie.

"Hi to you, too, wanker" a sullen Julie says, stomping past me in a huff.

My brows lift at her chilly demeanour. I've only met her once I think.

"I didn't realise you'd be here," I say, turning back to Vi and looking her up and down. A heaviness bears down on my shoulders that wasn't there before. Fuck me, she looks stunning. The flesh revealed on her abdomen and the curve of her slim hips beneath the stretching red fabric causes my dick to stir.

"I didn't know this was a combined party." She looks around awkwardly, seemingly trying to avoid eye contact. "I thought it was just a hen night."

Is she disappointed? "Uh, yeah. It was Liam's idea. This is where Theo and Leslie met, so…" I can barely finish my sentence as anxiety prickles all my senses.

She nods stiffly. "You look nice." She shoots me a cool, polite smile and tucks a nonexistent loose hair behind her ear.

I look down haphazardly at my clothes. I'm dressed in black jeans and a tight, fitted, blue button-down with my sleeves rolled up to my elbows. I've carelessly left a couple of buttons popped around my neck. My brown cuffs and watch are in place as usual. I look like a prat compared to how stunning she looks.

I swallow hard, trying to determine how to warm up her ice-cold demeanour toward me. I know we didn't leave things on the best terms last time we saw each other, but fuck. I'm not just some random bloke.

"You look…shocking."

Her face screws up. "Shocking?"

"Um, red. It's…your colour." My voice falters like a moron as I try to stifle the impending urge I have to toss her back into the cab and hide her from the rest of the world. Honestly, the possessiveness I feel combined with not knowing exactly what she's thinking right now is driving me mad.

"You okay?" She looks at me with confusion over my nervousness.

Fuck, Hayden, get your shit together.

I nod stiffly and gesture toward the door for her to lead the way. I place my hand on the small of her back out of morbid curiosity if that spark we had is still there. She shivers beneath my touch and it takes the strength of a saint to not curve my hand around her small waist, pull her back against me, and allow my eager fingers to grope until their desires are satisfied. I know she doesn't need my hand on her bare back to be guided to the VIP section, and that's not why I'm touching her. I'm touching her to send a message out to all the fucking tossers in this club that she is spoken for.

Is she?

Christ, Hayden. She's not bloody spoken for. You'd do well to get that out of your head if you want to do what's best for everyone involved.

I rip my hand from her as we reach the corner of the club where

STRENGTH

everyone is sitting on black leather couches. There's a glass coffee table with bottles and mixers in the centre.

Leslie is perched on Theo's lap and is giggling happily at something he's whispering in her ear. Finley and her husband, Brody, are seated next to them. The others who came out tonight for Theo's stag party consist of Liam and Theo's other two mates, James and Ethan.

Reyna's eyes find mine. I could feel her penetrative gaze as soon as I entered the VIP section. Liam has a lazy arm draped over her shoulders as he talks to Ethan. I can read her expression like a fucking book, and right now she's wondering how hard all of this is for me to be around. She raises her eyebrows at me in silent question. I frown and shake my head, telling her I'm fine. I look away, trying to conceal my annoyance. For starters, I'm not her concern anymore. Secondly, the alcohol is child's play compared to Vi in her red fucking dress.

Vi bends over to grab a bottle of water off the table and Ethan's eyes zero in on her. In seconds, he's detaching himself from Liam and approaching her slowly in a way that makes everything in me want to turn into a caveman. Ethan has definite sleazebag qualities. Of all Theo's mates, he's the worst. He's tall with caramel-chocolate skin and blue eyes that he thinks make him fucking Zeus, king of the bloody Greek gods. The way he expects women to fawn all over him gets right up my nose.

I turn away as he slithers up to Vi. I lean on the metal rail that's positioned above the dance floor, watching the swarms of people drinking themselves into oblivion. There was a time when I'd be right there with them, drinking so I wouldn't have to feel. But all that did was delay my feelings until they crashed in a mighty wreck all over my life. Now I'm content to be sober and deal with things as they come, one-by-one.

The night carries on, and all I can do is watch Vi laugh and have a great time while I sit and stew over how I feel about her. She doesn't drink alcohol like everyone else. She's had the same cocktail since she arrived nearly two hours ago, and she's gone through two whole bottles of water. I fucking love that about her.

"You're not fooling me, you know." Leslie's voice chirps quietly in my ear.

"What do you mean?" I ask, frowning at the fact that Vi has barely looked at me since we came inside. I'm sitting on the couch directly across from her as she's sandwiched between Ethan and James—the only other single blokes here tonight.

Leslie sits on the edge of the coffee table, blocking my view. "You're trying to act strong and confident. But I see right through you, baby brother."

I roll my eyes. "Stop calling me baby brother. You're only one year older than me."

She giggles dopily, her green eyes drooping in her happy, drunken state. She reaches out and pushes my sullen pout into a grin, and I can't help but laugh in response.

Shaking my head, I say, "The alcohol isn't bothering me. I actually quite enjoy being sober. All you sods are going to wake up with crippling headaches tomorrow and I'm going to hit the gym feeling great."

"I'm not talking about the booze." She shifts off the table and onto the couch, leaning back next to me. She rests her head on my shoulder and continues. "I'm talking about the blonde."

I shift my jaw back and forth. "It's like she doesn't even know me."

My eyes squint as Vi laughs at something Julie says from the other side of James. I know I rejected her, but I can't help but feel like her excessive shift in attitude toward me is some blatant form of judgement. Does she not want to be seen publicly with me? Is that it?

"You're not the easiest of guys to get to know," Leslie drawls sleepily.

That was true until I met Vi. Christ, what on earth have I gotten myself in the middle of? Originally, running into Vi at the gala felt like the universe's way of putting us together. That's why I thought she'd be perfect to help me with my countdown. I should have known better. The first moment I met her at The White Swan was the first time my body had responded to another woman since Reyna.

Fuuuuuck. What have I done?

"I've told her more than I've told most, Leslie," I admit in hushed tones.

She sits up and whispers right in my ear, "That must mean she's worth it."

Her words hit me just as the music shifts to a Beyoncé track. Leslie lets out a mighty cheer and Frank's head pops up out of nowhere. His eyes lock on hers and they sprint toward each other, connecting in an epic hug of jumping and squealing. They make a mad dash for the dance floor, grabbing people along as they go.

Suddenly, Julie sidles up to me. "Will you fucking dance with me, Hayden?" she purrs. "I've had a bastardly couple of weeks and I feel like a bloody loser."

I turn my surprised expression to her and see Ethan pulling Vi up out of the corner of my eye. They head toward the dance floor, so I quickly stand, grabbing Julie's small hand as I go. I drag her through the throngs of wasted Londoners grinding on each other. She hoots with excitement as we pass by Leslie, Frank, Theo, Finley, and Brody. I position us in a place where I can keep my eyes on Ethan and Vi, but not so close that I look like a tosser from *To Catch a Predator*.

Julie's hands grip my biceps and she sings along to the music as we begin moving. "You're not an ugly bloke, Hayden!" she yells above the roaring beat.

"Thanks?" I reply, frowning down at her.

"I've been in a bit of a bubble for the last couple of years. Mitch took a walk and I feel like my whole world looks different now. Know what I mean? Like, I've always been in a relationship. I jumped from one to the next, to the next. I considered getting a cat to keep myself occupied, thinking maybe a new companion might stop me from jumping straight into another relationship. But then I was terrified that might turn me into a permanent crazy cat lady. So I thought that maybe if I shag a new bloke, I'll feel better!"

"I guess that could help," I murmur halfheartedly listening while mulling over what Leslie said earlier. How can one sentence uttered by a drunken woman throw me so much?

"I think you'd do me properly, don't you?"

"Excuse me?" I look down, my brow furrowed at what I think Julie's just suggested.

She squeezes my biceps appreciatively. "No strings attached. Just a good physical effort. What do you say?"

"Uh, Julie," I begin, trying to find a way to let her down. But before I can finish my sentence, she yanks me down by my collar and connects our lips in a painfully awkward kiss. Her tongue forces its way through my teeth and the scent of alcohol blazes into my senses. It feels wrong. It feels like cheating in more ways than one.

I quickly break her grip on my collar and detach my face from hers. "I'm sorry, Julie, but that's really not a great idea," I say, doing my best to be kind.

"Why ever not?" She actually has the nerve to haul me down for another snog.

"Julie, I'm not in a place to be in a relationship right now. Really. I just…I'm focusing on my own life before I even consider diving in with anybody."

"Well, bugger," she whines, releasing me and placing her hands on the back of her neck. "I just need a proper servicing for bloody sake! Whose balls do I have to suck to get a proper dicking?"

My eyes widen in disbelief, and I glance around nervously at the people gawking at us. Vi's eyes draw me to her, and the hurt on her face is crushing. Ethan attempts to twirl her back into him, but she ends up pulling away from him and storming off the dance floor. He follows closely behind and my heart thuds with growing frustration.

"Fuck," I groan, feeling annoyingly out of control. "Julie, I have to go."

"Hayden, just be honest with me first. Are you not attracted to me? Be specific. I'd rather you be straight with me than have this whole weak, 'It's not you, it's me excuse.'"

"Julie, you're beautiful. I'm a fucking mess. Believe me. You don't want a thing from me."

I slip past Julie and head over to Finley and Brody to let them know they should go check on her. The last thing I want is for someone to take advantage of her. She's obviously going through something as well. Then I make my way through the crowd, back to the VIP section where I find Ethan completely wrapped around Vi, encasing her against the side railing and attempting to kiss her.

I see red.

Bright, angry, vengeful, frustrated, possessive red.

I don't think. I just react.

"What the fuck's going on?" I seethe through clenched teeth, grabbing Ethan by the shoulders and aggressively wrenching him backward.

"Oi, Hayden." Ethan's tone is light and playful, setting me more on edge. "Shove off. This has nothing to do with you."

I turn my back to Vi, inserting myself between them so I'm nose-to-nose with Ethan. "Yes, it fucking does." My words are slow and menacing.

"She hasn't mentioned a thing about you, Hayden," he sneers, giving me the look of a fucking righteous, self-entitled prick. "So I beg to differ, mate."

I step even closer to him, inhaling a large breath.

"Hayden, stop it right there." Vi's tone is a warning as she moves to stand beside me. I ignore her, nudging my chest into Ethan. Out of the corner of my eye, I catch sight of her heeled foot stamping on the ground in haste. "This is ridiculous. I can handle myself."

"You heard her," Ethan smirks cockily. Then he pats me heartily on my shoulder and gives me a light shove away from her.

Everything after that happens so fast. One second, I'm getting a light push from Ethan. The next, I'm shoving him using five times the force he did. He stumbles backward, clumsily tripping on his own feet. I can see what's about to happen, but I'm frozen in time, unable to change the ripple effect even if I wanted to. He lands on his arse right on top of the glass coffee table. It cracks loudly and shatters beneath him. His hands fly out to catch himself on the frame before he crashes through to the floor.

Everything and everyone stops all around us. I swear, even the music does that scratched record sound you only see in old films. I'm still stuck in the single, solitary moment where everything before me went from bad to worse.

"Hayden," Vi cries, bringing her hands to cover her mouth in horror at the mess in front of us.

I reach down and pull Ethan up out of the coffee table. A wetness covers my hand. I look down and see red, angry blood smeared all over my hand.

"Fuck, Ethan, are you hurt?"

Ethan's eyes narrow at me as he straightens his tie. "I'll live. At least mine wasn't *self-inflicted*."

My anger immediately falls as Ethan's cutting remark casts an instant shroud of darkness over my soul. His blatant insinuation has its desired effect as shame completely envelops me.

Suddenly, a hefty bouncer appears and grabs me aggressively by the arm. I don't even have the strength to look back as he twists my right arm behind my back with a painful crank. The only place my downcast gaze seeks is Vi. Humiliation and despair explode inside me, reflecting in my broken posture as her beautiful blue eyes look at me with utter sadness.

"You're done, mate. You're on the fucking shit list, and you won't be coming back here ever again," the bouncer growls as I'm dragged harshly through the club.

I shake my head, completely oblivious to what he's saying, only thinking about Vi and what I've just done. He gives me another hard shove out the door for good measure, and I look back at the building in shock. How the fuck did that all happen so fast? I look down at my hands in horror and quickly wipe Ethan's blood off on my jeans. I unsnap and re-snap my leather cuffs, nervously unsure what to do. *Fuck, fuck, fuck! What are you doing, Hayden? What the fuck are you doing?* I jam my hands into my pockets and pace angrily in front of the door.

A minute later, Theo's stocky frame barrels through the door. "What the hell happened, Hayden?" His eyes bear down on me accusingly as he adjusts his glasses on his face. "Ethan's fucking bleeding!"

"I know!" I shout. "I don't know what fucking happened. I lost it I guess!"

"Explain," Theo cuts at me sharply.

Furious, I bellow, "Your mate Ethan is a self-righteous prick. How the fuck are you friends with him?"

Theo exhales through a frown. "You don't know him well enough. He's got a story the same way you have a story, Hayden."

"He was fucking all over Vi!" I roar, wincing at the overwhelming urge I feel to sprint back inside and tear her out of there.

I don't give a fuck about his story. Ethan's a man-whore through and through. I need to talk to Vi. She deserves an explanation, and I need to make sure that twat isn't still mucking about!

"Don't even consider it," Theo warns as he catches my piercing eyes on the bouncers, contemplating a way to get past them.

Then the gods of sod's law seem to answer my silent prayers. I catch sight of a familiar figure in a red dress storming toward me, and she doesn't look pleased.

White Rabbit

26

Vi

I'M FURIOUS WHEN I FIND HAYDEN AGGRESSIVELY PACING OUTSIDE of Club Shay. He looks like he's raked his hands through his hair a thousand times since I saw him a moment ago. Theo stands to the side, properly glowering at his younger brother, who is clearly in the midst of an enormous tantrum.

"Are you fucking joking me?" I screech as soon as I'm out the doors. "Christ, Hayden! Tell me you are messing about and that was some elaborate bit you and Ethan planned for a laugh."

Hayden's hard grey eyes pierce me with his silent answer. I can't believe he's got the nerve to clench his jaw like he's got something to be angry about. He begins to speak, but I cut him off.

"Bullshit is what that was. Embarrassing as fuck, rubbish! What were you trying to do?" My eyes are wide and crazy, my hair messy and coming loose around my face, but I couldn't care less.

"Vi, he's a bloody wanker!" Hayden roars, gesturing wildly toward the club doors.

Theo scoffs loudly, clearly unconvinced of his brother's assessment of Ethan. I can't say I completely blame Hayden for thinking so, but I'm still not about to let him off the hook.

"You think I don't know that?" I exclaim, ignoring Theo's

brooding. "You think I can't see that from a mile away? Fuck, Hayden! I'm not some meek, stupid blonde, despite what you so obviously think. I can handle myself. I've done a proper job of it for twenty-five years!" I cross my arms over my belly, feeling a chill from the cooling summer night.

"Well, what was I supposed to do?" He grips his leather cuffs protectively. A trait I've noticed he does when he's feeling insecure. "I can read you, Vi. You didn't want him all over you like that. I can't just walk away and leave you to fend for yourself."

"Why the bloody hell not?" I nearly yell, stamping my Monolo Blahnik in barely contained fury. He's the one who continually pushed me away and stalked off, so why am I of any concern to him?

"I'm going back inside," Theo says as mine and Hayden's eyes remain locked on each other. "You two clearly don't need a third wheel."

As Theo heads back inside, I can't help but think about how the entire scene between Hayden and Ethan is all too familiar. It reminds me of how Gareth reacted to seeing Pierce at the pub that night. The anger, the rage, the over-protectiveness. It's frustrating as hell how men seem to insert themselves into my life at every turn.

"Hayden, you told me I deserve better, so I don't know why this is even a discussion. Moreover, it wasn't like Ethan was attacking me. He was just being a moron. I was actually putting him in his proper place when you showed up."

"Yeah, it really fucking looked like it." Hayden scrubs his hands through his hair and looks away.

My eyes narrow at his clear underestimation of me. I don't need this shit. I storm past him, yanking open the door to one of the cabs waiting along the curb for the club-hoppers.

"Oh, no you don't," Hayden bellows. He shoves me into the vehicle and ducks in behind me. "I'm not done talking to you."

I turn to face him in the dark backseat. "You cheeky bastard. Get your own cab."

"Vi," he fumes, closing his eyes and clenching his jaw so hard I'm afraid his teeth will crack. "Please let me take you home. I need to explain myself and then I swear I'll fucking shove off."

I scowl angrily as the driver asks me what I want him to do. "Drive," I grumble, crossing my arms over my chest. I angle as far away from Hayden as possible while looking out the window.

His breaths are heavy as he attempts to calm himself down in the painfully quiet car.

"So, speak!" I bark.

"I'm not bloody well doing it in front of this bloke."

The driver's head turns. "Ain't nothing I ain't heard before."

Hayden shakes his head and looks out the window as we make our way back to my flat. We manage to arrive at Brick Lane without killing each other. I hop out without looking back, but I can hear Hayden's long strides behind me. I reach my alley entrance and unlock the doors to the lift. He slides in beside me, remaining completely quiet, but is watching me warily. I glare at his apologetic reflection in the mirrored wall of the lift and roll my eyes. He's got a lot of explaining to do. I don't care how hot he looks inside my lift. I jam my key in and punch my fist on the button marked eleven, schooling my features to remain angry. One puppy-dog look isn't going to get him off the hook.

The doors open and Bruce dives into the lift, attacking Hayden with happy licks, and pants, and tail-wagging.

Bloody traitor.

"Do you have to take Bruce for a walk?" he asks.

My heels clack on the slate flooring as I go to flick on the lamp in my seating area. I glance at the clock and see that it's not quite one.

"I have a neighbour who walks him when I go out. He was here half an hour ago. I didn't expect to be home this early."

The light casts a warm glow on Hayden's sombre face. "I'm sorry," he says quietly.

I lift my brows, feeling an awful lot like I'm scolding one of my brothers for rowing on the pitch. "What for?"

"Vi," he says my name on a shaky sigh. "You aren't just some random bird to me." His voice is husky as he speaks slowly and carefully. "And you're not someone I can just forget about and walk away from."

I flinch at his shocking comment, which renders me at a rare loss for words. "But last week, you totally brushed me off. Told me to get stuffed."

He shifts his jaw back and forth in silent protest over my less than stellar paraphrasing. "I said all that because I don't want to ruin everything around me, Vi." He pushes a harsh hand through his hair and continues. "I'm finally feeling happy with life again, and I'm terrified of messing that up. It's like this…In rehab, they have a rule of thumb. After you get out and you want to start a relationship, you have to buy a plant first. If you keep it alive, then you get a dog. If you keep both of them alive, then you can consider starting up with someone."

"Okay…And?"

He purses his lips in disappointment. "It's been a year and I can't even bring myself to buy a bloody plant. I'm fucking terrified of failing and ruining everything I've gained back. Then I met you and you have a dog *and* a secret bloody garden on your roof!"

My jaw drops at his accusatory tone. "I pay someone to care for my garden!" I stamp my foot with indignation, feeling immediately defensive for some odd reason.

His eyes drift down my body, landing on my legs, and heat flourishes behind his hard grey stare. He licks his lips and his nostrils flare in challenge. "You have to stop stamping your foot."

"Why?" My face screws up in disgust over his ridiculous demand.

"Because it makes me want to throw you over my shoulder and spank the ever-loving shit out of you. And then I'm going to want to fuck you until you forget whatever it is you're angry at me for!"

My heart stops. Time freezes. "Hayden," I croak, not all together comfortable with how my body is reacting to his sexual threat.

As if reading me like a book, his chin drops and he begins walking slowly toward me. His hand grips his wrist so hard his knuckles turn white. "Before…I didn't think I could have you. But now I know there's no way I can't have you." I inhale sharply at the twinkling determination in his eyes. "I want to know you, Vi. I want to know why you stamp your foot. And what exactly you love to cook. Whom you have dated. Why you spent six hundred pounds on a keepsake box that you're going to give away." He stops in front of me. "I want it all."

"You're so confusing, Hayden," I reply, my voice embarrassingly breathy as he stands only a foot away from me. His eyes are glossy with obvious lust. Pure, undiluted lust. "You kiss me and run away, then kiss me and tell me I can do better. I don't know what you're even saying."

He licks his lips thoughtfully. "I'm saying that when you showed up tonight looking the way you did…" He pauses as his eyes drift down my body. His heated expression makes me feel every drop of hot blood coursing through my veins. "I wanted to have you right then and there, but not in a club full of people. I wanted you in the privacy of your bedroom where the curves of your hips, the rise of your chest, the moisture on your lips are for me and me alone."

I exhale at his guttural tone, and I'm embarrassed when a throaty noise comes out of my mouth. He takes the noise as permission and moves in closer, his posture hunched as he looks down at me. "So I'm sorry for some things, Vi. But I'm not sorry for interfering. Asking me to just walk away when a prat like Ethan Simmons worms himself within inches of your mouth…Your fucking mouth that I've touched with my lips and that I've claimed as mine in a thousand different fantasies…No, Vi. No. I'm not going to be sorry for that."

"But you said—"

"Stuff what I said. I can't stay away from you." The words rush out of his mouth as he harshly grabs me by the waist. His bruising, firm grip shoves up the stretchy fabric of my top as his lips find mine in a desperate, needy kiss. He greedily yanks the cups of my bra down and caresses my nipples in such a way that I rip my mouth away from his and let out a strangled cry. I'm not all together certain I've ever heard that sound come from my mouth before.

He releases my nipples to pull my top off over my head, revealing my lacy red bra tucked firmly beneath my breasts, pushing them up for his lustful perusal. He drops an open mouthed kiss on each of them before standing back up straight. Groaning in frustration, he pauses his assault and looks into my eyes. A warmth blossoms in his gaze as he wraps his arms around me, holding me close.

"I'm terrified, Vi…Of so much. But I don't have the strength to walk away from you again. You make me weak."

I exhale with relief and anxiety over his comment, feeling my emotions at odds. I've been wanting Hayden Clarke to let me in since he first kissed me outside my building. But what does it mean when he says he feels weak around me? Am I capable of hurting him?

I lick my lips and guide him down to my level. "Maybe with time I can make you strong." He swallows my words with his mouth and our lips move against each other more passionately than ever before. This kiss is less frenzied and desperate. Less lustful and hard. With this kiss, our lips mould in synchronisation, equally giving and taking, like two flames licking the night sky in perfect, rippling unison.

"Stay the night," I demand against his lips, forgetting everything that confuses me and wanting to keep him with me long enough to figure it all out. I moved into this flat to assert myself in my life and become more independent. I refuse to let my entire happiness rest in the hands of this stunningly complicated and somewhat broken man.

He swallows hard and nods as if he knows what he's agreeing to is huge and he's making a commitment to himself as much as he is to me. "Okay, but no spanking," he smirks and his chest rumbles beneath my hands with his silent laughter.

A grin splits across my face. "As long as I don't stamp my

foot, right?" I giggle softly. "How about some good, old-fashioned cuddling?"

He nods and allows me to take his hand and lead him through the French doors to my bedroom. I quickly pull the cups of my bra back up over my breasts, feeling a bit shy now that things have tamed down. Tamed down is good. I'm not ready to jump into the deep end with Hayden. Not yet. He's shared a lot with me, but there's still so much more I want to know about him.

Blue moonlight swirls with glowing orange city lights as they pour into my room through the floor-to-ceiling windows. That's one benefit of being on the eleventh floor. Curtains aren't necessary when you're in the tallest building for miles. Bruce's paws clack on the slate floor behind us as he trots over to his bed in the corner of my room. He's such a good dog, even if he is a slobbery beast. I make a mental note to give him extra cuddles in the morning since I haven't paid him much attention tonight.

Hayden lets out a huff of a laugh as he looks down at my bed.

"What?" I ask, smiling at him while rifling through my dresser for a nightshirt.

He shakes his head and rubs circles around his wrist. "From the second I saw your room for the first time the other day, all I could think about was you spread out and completely naked on this magnificent bed."

My jaw drops from both shock and excitement. "I love my bed," I croak, dropping the shirt on the duvet and nervously looking into his eyes. The butterflies in my belly can stop anytime now.

He swallows hard and glances down at my bra-covered chest and then to my skirt. "Are you sure you want this, Vi?" he asks, his grey eyes turning from sexual to serious in the blink of an eye.

I notice he says "this" instead of "me." I don't quite know what *this* even is to know how to respond. I'd be lying if I didn't admit that a very tiny, inconsequential part of me wants to run for the hills. Hayden's given me a laundry list of reasons he's not ready for a relationship, yet here we are, in my bedroom. Now all I can think about are his arms wrapped around me all night.

"I want what you're willing to give me," I reply, placing a gentle kiss on each side of his neck. "As long as that's just cuddling for tonight, of course."

He groans as I pull back. "Then you better toss this on, Bunny." He chucks my T-shirt at me and I let out a hearty laugh as I catch it.

"Bunny?" I ask mockingly. "So if I'm a bunny, what does that make you?" I reach forward and begin slowly popping the buttons of his shirt, feeling dizzyingly excited to see what's underneath.

He grins playfully. "A very rude rabbit."

Completely unable to keep up the sexy facade, I burst into giggles while removing his shirt from his arms and feasting my eyes on the lean planes of his chest. He grins cockily at me, clearly proud of his little joke.

"Give it here," he groans and yanks the T-shirt down over my head, smoothing back my blonde strands that come loose. He brushes his finger along the top of my nose with a warm affection in his eyes. "Off to bed with you."

I giggle and shimmy out of my skirt, leaving my red thong and bra on. It at least makes me feel sexy underneath the very unsexy nightshirt. I crawl beneath my crushed velvet duvet, and my eyes snap up when I hear the buckle of Hayden's belt. I follow the action and stare for a moment at his thick brown leather cuffs. Coupled with his watch and muscled forearms, the look is masculine and attractive in a style I've never seen on a bloke. But I know he doesn't wear them as a simple fashion choice, so I can't help but wonder if I'll ever see beneath them.

My thoughts are quickly distracted by the sight of Hayden standing before me, wearing only a pair of pure white boxer briefs. The material hugs his muscular thighs, and my eyes greedily rake up his body, taking in every trim line of his abs. He's not overly muscled, but he's lean and toned in all the right places.

"Not an innocent bunny at all," he purrs, crawling into the bed beside me. "Your bedroom eyes are making it really fucking hard to be good."

I smile in contentment as he tucks his arm beneath me. Snuggling in, I lay my head on that perfect place on a man's chest. The place that dips in just above their peck and below their neck, which allows you to hear their heart thundering beneath the surface.

"What's this?" I ask, touching the black ink on the side of his rib cage that I hadn't noticed before. It's a small tattoo with the digital time display of 11:11 in thick gothic font. It's resting on top of a flat line that shoots up in several peaks that look like waveforms on a monitor, like a heartbeat.

He stiffens slightly. "Just something I got after rehab."

"What does it mean?" I ask, wanting to push for more information about something that is clearly very important to him.

"Just a little superstition. It's nothing."

My brows lift curiously, but I decide to let it go. We still have a lot to learn about each other, but I want him to tell me everything on his own time. I nuzzle into him and pull the blanket up a bit.

"Vi?" he asks quietly into the night.

"Yes?"

"Thank you." He drops a soft kiss on my head and lets out a large sigh like he was holding his breath.

Rather than ruin the moment with a self-deprecating comment, I remain silent and close my eyes, allowing myself to drift away in the arms of this mysterious man.

Not the One

Hayden

A SOFT GIGGLE FOLLOWED BY CURSING CAUSES ME TO STIR. MY eyes crack open and I find myself alone in an enormous bed with bright daylight pouring in on me. This is definitely a first. My past experiences with women have included me ducking out before they woke up to avoid any awkward encounters.

Everything is different with Vi.

I chuckle, amused by how I must look wrapped in her duvet. Honestly, who has crushed velvet anymore? I throw my legs over the edge of the bed and stretch while ruffling my hair. Fuck, I slept well. That's quite different for me as well. I grab my jeans up off the floor and slide them on as I pad barefoot into the attached bathroom that I never even got around to seeing last night.

I'm stunned by the sight of a huge soaker tub resting in front of yet another floor-to-ceiling window. It faces north over the city, and a surge of possessiveness rushes over me as I envision Vi's naked body covered in bubbles, bathing out in the open for all of London Bloody England to see. Surely she doesn't use this bathroom. How the fuck does she think this is a good idea? I make a mental note to have a proper talk with her about window fixtures.

Fuck, Hayden. You need to put a pin in your brooding caveman.

A large, glass, walk-in shower with two stainless steel waterfall showerheads sits on the opposite wall. Straight ahead is a modern black and white double vanity sink.

"Bloody hell," I say, marvelling a bit over all things Vi. Her style and her personality are all over this flat. Minimalist and strikingly beautiful, with an edge of surprise around every corner.

I relieve myself and head over to the sink to wash my hands. She obviously is not hard up. Truthfully, as far as money goes, we are similar. My father's furniture distribution centre made us very comfortable growing up. My mother was able to stay home with us when we were kids, so we had a traditional English upbringing.

But Vi being raised solely by a former professional footballer turned manager had to be different. I know from news articles that her brother Gareth makes millions a year. It's not even the money that impresses me, or the fame. It's the lifestyle. I wonder what Vi does for fun outside of her brothers' very public lifestyles?

It appears she's trying to gain some independence from her family, whereas I'm relying on mine more than ever. Last night with her was definitely unexpected. I was trying to convince myself I had to leave her be and avoid her at all costs, but seeing her at the club with Ethan pushed me over the edge. I realised in that moment that if it isn't Ethan, it will be somebody else. That's when I knew just how tightly Vi has me in her grips. Possessiveness isn't a trait I'm familiar with, but fuck I feel it when it comes to her.

Vi is refreshing. She's beautiful and warm, a bit quirky, and a mess in some of the most adorable ways. And she's so fucking charming that I can hardly stand being away from her, even right now. I pop a new tip on her electric toothbrush, brush my teeth, wash my face, and then quickly head out to find her. My body actually aches to touch her again. Sleeping with her all night was oddly calming.

I used to sleep with Reyna occasionally during our dark and twisted time together. She'd have these horrid reoccurring dreams, and I was her anchor to help bring her back down to reality. I rarely fell asleep at her flat because all I could do was stew about the fact that I was falling for her and could never bring myself to tell her.

Now, after only one week with Vi, I'm laying everything out on the table. Fucking therapy has ruined my alpha bloke status.

The large glass patio door in the living room is wide open and I see Vi outside, walking carefully with a large dog bowl full of water. Suddenly, Bruce bounds toward her from the other side of the deck. She cries out for him to stop, but it's too late. His momentum is out of control. He clobbers into her, and the bowl and Vi both go flying into a slopping heap on the ground.

"Bugger…Fuck a duck, Bruce!" she cries as he pounces on top of her until she's forced back on her arms. He laps happily at her face, shoving his nose against her neck. "You vile monster! I'm getting you in classes. I mean it. You've pushed me for the last time!"

I chuckle quietly, crossing my arms and leaning against the doorway to watch her. She's dressed in a tiny pair of black spandex shorts and a loose white tank. My dick stirs when she stands up and turns and I get a full-frontal glimpse of her. A crystal clear outline of a pair of pert pink nipples shows through the wet front of her tank.

She starts giggling as Bruce licks water off her leg. "Stop buttering me up, beast. It won't work."

My eyes twinkle at her with an affection I feel everywhere in my body. "You know you're not fooling anyone," I say from the doorway.

She jumps and her blue eyes fly up to me in surprise. "What do you mean?" She awkwardly tugs her wet top away from her breasts. Her blonde locks are hastily scraped up into a high ponytail in that "I just rolled out of bed" way.

"You can call him all the ghastly names in the book, but it doesn't take a mind reader to know how much that beast means to you."

"Well, don't tell him." She covers his ears and whispers, "If he thinks I like him, he'll be even more of an arse."

I smile and stride out onto the patio, dropping down on one of the white lounger chairs, absently realising this is the most comfortable I've ever felt around a woman the morning after sleeping together. Or *not* sleeping together I guess you'd say.

"Where did you get Bruce?" I ask, propping my hands behind my head and squinting up at her. "I'd envision you as more of a Cavalier King Charles spaniel type of bird. Or maybe a pug."

Vi's eyes trail from my face, to my bare chest, to my unbuttoned trousers where my white Calvin Klein boxer briefs are revealed. Finally, she looks up at me, shaking her head and answers, "Sort of a favour to an old neighbour. She passed away last year. The family couldn't take care of him, so I offered. She was a huge Batman fanatic, so technically his full name is Bruce Wayne."

I half smile. "What a great name for a dog. Does he have super powers? Aside from the ferocious tackling and licking?"

"If by super powers you're referring to giant-sized craps, then yes, he is powerful." She huffs out a laugh and drops down on the seat next to me, mindlessly pulling her shirt away from her to dry.

I scrunch my nose up. "Oh, Bunny. You always manage to surprise me."

"What on earth is with the bunny nickname?" She pauses her action to place her hands on her hips. "Is it a term of endearment? Or shall I start calling you the schoolyard bully?"

"It's a compliment," I smirk. "You like to stamp your foot when you're frustrated, like a bunny. And I find it sexy as fuck."

She raises her eyebrows with excitement. "I can't decide if I find that creepy or charming."

I chuckle good-naturedly. "I do my best to walk the line in all things creepy and charming. Like right now, I'm not even staring at your sexy nipples that are showing off clear as day through your tank top. Never mind, I lied. Now I am."

Her eyes turn to saucers and she crosses her arms over her chest. "Shit, I had forgotten."

"No need to be shy now. I became well acquainted with your nipples last night if you recall." I waggle my eyebrows at her suggestively.

Her eyes narrow. "Are you this cheeky with all your girls?"

I cock my head at her in surprise. "Are you my girl?" I'm not asking because I'm shocked. I'm asking out of genuine curiosity. I want her to be my girl with every fibre in my body. But there's a layer of me that wants to repel away from her and everything she represents to me.

She swallows hard. "I didn't mean…Of course I wasn't inferring…We've just started—"

"Look, Vi. I'll stop you right there," I start, twisting so my feet are on the ground and we're facing knee-to-knee. "I need to talk to you before we go any further with whatever this is between us. I'd rather be open and honest about my past, which, surprisingly, comes rather natural for me when I'm talking to you."

"Surprisingly?" she asks just as Bruce trots over to her for a fondle. She mindlessly pets him while looking intently at me.

"I don't know if it's therapy that's changed me or you, but I never liked sharing things about myself. I never did it, as a matter of fact. Ever. I just kept things bottled up. Even with Reyna, whom I considered my best friend back then. She knew relatively nothing about me."

"What is the story with you and her? What kind of friends were you if you didn't share things with one another?" she asks, her eyes tightening around the edges.

"The physical kind," I reply honestly, watching her reaction carefully and feeling slightly annoyed that I don't see the green-eyed jealousy I was hoping for. "Rey and I always had this way of mucking through life together. Like a soldier on the battlefield, it's all a lot less scary when you have someone standing right beside you on the front lines. But out of nowhere, or at least it felt that way to me, Rey wanted out of the dark place we'd found each other in. She started pulling away from me."

"Reyna fell in love with Liam."

I shrug my shoulders and shake my head at the fact that Vi is completely oblivious to the pain those two names together caused me while I was in rehab. "Yes. That's exactly what happened. I wasn't even aware that Rey and Liam had a history of some sort. Did you know Liam used to date my sister, Marisa, back at Oxford?"

"I had no idea."

"Well he did. I don't know the details…It's probably a story that could fill an entire book. Regardless, it is funny we're talking about Rey right now, considering she's a large part of day one on my countdown."

Vi's eyes widen. "Your final countdown day? How so?"

I sigh heavily, feeling the familiar aching in my chest that I feel every time I transport myself back to that night.

This is it, Hayden. This is the final day of your Countdown Challenge. You're strong enough for this. Don't hold back now.

"The night of the gala, I was completely wasted. As you know from the other days I described, things had been going from bad to worse for me. I'd been drinking most of the day because I had it in my head that I was going to do it that night. I was going to kill my-self." I pause, swallowing hard. Damn, those last two words are still hard to say. "But I started having second thoughts. Namely because of Reyna and how awful we'd last left things. So I thought maybe if I saw her just one last time, something would click. Something would make sense again. She'd see me differently, or I'd see myself different-ly, and I could get out of that place in my mind."

"But it didn't work," Vi says softly. Her eyes are trained on my cuff-covered wrists.

"No. Our conversation was painful, horrid, awful shit." I shrug helplessly. "I fell in love with her. It's that simple. And she was in love with Liam. And Theo was in love with Leslie, and it just seemed like everybody around me was getting on with their lives except me."

Vi nods thoughtfully. "How are you with Rey now?" Her blue eyes watch me with a deep sympathy that I feel in my heart.

"Doc labels Rey as a trigger for me. He says it's best not to engage with her any more than casual acquaintances." I pause for a moment before I admit, "I have actually revealed more personal information to you in one week than I ever did in three years of friendship with Rey."

Vi inhales sharply. "How is that possible, Hayden?"

I shake my head. "Rey was a huge part of my life for so many years, but it was mostly our grief that maintained our friendship. Not our true selves."

"I'm so sorry, Hayden."

"That's why I have to protect myself, Vi. From alcohol, from pills, from depression—"

"From me?" she finishes my sentence.

I shake my head earnestly as I take her hand in mine, twining our fingers together. I note the difference in skin tones, from her creamy complexion to my olive tone, and silently marvel at this simple gesture. Feeling her soft hand in mine is a sense of life I might never have experienced.

"I don't want to protect myself from you," I whisper in answer to her question. "But caring for someone more than myself terrifies me. I can't slip back into the darkness, Vi. There are too many people here that I want to live for. Marisa, my family…you."

She looks up through her low, dark lashes. "But we've just met."

"I know, but I feel something when I'm around you that I have never felt in all my life, Vi. I want to dive in with you and figure it out. I want us to be *something*. But I don't want to fall into another Reyna situation where I use you as a crutch. You've heard my countdown. I've completed my challenge. I don't want to be seen as damaged anymore."

"I don't see you that way!" she exclaims and stands up. She moves over to me and pushes me back in my chair, straddling me so I can look straight into her ocean blue eyes. "I don't think you're damaged. I think you're beautiful."

I smile—genuinely smile—for what feels like the first time in years. "I think that's my new favourite thing about you. Mostly because it's about me."

She laughs and swats me across the chest while mumbling something about me being a narcissist.

I grab her hand before she can move off of me and stare deeply into her eyes. "My list of favourite things about you grows every time I'm with you."

Her head tilts to the side as she looks at me thoughtfully. "But what about your plant? And your dog?" Anxiety fleets over her face.

"Maybe I can just help you with yours."

She smiles. A soft, sexy, secretive smile. The kind of smile where she's not celebrating a win, but encouraging the removal of a loss. Her cheeks flush a rose hue that makes her look like she's just returned from a jog. I can't contain myself another second. I pull her lips to mine and push all of my feelings into this one simple act. All the feelings I've been hiding from the world. All the secrets. All the pain. All the loss…

…and I let it go.

And I realise with delirious happiness, that kissing Vi is different. Every. Single. Time.

Vi

As I walk Hayden to my lift, there's a small part of me that fears he'll change his mind about us as soon as he walks out the door. He'll decide I'm not worth the risk and that he doesn't want to pursue a relationship with me, if that's even what he'd call it. He sees himself as damaged, and I see him as beautiful. His soul speaks to mine on some deep, unnerving level and I crave him. I crave his presence, his mood, his smirk. Everything.

Instead of pushing the down arrow button, Hayden turns on his heel and pulls me into him, resting his back against the wall and holding me close.

"Are you close to your brothers?" he asks, his eyes scanning my neck as he begins dropping soft kisses on my shoulder.

My body tenses a bit, and I pull back to eye him warily. "Why do you ask?"

He shrugs halfheartedly. "Just curious. You said you go to your dad's with all of them for a Sunday dinner every week, and that seems like something a close family would do."

The curious look in his eyes makes me feel more comfortable about opening up about my family. I don't get the impression he's curious about my brothers. More so, he's curious about what our family dynamic is like to compare to his own.

"Well, it's best you know now that I am annoyingly close to my brothers. Like I said, I still see them every Sunday. Not to mention they like to pop over here whenever they feel like being little sods and want to torment me or need a mediator for one of their stupid fights."

He chuckles softly. "Do you have a favourite?"

I squint as I consider his question. "Not really a favourite. Rather, I appreciate them all for different reasons. I like Booker when I need someone to confide in; I like Cam and Tanner when I need a laugh; and I like Gareth when I need help."

"What do you mean by help?"

I shrug my shoulders. "He's my big brother. He's protective, and I know he will do anything for me at any time. Last year, I was in a crap situation with my ex, and Gareth nearly went to jail defending me. He could have ruined his career reacting the way he did. It was dangerous and scary, but it's touching to know he'd risk anything for me."

Hayden's eyes harden and he tightens his grip around me. "What happened?"

"Oh, God, nothing all that original. Pierce was this guy I had been dating for a while and he started cheating on me. The affair was all over Chigwell because the woman was the wife of a famous footballer. And, no, I will not tell you which one."

"Wasn't even going to ask," he replies, his eyes trained on me, silently urging me to continue.

His reaction gives me a secret thrill, knowing that what he cared about most in the story had everything to do with me and nothing to do with football.

"It was one of those 'everyone in town knew but me' situations, which made me feel like the biggest loser."

"Why would that make you feel like a loser? He's the prat in this scenario."

I shrug, feeling a tad too transparent. "It's nothing."

Hayden frowns and his eyes grow scarily serious. "Tell me, Vi."

Sighing, I look down at his chest and play with the buttons on his shirt as I reply, "It's a daft fear I have. My dad and brothers have always been great at showing me how much they love me…They didn't give me a complex or anything."

"But…"

"But growing up, I always felt a bit invisible."

"How is that even possible?" Hayden's eyes pierce me with an intensity I feel everywhere, but I can't look back at him as I continue my explanation. He sees me too well. I'm too exposed and this admission is too mortifying. But for some reason, I still want to share it. I need to share it. He's shared so much with me. This is something I need to give him.

"My brothers' friends would barely even look at me, let alone acknowledge my presence in a room. I sort of got it in my head that I was uninteresting. Generic, perhaps. I was content to live in their shadows and take care of things at home, so I just never felt it'd be easy for me to find someone to care about me. And the blokes I did date never had that special spark. I can't help but think, 'What is life if you don't have anyone extraordinary to share your wine gums with?'" I laugh to lighten the tone a bit, but my brain refuses to slow down. "That's why I was kind of happy to be lumped with Bruce. The little sod has become my best friend, and he notices everything I do. He's around to test my latest food experiment or pounce on me when I've tripped. Bruce Hugs are quite good, really."

I look up to see Hayden's severe expression and immediately wish I could gobble up all the words and stuff them back in my mouth. An annoying sting of tears pricks in my eyes. Christ, I need to pull myself together. I sink my teeth into my lower lip and do my best to stave off my emotions.

"Oh, God, I make myself sound like a sad, desperate cow. I'm sorry. I was just rambling away with the fairies or something. Ignore me. You better get going anyway because I'm going to be late—"

My words are snuffed out by Hayden's hard and urgent lips. He twirls us around so I'm up against the wall as he presses every determined inch of his body to mine with a force that he wants me to feel everywhere. His tongue tastes like man, and goodness, and desire all wrapped into the most perfect Hayden flavour.

The kiss is broken all too suddenly when Hayden pulls back and murmurs against my lips, "Remind me to send a thank you card to your brothers."

"What on earth do you mean?" I ask, out of breath from his assault on my blabbing mouth.

"Vi," Hayden replies seriously as he pulls back enough so I can see his whole face, "you are any man's fucking fantasy. The only reason you felt invisible is because your brothers probably threatened bodily harm to anyone who dared to look at you."

I scoff and roll my eyes. "They are certainly overprotective, but I promise you that even they can't scare away every man in existence."

Hayden purses his lips skeptically. "Tell me, did that Pierce prat know your brothers? Was he a mate of theirs?"

"Not at all! He was a slimy DJ who worked at a club in Chigwell.

He ran in a completely different circle." I blanch at my embarrassingly poor choice in a man, especially when I'm staring into the eyes of Hayden.

He chuckles. "I bet your brothers were big fans of him."

"Oh yeah, they're proper mates now. They go paintballing together every Tuesday," I giggle.

Hayden begins kissing me like it's a reflex. Like the sound of my laughter forces him to attack. But the attack is most welcome and quickly turning into a kiss that's going to end with clothing shed.

I lift my leg to wrap around his hip, but he pulls away. He swallows and punches the button to the lift. It opens instantly and he steps inside with a tortured, heated look on his face.

"I'll call you," he states, his voice gruff with arousal.

I nod stupidly. What else can I do with this mysterious, dark, sexy man of mine?

First Date

Vi

THE NEXT TWO WEEKS FLY BY WITH HAYDEN CLARKE. AT FIRST I thought he was going to change his mind and pull away. But every day he calls and every evening we spend doing normal, ordinary things together.

Our first evening, I make dinner for us. He comes over in his adorable button-down and jeans and perches on the stool while I busy myself in the kitchen. If I was worried he'd be bored, I was wrong. He's surprisingly content watching me work. I think he even likes it when I slap his hand every time he tries to sneak some food. I like it all, too. I didn't realise how much I missed cooking with a warm body around. It's like Sunday dinners with my family but with flirting.

God, I missed flirting.

Bruce helps keep the mood light, doing his duty of lapping up all of my spills that seem more frequent when I have a hot guy in the room. I swear his ears are hardwired to register the sound of the smallest crumb hitting the floor. Never mind the fact that he trips my feet up at least once every evening as an assurance for an ooey-gooey mess.

Hayden seems to love watching me and Bruce argue because

he keeps coming back. Sometimes with takeaway. Sometimes with groceries. Always with a sexy smile.

Our conversation flows effortlessly, too. It's lighthearted, getting-to-know-each-other stuff. But one evening, he turns it more serious.

"Don't you ever cook and drink?" Hayden asks from his seat at the kitchen island stool.

"What do you mean?" I ask curiously, pausing the chopping of stir-fry veggies.

He looks down at my work and says, "Most proper chefs I know enjoy a glass of wine while they cook."

My brows arch. "Well, I didn't want to make you uncomfortable." I look back at him, feeling almost guilty for admitting that.

Hayden strides over to my wine fridge and grabs a bottle of white that I was cooking with earlier. He pours a glass for me and then pops the cork back into the bottle with a huff.

"I'm not fragile, Vi. I'm not going to crumble."

Well, okay then.

I hadn't realised that I was behaving differently around him until he made that comment. I feel a little silly about my assumption. Hayden shouldn't have to remind me he's okay. Just looking at him the past couple of weeks we've been together, I know he is doing wonderfully. However, I think he is definitely in the small percentage of recovering addicts who don't fear relapsing every day.

He explains to me that his alcoholism is a bit different than most as it didn't take shape until Marisa died. "I struggled with survivor's guilt after Marisa's death. That was the start of my problems. It wasn't a brain chemistry issue or heredity inheritance. It was an environmental event that affected me deeply. As a result, I turned to drinking and other dangerous behaviours. But alcohol is a depressant. It stoked my guilt and caused me to drown in my own self-pity. Continuing to drink could essentially lead me back to that dark place in my mind. That means avoidance of all alcohol is paramount if I don't want to slide down that slope again."

I have no clue why, but I stop what I'm doing in the kitchen, walk over to him, and kiss him with a fierce pride that I've never felt before.

He seems taken off guard, but his arms wrap around me instinctually and he gives as good as he gets.

The more I learn about Hayden, the more I want him. Every day, he surprises me with all he is willing to share. Even his lighthearted family stories are showing me what kind of man I have in my grasp.

One evening, we take Bruce for a walk, and he tells me a hilarious story about his mum catching Theo and Leslie butt-naked in the hallway of their family home last year. I laugh so hard at the image that we have to stop walking so I can catch my breath. Then I proceed to peg him with tons of questions about his mum. The way he describes her sounds so delightful.

Following his story, I tell Hayden all about how when I was growing up, I always paid close attention to other people's mums. My friends at school would invite me over and, instead of going up to their rooms to talk about boys, I would ask if I could help their mum make tea. It's probably a large reason why I didn't have many friends.

I admit to Hayden that even to this day, I watch mothers at supermarkets and fantasise about what they're preparing their family for supper. I dream about what it would have been like growing up with someone like that to care for me. I find myself so envious of the behaviours of mothers that I have completely turned into a weirdo who stalks middle-aged women in the supermarkets.

Hayden never once judges me. In fact, he says it's his new favourite thing about me.

Each simple moment with him feels like nothing and everything at the same time. I am completely smitten.

And I think he is, too.

His warm grey eyes seem like they get brighter the more we see each other. It's a beautiful sight. And I can feel myself reflecting that same inner happiness that makes my insides swirl with anticipation.

All of it is an aphrodisiac, and the sexual tension between us is far more potent than my cooking.

Hayden fits into my home and my life so perfectly that I find myself growing more and more desperate to take things to the next level…physically. He seems like he's trying to be a gentleman and I am trying to respect that about him. But deep down, I want him to be bad. Very, very bad.

It's been two weeks of this nightly routine. It's time! I decide to make us oysters in hopes of setting the mood and making my intentions known. I think Hayden can tell I'm up to something when he shows up. I watch his eyes take in my tight white tank with no bra.

But all through dinner, his eyes seem glued to either my face or his food. They never drop below my damn chin, and I worked so hard to put on something that made him think of sex! This man has the control of a saint. While I stand at the sink washing dishes, I begin contemplating what might happen if I throw myself at him.

In the split second that it takes to place the pan onto the drying rack, I feel Hayden step up behind me. His body is warm and firm, and somehow soothing and erotic, like I conjured him right to me to fulfill all the needs I've been mulling over while scrubbing that stubborn pan.

"Dinner was delicious," he purrs into my ear as he wraps his hands around my waist and then slides them down my bubble-covered arms into the water. "But I told you I was going to do the dishes."

My breath inhales slowly because, while many kisses have been stolen between us the past two weeks, he's never done full-body contact quite like this.

"I'm glad you enjoyed it," I reply, my voice a bit trembly as I twine my wet fingers with his under the water. It feels naughty and makes my nipples harden from the erotic contact. "But you were in the loo, and I had time on my hands."

"What if I told you I have a surprise for you in the bathroom?" he asks, moving his wet hands up my forearms and back to my waist, dampening the bottom of my tank top.

My head drops back onto his chest, and I pray like hell my prayers have been answered. "What kind of surprise?" I croak, sounding so obvious I should probably be embarrassed.

He steels his hands under my shirt and slides his wet palms up my sides. My breath inhales sharply when he greedily cups my breasts. "You've been tormenting me all night, Bunny."

I swallow slowly. "Have I?"

He hums a low tone of warning and runs his lips along my neck, nibbling in a way that drives me completely wild. "Walking around in this see-through tank top and looking at me with those sexy eyes of yours. I've been going completely mental trying to keep my hands off of you."

"Then stop resisting," I husk, needing to hear his voice again because I swear I could spontaneously combust if he says the right words right now.

"Is this resisting?" he asks, pinching my nipples and rolling them gently between his fingers.

"No," I cry out breathily, a light groan slipping out between my lips.

He releases my hardened buds and palms my breasts in a possessive grasp as he presses his groin into my bottom and almost growls. "Are you ready for your surprise, Bunny?"

His firmness against me is so glorious, wonderous, and marvellous, I can hardly form coherent thoughts.

"Good God, yes," I all but moan, shamelessly jutting my rear into his erection.

"Come with me," he replies and removes his hands from my breasts to take my wet hand in his.

He leads me through my bedroom and into my en suite where he's drawn a bubble bath in my soaker tub that overlooks the city.

"We're taking a bath?" I ask with an excited smile.

"Something like that," he replies, stepping toward me and

instructing me to lift my arms so he can remove my tank top. He drops his hands to remove my shorts and I want him to look at me. I want him to see me completely naked. I want his grey eyes all over my body.

But he doesn't take his eyes off of mine.

The cheeky bugger.

He offers me his hand and helps me into the bath. I sink down into the hot water, and a pressure builds between my thighs from the heat of his eyes and the heat of the water hitting me all at once.

The bubbles cover all of my bits, and I bite my lip coyly and toss a handful of suds up into the air. "Aren't you joining me?" I ask, as he looks down at me with so much heat in his eyes, he could have cooked our food tonight.

He bends over and brushes his finger down my nose. "Not tonight, naughty bunny."

I deflate, my thighs clenching together with need. "Are you joking?"

He shakes his head and squats down beside the tub, crossing his cuffed wrists on the edge and staring into my eyes. "This bath is just for you. As a thank you for two of the best weeks of my life."

His words make my heart skip a beat as he gazes at me with so much sincerity, I have to believe him. I have to believe that he's telling me ordinary nights in my flat were the best of his life. Who is this man?

"Are you free tomorrow?" he asks.

I huff out a laugh at the massive change of topic. "Um, I'd have to check my diary."

He chuckles at my frustrated eye-roll. "Good. Because I'm taking you out on a date."

"What kind of date?" I ask, hoping he's going to say the kind of date that ends with sex because, even though his words are full of romance, I'm one hundred percent ready for more than talk.

He gives me a wicked smile like he can read my mind. "The

kind that allows us to take things to the next level. No countdown. No suicide talk. No painful past stuff. Just a date. A single, solitary, and somewhat boring date with dinner and a film. Will you come?"

My brows rise. "I sure hope so."

He shakes his head. "You're going to pay for that one."

With a wink and a smile, he strides out, calling over his shoulder that he'll pick me up at seven.

Sounds like I should have saved those oysters for tomorrow.

The next night, I'm positively buzzing with anticipation. I have my main mutt, Bruce, standing guard at my door, watching me with sad puppy-dog eyes that probably resemble what mine looked like in the tub last night after Hayden left.

I'm dressed in a simple black and white striped, short-sleeved, cotton dress. It's rather modest, aside from the shorter length, but I paired it with my favourite white Converse to give it a more casual appearance. Keeping to the theme, I left my blonde hair loose down my back, adding a bit of soft curls to the ends, and my makeup is light and elegant.

I turn to Bruce. "How do I look?" I ask, tossing my hands out to show off my outfit. He huffs and drops his head down on his pillow. I took him on a good long walk after work today, so he's properly knackered now. "Much help you are," I grumble.

Just as I finish tying my laces, my buzzer goes off. I jog over and breathe, "Hiya," into the monitor like a smiling loon.

"Vi, let us up! We have to talk to you."

I frown. "Camden?"

"Of course it's fucking Camden…and Tanner. Who else would it be?"

My heart drops. Hayden should be here soon, and the last thing

I need is for him to get a glimpse of the Harris Brothers. He's so not ready for that.

Panicking that Hayden could be walking up at any moment, I buzz them up. *Shit, shit, shit! How am I going to get rid of them? What the hell do they need?* As the lift doors open, my two owly brothers are standing face-to-face, arguing as usual. They are kind of a hilarious sight. One is a clean-cut, playboy-looking type. The other is a scruffier slacker-boy. But their faces are similar, so it's quite comical.

"That is your perception of how the night went. You are off your bloody rocker, bro," Tanner challenges.

"I'm about to fucking pummel you in the face if you don't watch your tone." A vein in Camden's neck bulges angrily.

"Oi, oi, oi! What's the problem here?" I stand with my hands on my hips, greeting them in the foyer. I don't want them coming in and making themselves comfortable. This is a quick fix and then I'm sending them on their way.

Tanner looks at me and flicks his head back to get his blonde hair out of his eyes. "Here's what happened, Vi. We were at a club last night, right? And all these little slappers were flocking on us like flies on shit."

"Tanner!" I snap.

"What?" he asks, looking at me in confusion.

"First of all, you're disgusting. Second of all, *women*, not little slappers. They are females who deserve your respect. I don't care how loose they are," I reprimand.

"All right, all right. *Women*," he groans with his jaw jutted out defiantly. "Hell, they could've been Kate fucking Middleton for all I care. Anyway, this gorgeous redhead was on me. Like, super on me. I was thinking, 'I got this in the bag.'"

My eyes close in pain over where I see this story going.

"And I was about to seal the deal, but I had to nip off to the loo because I'd been drinking a lot and needed to piss. But before I left, I suddenly got nervous because I could tell Camden was sniffin' about."

"I wasn't sniffin' about! Your slapper—*woman*"—Camden corrects when I cut my eyes at him—"was eyeing me like she could see my package through my trousers. I can't help that, bro! She liked what she saw."

Tanner rolls his eyes and continues. "Anyway, I could see Camden had ideas, so I thought bacon sandwich, right?"

"Bacon sandwich?" I ask, my brows puzzling.

"Yeah, like, lick my bacon sandwich and then it's mine and no one can touch it."

My jaw drops. "Is the bacon sandwich the woman in this story?"

"All right, you got it now!" Tanner crows proudly. "So I leaned in and gave my bacon sandwich a good lick. She liked it, too, let me tell you. You can always tell when the flavour suits them. She was into my flavour, Vi. So I nipped off to the toilet, and when I got back, Camden was all over her. Like, they were practically having sex on the couch. His tongue was so far down her throat I thought she was going to need resuscitating!"

"I took her breath away, all right," Camden jeers with a naughty twinkle in his eyes. I stare at him, clearly not impressed.

"Fucking wanker," Tanner mumbles. "He was wrong, right, Vi? I mean. Bacon Sandwich Rule…Clearly he was wrong!"

"All is fair in love and redheads, mate." Camden pats Tanner on the shoulder, and Tanner swings back and shoves him away from him. It only makes Camden laugh harder.

Sighing heavily, I close my eyes shut before I say, "I am not even sure where to begin with this ridiculous story and your appalling behaviour. For starters, Bacon Sandwich Rule…Not a thing!"

"What do you mean?" Tanner barks.

"I mean, that is not a thing. If you're talking about humans, then the bacon sandwich idea is horrifying on many levels. Moreover, Camden, get your own girls and stop interfering with Tanner just to get a rise out of him."

"I can't help it if—" he starts, but I cut him off.

"They don't like you better. You're just a pig. You're both pigs. You both need to stop looking at women like conquests and start treating them with respect. If I was that redhead and a couple of horrid blokes like you two were talking about me like this, how would you feel?"

Both their faces drop.

"Exactly! Bugger!" I snap. "This disappoints me, like I taught you guys nothing growing up."

"Vi, these women know what they're getting from us. We don't make them any promises," Camden argues.

"I don't care. I can't hear any more of this. Seriously. You guys need to leave." I push the button to my lift and it opens instantly. I point.

"But, Vi," Tanner starts, his face crestfallen.

"No. You need to go. I'm so sad to hear you talk about women like this. I won't forget it."

"Vi, come off it," Camden cajoles and tries to pull me under his arm, but I resist his embrace.

"Talk to me about your women troubles when you each find someone who makes you feel something north of your damn penises."

My phone dings in my hand, and I see a text from Hayden that he's on his way. I hustle my twin brothers out of my flat with their tails tucked properly between their legs. Good. Serves them right. I'm tired of them talking about women like they are candy to quarrel over.

I rush into the bathroom and give myself a final once-over. Then I grab my clutch and denim jacket and hop into the lift. As I descend, I can't help but hope that my brothers someday find girls who make them feel giddy and excited like I feel right now.

I stride out to find a relaxed Hayden leaning against the opposite brick wall. I glance up and down the alley nervously and exhale when I see no sign of my brothers. My heart does a double beat as I look back at him and take in his muscled, denim clad leg tossed over the other. Hayden Clarke takes jeans to a whole new level. Every pair he wears is fitted and slim, but faded and masculine in all the right places. Today, the bottoms are cuffed, revealing really sexy leather boots. My eyes move up to find him in one of his half-buttoned, grey, blended shirts. It's pulled tightly across his lean chest, and his sleeves are pushed up on his arms, revealing his manly blonde fuzz-covered forearms and the standard leather cuffs and watch that I hardly notice anymore.

"Fuck, Bunny," Hayden groans under his breath, lustfully eyeing my legs. "Probably a good thing you didn't play football."

"And why is that?" I ask, putting my hand on my hip in defiance.

He shrugs his shoulders. "You've seen footballers' legs. Why mess with perfection?"

I shake my head and accept his ridiculously cheesy compliment as he pulls me in for a sensual kiss.

"Miss me?" I ask, giggling as he tries to stop me from pulling away.

"You could say that." His eyes are hooded as he bites his lower lip.

He sighs heavily and grabs my hand in his as we make our way over to Pizza East located in an old tea warehouse near my neighbourhood. I've been here a few times for takeaway. It's got a cosy cavernous feel inside. Furthermore, the wood oven and comfort of the home-style foods they serve make it the perfect place for a relaxed evening out.

We order a couple of pizzas to split, and Hayden baulks when I ask for an Italian soda.

"You can get wine," he mumbles, frustration radiating off his stiff posture.

"Oi! You need to start letting me make my own choices. I'm not that big of a drinker, Hayden." I take the glass bottle of grape soda from the bloke behind the counter. "Can you get him one, too? He needs a bit of cheer. What kind do you want?"

Hayden frowns and grumbles, "Strawberry."

I conceal my snicker as the man hands him the bottle of pink liquid. "Nice choice."

Hayden sullenly takes a sip. "It's bloody good, too." A grin splits across his face and he winks at me. We both laugh and make our way to a cosy red booth by the wall covered with wood logs for the pizza oven.

"I noticed that you didn't drink much at Club Shay, actually." Hayden says after we settle into our seats.

I nod feeling slightly pleased that he was watching me so closely that night. I did everything in my power to not look at him and it obviously worked. "I like an occasional drink, but I prefer to keep my wits about me when I'm around a lot of people."

Hayden narrows his eyes at me. "Did you have your wits about you when you were giving Ethan all that sodding attention?"

My jaw drops in mock indignation. "You're one to talk. I seem to remember you receiving a proper snog from Julie!"

He flinches. "That was awkward. I only danced with her so I could keep an eye on you, but she pounced on me like a tiger in heat."

I laugh at the visual imagery. "You were keeping an eye on me?" I shoot him a coy look.

"Bloody hell right I was," he barks, knitting his brows at me. "You were killing me the whole night. Looking the way you looked. Christ. I didn't think anything could top the white dress you wore the night of the gala, but red is definitely your colour."

I giggle happily, his compliments blooming inside my heart.

"Then you barely looked at me after we got inside the club, never mind speaking to me," Hayden adds with a growl. "It was fucking torture."

"Well, you tortured me on my rooftop if you recall," I rebound, still somewhat smarting over the number of times he tried to walk away from me.

He blanches, his face turning serious. "I know, Vi. The only thing I can say to that is that my feelings for you surprised me. I'm not sure I was ready for them. And you're just so good, and kind, and pure. I was terrified of ruining you. I still am sometimes."

I frown and shake my head defensively. "I'm not as perfect as you're building me up to be in your head, Hayden. You want me to stop treating you like you're fragile, andI want you to stop treating me like I'm Her Majesty the Queen. I'm far from it." I laugh as I think of a way to prove my point. "I was the type of kid who played hide-and-seek and yelled to the seeker where I was hiding! Kids hated playing with me on the playground because I never played games the way everyone else did."

He roars with laughter at my sudden lighthearted change of tone. Despite my urgency over breaking his twisted view of me, this reaction still pleases me, so I continue. "It's true. I'm always going to be that person who never quite gets it all done perfectly. I might send a gift, but it won't be wrapped. I might remember your birthday, but you probably won't get a card. I might want to send out Christmas cards myself, but I just won't ever get it done. I'm not crafty at all. Pinterest looks like prison to me. I'm probably going to over-bake the biscuits the one time of year when someone actually needs them for something. Even though I love cooking, I love picking up take-away just as much. But I'll probably call ahead and go to the wrong shop first. I'll always be home late because I'm a horrible judge of time—"

"If you're trying to put me off, you're failing miserably, Vi," Hayden interrupts. His brow is furrowed and there's an oddly serious heaviness to his posture.

"Aren't you listening?" I exclaim. "I'm a mess."

He shakes his head and slides out of the booth to tuck himself in next to me. He rests one arm on the back of the seat and cups my cheek with his other hand. My eyes flutter closed as I become intoxicated by the overwhelming sawdust and shower scent that's so deliciously Hayden.

A secretive grin plays on the corners of his mouth. "Everything you said sounds utterly charming, deliriously adorable, and, because it's about you, sexy as fuck."

I roll my eyes. "You're hopeless."

Without warning, he holds my face in place and presses his lips to mine. "I am hopelessly falling for you, Vi Harris."

My chest shudders at his declaration. "Feeling's mutual, Hayden Clarke," I reply on a swoony sigh that would embarrass me if only I gave a shit right now. Bloody hell, Hayden wanting me more after unloading that lot is a turn-on of epic proportions.

After we devour our pizzas and more fizzy bubbles of Italian soda, we walk hand-in-hand to the cinema that sits only a couple of blocks away from my flat. Grabbing two seats in the far back row of the nearly empty cinema, we cuddle up, preparing for a simple movie-watching experience.

I'm not sure who started it or what atmospheric shift occurred, but somewhere along the way, things changed. Hayden's grip on my hand shifted ever so slightly, and I knew instantly that he was no longer focusing on the flick.

I turn and our eyes connect in the dim, flickering theatre lights. Biting my lip, I get turned on watching his eyes on my mouth. A hunger, thick and rich, implodes inside of me when he releases my hand and moves his warm touch to my bare legs. I could scream with joy that there's nobody sitting anywhere near us when I brazenly uncross my legs.

I've never been sexually promiscuous. Like, ever. I had never even seen the majority of the items at Leslie's hen night party. I also never would have called myself an exhibitionist, but what's happening to my body right now is not up for debate. It's intense and heavy and I want it right the fuck now.

"Vi?" Hayden whispers my name in question, tickling my

inner thighs.

I bite my lip and nod shamelessly as I shift down in my seat. I snatch my denim jacket off the chair next to me and toss it over my lap to conceal the place that his hand is currently en dangerous route to. Definitely a place I wouldn't normally have opened for visitors in the middle of a public theatre, but fuck. This is Hayden we're talking about.

I drop my head back on the chair and turn to him to whisper in his ear. "I need you, Hayden. Right now."

He clears his throat, and my inner thigh muscles clench with satisfaction from his blatantly ruffled feathers. He slides down in his seat a bit, too, allowing him better access, and resumes his travelling pursuit between my thighs. His fingertips are firm and slightly rough, only further intensifying all of my sensations. They finally reach my centre, and he begins stroking me through the flimsy fabric of my thong. I stifle a moan and grab his wrist aggressively just as he pinches my clit. He freezes and tenses, but I'm not worried about him right now. I maintain my ironclad grip on his leather cuff, doing my best to gain control over myself. Finally, when I think I can handle more without screaming out in ecstasy, I release his wrist and trail my fingers up his forearm, gliding them along the crook near his bicep.

Slowly, he slips one finger around the fabric and brushes against my bare slit. My teeth crush down on my lower lip so hard I can feel the bumpy muscle beneath the skin. I should feel embarrassed by how soaked I am already, but fuck. Everything he does to me feels so good. All I can feel in this moment is excitement. Excitement from the naughtiness. Excitement from the location. Excitement from fucking Hayden.

Fucking Hayden.

"Christ, Vi," he groans with a stiff, husky voice.

He plunges his finger as far as he can from this angle and, oh my God, does it feel incredible. I pump my hips like a wanton sex siren, calling him inside of me, aching for him to continue his quest. He honours my call. He pushes a second finger in me and I turn to bite down on his shoulder, overcome by the deliciousness of his touch. He pumps in and out in steady, purposeful swells. My breathing turns laboured and frenzied as he works me closer and closer to climax.

Desperate for something to do with my hands, I touch his huge, firm bulge concealed beneath the tight denim.

He grabs my wrist with his other hand. "There's time for that later," he croaks.

"I want you, Hayden," I say, my eyes opening and landing on his, which were watching me with a sexy, thinly-veiled intensity that I feel everywhere. Oddly, tears prick my eyes from the powerful force being transferred between us right now.

Suddenly, my body distracts me from my emotions as his finger twists to a location that has me toppling over the edge. I throw my arm over my face and silently scream with wild, orgasmic conviction as I feel the climax reach every single inch of my body.

"We need to leave," Hayden says, yanking his hand from between my legs. He snatches my jacket off my lap and covers himself while hauling me up from my seat. My legs feel like gelatin as I tug my dress down and he guides me through the darkened theatre toward the green exit sign.

My mind is in a complete fog, so I'm surprised when we step out of the theatre to see that it's completely dark out. I lose track of time so easily with Hayden.

"Fuck," he curses quietly, taking note of the pouring rain and glancing up and down the street for a cab.

"My flat is only two blocks, Hayden."

"It's raining," he says to me, obviously agitated by the situation.

"So?" I say putting my hands on my hips, feeling a bit more of my strength return in the fresh and wet night air.

"You're not fucking walking in the rain, Vi," he growls in

frustration, looking up and down the empty street again.

"Hayden," I say in a warning tone, but he ignores me and pulls his phone from his pocket. "Hayden!" I exclaim, stamping my foot on the wet pavement in annoyance.

His eyes flash to my bare legs and a hardened look shutters over his face. "Bunny."

I shake my head and begin walking backwards away from him. "We don't have to walk…We can run!" I screech and turn, taking off in a dead sprint through the downpour.

"Vi!" Hayden shouts.

Excitement flies through me as I feel his approaching footsteps behind me. The rain clings to my dress as I grip my clutch firmly and continue running while squinting against the heavy pelts of water.

He catches up to me in seconds, glaring angrily at me in the rain. "You stubborn woman." An odd smile spreads across his face as he tries to look mad but fails. There are those sexy crinkles again.

"It's raining cats and dogs!" I bellow, throwing my hands out wide and smiling as if it's just another Thursday.

He shakes his head in admonishment. "I thought you'd be faster, Bunny. You're a Harris footballer's daughter for Christ's sake."

My eyes narrow with a renewed sense of determination. I do my best to pick up the pace, but it seems useless. Hayden doesn't even look like he's trying. A giggle erupts from my mouth when I hear him chuckling at me.

We make it to my neighbourhood, passing the bustling Hookah Lounge, and round the corner down the alley to my flat. I fall backwards onto the brick wall beside my lift, completely drenched, and push the wet strands off my face. My chest heaves while my laughter dies down and I attempt to catch my breath. Hayden comes to a stop in front of me, propping his hands on his knees as I dig in my clutch for my keys. He watches me out of the corner of his eye. My hand freezes on my keys as our gazes lock through the sheet of rain separating us. A loud crack of thunder causes me to flinch and a huge burst of lightning illuminates the darkened alley, shedding a clear blue light on the true, unbelievable, and intensely gripping face of Hayden.

My breath is gone. Sucked straight from my lungs and slammed into my chest. Into my heart, like a lightning bolt. He slowly stands upright. Something simmering deep and hungry in the grey pools of his eyes makes me gasp.

He swallows hard and nods as he steps closer to me. "I want this," his voice cracks as he trails the backs of his fingers from my cheek, to my breasts, to my belly, then to my hip. He yanks me into him so our bodies are flush against each other. With his forehead resting against mine, he whispers as if in pain, "I want you."

I shake my head, confused by his sudden comments. It's as if he was having an entire conversation with himself during our run here. Now he's finally made up his mind and is putting it out into the universe for acknowledgement.

"I want you, too—" I start, but I am immediately silenced by his mouth on mine in a painful, biting, and frenzied kiss.

He shoves me up against the wall and grabs my legs so they wrap firmly around him. His hardened erection presses against me, and I cry out into his mouth as a desperate ache explodes inside of me. Fisting my hair in his hands, he holds my face just where he wants it to kiss me…and kiss me…and kiss me. God, he kisses me like a starved man who's found the only item in the world that could ever satisfy him.

"Let me in, Vi," he commands while dipping his head to nip along the edge of my jaw. "Let me up and let me in. Please."

His request stings my eyes. I swear I could cry real, wet tears from his words. Everything south of my waist is screaming at me to let him in. But the one organ I'm most terrified of—the one I'm not sure he's asking for—is the one cracking at his raw and guttural words.

He releases me and I shakily open the lift doors. The moment we step inside, we collide. He licks and sucks my neck and collar bone as I punch the button for the eleventh floor. As we begin our climb, he pulls my soaked dress up over my body, revealing my white, lacy bra and thong, both also soaked from the rain…and other things.

"Bunny," he murmurs. He hunches over and grabs hold of my nipple with his mouth through the sheer fabric while aggressively caressing my other in his palm. Then he glides his hands down my hips and hisses as he slides his fingers beneath the edges of my thong.

The doors open suddenly and Bruce barrels in, pouncing on the back of Hayden. Hayden widens his stance to protect my nearly naked body from Bruce's assault. Bugger!

Hayden chuckles and turns, telling me to hop up on his back.

Well, this is a first.

He carries my nearly naked butt, still wearing my soaked Converse, through my flat and into the kitchen. I tell him which cupboard the bones are in, and he grabs one and tosses it into the living room where Bruce tears after it.

Hayden continues to my room and closes the French doors on a besotted-looking Bruce with a bone hanging from his mouth. *Sorry, buddy. I'll make it up to you! Promise!*

He releases me, slowly sliding me down his back and turning to face me. He smiles sweetly and kisses my lips, brushing my nose as he pulls away. The crinkles around his eyes return just before a look of nervousness takes hold. "We don't have to, Vi. If you're not ready, or if you think we shouldn't."

"What was it you said you'd do if I stamped my foot again?" I whisper into his ear and lightly trail my tongue along his lobe. It's cold and wet from the rain, as is the thin shirt concealing his body. I'm normally not so sexually bold, but everything with Hayden is different.

Everything with Hayden is different.

He draws back and grins naughtily at me, revealing so much about his happiness in this moment. "There's a lot I'd like to do about that little habit of yours."

With a sense of needy determination, I grab the bottom of his soaked shirt and peel it up over his head. I feast my eyes on his firm build and place a row of soft kisses across his chest.

"Bunny, you don't even know what you're in for."

"Bunn—" I start with a snarky reply in mind, but he promptly leans down and tosses me over his shoulder with a thrilling crack right on my bum. An excited yelp bursts from my mouth as I brace myself on his firm back.

"Don't talk back, Bunny. I promise you're going to enjoy this," he groans as his hand grazes all the way up the back of my leg to my arse. He tugs at the strip of fabric between my legs. "Perhaps not as much as me."

He flops me down on the bed, and the crushed velvet feels wildly sensual beneath my bare skin. I watch him as he reaches to his back pocket and pulls a condom from his wallet and tosses it on the bed. A fission of excitement pulses between my legs as he begins unbuckling his jeans. I'm pleased to see a pair of black boxer briefs this time. Still Calvin Klein. I must remember to write Mr. Klein a letter of appreciation.

Hayden crawls up on the bed and hooks his fingers on the edge of my knickers, pulling them down my legs. His eyes hood with arousal from seeing me bare for the first time. He continues inching his way up my body and finally reaches my face. Leaning down, he steals my lips for his own. *They're yours, Hayden. All fucking yours.*

His fingers trail slowly down my side as goosebumps erupt on every surface of my skin. After removing my bra, he finds my pulsing, wet centre. I writhe beneath him as he continues to tickle me softly everywhere except the one damn place I want him the most.

I pull my mouth from his and moan, "Hayden, please!" I thrust my hips up greedily toward his hand and, without thinking, reach down and attempt to touch myself for some semblance of relief.

"No, no," he chastises and then bites his lip. Whispering against my mouth, he says, "When I'm here, this is mine." With that, he plunges his fingers deep inside of me.

My eyes slam shut as I cry out, relieved that the torture is over. "God," I moan with wonton abandon. The foreplay from the cinema and then here is the most intense I've ever had. Every passionate encounter I've had with Hayden flashes before my eyes. The fighting, the spanking, the kitchen kisses, the striptease, the pussy tease. It's all so…heady.

Hayden pulls his fingers out and flicks my swollen and drenched clit. I yelp in delirious agony as he quickly pushes up on his knees all the while tossing me over onto my belly in the same fluid motion. He leans over top of me, wraps my wet locks around his fist, and then uses his other hand to drop a swift slap to my bottom that I was already shamelessly pushing into the air toward him, ready and waiting.

Fuck, this is too much. I need him inside me right the bloody hell now.

"So fucking sexy," he moans, affectionately stroking the area he swatted. He releases my hair and grips my hips, positioning me so I'm up on my knees, but my chest is still resting on the bed.

I hear him rustling with the condom wrapper, so I look over my shoulder to watch just as he pushes his briefs down. His penis is exactly as I pictured. It's thick and pulsing, clearly showcasing every bit of hard desire he's got for me.

He rolls the condom on and looks down at me with lust deep in his eyes. "You ready?" A half-grin teases the corner of his mouth.

I nod and bite my lip, and he surges himself inside me with one swift push. I'm already soaked, so there is very little resistance, aside from the tightness, as he fills me completely.

"Hayden," I nearly scream, looking out the window and thanking fuck this is my life right now. God, it's been too long since I've been properly shagged.

"Vi," he groans, pushing and pulling himself in and out of my channel in slow, long strokes. "Vi, I want to try so many things with you and your hot fucking arse. But tonight…Christ, tonight I'm just going to give it to you fast and hard and hope to fuck you're okay with that because I'm not sure I can manage it any other way."

"Sounds like the best thing you've said all night," I shamelessly admit, my mouth muffled against the duvet as I feel my impending climb to release approaching already.

And that's exactly what he does. He slams into me for who knows how long because time ceases to exist when Hayden Clarke is inside of me. I am suspended in the time and space continuum, floating and completely oblivious to the number of seconds that tick from present to future.

Completely oblivious to the number of seconds it takes my body to slam into a roaring climax.

Completely oblivious to the number of seconds I scream out his name in utterly blissful pleasure.

Completely oblivious to the number of seconds that it takes me to fall for the brooding, broken, complicated, demanding, and sexy as fuck Hayden Clarke.

23

11:11

Hayden

I LIE AWAKE, NERVOUSLY CHECKING MY WATCH AND WAITING FOR 11:11 to approach. Vi is asleep, draped completely across my chest. Her bare breasts soft and supple against me. I watch her back rise and fall with each breath, relishing in the feeling of her faint heartbeat pattering against me. I play mindlessly with her drying blonde hair that's fanned out on the grey sheets.

Exhausted from our exertions on her bed, in her shower, and then on her bed again, she's been out for nearly an hour. But her last noises weren't those of sexual ecstasy. They were the sexiest fucking noise I've heard come from her lips yet. Her giggles over some daft joke I made about rude rabbits.

She fell asleep so easily, so trustingly. *Nothing troubles Vi*, I think as I've been lying here, watching her and trying to figure out how I can slip out of bed. I hate that I have to leave her. I hate that my body forces me to feel the tick of 11:11 like the timer on a really hot oven. Like if I don't get up and deal with whatever is cooking inside, everything will go up in flames.

Aside from our first night together after the gala, I've managed to avoid being around her at 11:11. But there is no way I could connect with her the way I did tonight and manage to leave her flat. I

195

ache for her closeness. For her comforting warm breath against my body. A possessiveness seizes over me at leaving her alone in this big bed. She shouldn't be alone. Ever. She is mine to care for.

But with the time creeping closer and closer, I feel myself growing tenser and tenser. I attempt to slide out from beneath her, but she stirs. I freeze, hoping she'll fall back asleep, but my prayers aren't answered.

"Why aren't you sleeping?" she croaks with a raspy, sleepy voice and looks up at me, rubbing her eyes.

"I just need to pop outside for a second," I reply honestly. I can't tell her I'm going to the loo because I have it in my head that what has to be done needs to be done outside.

"Pop out where?"

"Just to your patio. Stay here. I'll be right back." I jostle her a bit more roughly than I mean to but manage to break free. I grab the towel I used earlier and wrap it around my waist, padding quietly out of her room and hoping to fuck she doesn't follow.

Bruce is up and trots out to greet me. "Go back to bed. Lie down," I command. He doesn't listen. He follows me to the door that goes out to the deck. "Go on, old boy." I shoo him back from the door and close it behind me as I step outside into the cool night air.

London city lights twinkle all around and it's chilly from the rain, but I hardly notice as I'm too focused on the task at hand. I cinch my towel and glance down at my watch just as it ticks over to 11:11 like a gunshot. I grip the edge of the railing and hang my head low while closing my eyes tightly.

Please take away my past. Change my past. Alter my past. Go back and make the accident never happen. Go back and make it so Marisa didn't die. Go back and make it so I never tried to kill myself. Go back and take me instead of her.

"What are you doing?" Vi's voice asks from behind me as I stand up straight, finishing what I came out here to do.

I shake my head, avoiding her eyes, but I know it's useless. "It's nothing, Vi. Please, let's go back to bed."

"It's not nothing." She strolls out dressed in a baggy nightshirt. Her blonde hair is loose and wild around her face, but she still has never looked more beautiful. "Tell me."

I look at her and instantly fear everything exploding all around us if I don't explain this properly. "It's just a stupid superstition I've had for ages."

"For how long?" Her brow furrows.

I swallow hard. "About four years."

Her eyes blink knowingly. "Since Marisa died."

I shrug sheepishly. "Told you it's stupid."

"What do you do?"

I sigh heavily. "I'd rather not talk about it, Vi. You're going to think I'm crazier than I've already proven."

"I want to know." She leans against the railing beside me. Bruce follows on her heels, shooting me a wounded puppy-dog look over blowing him off a bit ago.

With a deep breath in, I place my forearms on the railing, choosing to watch London's reaction to my story over Vi's. "I just have a little ritual I do every time 11:11 hits. It's developed into a bit of OCD I guess. 11:11 has always been important to me. I've always seen it in my life, represented in one way or another. License plates, mileage on a speedometer, final amount on grocery receipts. It always randomly appears to me." I cut my eyes to hers. "The floors of people's flats."

Her eyes turn into saucers and her jaw goes slack.

"Before my attempt, Daphney said it was lucky and that I should make a wish whenever I see it. So that's what I do because it's better than the eerie sensation I get every time it appears to me. It has become even more important after Marisa's death. Some people pray before bed. I do this."

An unnerving look fleets across Vi's face, but she shakes whatever thought she was having away. "So, what do you wish for?"

"Vi, really—"

"Tell me," she insists.

I clench my jaw in frustration. Being open with Vi has never felt like an obligation until this very moment, but I don't have it in me to tell her no. "First, I wish the accident never would have happened. Then I wish she never would have died. And since rehab, I began wishing I wouldn't have slit my wrists. And…" I look down, suddenly shrouded in shame.

"And?"

"I wish I would have died instead of Marisa." My voice is hard and cold. Cutting. It's best she knows the darkness that still lives in me.

Her face falls. "Is that really an option you wish for?"

I nod.

"Still?" Her blue eyes are swimming with anxiety.

I nod again.

She swallows hard. "I see." She turns around, mumbles something at Bruce, and walks back into her flat. Her posture hunched.

My heart fills with despair.

"Vi," I plead, following her inside. When I touch her shoulder, she turns and flashes her wide, challenging eyes at me.

"What?" she snaps, grabbing her hair and balling it around her fist.

"You have to understand that I battle years' worth of demons. Demons I still fight inside my mind. I can't just blink all of that away."

"Why don't you wish it away?" she quips, her tone snotty as she chucks her hair behind her back.

"What the fuck is your problem?" I growl angrily, pacing the room. "I stepped outside to do this. I get that it's strange and stupid, but it's something I have to do. I'm not sure where you get off acting all self-righteous over it."

"Hayden!" she exclaims, balling her fists beside her. "You tell me you're not weak, but this sounds scary. And I just found out the guy I'm falling for wishes his life away. How is that supposed to make me feel?"

Her words hit me like a punch to my gut. Weakness is representative of all that I want to leave behind. Picturing Leslie's face the moment she found me after carving into my wrists was the lowest I ever felt. To hurt someone like that...To put her through it all. I hated it. Is making these wishes at 11:11 considered weak?

"These wishes make me feel safe," I croak, not knowing how else to explain myself.

"Safe, how?" she asks, her tone nearly a shrill.

I inhale slowly through my nose and tell her yet another thing I've never revealed to another person. "A few years ago, I was pissed out of my mind on both booze and pills. I was driving, like a fucking moron, and I looked down at my speedometer. The miles on my car switched over to 1111 just as the clock struck 11:11. It shook me to my core. The next thing I knew, I wrapped my car around a tree and spent several weeks in the hospital."

"Hayden—" she starts, but I cut her off.

"That was the first time people started throwing the word *suicide* around with my name. That was when Mum started the charity. That's when I became the fucking family charity case." I suck in my cheeks and bite down, ignoring Vi's reaction all together. "This is the one thing that brings me comfort with my recovery, Vi. So I do it."

A painfully quiet and charged moment passes between us. Her blue eyes look like they are searching mine for something. Something I don't have inside of me to give away.

As if defeated, her soft voice utters, "Okay."

I blink at her, my eyes squinting in confusion. "Okay?" I ask for confirmation.

She nods woodenly. "Okay." A sombre, yet helpless look crosses over her face, and whatever it was she thought just then forces me to eliminate all space between us. As I take her in my arms, she looks up at me with watery eyes. "I'm sorry, Hayden. This is hard for me, too. This is your journey and I can't walk it for you, but I hope you know that you don't always have to fight alone."

My heart soars and sinks with that one profound statement she just spoke. The look in her eyes as she stares back at me is a look of surrender. As if she's got no other choice but to give herself to me completely. As if her level of interest in whatever it is we have between us trumps all bad habits and it terrifies the shit out of her.

Her arms wrap around my waist and I clasp them firmly behind my back. The trembling in her body hurts my heart. "Please, Bunny," I murmur into her hair. "Trust me to figure this one out. I promise, I just need time." I kiss the top of her head and wish the vow I'm making to her be true with every fibre of my being.

The next morning, I walk back home, or to Theo's flat I should say. As soon as I swing open the door, I'm greeted by a beaming Leslie.

"Welcome home!" she sings from her place at the dining room table with Jaci. They have several binders spread out all around them.

"I'll be in touch," Jaci says with a huff of annoyance, like my mere presence alone could spoil all their work. She stands and bustles past me, pausing to give me a nasty once-over. "Has he been fitted for a suit?"

Leslie nods. "Yep! We'll get him cleaned up, don't you worry."

A painful smile splits across my face as I scratch my whiskered chin. Jaci makes her hasty exit. I lift my brows, giving Leslie an "are you serious" look. She shrugs her shoulders good naturedly while eyeing my clothes from last night.

"Where's my favourite girl?" I ask, attempting to delay the conversation that I've felt coming the last couple of weeks.

"Sleeping upstairs with Theo."

"Another rough night?" I guess, striding over to the kettle and pouring myself a cup of tea.

"You guessed it. But you wouldn't know because you've been MIA the last two weeks."

I flinch, touching my right cuff self-consciously. I pour some milk in my tea and walk over to join Leslie at the table. "Sorry about that."

"No need to be sorry, Hayden. You're a single, twenty-six-year-old man. And, hey, I have Jaci in my corner. That broad may be a crusty, British, upper-lip, tight-ass, but she's my wish come true." Leslie's eyes narrow from behind her mug. "But no one cares about that. Let's hear it, Hay Day. Did you get way laid?"

Frowning, I shoot a warning glare at her. "So not funny, Leslie."

"What? I thought it was funny. I rhymed!" Her sea green eyes are brighter and happier than I've seen them in months. Maybe Jaci no K is a miracle worker after all. I smile to myself at how Vi can make even the happiest of people happier.

"This is awkward enough without you making it more awkward with lame sexual jokes." I slice one hand through my hair and prop my head on it, my thoughts scattering all around me. It's strange that I haven't been confiding in Leslie about all matters concerning Vi. Since my attempt, there's an unspoken openness between us that makes Leslie the one I go to the most when I'm feeling troubled. I talk to Theo some, but there's an ease with Leslie. She was in the trenches with me. She's my sister in combat. She saved my fucking life.

"What's awkward about it?" Leslie asks. "I love Vilma. I think she's perfect for you." Leslie's tone is bright and excited, obviously feeling everything I'm trying to *avoid* feeling.

I sigh heavily. "Do you really think this is a great idea? I mean, how could you? She's a mate of yours and I'm…well, fucking crazy."

"Hayden!" she snaps. "You're not crazy and I will smack you if you call yourself that again."

I roll my eyes. "I was in a loony bin for thirty days, Leslie. I'm a mess and Vi is…Vi."

"You were in rehab, Hayden. Hell, Ke$ha went to rehab. It's practically a trendy hot spot these days." I eye her harshly and her light tone falters a bit. "Hayden, look. I know you. If I tell you you're worth it, you're worth it!"

"This is different, Leslie. Vi's special. She deserves more." I bite out the last word and swallow hard thinking about the impending doom I feel every time I consider that thought I know to be true.

"Deserves more than a Clarke brother? No such thing! You guys have super powers."

I shake my head, putting a pin in this conversation for now. "I'm being stupid," I scoff and offer her a cocky smirk that symbolises the complete opposite of what I feel on the inside.

"Hey!" Her eyes flash with excitement. "Why don't you bring Vi over to Frank's tomorrow night? It's family flick night. Could be fun!"

My face recoils. "I don't know, Leslie. I think it might be a little soon. Won't Rey and Liam be there?" While it wasn't horrid being around them a couple of weeks ago, avoiding them is a lot better for my own sanity.

"No, they haven't come since the pub's been up and running. And what do you mean, too soon? You guys have been hanging out together for a couple of weeks. It's not like you're asking her to marry you. Vi's my friend! It's just a casual evening with some friends."

I nod silently, mulling it over for a moment. "I guess it couldn't hurt."

Leslie cheers at her win. She immediately starts texting Frank while I attempt to snuff out the painful ache of insecurity hurtling through me. Feeling everything I've allowed myself to feel for Vi isn't just scary for me. It's dangerous.

The next night, Vi meets us at Theo and Leslie's flat so we can all ride over to Frank's together. I feel a bit like a couple of pubescent teenagers stuffed into the backseat of Mum and Dad's car on our way to a school dance, aside from Baby Marisa nestled snuggly between us in her infant seat.

"Everybody all buckled up?" Leslie crows from the passenger side as Theo slides in behind the wheel.

"You're seriously wearing that?" I ask Leslie, my tone flat and clearly unimpressed.

"I wear it every time."

Vi giggles. "You should have gotten me one, Leslie. I would have joined you." My eyes swerve to her, and I can't tell if she's joking.

"I'll place an order for future flick nights, Vilma!" Leslie fist bumps Vi moronically, then cries out, "Boom. Converted another!"

"Still won't get me," Theo grumbles as he buckles up.

"Hey, I got Frank, I got Finley, I got Julie. Hell, I even got Brody!" She turns and nods her head eagerly, clearly impressed by herself. "It's only a matter of time before you Clarke brothers submit to my redheaded superpower wiles!"

Leslie is referring to her cheetah-print, onesie, footie pyjamas. She's actually wearing them in the car with trainers on over them, clearly not the least bit embarrassed to be riding through the streets of London in the getup. Apparently they all wear onesies on family flick night. It's part of their thing. I didn't tell Vi about it because I was certain she wouldn't want one. Clearly I was mistaken.

"Brody is whipped," Theo grumbles. "You got enough leg room back there, Hayden?" My brother's cocky chuckle gets right up my nose, but I let it pass. "How about you, Vi?"

"I'm good!" she chirps in response and I smirk at her happy demeanour.

When I pitched the idea of family flick night to her last night on the phone, she seemed shocked that I'd want to hang out with friends so soon. Then I told her I was prepared to meet her brothers any time, which I think really floored her. She keeps going on about how scary they are, but frankly, they are the least of my concerns.

Theo pulls out of the carport and drives us through the dark streets of London like one big happy family. I peek down at Marisa, who has hold of my finger and is attempting to yank it into her mouth repeatedly. Her eyes are wide and curious as she takes in the flashing lights.

I glance up to find Vi watching me. She smirks. I smirk back. She licks her lips. I lick mine. As if we are being drawn together by some outside force, our heads lean into each other and our mouths connect in a soft, sweet kiss. It's the kind of kiss that leaves me wanting more, but also completely satisfies everything inside of me like I've never had better.

Marisa's sudden cry interrupts our tender moment. I pull back from Vi, laughing. "Don't be jealous, Marisa. You're still my number one girl."

"Number one is it?" Vi tsks in mock offence, her grin still permanently in place.

"She's *my* number one girl," Theo objects from the front seat. Leslie's hand reaches over and strokes his. "Tied for number one," he adds curtly and cuts a heated squint at her that forces me to look away.

We arrive at Frank's and waltz through the large purple door framed in climbing ivy. I've never been to Frank's, but it somehow suits him. It's a large, imposing home, but when you walk in, there's an energy unlike any other.

Frank bounds out of the living room on our left. "The bloody Clarkes are here! Hide the family jewels!"

Leslie's eyes turn into saucers. "I believe it was my jewels that you always stole, Frank and Beans. Along with my Bedazzler."

"Christ, gingers sure can hold a grudge." He glares meanly at her, then looks at mine and Vi's hands clasped together. He ropes his arm with Vi's and pulls her away from me, leading her toward the dining room. His voice trails back into the foyer as he says, "Why, Vi. Hopped from Ethan to Hayden faster than you can say Frank's your uncle! I have to say, I'm impressed, dear girl."

My face falls and I move forward quickly, but Theo stops me in my tracks with a hard hand on my shoulder. "Don't be a fool, Hayden. It was a joke." He gives me an annoying matey pat on the shoulder. "You're better than that."

Am I? I swallow hard, my clenched jaw rocking side-to-side in frustration. Just thinking about Ethan and Vi makes my blood boil. But fuck, Theo's right. I know what Frank's like, so why is it bothering me so much?

Finley and Brody join us in the living room, both wearing their own footie pyjamas. They sit cosily next to each other on the couch as Brody holds Marisa somewhat awkwardly, and Finley looks so happy she might burst into tears. They've been married for about a year now, and Leslie has mentioned to me that children won't be a part of their future. But watching them right now, I'm not sure they know it.

"I think we should do it now," Finley says, looking up at Frank sneakily as he readies some snacks on the coffee table.

Frank's eyes alight knowingly. "All right. Everyone remain calm. This is not a drill. We have a bit of a surprise for Marisa, so if you'll all follow me."

Finley passes Marisa back to Leslie, and I find myself so intrigued that I follow the group up the large staircase to the second floor. Frank stops in front of a closed bedroom door and turns back to us while dramatically coiffing his puffy red hair.

"This was my idea," Frank starts.

"Bullshit! It was my idea!" Finley interjects, standing shoulder-to-shoulder with him. The two of them are wearing footie pyjamas, looking like the biggest fools as they bicker over whose idea whatever it is we're about to see was.

"Oi, all right, Fin-Bin. It was your idea, but you need to thank fuck I was around for the design process or you would have had it decked out in K-State University drivel."

"Frank!" Finley cuts.

"Why don't you guys just open the door," Brody asks calmly.

Seriously, Brody is a big, brawny, man-type of bloke and seeing him in his onesie is disturbing. Finley must have some serious pull over him to get him to wear one of those.

Finley smirks and opens the door. Following her lead, we all walk in to one of the most beautiful nurseries I've ever seen. Not that I've seen many. Honestly, I feel a bit poorly because I'm in the bedroom that would normally be Marisa's perfect little nursery at Theo and Leslie's flat if it wasn't for me. But Leslie says she wants to keep Marisa close for a while anyway, so having her crib upstairs next to them works best for everyone.

I take note of the expensive-looking crib covered in a funky, loud, floral-print of fuchsias, pinks, reds, and oranges. Next to it is a safari baby bouncer, a fire-engine-red changing table, nappies, wipes, the works. The walls are a soft cyan colour with white crown moulding everywhere, allowing the decorations to make the statement. A modern, grey, upholstered rocker is nestled perfectly in the corner. It's a trendy baby's dream come true nursery. A day bed even rests along the window making it not just a nursery, but a place for mum and dad to stay when they visit as well.

Leslie hands Marisa off to Theo and does a complete survey of the room, remaining completely silent. I think we're all waiting to hear her reaction as she runs her hands along the crib. Finally, she covers her mouth as she turns to look at Theo. Her eyes are drenched with tears and, without pause, Theo rushes over to her and hugs her with his free arm—an unknowing Baby Marisa smashed happily between them.

I look away and rub my face annoyingly as my own damn eyes start to prick. Vi catches sight of me and I frown, grabbing her hand and pulling her out of the room.

"You okay?" she asks softly.

I nod. "Yeah. That's just…I know that means a lot to Leslie. Her family isn't the best." I don't offer any more details on the matter because it's not my story to tell.

"You're really close to her, aren't you?" Vi's eyes squint curiously as if she's trying to piece together why I'm reacting so strongly.

Feeling strangely, like I need to minimise what Leslie means to me, I huff, "It's nothing. Let's go downstairs." I take Vi's hand in mine and lead her toward the flight of stairs. I freeze in my tracks when I see Reyna standing below.

"Hey," she says, looking up at me in surprise and pausing her climb up the steps. "I didn't expect you to be here." Her eyes cut down to my hand in Vi's and, for some reason, I quickly let her go.

I swallow awkwardly. "Leslie invited me."

Reyna looks at Vi, her eyes narrowing. "Vilma, right?"

"Yeah. It's Vi, I told you before. Hi, Reyna. Nice to see you again." Vi tucks her long blonde strands behind her ears, her eyes squinting with speculation.

Reyna's grey eyes chill, which puzzles me.

Suddenly, we're all distracted by a huge commotion behind us.

"FUCKING CUNT-FACED SPUNK BUBBLE!" a woman's voice screams from the bedroom down the hall from the new nursery.

Frank, Leslie, Theo, Finley, and Brody dash out into the hallway just as a box of men's clothing is launched out of the open bedroom door. Next comes a mobile. It strikes the hallway wall and crumbles to several pieces with a cringe-worthy crack.

A besotted Julie storms out of the room dressed in a lime green onesie. Her almond-shaped eyes are wide, her black hair is tangled, and her stance is braced with a menacing gait that makes me fight the urge to cover my balls.

"Men are fucking PIGS! The lot of them!" she screams.

My eyes flash to Baby Marisa, who begins fussing in Theo's arms.

"Fuck, I'm sorry. But they are. Men are fucking spunk bubble twats. I will tell all of you this right now. You're all in love and you all think love can conquer the universe. It fucking doesn't. The only men you can trust are the arseholes who have no feelings. They just have ARSEHOLES!"

She turns and storms into the bathroom at the end of the hall, slamming the door loudly in her wake.

"Well, there goes our tender family moment," Frank huffs as he sashays down the hall to console whatever is eating at Julie.

Finley turns and sees Reyna and rushes to welcome her surprise visit. I overhear Rey tell Finley that Liam is running the pub tonight and that she needed a night of relaxation. Leslie joins in the greeting but watches me nervously. I try to give her a look that tells her I'm okay because I know she tries to hide her friendship with Rey from me. But I'm not an idiot. Theo and Liam are best mates. I know Leslie has naturally grown closer to Reyna as a result. It's not just that, though. Having Rey around with Vi here makes me uneasy. Last time I properly spoke to Rey, I told her that lust and recovery don't mix. Now I'm standing here feeling like a hypocritical prat. Although, a quiet, annoying voice in my head knows it's more than just lust with Vi. But admitting that thought is more terrifying than tempting my recovery.

We make our way to the living room and begin watching a film. It's charged and awkward and I feel horrid because I'm not touching Vi like I normally do. My body yearns to throw a claiming arm around her, but Rey's presence and the thoughts rattling off in my head make me feel disjointed.

Eventually, I remove myself to pop out to the kitchen for a drink. Maybe if I can give myself a silent pep talk, I can stop acting like such a wanker. Just as I close the fridge door, Rey's face appears from behind it.

"So, you and Vi?" she asks, leaning her back against the fridge and crossing her inked arms over her chest.

I crack the top on the can of soda in my hand. My jaw clenches in annoyance because this feels wrong on so many levels. I shrug my shoulders, dismissively opting to remain silent.

She frowns. "What? You're not going to tell me anything?" Her tone is defensive.

"I don't see how it's any of your business." I turn and lean back on the counter to face her, taking a cool drink.

"I just think it's odd that you told me only a couple of weeks ago that you're putting yourself first and focusing all your efforts on you. Then I see you holding hands and cosying up to some blonde you barely know." She gestures flippantly toward the living room where I left Vi with everyone else.

My temper flares. "She's not just some fucking blonde, Rey. She's got a damn name and you bloody well know it. Stop acting as if she's some random bird I picked up at a pub. And you're one to talk!"

"What do you mean?"

"You were a fucking mess, too, and you got engaged!" I accuse, not because I'm jealous, but because I'm defensive. "What did your therapist say about that?"

She recoils. "Liam and I had history."

"Don't remind me." I cringe thinking about the fact that Liam and my sister nearly got engaged when they were together at Oxford. It makes me ill to think about Rey with him, truthfully. I'm all for unconventional love stories, but fuck me. Don't act all self-righteous when you're the pot calling the kettle black. "Regardless, none of it is your concern."

"Oh, excuse me for being a friend!" she snaps.

"You and I aren't friends anymore, Rey." I set my can down and cross my arms, mirroring her subliminal shield of armour.

"Not by my choice!" she shouts. "I miss you, Hayden!"

"Oh, please," I laugh with shock. "You wouldn't even be talking to me if Liam was here and you know it. If he were here, he'd be sulking in the corner, watching us like a hawk."

"Knock it off. Liam isn't like that. He understands what you and I are."

"You and I *were* a fucking mess, Rey. Were. Don't build us up to be more than we *were*."

Her eyes narrow with barely contained fury. "We were best friends, Hayden," she says in slow, warning tones.

"You made me weak, Rey!" I roar, feeling like, for the first time, I've finally pegged exactly what Reyna Miracle was to me all those years. "You made me fragile. And you bring me right back to the sod all mess I was all those years ago, and I don't fucking want it." Her jaw drops in shock, only infuriating me more. "We were *never* best friends. You said it yourself on that park bench. We know nothing about each other, so you can't possibly throw that card at me now."

Her grey eyes well with tears. I flinch. "Fuck, Rey. I'm sorry. I'm not blaming you for everything, especially not for what I did to myself. It was my own fault. I just need you to understand that you cannot have a say in my life anymore. And you cannot use our past against me."

She swipes hastily at her eyes, and I have to fight every urge in my body that wants to go to her and comfort her. Rub that spot on her neck that I know soothes her almost instantly. It's a reflex with Rey. Comforting her. She craves my comfort like a crutch, and I let her use me that way for so many years. Maybe we both have addictions to fight?

She sets her jaw angrily and turns, storming out of the kitchen. When I watch her leave, I find Vi and Leslie standing in the entryway staring at the scene that just transpired. Both their jaws are dropped.

Fuck.

Anger pulses through me from the fact that Rey can go off on me and then act all wounded when I get real with her. I stride over and motion for Leslie to follow me. I can't even bring myself to look at Vi right now.

"Hayden, what the fuck?" Leslie says, following me out the

front door and into the gated patio area on the face of the house. It's completely shrouded in ivy, similar to how my heart is shrouded in shame.

"Fuck, Leslie. I don't know what to bloody do!" I exclaim with a forced whisper so no one can hear me. "My mind is spinning and I'm a fucking mess. A lot of what Rey said was true. I was going to focus on myself, yet here I am, acting like a normal fucking bloke with a new girlfriend!"

"You are a normal bloke, Hayden!" Leslie cries. "Don't let Rey's insecurities tell you otherwise. She has her own demons to fight."

"I swore I'd never let anyone become number one over me again. I gave Rey so much power over my moods and my heart. Now I'm doing the same damn thing with Vi!" I shove my hands forcibly through my hair. All of this is too much too soon. How did I let Vi get so close so fast?

"Stop. Right now. Stop everything." Leslie sticks out her hands like she's trying to calm a wild beast. "You're letting Rey get in your head. You don't need her there. She's a trigger for you. Don't let her make you crumble. Don't give her that power."

I nod, seriously absorbing everything Leslie is saying but feeling a pit of despair in the bottom of my stomach like I could be screwing everything up for myself again.

"Hayden. You deserve to be happy," Leslie adds. "It's been a year."

"Right!" I whisper scream, my voice bordering on a manly shriek. "It's been a year. You've seen me through it. I'm a completely different person than I was fresh out of rehab. Aren't I?" I grip my leather cuffs and ache for the pressure thundering through every part of my body to dampen. I want this to be true. I need it to be.

"You are different, Hayden. Calm down," she says soothingly.

"Fuck. I just wanted a normal night out." I crouch over a chair and drop my head down to my chest. "I'm so tired of feeling broken."

"You're not broken. You're changing. Change is hard. But from the looks of it, you're making all the right changes! That's what matters."

I nod silently to myself. I am doing this properly. I can't let Rey rattle my confidence. Vi and I are taking things slow. We're not rushing into anything. We're not saying "I love you." We're just together. Meeting friends. That sort of thing. Nothing major…

…even though there's a heaviness in my heart that's screaming at me to stop ignoring it.

A sensation that I've never felt before…Even with Rey.

The car ride back to Theo and Leslie's is quiet and charged with tension and unspoken words. Vi has hardly looked at me or touched me since Rey's hasty departure. I know she's probably angry about how I treated her all evening, but surely she can see why I acted as I did. She's got to understand that all of this is still difficult for me.

She offers polite goodbyes and I begin walking her back to her flat.

"You don't have to walk me home, Hayden," she croaks under the dark streetlight.

"Don't be ridiculous," I snap with exasperation as we walk at a quickening pace down the sidewalk.

"I'm not being ridiculous. I'm perfectly capable of walking my own arse back to my own flat. I don't need you."

My hand wraps around her elbow, bringing her to a halt so swiftly that she stumbles into my chest. "What are you doing?"

She refuses to look up at me even though we're pressed tightly together. "I'm just reading the writing on the wall."

"Stop," I demand and force her chin up so she looks at me. The hurt, and confusion, and pain swimming in her glossy eyes crushes me. My anger melts to heartache. "Vi, stop," I beg.

She shakes her head. "No. You hurt me tonight. I was on cloud nine with you until Rey showed up. You wouldn't even hold my hand! Are you still in love with her?"

"No, don't be daft," I scoff, looking away to hide my irritation but refusing to let Vi go.

"Well, who am I to be jealous of then? Am I jealous of Rey, or am I jealous of Leslie? I can't keep up! I'm sure Julie would be in line for a quick shag if the mood struck you!"

I swirl her around and press her up against the nearest flat surface, both my hands braced on the stone wall on either side of her head, caging her in so she remains in front of me. "This is complete shit and you know it, Vi. You know me. You know me better than anyone!"

"I thought I did, but that was before you chose to run off and confide in Leslie instead of me! That shit hurt, Hayden. How on earth do you think that makes me feel? Are you in love with your brother's fiancée?" she snaps meanly.

"Don't be ridiculous," I growl, clenching my fists in anger.

"Then why can't you talk to me?" Her voice rises to a pitch that jolts me.

"I can't tell you these things," I grind out through clenched teeth, slamming my eyes shut in utter fear.

"Why?"

"Because I don't want to scare you away!" I bark and finally look at her. Her jaw actually closes and her defiance morphs into a simpler, moody scowl. "Everything is different with you, Vi. The stakes are higher."

Her jaw shifts as she absorbs my outburst, but I can tell it's not enough. Her eyes narrow in willful determination. "I need to understand your relationship with Leslie more, Hayden. It hurts me to see you confide in her over me!" she exclaims.

"She stopped the blood!" I roar, billowing over top of my last shred of self-control. "The blood wasn't just coming from my wrists, Vi. It was coming from my heart and my soul. I hurt everywhere, but Leslie was the one to put pressure on the wound and make it stop. She made it all stop." Shocked at what I've just revealed, my hand grips Vi's hip as a painful emotion bubbles up from somewhere deep and dark inside of me. "Leslie held my head in her lap and my life in her hands. That is something a person can never forget."

Tears slide down Vi's face, and my own screws up in pain over what I keep doing to her. God, I keep making her cry over and fucking over again. But I need her to understand. I need her to keep *looking at me*. I take my hands and cup her cheeks, wiping away the tears as if the act alone can wipe away her pain.

"I will always have a certain attachment to Leslie. She helped me understand reality. She saw into my soul that night so long ago. A place that I didn't think anyone else could see…until you." I look down to try and stifle the fear ripping through my body.

Vi inhales a shaky breath and her head nods in my hands, forcing me to look up in shock at her approval. "I'm sorry, Hayden," she croaks, her voice thick with emotion. "I can't understand something like that, but I'll try. That's all I can do. I just wish…I wish I could have been there for you."

I exhale with relief and lift her chin with a gentle nudge of my knuckle. "You have no idea how much I wish the same thing. I'm the one who should be sorry. As much as I've shared with you, I struggle to share things that I still don't fully understand myself."

She nods woodenly.

"The thing is," I start, dropping a needful kiss on her forehead before pressing my own against hers "I thought I already knew the reason why I was grateful that I hadn't erased my life forever that night until you. You, Vi…*You* make me want to fight even harder to be the man I want to be."

Her taut, emotional expression softens into a look of lust and desire. She grabs my neck and pulls me down to her lips. The relief.

The absolute, ecstasy-encompassing relief I feel with her mouth on mine and the understanding that one simple act proves to my heart right now is life-changing.

"Take me home," she whimpers against my lips, sliding her hands down to grip my biceps in her small grasp. "Take me home and show me how strong you are."

I release a husky laugh against her lips. It's a laugh that makes everything inside of me lunge for her. Even with all this drama—all this fucked-up confusion—she still doesn't see me as broken. She's just a woman who wants me to fuck her senseless.

We're still us…Whatever we are.

"Are you asking what I think you're asking, Bunny?" I grin wickedly down at her, thinking about everything I could do to her.

She giggles. *God, she fucking giggles.*

"Show me rude rabbit, pretty please." Her eyebrows waggle at me suggestively.

I'm instantly hard.

The way this woman can look at me—a frail, weak, broken, and emotional fucking mess of a man—and still want me to take her home and have my way with her…Christ, if she's not it for me, no one is.

I stand behind Vi as she perches on the edge of her large, baroque-style bed. Her blonde hair cascades down her fresh, alabaster skin that is glowing in the dim evening light that pours in from the windows of her flat. Her posture is straight and perfect. Poised and ready for what I'm about to do to her. *Vi takes direction really well*, I think, smirking to myself as I crawl up behind her on the bed. She's sitting completely naked except for her cobalt blue thong that I told her to leave on. I kneel behind her. My front to her back. I nudge my erection into her back, shrouded only in a pair of black boxer briefs. She shudders out a quick, shaky breath, and it makes me smile. I reach around and stroke my fingertips from her breasts, up the front of her neck, and finally to her chin. I pull her mouth up to meet mine, her head thrown back as I tower over her.

She gasps as I drop a soft kiss on her lips. The anticipation is killing her already. Fuck. This is going to be fun.

"See these lips?" I whisper huskily against her mouth, dragging my thumb across them and watching hungrily as they plop back into place. "They're mine. Every centimetre down to the little divot right here should only crave my lips. My taste. And my power. This lower lip is for my teeth to sink into whenever I feel like it. Understand?"

I nip at her bottom lip and she lets out a husky laugh, our breaths intermingling in a heady sexy exhale of happiness. "Yes," she submissively agrees.

I kiss her firmly, cementing my point before dragging the white scarf I found in her closet across her lap. I move it up her body and over her face, draping it across her eyes as her face remains angled toward the chandelier above us.

"I'm going to lay you back, Bunny. But it's your job to hold this scarf across your eyes. We're not tying it. This is your one job. Think you can manage?"

She lets out a throaty giggle. "I'll do my best, sir."

I shake my head, grinning at her sass and mumble about her being a naughty bunny. I slide off the bed and push her back onto the mattress so her feet still remain on the floor. She holds the white scarf to her eyes by gripping each side with her fists. She squirms nervously.

I stand back and admire the scene before me. Perfect, pert breasts with the pinkest nipples I've ever seen. Creamy, smooth skin that dips in all the right places, and sexy sculpted legs that I can't wait to have wrapped around my face in two seconds.

The bed dips as I lean over her and take a nipple in my mouth.

Her hand releases the scarf and cups the back of my head. "No, no, Bunny. Hold that scarf."

She groans out in frustration, and I smile as her legs wrap around my upper body. I nip my teeth from her shoulder to her nipple. She's greedily thrusting herself up toward me, her arse rising off the bed, giving me just enough room to…

Smack.

Her lips part with a mighty groan as my palm connects with her arse, proving she was made for a rude rabbit like me. Growing impatient myself, I continue my nibble down her body until I reach her centre. She continues to squirm and writhe on the bed as I blow cool air all around her. I take my hand and push aside the strip of blue fabric that covers her. I exhale my hot breath right on her slickened nub. She moans out my name loudly. A deep throaty sound. I snap the thin strips of her thong on her hips before sliding them down her legs and tossing them on the floor.

I drop down onto my knees and grab her by her hips, yanking her to the edge of the bed so her thighs rest on my shoulders and her arse is suspended in the air for my greedy hands to fondle. *Fuck, her arse*, I think with a throaty growl. It's the most magnificent arse I've ever seen. I inhale deeply before pressing my mouth happily to her vertical lips.

A frenzy takes over as I taste her. Never in my life has a woman's scent called to me like such a siren before. Her scent was fucking made for me. Like a starving man, I devour her with all the passion I feel for this sexy, beautiful, understanding, and surprising woman.

Any time her hands stray from the blindfold, I give her pert bottom a punishing slap. I'm beginning to think she likes it based on the frequency of her disobedience. In a shorter amount of time than I anticipated, her body hardens like a bullet as she hits her climax at an alarming velocity. She screams out my name and, just as quickly, her legs sag with relief.

After a moment, she props herself up on her elbows, and I

chuckle proudly as she tosses the scarf at my face. My cock strains against my briefs as I take in her messy blonde hair that makes her look properly fucked. The pink of her cheeks glows rosy and healthy. Her lazy smile, the perfect expression a man wants to see after he's just properly serviced his most prized possession.

"Well, what do you have to say for yourself?" I ask, my smirk turning into a lustful gaze as I fantasise about how good it's going to feel when I push myself inside of her.

She smiles broadly. "If fighting with you gets me that, remind me to do it more often."

"We're just getting started." I tenderly kiss the inside of her thigh and surprise her with a playful nip.

Her giggles set the mood for our rousing round two in her shower that ended happily for both of us this time. It was the kind of fuck that would put even the sexiest pornos to shame. But it was better because it was Vi. There are no rules with her. Sexy and silly moments ebb and flow seamlessly, never once pulling us from the glorious moment.

Now I lay, once again, entangled in crushed velvet with a stunning Vi draped across my chest. I alternate twining the blonde strands of her hair between my fingers and trailing my fingertips up her bare spine while she plays with the cuff on my wrist—a custom I've noticed she enjoys doing. It took a great deal of effort on my part to allow her to do so at first, but now I can rest into it.

"How do you see me so differently, Vi?" I ask, quietly staring up at the chandelier above her bed. At times, I still can't wrap my brain around how normal she makes me feel. How normal she looks at me despite my past.

"What do you mean?" Her voice is soft and sleepy as she continues picking at the seam of my cuff without looking up at me.

I squint my eyes and elaborate. "I look in the mirror and I see a broken, suicidal screw-up with a laundry list of vices all working against him," I quietly admit. "What do you see?"

Her hand stills on my cuff and she turns to look up at me, propping her arms and head on my chest. Her blue eyes lock on mine for a long, painfully quiet moment. I stroke my fingers down her cheek as I wait on bated breath for her answer.

Finally, she tilts her head and replies with a sigh, "I just see My Hayden."

The Ruse

Vi

"I THINK I'M READY," I SAY TO BRUCE AS I WALK OUT OF MY EN suite bathroom. My jittery nerves could pipe down any time now. I smooth down my black cotton dress that's smart and hopefully good enough for what Hayden and I are about to go do. After the family flick night drama, our reconnection the last few days has been pretty mind-blowing. It's a new level of intimacy that causes me to daydream about him all day at work. The only thing that's bothered me is his continual insistence on stepping outside at 11:11 every night. I've given him his space to do so, but I have something planned for tomorrow that I hope he'll be open-minded about and not take offence to. But I'm too scared to tell him what it is quite yet.

As I walk out of my bedroom, I find Hayden stretched out on the sofa in my dark living room, staring up at the ceiling as if deep in thought. He looks like a damn model lying on a beach, except for the clothes part. Thankfully, I have a very good memory of what he looks like naked, so my imagination can fill in the blanks.

"You ready?" I ask as Sleeping at Last's cover song "500 Miles" swells in the overhead sound system.

He turns his head toward me, and the look in his eyes makes me stumble. The grey irises swirling around his pupils heat with a longing that causes my smile to fall. The city lights streaming in the windows reveal a tenderness in his expression that I don't think I've ever seen before. He stands up slowly, his eyes never leaving mine.

"What are you doing?" I ask, surprised by the trembling in my voice.

"Dance with me," he says, moving closer to me with his hand outstretched.

"What? Here?" I look around stupidly like there are people here to feel embarrassed by.

He nods. "Right here. Right now. I want a living room dance, Bunny."

A fleeting look of sadness streaks across his face, but it's replaced by a half-smile before I can be sure I even saw it. I swallow nervously as he twines his fingers through mine. His other hand slides gently around my waist, stopping at the small of my back. I place my free hand on his shoulder and he pulls me against him so our bodies are flush with each other.

With the perfect measured strum of the acoustic guitar riff in the song, he begins moving us in a slow, gentle dance. We are barely rotating, but we're swaying just enough to swirl the emotion of the music straight into my heart. The familiar scent of sawdust and Hayden invades my nostrils. I tuck my face into his chest, relishing in his entire aura that feels custom-created just for me. The song fills the room and our souls, touching us in every crease and crevice hidden to the rest of the world. In this moment, we are one.

After a few more sways, he crouches over enough to press his cheek to mine. "You're beautiful," he whispers. His voice catches just as he tucks our clasped hands between our chests.

My eyes prick with tears from the blatant display of vulnerability in his voice. "You, too," I reply because I am too electrified by him to think of anything more original. We're shrouded in our own little cocoon of affection, and everything he says and does is unexpected in the most magical way.

"You are a dream, Vi." He nuzzles into my ear, inhaling deeply as he smells my hair and the spot just below my ear. He drops a soft kiss right there and says, "Every part of you feels like a dream."

I suck in a shaky breath, remaining silent as he continues to move us in calming sways. I swear I can feel his chest shuddering beneath mine, but I'm frozen in silence, my voice refusing to speak. I have no words because this moment isn't meant for filling with obligatory exchanged words. This moment is for listening and accepting whatever grey storm he's got brewing in his stunning, cloudy eyes. He needs me right now, and it makes my heart split down the centre completely. I pray to God that Hayden Clarke will be the man to give me his other half. Two halves, making one whole.

When the song ends, his hands are in my hair and his lips are pressed to mine, soft and sweet, passionate and meaningful. His demanding tongue caresses my own as his fingers rub along the back of my neck. Just when I think my legs are going to give out, he pulls away. My eyes flutter open with slow blinks. I feel lightheaded and dizzy as he rests his forehead against mine and says, "I'm ready."

Thirty minutes later, we're standing in front of Welly's Pub. I'm grateful for the quick walk over because I needed the fresh air to gain some of my senses back. Hayden's expression is pensive. His introspective mood from earlier is somewhat lifted, but there's still something happening beyond his eyes that puzzles me.

"You sure you're ready for this?" I ask, glancing over at Hayden nervously.

"I'm not afraid of your brothers, Vi." He furrows his brows and pins me with a sobering look. "I'm afraid of you."

My face falls. "Hayden—" I start, but he pulls me through the door before I can finish.

A familiar voice calls out, ripping my attention from my Hayden bubble.

"Vi!" Tanner jogs over with a pint in hand. He tosses his head back to flick his shaggy blonde locks out of his eyes. He passes his pint off to an unsuspecting Hayden so he can yank me into his arms for a brotherly hug. "Who's this wanker?" he asks, laughing and snatching the pint back from Hayden.

"Just kidding, mate. This one's yours." He tries to pass it back.

I roll my eyes. "Hayden doesn't drink, Tanner. I told you."

"Oh yes, that's right. Vi hardly drinks either. One pint and she's pissed. I don't know what's with people like you."

I reach out to give him a shove and he dodges me easily. Hayden laughs good-naturedly, but I'm cringing inside.

"Hey, Booker!" I exclaim and smile sheepishly as he walks over. I swear his tall, muscular frame seems to grow every time I see him. "This is Hayden."

Booker shakes Hayden's hand, his eyes narrow as he scans him up and down. He looks downright impolite, which shocks me. This whole brotherly meet-and-greet was his idea. His demand, really. I had made the mistake of telling Booker that I was seeing Hayden, and he sussed it out that Hayden was the same guy I'd told him called me a "blonde distraction." He said the only way he could be convinced Hayden isn't a prat was to meet him. And there's no such thing as one Harris Brother. One goes, they all go.

Hayden and I make our way over to the booth where Camden and Gareth are seated, while Booker heads to the bar for more drinks. Gareth is properly moody toward Hayden, which doesn't surprise me. I'd warned Hayden about that. Camden is indifferent, and Tanner is Tanner. Nothing fazes him. Booker rejoins us and passes a beer to me and a water to Hayden.

"Tell us how you two lovebirds met," Tanner sings in a high-pitched feminine voice.

Camden picks up where he left off with a flick of his wrists and a happy clap. "Yes, and don't leave out a single scrumpet of detail!"

Hayden laughs and looks to me for an answer.

"Well—" I start, but he cuts me off.

"Her dog attacked me." The pleased grin on his face as he eyes me with contempt makes me giggle.

"That a boy, Bruce," Gareth mumbles and takes a drink.

"Bruce didn't attack him…More like his lead attacked you," I add, shoving Hayden in the side playfully. "We were going to a pub opening and sort of smacked into each other. The pub owners are friends with my coworker, Leslie. You guys know Leslie."

"Leslie is marrying my brother," Hayden adds helpfully, and I briefly realise the wedding is next weekend and we haven't discussed whether or not we're going together.

"Sounds like destiny," Tanner sighs dramatically and flutters his lashes. We all laugh. Tanner's always the clown.

"And just like that, smooth sailing love story," Booker states with an edge to his voice. "So, Hayden. What do you do? Like, for a living?"

Hayden's brows lift and a small smile plays on the corners of his mouth at Booker's blatant challenge. Built-wise, Booker is maybe a touch larger than Hayden, but they are very nearly evenly matched.

"I am a partial owner of a custom furniture business with my brother. C. Designs? Theo's the designer and creator. He's got a pretty large following. I'm the bookkeeper."

I frown. "Hayden's very talented as well. He's got a great eye for designing smaller detailed pieces."

Hayden pulls a face at my defensive addition to his story. "None of that is making me money yet. I just do it as a hobby for friends. For now, my brother's business keeps us very busy."

"And that earns you a proper living?" Camden barks, taking a large swig of his beer, all evidence of playing vanished. I down a gulp of mine as well.

Hayden nods. "Yeah, I'm living with my brother right now, but not because of financial reasons."

"His brother just had a baby," I interject. "She's four months old and beautiful. Hayden is great with her."

Hayden frowns at me again. "She's a great niece. I'm very attached."

"So you're close to your family then?" Tanner asks kindly.

His question makes me nervous. Diving into family details so quickly wasn't expected. I thought they'd start talking football to be honest.

Hayden swallows but keeps his tone light. "My family is great. My parents and youngest sister live in Essex. I live with my brother not far from here, and I had an older sister who passed away four years ago."

My brothers all look at him in stony silence.

"Fuck," Camden says first, his face paling slightly as he looks at me with a renewed sense of appreciation.

Gareth's moody expression turns cold and bleak. Tortured. I lean forward when his eyes start to look glossy, but Booker's comment distracts me.

"Is that why you don't drink?" Booker's prying voice is challenging and cocky, clearly not worrying over any ounce of decorum.

Hayden cuts his eyes to Booker and I see Booker actually shrink in his seat.

"Partially. It's complicated," Hayden replies, sipping his water. "So, what about you lot? Can I ask you questions, or am I the only one under fire here?"

Tanner laughs and they eagerly start discussing football. This feels better. Talk of emotions at a table full of British lads is never top on anyone's list of hot things to do in London. Gareth remains eerily silent the entire time, though, staring at his glass with morbid intent.

"Wanker," I hear Booker mumble as Hayden answers Camden's question about who his favourite footballer is.

"Booker, a word," I hiss, knowing I can't take another second of his pouty teenager act. I pop out of the booth, motioning with my head like a maniac. "Can I trust you guys not to be arses while I'm gone?"

"Probably not," Camden replies, taking a swig. "But it's worth a shot."

I roll my eyes and Booker follows me to the loo hallway. I stop and turn a murderous gaze on him. "What the hell, Booker?" I seethe, barely able to contain my temper.

"What?" he barks back defensively.

"What are you trying to do? Win the award for the biggest arse of a brother? Christ! I expect it from them, but not you. You're supposed to be on my side."

"He's not good enough, Vi," he snaps back, shoving a hand through his short brown hair.

"You've barely spoken to him!"

"I don't have to. I can tell. He doesn't drink *at all*," he growls. "What is he? A recovering alcoholic? Boy, you really picked a winner."

I shove him hard and catch him off guard enough that he stumbles back into the wall. "You listen here, baby brother. I'm still your big sister. I practically raised you. If I tell you someone's important, they're bloody important. End of."

"Everything okay?" Hayden asks, coming around the corner. He narrows his eyes knowingly.

I cut one more withering glance at Booker. "Everything's fine."

"Okay, well a pack of fans have descended and Gareth told me you'd know what to do?" Hayden looks at me and shrugs his shoulders.

I nod and sigh. Welly's is supposed to be sacred. The pub owner loves the guys and keeps a lid on the fact that they stop in regularly. Most pubs broadcast it for business, so I suppose it was bound to happen eventually.

"All right, just hang back here with Booker. It'll be easier for us to get out that way." I throw a warning look at Booker, and he nods subtly knowing that Hayden is not to be messed with right now.

I pull off my denim jacket and toss it haphazardly at Booker. Hayden eyes me in confusion as I crack my neck and put on my own game face. I stroll over to our booth and blanch at the larger than expected crowd swarming the table. There are at least six middle-aged blokes decked out in football fan gear. Super fans to be sure. Two have slid into the vacated side where Hayden and I were seated. Gareth seems to be blocking anyone from sitting down next to him.

I clear my throat loudly as I approach and poke one gentleman on the shoulder. "Oi! Pardon me, but I need to talk to that bloke right fucking there." I hitch up my accent to sound thicker and more Manchester by dropping off the ends of most of my words.

The heavier-set man of the bunch turns on me with his nose wrinkled. He reeks of alcohol and fish n' chips. "Get stuffed." He turns back to the table like I don't even exist.

I could be offended by his cheek. However, I'm a Harris, so I'm not easily derailed. I tap the man next to him. This guy has to be pushing fifty and idolising Gareth like he's fucking royalty. "That fucking footballer has loads of explaining to do, so I fucking need to get in there. Get out of my way!" I exclaim, ramping up my performance to be a bit more dramatic.

Several of the guys turn to look at me, clearing a path for me to slide through. Gareth's eyes land on me with a silent cheer of appreciation. Then he realises he's on, so he's got to react.

"Freya! What on earth are you doing here?"

"Don't you Freya me. Your arse is coming with me, mate. You haven't rang me in weeks!" I crow out in my best jilted female voice. "And bring those worthless brothers of yours. All of you are about to get it good from me and me flatmates."

"Oi, shove off ya bird," one bloke croaks from a few bodies over.

I frown and motion for Gareth to come along. He attempts to slide out, but the older man steps in front of him. "You don't have to shove off just 'cause of this fucking jersey chasing slag!"

My jaw drops and Gareth's eyes turn a menacing shade of brown. I've done this little song and dance for Gareth several times before, and most blokes are keen to sit back and enjoy the show of a pro footballer getting his butt chewed from a relationship gone array. Gareth and I have become quite good at our performances. He even lets me slap him across the face if we get going really well. This has satisfied years of oppression that I suffered for being the only Harris in our household who could never break out of a headlock.

"She ain't no jersey chaser," the heavy one says. "I think she's a proper tart. How much for a rub and tug, blondie?"

The man lays his sweaty palm right on my arse, and Gareth's eyes turn to flames as he lunges across the table. But before Gareth's hands connect with his throat, the man's body is wrenched backward and out of the throng of people.

Shouting begins all around me, and I shove past the gawking crowd to see what's happening. My eyes turn wide when I realise it's Hayden who has the man in a painful-looking headlock. It reminds me of the full nelson wrestling hold they do in America. The man's lip is bleeding and one eye is partially closed from a fresh punch. His obese belly is hanging out from beneath his jumper as he struggles to breathe against his arms that Hayden has gripped up under his ears.

"Fucking apologise to her," Hayden roars, his face beet red with a fury I've never seen in him before. His arms bulge angrily beneath his shirt as he holds his restraint firmly.

The other men make a move for Hayden. In a blink, Gareth twists one guy's arm behind his back, causing the man to drop on the ground, writhing in pain. Tanner and Camden shove a couple others away from Hayden and stand as a protective barrier between them.

"She's a fucking jersey chasing cow! What the fuck are you on about, mate?" the man grumbles, causing Hayden to crank his hold on him. The guy cries out with a high-pitch squeal that would be comical in any other setting.

"Fucking apologise!" Hayden roars again, a vein popping out

angrily on his forehead.

"All right! I'm fucking sorry! I'm sorry!" the man screams. Hayden releases him and gives him a swift kick in the arse, toppling him into the feet of his mates.

Just then, Booker shows up, joined by the bar owner with a menacing-looking bat. "Don't try a thing, or I'll call the cops on the lot of ya."

Everyone freezes but Hayden, who moves toward me and places a hard hand on my back. He quickly walks me to the door. I glance back and see the bar owner pointing the bat at the football fans with a look that says not to fucking try a thing.

"Hayden," I say as we step outside into the night.

He avoids eye contact with me as he nervously looks up and down the street. As if some divine intervention has been bestowed upon us, a large fifteen-passenger taxi van is parked on the corner letting out another group of football-looking fans. Why the hell are these guys all coming out of the woodwork tonight? Is it fantasy draft night or something? Regardless, we have a getaway vehicle now.

Hayden grabs my hand and pulls me down the sidewalk just as my brothers barrel out of the pub. "This way," he shouts over his shoulder to them.

We get to the open door of the van. The driver looks like he's about to argue, but Hayden says, "Two hundred quid for a quick lift."

"Five hundred," Gareth says, hopping in past us without pause.

The driver's eyes grow wide as the rest of my brothers barrel in after him.

Hayden holds my hand to help me up, but I pause at the step. "Are you okay?" I ask, touching his face.

He yanks away from me and snaps with an acerbic tone, "Fine, get in. We need to leave."

Hayden folds in behind me. "We should drop you guys first. I don't want them seeing where Vi lives if they get it up their arses to follow." He turns to look behind us but seems satisfied enough to turn and face ahead again.

"Smart thinking," Camden says, then leans forward to give directions to the driver.

"Vi, I'm so sorry," Gareth starts, punching the back of his seat angrily. "I never would have had you do that if I thought those wankers were that belligerent."

I shake my head and start to reply.

"She shouldn't have done it to begin with. Belligerent or not." Hayden's voice is cold and threatening.

"Look—" Gareth starts, leaning forward to get in Hayden's face, but Booker's voice stops him in his tracks.

"He's fucking right, Gareth." I turn around to see Booker staring angrily out the window from the far back row. "That's the last time you have Vi get you out of a fan jam. Get a fucking bodyguard. It's not like you can't afford one."

The van grows eerily quiet as our baby brother's chastisement descends over us.

"It's not all Gareth's fault. I'm a big girl. I chose to do it," I say, coming to his defence.

"Well, you chose wrong," Hayden growls. "Had I known what you were doing—"

"I still would have done it! You're not my boss, Hayden," I snap.

"Vi," Camden warns.

"What? It's true. I'm not going to let you all manhandle me into what you think is best for me. This is horse shit. I'm a fucking adult. I'm tired of you all interfering."

"Vi!" Tanner snaps out of nowhere. "I'm bloody grateful Hayden was there tonight. That scene was rubbish and scary as fuck! I for one am glad you have him. Just stop with the independent woman, feminist shit and say thank you to your bloke for defending you the way he did. It could have been so much worse."

Tanner's outburst stuns me. He rarely gets ruffled feathers and holy shit are his feathers ever ruffled right now.

"I am thankful you were there, Hayden," I whisper to him. He still hasn't looked at me. I want him to understand, though, that I don't have to be taken care of all the time or scolded like a child. My independence is important to me. But he looks like he's warring over something bigger than the pub skirmish. I want to push the issue, but I need him to come back to me first. "I'm sorry," I say softly. He still won't look at me and the lower part of his jaw shifts as if he's in pain. I grab his hand and twine my fingers with his. His shoulders drop, and he finally turns his glossy eyes to me. "I'm really sorry."

The anxiety and fear-stricken look on Hayden's face makes me feel ill. I rub the backs of my fingers down his cheek, and he exhales a breath he's been holding for miles. He leans into me and rubs his nose on my temple, sucking in a shaky breath. The touch feels important, like he's telling himself that it's okay for him to care about me.

After a few moments of driving in silence as we all stew about how bad that could have been, Tanner lightens the mood.

"Think you might have lost some fans tonight, bro."

We all burst out laughing, and I glance over and see the corners of Hayden's mouth turn up. Eventually, we pull up to our dad's Chigwell house. My brothers each give Hayden a matey pat on the back before exiting the vehicle. Gareth stops and makes it a point to shake Hayden's hand. They exchange a silent, heavy look and then we depart, back to Brick Lane.

Scars

Hayden

SEEING THAT DISGUSTING SPECIMEN OF A MAN PUT HIS HAND ON Vi made everything inside my body snap. My mind, my temper, my muscles, my sanity.

My heart.

The word "mine" screamed in my head as I bulldozed through the crowd and wrenched him away from her. The scene was so much worse than the one with Ethan at Club Shay. I actually feared for Vi's safety tonight. A fear that ripped through me like a pain that I've never felt before.

Fuck.

Fuck!

This is all happening too fast. Too quick. Too much. She's just so open, and trusting, and giving. She's got no idea about the deeply rooted fear that lives inside of me every time I'm with her. We make our way up to her flat in a heavy silence. A silence that I'm not even sure how to fill at this point.

I'm fucking falling for Vi. And it terrifies me so much because she somehow turns me into a loose cannon. I lose all my control and all my sense. The immense possessiveness I have inside me regarding her safety and well-being is terrifying.

"Do you want to talk about tonight?" she quietly asks, squatting down in the dark kitchen to pat Bruce affectionately as he laps at the fresh water she's just poured for him.

I sigh heavily and ruffle my hair. "To be frank, I just want to take you to bed and bury myself inside of you until I can't think anymore." I don't tell her that being inside her is the only time I feel like I truly have her.

She rises to her feet, watching me with a sombre expression. Then she bends over and peels her dress up over her head. Her hair cascades around her shoulders as she stands before me in nothing but a black strapless bra, a black thong, and her black heels.

Desire throttles me as she drops the dress on the floor. In four strides, I'm on her. Kissing her harshly and painfully. Roughly, I toss her up on top of the counter, and she flinches at the cold granite against her bare arse. I grab her jaw gruffly, squeezing tightly as I cut my narrowed eyes to hers in warning.

Her head tilts back as her pink tongue darts out to wet her lips. I place my finger in her mouth to jerk her face back down. She responds with a firm bite into my flesh and then soothes the connection with a deep suck on my digit from root to tip. I pull it out and punish her harder with my tongue, thrusting it deep into her mouth so that she only feels my presence in her, snuffing out any sensation of her own returned kiss.

When I break away from her, arousal floods into the pools of her eyes. She wants it. She feeds off of it. My aggressive passion. She bites her lip and grips my shirt, ripping it open with one harsh yank. The sound of buttons hitting the counter and floor don't slow her from tearing off my shirt. She kisses my peck and rubs my bulge through my denim pants, releasing a sexy as fuck moan as I thrust my cock into her greedy hand.

Unable to wait another second, I cup her arse and lift her up so she wraps her legs around my waist. They grip me tightly as I walk us into her bedroom, shutting the French doors on Bruce's crestfallen face.

I toss her sexy fucking body down on the bed and lie on top of her. "What do you want, Bunny?" I ask, my voice husky. "Tell me and I'll give it to you." *I'll give you anything*, I think to myself.

Her long lashes lift and her blue eyes twinkle, piercing me with something I didn't expect. "Make love to me," she says.

My heart seizes in my chest and I huff out a nervous breath.

Her face falls as she stammers, "I didn't mean—"

I cut her off, kissing the doubt right off her mouth. I swallow it whole and bury it deep inside of me to live with the self-doubt that is commonplace in my own soul. I frantically tear off the few pieces of fabric separating our skin-to-skin contact and work toward kissing every bare inch of her luscious body. Finally, our mouths reconnect as I rest my back against her grand headboard and she straddles me. My bare cock pulses with need against her slickened folds.

Assurances that condoms are no longer necessary happened the last time we were intimate, so I'm rock-hard with anticipation of feeling her bare on me for the first time. She places my tip at her entrance and quirks a sexy brow as she slowly slides down on top of me. I groan loudly at the incredibly intimate wetness gripping my shaft. My fingers bite into her lush thighs as I breathe deeply to maintain some control of myself.

Fuuuuuck. She feels so fucking good. So fucking right. So fucking everything.

I bring her mouth down to mine, desperate to connect our bodies even further as she gyrates against me. Her tight nipples brush against my chest and I cup the heaviness of one breast in my hand. Needing to taste her everywhere, I break our kiss to pay homage to her perfect, pink bud. I suck hard and tap my teeth down lightly. She cries my name out with a throaty moan.

Hugging her tightly as she sits astride me, I swallow hard at the glorious intimacy of this encounter. The closeness I feel having her like this.

Suddenly, my leather cuff catches in her hair, and I quickly detach it to bring my hands forward to continue their exploration of her body. She stops my action by gripping both of my wrists in her hands. Her small hands clasp around the worn brown leather.

My eyes find hers in confusion and she gives me a look that scares me. "No, Vi," I say in a warning tone. I attempt to pull my wrists free, but she isn't easily deterred.

"Please, Hayden." She says my name so reverently that I close my eyes, begging for my will to be strong. I want to give this woman everything, but only what I have in me to give. She has me. She has all of me, yet she still asks for more.

Sudden tears burn in my eyes. I open them to find her watching me with a soft, warm expression. She leans in and kisses both of my cheeks comfortingly.

"Please, Vi," I beg, my voice quaking with fear. "I don't think I can."

Her face remains calm, serene, loving. "I'm here, Hayden," she says. "You can."

Her blonde hair fans a wall beside us as she looks down and takes one of my wrists in both of her hands. With my palm facing up, she releases one snap of the leather cuff. A sharp intake of breath on my part has her eyes looking up at me. She nods slowly before releasing the second snap, then the third, all the while maintaining eye contact with me. My hand tremors as she opens the cuff to reveal the bumpy ridge of the scar along my wrist. I look away ashamed, traumatised, and completely fucking sickened.

Two wet lips touch the scar, and I hiss in horror as my eyes find hers. She leans back again and takes my other wrist in her hands, popping the buttons on that one and repeating the same soft kiss.

I shake my head and sniff. "They're hideous."

"They're mine," she says, kissing them softly again and holding them to her bare chest over her heart.

My eyes look to hers in a pleading surrender. I've given her so much. So much she still can't even possibly understand. But the intimacy of this is overwhelming. I can barely look at the scars myself and this woman…This woman worships them.

She strokes my hands over her chest and adds, "Your scars make you My Hayden." She inhales a shaky breath and utters three soft words that I'd never imagine hearing from a woman seeing me this way. "I love you."

Sadness lifts from my soul at her proclamation and the absolute devotion swimming in her eyes. She loves me? How? How can she possibly love me after everything I've told her? What kills me-—what completely guts me—is the attachment and love she displays for every part of me. All of my flaws. All of my darkness.

She looks at me as if my scars allow her to love me even more.

My voice is gone. Unwilling or unable to reply and return her feelings. Probably both. A knot creeps up my throat because I'm not even sure I have that emotion in me to reciprocate in the way she needs me to. It died inside me a long time ago, and I have nothing more to give her. And fuck! She deserves it. Vi deserves *more*. So much more.

Instead of watching her loving eyes turn to pain from my silence, I yank her to me, slamming my lips to hers in a hard, all-consuming kiss. It's all I can give her right now.

My touch. My passion. Even my pain.

As I hug her body to mine, the silky skin of her back feels foreign as it brushes against my bare wrists.

Scars against flesh.

Hearts against souls.

And it's in that one moment that 11:11 ticks by and I physically choose to live in this moment and not wish for another.

If only it didn't make me feel so wrecked.

Everything in Numbers

Vi

I GLANCE OUTSIDE MY PATIO DOOR TO SEE HAYDEN LEANING OVER the railing. His head hanging, his posture sagging. I turn to the clock.

11:11.

I watch him carefully and can tell he's doing his ritual. As much as I wish it didn't, it feels like a personal strike to my heart. Last night was so tender, so meaningful, so completely intimate.

And then it wasn't.

He held me afterward and asked me if I would be his date for Theo and Leslie's wedding next weekend. I even laughed when he begged me to wear a red dress. He continued to whisper the most beautiful things in my ear as I drifted off to sleep, but never the three words I wanted to hear most from him.

God, how could I be so stupid? I held him over a barrel last night, asking to see his scars. Then I had to ruin everything by saying I love him. I thought once he opened his cuffs to me, things would change. No more barriers. No more shields. No more rituals. But there he stands, outside my flat, wishing away his past and his current life.

My stomach drops. My only hope is that what I have planned for today will be a turning point for him. If it is, I hope he'll come home with me for family dinner tomorrow night.

"You ready?" I ask as he strides back inside. I paint a happy smile on my face.

It feels forced until his hard grey gaze lifts to mine and his eyes warm with affection. God, his smile. It makes me want to forget everything that happened last night and take him to the movies.

"Still not telling me where we're going?" he asks, sliding his feet into his shoes. What is it that's so sexy about a man walking around barefoot in your flat?

"It's a surprise," I wiggle my eyebrows playfully.

The cab drops us off in front of a familiar building in Notting Hill, and Hayden cuts me a skeptical look. "Is Benji pissed again?"

I chuckle. "Nope."

"Are we here because he wants to re-ignite our love connection?" he asks with a smug tone. "He was a pretty good kisser."

I giggle and slide my hand into his. "Nope. Just have to trust me!"

We check in with the doorman and head up to the second floor toward Benji's aunt's flat. I smirk thinking about how cross Hayden was the night he helped me get Benji home after the gala. So much has changed in so little time.

I knock on the door, and Agitha Abernathy opens it, looking a bit more put together than the last time we saw her. She's a short, round woman with ample breasts concealed beneath a pink sweater set with cream trousers. Her hair is permed and sculpted to the shape of her head, looking as if an entire can of hairspray has set it to be so.

"Aunt Agitha," I smile broadly. "Vi Harris. Thank you for

agreeing to do this!" I shake her hand. "This is my…boyfriend… Hayden Clarke." I bite my lip realising it's the first time I've referred to Hayden as my boyfriend. The slip wasn't lost on him either as the corner of his mouth lifts in appreciation.

Her chubby fingers grip Hayden's large hand. She looks between the two of us. "Glad to see you two figured things out."

I frown. "What do you mean?" I ask curiously.

She beams happily. "We'll get to that. Come, come! And please, call me Aggie." She bustles us into her flat that looks like it's a snippet of English Home and Country Magazine. My eyes widen as I see hutch, after hutch, after hutch filled with…

"Salt and pepper shakers!" she sings, answering my silent question. "I'm a bit of a collector. I have a set dated back to King George the III! Do you want to see it?"

After a polite amount of time oohing and aahing over her collection, she leads us into her kitchen. Benji is out of town, apparently at a comic book convention, which is extra convenient for me. I prefer to not have him around while we do this.

She offers us a seat at her round, retro-style table with sea foam green chairs and a white and green designed top. It's a bright room with lots of natural light streaming in from the pigeon-scattered window. On the table, she's got some votive candle holders, a deck of tarot cards, and what appear to be some tuning forks.

"I haven't told him why we're here yet, Aggie, so just one second." I look at Hayden's quizzical expression as he adjusts in his chair to face me. "Hayden, Benji's aunt is a psychic."

"Okay," he replies slowly, his expression wary.

"She specialises in numerology." I touch his arm encouragingly and he instinctively shifts closer to me.

"Interesting," Hayden says politely, crossing his cuff-covered wrists over each other on the table.

"I thought we could talk to her about 11:11 a bit." My eyes watch him as I see it all click together.

His jaw clenches.

"All due respect, Miss Aggie, I'm not sure this is necessary." He moves to stand up, so I hold him down.

"What could it hurt to get a little background information on the number, Hayden? It could be really interesting."

His jaw shifts side-to-side, but I see that look in his eyes. That look that shows how utterly difficult it is for him to say no to me. "Fine," he snaps and shifts in closer to the table.

Aggie beams. "Brilliant! So tell me, what specifically do you want to discuss today, love?"

I look at Hayden, who is doing his best to remain polite but is visibly struggling with this idea.

"Well, Aggie, my boyfriend here has a strong connection with the time 11:11, and I wondered what kinds of things you can tell us about the meaning behind that number. I assume you may have some insight."

"Oh yes, certainly. I've studied numerology for many years and it is incredible how much it plays a part in our everyday lives." She moves her glasses to the top of her head and leans her plump arms on the table as she continues. "Some say that 11:11 is the angelic hour. It's when your angels can send you messages. Specifically noticing it on a regular basis is often times the Universe's way of providing a wake-up call so to speak. It's a sign that you're about to embark on a journey of discovery."

"How do you mean?" I ask, glancing at Hayden, who seems to be listening intently.

"Well, often times, 11:11 can help you unlock parts of your sub-conscious that you have maybe been hiding from yourself or not sharing with anyone. It's a symbol to help you get in sync with the greater workings of the Universe. The Universe has a purpose for you. Whether you believe it or not, there's a reason you're alive!" She chuckles gaily.

I cringe recalling how in Hayden's speech, he said he chose the time 11:11 to slit his wrists. I want to ask her about the meaning behind it, but I don't want Hayden to feel completely ambushed.

"Why do people say to make a wish at 11:11?" Hayden demands, surprising me. I look at him, and he's eyeing Aggie very seriously.

"Oh yes, that's definitely what lots of people do when they see that time, isn't it? Make a wish!" she snickers. "I think that began because 11:11 is a sign that our innermost thoughts are turning into reality, so you see it and you take control of making blessings in your life happen."

"But what does it mean if you're only wishing to change the past?" Hayden's hand finds my knee beneath the table, and he squeezes it for reassurance. I place mine over his.

Aggie's face turns grave, and I notice the stunning clear blueness of her eyes, almost as if they are colourless. They were so small when she was smiling before that I never got a good look. She reaches out and touches Hayden's hand. The loose skin on her cheek tremors ever so slightly. "Your heart is heavy with a large burden, love. But you are seeing 11:11 for a positive reason that has everything to do with the present and your future, and nothing to do with your past."

She cuts her eyes to me with a meaningful look. I pull back slightly. "What is it?" I ask.

"Her." She gestures to me while looking at Hayden like he will get it. He remains still, so she looks to me again. "Tell me, Vi. Does 11:11 hold any significance to you?"

My face freezes. I didn't expect her to turn this on me. I'm even more floored that she knows to ask me anything about it. I refuse to lie to Aggie when she was generous enough to do this for me, but I'm kicking myself for not telling Hayden all of this before we got here.

I nod.

"Well go on then, love, tell us." She nods encouragingly at me, her transparent eyes sparkling with anticipation.

I swallow hard, the room suddenly feeling very still and quiet. The hum of the fridge halts and even the pigeons outside her window stop flapping about. "My mother died on November eleventh."

She smiles knowingly. "And you have a special connection to your mother, correct?"

Nodding, I add, "I share my birthday with her."

"And the two of you are Geminis, correct?" She beams.

My mouth opens. "Yes, my birthday is June fifth."

"Oh, how funny," she replies. "Six plus five equals—"

"Eleven," Hayden finishes.

Aggie chuckles and begins shuffling through her papers. She pulls one out to show us. "Gemini is the Zodiac house of twins, symbolised here." She points to the sheet. "See? Two pillars joined at the top and base, which is a representation of the twins seated side by side with embracing arms. Similar to an eleven, don't you think?"

Hayden's hand moves from my lap. His eyes are wide and accusing when I turn to him. "How could you not mention that about your mum?"

I shake my head nervously. "11:11 seemed so important to you, and I didn't want to scare you. You were already spooked by the fact that I live on the eleventh floor."

"Oh!" Aggie chuckles. "The Universe is a wicked creature sometimes, isn't she? This is all so perfect."

"Perfect? Why?" I ask, looking back at her.

"Because you two are each other's twin flame, of course!" Hayden and I stare at her in confusion. She chortles, "I felt it plain as day when I first saw you the night you brought my naughty rat-arsed nephew home. Surely you two have sensed it since then. I couldn't believe you held out as long as you did. That deep, burning, pulling connection is intense, isn't it?" She twines her hands together in a powerful grip to visualise.

"What do you mean? What are twin flames?" I ask, my mind reeling.

"It's like this…You've heard of soulmates, right? Well, twin flames have an even deeper connection that supersedes soulmates.

The moment you meet your twin flame is the moment the earth beneath your feet begins to shift."

My memory flashes back to the night Bruce knocked Hayden over outside The White Swan Pub. The energy between us was just chemistry. An obvious physical attraction, nothing more. Yes, it was intense. More intense than with any man I'd ever met. But I thought that was because it was Hayden. And Hayden is well…Hayden. I'm not all together sure I believe whatever it is Aggie is trying to say we are.

"I've never even heard that term before," I state dismissively.

"Twin flames are mirrored souls because they essentially reflect the deepest needs, desires, dreams, and even the dark elements of our souls. The yucky stuff. They can accept and absorb."

A loud scratch echoes in the small kitchen as Hayden shoots up from his chair.

"Hayden!" I exclaim as he turns and strides out of the room. I look at Aggie with wide, apologetic eyes. "I'm so sorry."

Her face looks crestfallen. "I'm sorry if I've spoken out of turn, love."

"No, you did just what I wanted you to do. It's been a very enlightening day. I think he's just overwhelmed. Truly, though. Thank you."

She nods, but her face still appears sympathetic. "It's all right, love. You two take care."

I nod and run after Hayden, hustling down the stairs and out onto the busy Notting Hill road. Traffic whizzes by nosily as I step around a group of tourists hopping off a red, double-decker bus.

"Hayden," I shout when I see him storming down the sidewalk.

His shoulders tense at the sound of my voice, but he slows. When I get nearer, he turns his head and barks at me like a wild animal. "I hope you're fucking happy, Vi."

I recoil, clearly underestimating his reaction to Aggie's reading. "What do you mean? Happy about what?"

His face pulls a menacing expression as he stops and turns to look at me. "We're destined to be together, so now I'm all better. All healed. Isn't that lucky for you."

"Hayden, stop it." I reach out to touch him, but he pulls away from me.

"I don't know what you were after in there, but whatever crap that scamming quack just told us is rubbish." He grips one of his cuffs and shoots accusing daggers at me.

"She's a nice woman, Hayden," I retort, my tone defensive. "It wasn't a scam. She did it as a favour. I didn't even pay her."

He scoffs loudly. "So now what? I'm just supposed to accept you as my twin flame and we go run off into our mythological future together, happily ever after? Life doesn't fucking work like that, Vi."

"I never said it does!" I exclaim, crossing my arms over my chest for some semblance of comfort. We've argued before, but never like this. "I was only trying to help you understand. I didn't know she was going to say all that."

He huffs out a mean, menacing laugh and a scary, dark cynicism shadows his eyes. "You don't get it, Vi. You haven't suffered as I have. There's no quick fix for me. There's no easy bandage for my kind of pain."

"Pain is pain, Hayden!" I screech in frustration and mindlessly stamp my foot. His eyes glower down at the action. "You don't have to have suffered through the worst of pain to have empathy."

"I don't need your empathy!" he shouts, his tone reaching a high, manic level. I think I prefer the dark, ominous Hayden better. He shoves his hands through his hair, yanking at the roots before letting go. "I've been trying to protect what I have going here. Telling myself that I don't need you in order to be healthy because I'm doing this all on my own. Then you take me to that crazy bird who tells me you're my life mate!"

"Stop," I grind out through clenched teeth, but it falls on deaf ears.

"It's fucking mental, Vi! All of it. One person can't depend on another that much. Soulmates? Christ. We ran into each other. I thought you were hot. End of. Let's not magic this into something bigger than it is."

My legs feel like they've been kicked out from under me, but he still doesn't slow.

"And what's with you hiding shit from me? I've told you so much, Vi. So much that you could write a damn book about me. You hiding that stuff about your mum feels like I've been lied to all this time."

My stomach convulses in response to his spot-on accusation. "I wanted to mention it, but I was scared, Hayden. I never knew much about my mum, and it's always been an odd feeling to share my birthday with someone I barely remember. So to have her death anniversary mean something to you would mean another part of my life is tainted by her. And 11:11 is important to you. Not me."

"Oh, whatever," he growls. "I was doing fine on my own until you came along. I made it through Reyna, through rehab, through living with my parents, through a bloody speech at the gala. I'll make it through you. I don't need to depend on anyone in order to be healthy."

Needles prick behind my eyes.

"And what happens when I go off the rails again? What then?" he snaps, his gaze glacial as he steps within inches of my face, towering over me with his most intimidating stance. His scent toys with my emotions as his hot breath on my face speaks in acerbic tones. "I'm going to crash, and I'll take both of us down with me. You're going to get caught in the crossfire, and I will ruin you. If what that woman said has an ounce of truth to it and you are my twin flame, then that means anything I do has the potential to fucking kill you. It might not be with a blade across your wrists, but I promise you it will hurt."

I bite my lip as tears flood my vision. I look away, my face fixed and frozen. I need to remain silent so he stops.

Just wait until he's finished, Vi. Just wait. He's just processing. Saying anything right now would be like poking a bear. Don't poke the bear.

He moves to walk away, but I catch his arm as quiet words escape my constricting throat. "Getting hurt is part of being alive."

"Alive?" He swerves back to me with a haughty bark of a laugh. "That's a joke when you're talking about me." He slides his hands up my wrists and clutches my arms harshly. "Look at me, Vi. You don't have anything good with me. It's best you find that out now."

His face crushes me. His eyes are merely hollow shells of the man who's been opening up to me the last few weeks. He moves to turn away from me, but before he lets go of my arms, an explosion erupts from the very depths of my soul.

"You don't get to keep forever to yourself!" I scream loudly into his face and shove his chest with all my might. He blinks hard as if the outburst broke some protective shell around him. My emotional shove proves more effective than my physical. Acidic tears slide over my lips and into my mouth, the salty liquid doing nothing to quench the burning in my chest. My spit is thick in my throat as I touch my hands to his face. He flinches like the tips of my fingers are made of razor blades. My voice trembles as I utter, "Hayden, I love you."

His expression turns grim, and he deftly yanks free from my grasp. "Vi, I need to be on my own." His voice is calm and professional as he backs away from me, like he's addressing a business transaction. "This isn't good for my recovery."

I swallow back the thickness bubbling up as every insecurity from my entire life starts pulling at me like quicksand. Like the underworld is reaching up from beneath the ground and dragging me down into the depths of Hell. "Hayden, if it's that you're scared or you're unsure, I get it. But if it's me, have the courage to tell me. If you don't love me, then that is something I *can't* help you through." I fist my hands against my chest in agony over the doom I feel coming. "At this point, either you love me or you don't. There is no way you don't know by now."

Sobs crack from my throat as I look at Hayden and all he offers me is a pitying expression. All the days we spent revealing the deepest parts of our lives, gone. Vanished. The pain is horrifying.

I look into his eyes one last time, and everything I love about him is magnified. His heart, his pain, his passion, his temper. I'm looking at everything I want.

And he's looking at me like a charity case.

Without waiting for his verbal confirmation, I walk to the edge of the sidewalk and wave down a passing cab. I slide onto the smooth leather and crumble inside the quietness.

I don't look back. I can't look back.

My broken man…

…just broke me.

Relapse

Hayden

MY KNUCKLES TURN WHITE AS I GRIP A BOTTLE OF BEER nestled inside the cooler door amongst a sea of other brown bottles. I blink furiously against the flickering neon lights casting a putrid green glow on the back of my hand. On the back of my scarred, mangled, fucked-up hand. I didn't even make the conscious decision to step inside this rundown corner shop that has the faint smell of ammonia and urine. I barely even noticed the foreign man behind the counter shouting into his mobile in another language.

But, here I am, staring at row after row of assorted booze inside a supermarket cooler section.

Seeing the bottle in my hand, my eyes narrow. I squeeze the base of it. Hard. Harder. It doesn't break. I'm not strong enough. *I'm fucking weak.* I have to choose between climbing up an enormous mountain or falling down a slippery hill. Rage explodes inside of me over that realisation. I yank the bottle from the cooler. The door slams shut as I swing my arm back as far as I can and launch the offensive bottle onto the ground by my feet. The scent of beer invades my nose as the amber liquid splashes on my pants. My boots crunch the shiny glass as I move back into the fridge to grab two more bottles that are staring me down at eye level. I hold them in place and squeeze them as hard as I can, letting out a garbled grunt when I still can't break the fucking glass.

The man at the counter begins shouting in a foreign language. I release the bottles in frustration and, without pause, storm down the aisle, chucking a twenty-pound note on the counter as I stride out the door. My walk turns faster and faster, eventually shifting into a full-on run. I sprint through the busy and narrow streets with cabbies honking at me at nearly every intersection. I run and run until my lungs are about to explode. In the end, I find myself back in Shoreditch in front of C. Designs. My stomach roils as I hunch over, propping my hands on my knees for support. Silently screaming in agony, my chest rises and falls in terrifyingly fast measures.

Theo's eyes catch sight of me through the window while he works a skill saw on a slab of raw wood. His expression drops, and he sets down the saw and runs out to me.

"Hayden, what happened?" His footsteps come to a thundering halt beside me, and he squats to look up at my face. I continue panting, unable to respond, and his eyes frown down at my wet trousers. He sniffs. "Have you been fucking drinking?"

I scowl and shake my head aggressively, standing up and clutching my side as I continue to heave huge gulps of air into my lungs.

"You're lying. You reek of alcohol," he accuses, his brown eyes icy slits as he rises up to his feet. "What the fuck, Hayden? How could you?"

"I didn't!" I snap, shoving him in the chest angrily just as Leslie appears over his shoulder.

She's pushing Marisa in a pram. Her green eyes widen with fear as Theo grabs me by my shirt and pulls me to his face. "Goddammit, Hayden! You're going to throw it all away again. A fucking years' worth of work, and for what?"

I go limp in his arms, and he stares back at me in confusion as I gesture over his shoulder with my chin. His head turns and lands on Leslie. Instantly, his grip releases my shirt.

"Tell me what I'm seeing isn't true," Leslie says, her voice shaky, further penetrating my aching heart.

Theo clasps his glasses and eyes me harshly. "Hayden's been drinking."

"No I haven't!" I roar and fight the urge to punch my fucking arrogant arse of a brother in the nose. I glance briefly at the pram, and it snuffs my burning rage when I hear Marisa begin to fuss. My heart bleeds inside my chest at the sound.

"Leslie," I beg. "Please, you have to believe me. I haven't been drinking. I swear to you. I broke a bottle at the corner store. I was going to buy it. I wanted to buy it. I wanted to drink the whole bloody thing, but I smashed it instead." My eyes slam shut at the fact that, in a flash, I'm back to being the sad, pathetic baby brother whom everyone feels sorry for. And it didn't even take me getting drunk to do it.

Leslie pushes the pram over to Theo, who exhales deeply, attempting to calm down with Marisa closer to him now. She walks over to me and cups my face in her hands. Her green eyes are glossy as she sniffs my breath. I begin to moan, feeling like the fucking spit on someone's shoe, but she catches me off guard when she pulls me down into her arms...

...for a hug.

She hugs me.

She tucks my head to her chest and she fucking hugs me.

Just when I thought I was already broken beyond recognition.

My heart splinters.

I begin quaking in her arms and squint at my watch through my tears even though I know there's not a shot in hell that it could be 11:11. But I wish it were. I wish so much that it were. I wish my own sister were here holding me. I wish I weren't shattering into a shred of the man I was before. I wish so many things, but the one wish I want the most is something I possibly just ruined forever.

I let everything in my life get so fucked, and now all this tiny redhead wants to do is hug me.

After an insurmountable amount of time, Theo interrupts my strangled sobs with a soft tap on my shoulder. I release Leslie with a loud sniff and wipe aggressively at my eyes. I look up and see Marisa's wide, beautiful baby blues staring back at me. I release another throaty sob as Theo holds her out for me to take.

I slide my hands beneath her small arms and tuck her against my chest, pressing my cheek on the top of her head. My arms tremble as I purse my lips into a thin line to conceal the emotional pain of the trust he's just given me in this moment. Exhaling a few more aching cries, I allow my heart to regulate with hers...

Calming...

Soothing...

Beating...

Alive.

"Where's my fussy girl?" I joke, and Leslie and Theo burst out into an emotionally thick laugh.

Theo tucks Leslie under his arm, and the two of them look at me with all the undiluted love and trust in their eyes that they can muster.

I swallow hard and kiss Marisa's soft head. She fusses and it brings a smile to my face. "There's my girl. I got you."

"Still my girl," Theo mumbles under his breath, and Leslie elbows him sharply in the ribs.

I nod a silent thank you because, for the first time in years, I allow myself to be loved.

Two days later, the words Vi uttered to me on that Notting Hill street corner continue to echo in my ears over and over as I dress for my therapy session with Doc.

Hayden, I love you.

"Hayden, I love you."

"Hayden, I love you."

I turn away from my reflection in the mirror, unable to look at myself a moment longer. You'd think after forty-eight hours, I could control my thoughts. But, no, I'm still obsessing over all things Vi.

I shouldn't have been so stunned by her declaration. I saw it coming. I sat back and allowed her to break down all my defences, just as I allowed her to pop open the cuffs on my wrists and kiss my scars.

I gave myself to her. All of me.

Or so I thought.

Then, something triggered me. Maybe it was the words of the psychic putting too much pressure on the future, or maybe it was just me not believing I am good enough for Vi. But for some reason, those last three words from Vi cut through me ten times deeper than the blade I drew across my wrists over a year ago.

The past two evenings have been spent on Theo and Leslie's sofa, clutching a sleeping Marisa to my chest while Leslie popped popcorn and Theo selected a film for us to watch as a family. It was nice. It was simple.

Like a normal, loving family.

Which is impressive considering how dark I was after I left Vi on the street. I felt like I was six feet under. My world was coming down all around me as I ran through the streets like a mad man.

Somehow, I managed to pull myself out. Somehow, I allowed myself to really accept that hug from Leslie and that meaningful look from Theo. And when tiny Marisa's finger wrapped around mine, the armour I'd been holding onto so tightly suddenly fell away.

Because I allowed my family to catch me.

My family.

They didn't hold my breakdown against me. They didn't rush me off to therapy, or a meeting, or rehab. They just sat beside me and allowed me to breathe their air and feel their presence.

That sense of family devotion was something I thought was long gone after Marisa died. In truth, it's been here all along. I just haven't allowed myself to accept it.

I stride out of my room and see Leslie bouncing Marisa in her arms as she warms up a bottle. Her green eyes find mine and are full of so much warmth and compassion, I feel it all the way down to my toes.

"How did you sleep?" she asks, dropping a kiss into Marisa's red, fuzzy hair.

"Like a dead man," I deadpan.

She eyes me sternly. "You're a clever boy. Let's go for a different analogy."

I roll my eyes. "I'm fine, Leslie."

"Are you sure?" she asks, walking over to me and fixing the collar of my shirt in a motherly way. "Because you still look sad."

I swallow slowly, a knot forming in my throat as I instantly picture Vi. "I…I'm fine."

"Hayden, why don't you go to her?" Leslie asks, her brows knit together in worry. "You obviously miss her."

I grip the cuffs on my wrists and shake my head. "I don't know if that's what's best for her…or me. I need to figure out my head first. I have an appointment with Doc now to try to help with that."

"Good. I hope he tells you to listen to your heart, not your head. Your head can be very dull."

I huff out a laugh at her small attempt at a joke, but deep down I want to scream at her that my heart is ten times more terrifying than my head. My head is predictable and in control. My heart is irrational and desperate. I don't know if I'm strong enough to trust it yet.

"I guess we'll see," I reply with a half-smile. I step closer to her and drop a kiss on Marisa's head before making my way out the door of the flat.

As I step out of C. Designs, something unusual catches the corner of my eye. I turn my gaze across the street, and that's when I see them.

All four of them.

The Harris Brothers.

Gareth, Tanner, Camden, and Booker are standing in a straight line, their arms crossed over their chests. All eight of their blazing eyes on me.

My steps falter, my heartbeat picking up from their mere presence. No one could help but be intimidated by them all lined up in a row. What do they want? Are they here to kick my arse? Have they come to knock some sense into me? Talk to me for Vi? Or, are they just here to make me regret the day I ever spoke to their sister in the first place?

Well, I don't regret it.

And I never will.

Vi is the best person I've ever known.

For that reason and that reason alone, I straighten my shoulders, push out my chest, and stride across the street toward them.

"Can I help you guys?" I ask, my voice low and doing its best not to show my fear.

They say nothing.

I look at Gareth since he's the oldest. His face looks as if it's made of granite, and I swear his muscles grow in front of me. "What are you doing here?" I ask.

No one is talking.

I eye the twins, and both of them are shooting daggers at me as well.

"If you guys have something to say to me, just say it!" I snap and turn my eyes to Booker, who has hated me from the moment I met him. I move down the line to stand in front of him, coming nose-to-nose with him as I add, "You can't protect her forever."

Booker lunges at me, but Camden grabs him by the shoulders and yanks him back into place. I shake my head and laugh, causing Cam to shoot his murderous-looking eyes at me in warning. But I'm not scared. Not a bit. When you've reached rock bottom, there's nothing that can make things any worse.

I step back and slide my hands through my hair, my head shaking back and forth in frustration over the ridiculousness of their silent message. "You guys think I don't know what I did was fucked-up? You think I'm not already punishing myself twenty times more than this little display? Well, you're wrong! I regret it all. Everything I said and did."

Tanner's hands tighten into fists as he takes a deep breath, his chest muscles puffing out even further. I scoff and continue my rant because it's clear these oafs aren't about to put sentences together.

"You know what, though? I don't regret meeting her. I don't regret letting your sister into my life. Maybe it was a mistake for me to get involved with her, but you guys don't give her enough credit. She has more strength in her tiny stamping foot than the four of you have combined. And that's the most beautiful thing about her. So, fine. Stay out here. Silently intimidate me, stalk me at my place of work. Do whatever you need to do, but know this. If I had an ounce of the strength Vi has, I wouldn't be here talking to you lot. I'd be at her place, making sure she knows just how incredible she is inside and out. Because, despite your protection—despite your family devotion and support—she will need the love of her life to make her believe it."

"And you think that's you?" Booker nearly spits, his tone acerbic and disbelieving.

I swallow hard, my face falling in pain as I step away from them and into the street. "I honestly wish I knew."

Without another word, I turn on my heel and walk away, my chest heaving with fear. And that fear has nothing to do with the Harris Brothers.

"So you've turned the person whom you completed your challenge with into a full-fledged relationship," Doc states, eyeing me seriously from his armchair and not giving anything away. If I didn't know any better, I'd swear I see a laugh quirking the corners of his mouth.

I squirm in my seat after revealing everything I've been up to since last seeing him. I can't help but feel like a kid who's just told his mum that he broke Grannie's vase.

"It was a relationship. Now it's not I guess."

My memory briefly flickers to the terrifyingly intimidating glowers from her brothers this morning. The four of them didn't look like they'd be done casing my flat any time soon, but I don't care. Deep down, I know I deserve it.

"Why isn't it a relationship anymore?" Doc asks curiously.

"I'm sure I don't have to tell you what a horrid idea that was. I mean, it's not exactly extra credit to take the assignment you gave me and turn it into a relationship. I've not watered a plant or gotten a dog. I sure as hell didn't need a relationship messing up my recovery."

Doc tilts his head. "How did the relationship make you feel?"

"Out of bloody control," I snap aggressively. But, in one blink, I remember the deliriously amazing moments I shared with Vi as well. Even the painful times with her were beautiful because she was with me.

"Is that all?" he asks.

I shrug. "It was too much. It was really intense. I don't need that right now. I need to focus on myself."

Doc's brows lift. "You need to focus on moving forward, Hayden. Above all. Being alive and living life is taking steps forward." I swallow hard and he leans closer as if he knows he still hasn't gotten through to me. "It's allowing yourself to live, not just be alive. Staying sober and functional shouldn't be your only goals. Embracing all of your emotions—good and bad—is the greatest challenge of all."

Substitution

Vi

A WET NOSE NUDGES MY FACE. NOW A TONGUE. NOW ANOTHER tongue. "Bruce! Off with you, or I'm giving you another bath," I groan, refusing to open my swollen eyes. His nails clack along the floor in a hasty retreat from me threatening him with the one thing he hates more than getting his nails clipped.

"When was the last time you had a bath?" a familiar voice asks from inside my room.

My eyes fly open and land on Gareth sitting at the foot of my bed. "How did you get in?" I snap, sitting up and rubbing at my crusty eyes. I inhale a sharp breath at the tender skin around the edges.

"I stole Dad's spare key. He wouldn't give it to me either. Said I needed to let you sort this one out on your own. But after ten fucking un-returned calls, I'd had it up to here, Vi." Gareth's arm flexes as he demonstrates just how far up he's had it.

I roll my eyes and scowl as I take in his appearance. He's freshly showered, his dark brown hair still wet on the ends. It's annoying.

"You didn't need to come over," I grumble, throwing the covers off myself and waltzing into the bathroom. I leave the door open while I stand at the sink and splash cold water on my face.

"By the looks of it, I needed to come five fucking days ago." He leans on the frame of the door, and his penetrative glower reflects at me in the mirror.

I wince at my own reflection but refuse to confirm his fears. "I don't want to talk about it."

"Too fucking bad," Gareth barks, standing up straight. "You look like you haven't eaten or showered in days. Have you even been in to work?"

"I worked from home." I glare at his reflection. "See? I'm not a weakling, Gareth. I'm doing just fine. I'm making my deadlines, answering emails. I'm a proper grown-up."

"Oh yeah, it really looks like it." Bruce trots over to him and nudges his hand for a pet. "Poor bastard. Bruce probably hasn't seen the light of day all week."

"Stop," I demand, turning around to face him. "I don't need to hear this, Gareth. Bruce has been well taken care of. Spoilt rotten with my daily presence. Does he look neglected?"

As if on cue, Bruce's jaw drops wide into a squeaking yawn and he lies down right at Gareth's feet with a sad huff.

"I've been by C. Designs," he says out of nowhere. My eyes fly wide. He crosses his arms over his chest and leans on the doorjamb as if he told me it's raining outside. It's fucking London. It's always raining!

I storm over and poke him in the chest. "You haven't really been over there, have you?"

He nods defensively. "If not me, it's Booker, Cam, or Tan. One of us has been driving by there every fucking day."

"And doing what?" My jaw is slack.

Gareth's eyes narrow as he continues that infuriatingly cocky, footballer nod. "Don't worry. I haven't laid a hand on him. We've just been watching."

"Watching for what? Has he seen you?" My voice rises with panic.

"Oh, he's seen us," he chuckles.

"Oh my God, Gareth!" I shriek. "No! What do you think you're doing?"

"We're sending him a fucking message, Vi." He points his finger in the air to accentuate his point. "He's got a hell of a lot of nerve acting noble in front of us one night, then slagging you off the very next day. He's a wanker. You're better off."

My eyes sting, but there is no sign of actual tears. My tears are completely dried-up. "Gareth, this has absolutely nothing to do with you!" I rake my hands through my ratty hair and grip the back of my neck as I walk back into my bedroom. "Why? Why do you guys keep doing this stuff?"

He follows, towering over me as I sit down on the bed. "Look, Vi. My season's almost starting again. I don't have to tell you that, that means I'm leaving for Manchester in two weeks. I can't leave you here with that fucking prat sniffing about."

"It's my life!" I cry out and stamp my foot. "I don't need you tousling every man who jilts me. At my rate, it'll become a full-time fucking job."

"Oh, stop," he scoffs. "You're just doing a proper job of picking morons."

"I don't, Gareth." I groan at the deep pain I feel every time I think about Hayden. "Hayden isn't a moron. He is everything, but he didn't see that. He didn't want it. He trusted me with so much of his life, but in the end, he still couldn't manage to fall in love with me. He walked away." My chest shudders into an awkward dry sob as I keel over and cry into my hands. God, this is pathetic. I can't even cry properly.

Large warm arms wrap around me. Gareth begins shushing and rocking me back and forth as I somehow hit a new well of tears buried in an un-tapped crevice of my body.

"It's not the men who are the issue, Gareth. It's me. And it's embarrassing enough having men not give two shits about me. I don't need you guys adding fuel to my pathetic flame. Just stop trying to protect me."

"I can't do that, Vi," Gareth groans, the deep timbre of his chest rumbling against my ear.

"Why not?" I lift my head and shove the hair out of my face. "Tell me, Gareth. What is the reason that you have to continually insert yourself into my life?"

He frowns and eyes my blotchy skin with a thoughtful expression. His hazel eyes soften, replaced by a deep sadness that makes me realise that his over-protectiveness isn't a superficial choice. He exhales sharply, his face wincing in silent pain.

"What is it?" I ask, my voice nervous and pensive.

"I don't think I knew why I do it until just this moment," he says, his expression in thoughtful awe.

"What do you mean?"

He sniffs and his eyes are glassy with unshed tears. "You look just like Mum, you know that?"

I swipe at my tear-stained face self-consciously. "Thanks a lot."

"She was beautiful, Vi. Even at the end. Did you know I was alone with Mum the day she died?" he asks and drops his elbows to his knees, gazing hauntingly off into the distance.

"The day she died? What do you mean? Where was Dad?" The image of Gareth as a small boy dealing with that all by himself horrifies me.

His Adam's apple bobs as he swallows. "Dad could hardly come into her room at the end. He was a wreck. It was painful to watch." He rubs his lips together before he continues. "I think he was just overwhelmed. I was only eight, and it seemed like all you guys did was cry. Booker was still a baby, and I didn't know how to change a nappy. No one ever showed me. And Dad was making do, but completely losing it, too." He pauses to shake his head, a look of shame casting over his features. "When he was around Mum, he shouted at her a lot. She lay in bed and cry every night because of how angry Dad would get."

Tears. More tears flood my eyes.

"She made me promise not to be cross at him for it. She told me that he was her bestest friend in the whole world. That he was going through a really hard time and she couldn't help him, and it is hard when your bestest friend isn't there to help you."

My fingers dig into Gareth's bicep as he continues.

"I didn't fully know what she was going on about. I just knew I loved our mum. And I was sad, too." His voice breaks on a garbled cry. "I decided then and there that if Dad couldn't be there for her, I would be. I would be her new best friend."

"Gareth," I cry, my belly shaking with quiet sobs. But he doesn't stop. He keeps looking forward and continuing his story.

"So I was her best friend, and I was there when she died. I held her hand and watched it go limp. It's strange, but I can still feel the softness of her hand." He takes my hand in his. Mine looks so small and fair-toned next to his large, rough palm. "She had these long, elegant fingers, just like yours. You have Mum's hands, Vi. Did you know that? I've probably never told you." He sniffles and clasps my hand between his two. "I was eight when I lost my best friend and my mum all in one shot."

I shake my head in defiance. I can't believe all of this happened and I wasn't there for him. I was four, but still. I should have been there for him.

"I'm sorry, Gareth."

"Don't be sorry, Vi. Just understand me. Understand that protecting you and loving you feels like I am doing it for my best friend. It always felt like I had something to prove."

"I understand now, you daft cow," I croak and pull him in for a hug that feels different. It feels different because, for the first time, I finally understand my brother and maybe even a little bit more of the stranger who is my mum. "You can be a meddling bruiser of a brother any time you want." I sniff and back away, wiping the tears from my eyes again. "I'll be fine, though. Really."

"Damn right you will." He rubs my shoulders soothingly and then frowns as his gaze narrows on my closet door. "What's that?"

I roll my eyes. "Oh, God. It's a stupid dress I ordered for Leslie's wedding this weekend. I was staring at it and feeling sorry for myself."

"Why?"

"Because I'm not going now, of course."

"The fuck you're not. You're going to that wedding, Vi."

"What?" I ask. "No. Why on earth?"

"Because best friends fuck up. But it doesn't mean they don't love you."

My face falls. "Gareth, stop. It's over between Hayden and me. I'm not going to allow myself to hurt like this again. He's crushed me one too many times."

"You're still going to the wedding." He drops his chin with a glower.

"No. I can't face him alone."

"Good thing you won't be alone," he retorts with a cocky grin.

Déjà Red

Hayden

Red. All I see is red. I close my eyes, and the backs of my eyelids still only show me red.

I stand next to Theo at the altar and attempt to focus on what the pastor is saying, but then the fucking red again.

A flush moves up Vi's neck. The urge to kiss the heat beneath her skin is so powerful, I actually glimpse over at Liam to make sure that I haven't moved from my position as best man. In my mind, I'm crawling over the top of every one of these arseholes in the church and covering Vi with my entire body. The urge I have to club her over the head like a caveman and shout out "mine" is problematic.

And probably a bit psychotic.

Her brother Gareth cuts me a homicidal look as if he can read my thoughts. My eyes twitch nervously, but I still can't bring myself to tear my gaze away from Vi. She's dressed in red. Just as I requested back when life was bearable. I silently chastise her fucking git of a brother for letting her out of his sight in that getup. I don't care how famous of a footballer he is, he's a fucking moron. Her red dress is short and flowy with a dangerously low neckline. It's held up by two floss-like straps that look like all you'd have to do is blow on them and her dress would go slithering to the ground. Gareth's hatred toward me must be immense for him to allow her to wear that bloody dress just to torture me.

The past week without Vi has consisted of a lot of angry grunting and snarling. Namely at Theo because he's my brother, and he's got it coming for the years of suffrage he has inflicted on me. However, Theo—being the older and apparently smarter brother—must have figured out my mood stabiliser is Marisa because every time I'd growl at him, he'd silently pass me the baby.

God, I'm a transparent softie.

The corner of my mouth turns up as I eye Marisa sitting in her white linen-covered Bumbo seat nestled safely inside a wagon drenched in yards and yards of white tulle and taffeta. Leslie and Theo keep grinning down proudly at her, only halfway listening to the sermon. I think all of us are amazed at how long she's lasting up here. The plan was for her to come down the aisle with Finley and me. Then, the minute she started to fuss, Finley was going to whisk her over to Brody, who got a hefty lesson from me on how to soothe Marisa.

I chuckle softly to myself at what an odd wedding party we must look like up here. Leslie's side consists of Finley, Frank, and Brody. Theo's side is me, Liam, and Daphney. Jaci no K probably developed a new vein in her forehead when Leslie informed her of their non-traditional plans. And Frank about sent her completely over the edge when he told her he was wearing a dress as well. The cheeky bugger.

I look down and fiddle with my leather cuffs, begging myself to stop looking at Vi. God, she makes me weak. Everything about her makes me liquefy to a puddle on the ground in her presence. Why did she have to bring her fucking brother?

I groan inwardly, and Leslie's eyes flash to mine as she glances past Theo. I swallow awkwardly and calm myself down just as the pastor asks me for the rings.

My hands tremor as I reach inside my suit coat, then hand him the rings that are to represent Theo and Leslie as one. A symbol of their eternal love that has no beginning and no end. Just as Theo reaches for Leslie's hand, Marisa lets out a mighty cry. Finley jumps to action, but Leslie stops her in her tracks, bends over in her beautiful wedding gown, and picks up my niece. Theo's eyes are watching her affectionately the entire time, devouring every flicker of her movement. She tucks Marisa against her stomach so she's facing out and resumes her position at the altar. Family complete now, Leslie beams at my brother with the happiest, most content, albeit wobbly-with-emotion, serene smile I've ever seen in my entire life.

My eyes prick as I glance down at Marisa, who's managed to tuck a piece of her lacy dress into her mouth for a good chew. She looks up happily, clearly much more content to be standing up here in Mummy's arms and looking at Daddy than down in that bloody wagon by herself.

The pastor attempts to resume, but Theo coughs loudly and looks down, pulling his glasses off his face and pinching the bridge of his nose. I want to offer a reassuring pat on his shoulder, but I refrain. As if sensing my support, he glances back at me, giving me a glimpse of something I'm not all together sure he wanted me to see.

His weakness.

My brother's crumbling, love-spilling-over-the-top vulnerability is exposed on every raw flicker of his face. He smiles at me knowingly and nods, a moment of thoughtfulness exchanged between us. He looks back at his wife and daughter and readies himself to solidify his happily ever after.

He's feeling. He's doing exactly what Doc said is the hardest challenge of all, and he's making it look bloody good. He looks happier than I've ever seen him.

As I watch them, my heart pounds like it's going to burst out of my chest at any moment. It already felt like it was holding on by a very thin thread all week. But now, that thread is cinching up around my heart, tighter and tighter with every second I'm forced to stand up here and not next to Vi touching her and telling her everything I've wanted to tell her since the first time I met her.

Poker Face

Vi

WHEN THE PASTOR TELLS THEO HE CAN KISS HIS BRIDE, I SLAM my eyes shut, unable to observe the end of the most vulnerably raw and absolutely beautiful wedding I've ever witnessed. Tears slip out from beneath my lashes because, even though I can't see their kiss, I can feel it. I think everyone in this tiny chapel can feel it.

Finally, I open my eyes and I can't help but smile at Leslie as she beams from ear-to-ear with tears in her eyes. She lifts Marisa up between her and Theo, and they both kiss either side of her cheeks simultaneously. Cameras flash wildly as the small congregation of less than fifty people all "aw" in unison at the perfectly beautiful little family.

The wedding was gorgeous. Simple, but in no way understated. That wouldn't be Leslie. Punches of colour explode everywhere from the wildflower bouquets, to the bold multi-coloured bridesmaids' dresses, to the unique fitted men's suits.

Hayden wears his better than every man up there.

Damn him all to hell.

I spent the last couple of days psyching myself up for my first sight of him. I envisioned him looking cold and detached, similar to how he appeared the night of the gala only six weeks ago. How could our story have only lasted six weeks? Somehow it feels like no time and tons of time all at once.

My expectation of him today was that he'd continue to block me out and further drive the stake through my already hardened heart.

What I didn't expect was for him to look so...concentrated.

The three times I mistakenly locked eyes with him during the service felt like we were frozen in time. In those moments, he was showing me the same passionate, intense, brooding, possessive man who threw a fit over me nearly kissing Ethan. I thought I could be strong enough to not let his presence consume me, but he's messing everything up by looking at me the way he is. I think he stared at me through twenty-five of the thirty minutes worth of ceremony. I have no idea what he's after, but I pray that he knows the damage done last week is irreconcilable.

Irreconcilable.

The congregation stands to file out of the church. I catch sight of Leslie and Theo, along with the rest of the bridal party forming a reception line in the narthex.

"Great," I groan quietly.

"You're fine. Only a couple more hours to go," Gareth mutters under his breath.

I offer a shaky smile to my brother who's dressed in a black fitted suit. Several people turn and gawk at him as we meander through the line.

"You could have dressed down a bit. I told you this would be a small, casual wedding."

He frowns down at me. "I'm not wearing a tie."

I roll my eyes. "Gucci is hardly casual."

His eyes narrow as he looks over my shoulder. A playful smirk teases his lips, so I turn to see him catching a sensual gaze from a tall, busty brunette.

"Nice," I croak.

"Hey, I'm here for moral support, but I'm no bloody saint." He flashes Busty a megawatt smile.

"Can you at least keep it in your pants until we get through the reception line? Hayden is right there." The pain I feel saying his name is acute.

Gareth frowns and his flirty eyes suddenly turn serious. "You've got this."

Do I? I think to myself just as we reach Leslie.

"Vilma!" she sings happily. "I'm so glad you're here." She yanks me into a tight hug. Her arms are firm and solid around me. She pulls back and looks into my eyes with a pensive expression. "I was worried you wouldn't come."

I shake my head dismissively. "I wouldn't miss your wedding, Leslie," I say just as Theo finishes with the couple in front of us and looks at me. "You're too damn needy for me to avoid anyway."

Theo laughs and casts his twinkling, happy eyes down at his blushing bride. "I can vouch for that. And now I have two of them."

We glance over at Marisa as she smiles from the arms of Theo's parents, whom I met briefly at the gala last month.

"Guys, this is my brother, Gareth Harris. I'm not sure you've all met." I turn to my brother as he moves in closer.

Theo's eyes fly wide. He pulls his glasses off as if to confirm that who he's looking at isn't a mirage. "Gareth Harris, for Man U? Bugger. I'm…Yeah, I'm a fan." Theo stammers as he cuts accusing eyes at Leslie. "Leslie, how could you not mention who Vilma's brother is?"

She purses her lips and shrugs as if the thought never once occurred to her. "I don't watch soccer! How am I supposed to know he's a big deal?"

"He's like…Beckham big deal, babe."

"Posh Spice's husband? Oh, shit! He's hot!" Gareth and I burst out laughing, and Leslie bites her lip and covers her mouth. Theo shakes his head at her as she says, "I'm sorry, Gareth."

Gareth chuckles. "No offence taken. I'm not as big as Beckham," he winks playfully.

"You should be offended. I'd like to apologise on behalf of my wife for this entire encounter. Keep up the great work. And good luck this season." Theo and Gareth exchange a matey handshake. I attempt to walk by him, but Theo surprises me by pulling me in for a hug. "Don't run," he whispers in my ear. I pull back, my brow furrowed. "Just don't run. It's worth it," he repeats, clearly unfazed by Gareth, whom I can feel shooting daggers behind me.

Doing my best to shake off Theo's unexpected propaganda, we greet the rest of the bridal party, including Frank. "Christ, Vi. You look as if you belong on every teenage boy's splattered ceiling!"

"Frank! You're disgusting," Finley crows and whacks him on the arm. "Hi, Vi! You look beautiful."

We exchange pleasantries with the rest of the family. But just when I think we're going to graze right past Hayden since his back is turned, Frank clears his throat loudly and unsubtly barks out, "Hayden, you wanker!"

Hayden's head pops up curiously and he turns. His serious grey eyes find mine instantly. Heat blossoms between us, and I feel a blush move up my neck and fill my cheeks. I glance down at his white button-down dress shirt, beige tweed-fitted trousers, and brown braces that Leslie says Americans call hipster suspenders. I'm going to ignore the fact that his trousers are tailored to his build within an inch of their life. I'm not going to notice the taut fabric of his cotton shirt around his muscular biceps. I don't care about how he's not wearing a tie, so two popped buttons reveal just enough of his sculpted chest to remind me of how he looks shirtless. And who really cares that his copper blonde hair is dishevelled in an artful way that makes it look like he's just fucked someone's brains out.

Deep breath.

"Vi," he begins and reaches his hand out to me.

Before his fingers can graze mine, Gareth swoops in, turning his back on Hayden and firmly gripping the side of my arm. "We need to keep the line moving." The set of his jaw is demanding, but looking at Hayden's hopeful expression on the other side of him makes me pause.

"Just a minute, Gareth," I say softly, my eyes never leaving Hayden's.

"Vi," he warns.

Ignoring him, I shove past his enormous frame and see a flicker of relief smear over Hayden's face with my approach. Shooting him a tight smile, I stick out my hand.

"What?" Hayden asks, frowning down at my outstretched hand.

"A platonic handshake," I offer, wiggling my brow.

He huffs out a laugh. "Don't be ridiculous. There's nothing platonic about you and me, Bunny."

I paint on a forced half-smile and grab his hand, clutching his cuffed wrist firmly with my other in warning. I move in so my voice is a mere whisper on his mouth. "Don't call me that. You lost the right to call me that the moment you stomped all over my heart last week."

Hayden's face falls. "I need to talk to you," he replies, eyeing my pink lips with a hunger that makes my inner sex kitten stir.

"You lost that right, too, Hayden," I say, my belly fighting hard against the annoying fear of rejection that I still feel in his presence even though it's me pushing him away right now. "You see, I've realised something this past week that you should know."

"And what's that?" he barks, annoyed.

My eyes turn to slits. "You're no different than all the other men who've cast me aside for dead."

His frustrated eyes turn glossy and panicky. "Of course I'm different," he croaks. I move to step away from him, but his hand grips mine to the point that I could wince. "No, Vi," his voice trembles.

I smile sadly at him. "None of this matters, Hayden. Just as I feel unlovable, you can't accept love. Let's not make this harder than it has to be." I move to walk away again, but he yanks me back toward him, his hand crawling around my waist in a desperate attempt to pull me against his body.

In a flash, Gareth is beside me, gripping Hayden's forearms so hard I can see his knuckles turning white. "You're done, Hayden," he threatens.

Hayden instantly lets go, staring at me like I've just committed the ultimate betrayal. With that, I walk away, holding my head high and praying to the good Lord that he can't see my shoulders shaking with my silent sobs.

31
Plan A

Hayden

WELL THAT WENT AS GOOD AS FUCK ALL, I THINK TO MYSELF AS
we pull up in a limo in front of the Bleeding Heart Tavern in
Farringdon where the reception is already in full swing. I was moody
the entire joyride around London. Thankfully, Leslie and Theo just
let me stew. One way or another, I have to get Vi to listen to what I
have to say. If I could just get past her thick fucking brother.

Her four brothers did a proper job of scaring me off all week.
They parked outside of C. Designs or drove by over, and over, and
over. Any time I had the urge to walk to Vi's and beg her forgiveness,
one of them was there, staring me down like they wanted to use my
head as a football. So, much to my great dismay, I withheld calling
Vi and ruminated over it the entire week. I anticipated tonight being
the night I'd get her to hear everything I need to say. I never once
suspected that she'd bring a bloody bodyguard with her.

Round one goes to Bunny.

We waltz into the tavern and Jaci no K is here to greet us. "Okay,
everyone, you're going to follow me. We're going to enter the reception where Theo and Leslie will cut the cake and then immediately
begin their first dance."

"What about refreshments?" Frank croaks from somewhere

behind me.

Jaci cuts him an evil glance. "There is a bar downstairs. You may grab a beverage as soon as the first dance begins. Not before. *Not. Before.*" Her eyes turn glacial.

"Blimey," Frank murmurs beneath his breath. "Scary bird."

Leslie giggles into Theo's shoulder as he whispers something in her ear. The two look like a couple of horny teenagers while we wait for Jaci to walk us down.

"You...The brother," Jaci says, snapping her fingers in my direction. "You will hold the baby during the first dance. The mother of the groom has her down there now. We want her to be able to enjoy her son's first dance, so you shall fetch her."

"Her name is Marisa," I mumble.

"I know!" she snaps back defensively. "Marisa Winifred Clarke. Her birthday is March eleventh, and she has two teeth coming in already, which is unusually early for a four-and-a-half-month-old baby but not unheard of."

My brows lift. Round two goes to Jaci no K.

She whisks us down to the lower level, six-hundred-year-old converted wine cellar. It's apparently where Henry VIII and Catherine of Aragon hosted a five-day party in the 1500s. It's an impressive crypt full of exposed beams and candlelit oval tables. Every table is overwhelmed by spreads of wildflowers, as well as overflowing baskets scattered throughout the cosy room.

Jaci walks us by the filled tables where people have been eating hors d'oeuvres and sipping champagne for the past hour. We pause near the head table at the front of the room and wait patiently as Leslie scoops Marisa up into her arms from my mum. Leslie presses her lips to Marisa's chubby cheeks, and I can't tear my eyes away from my brother as he watches Leslie with a fondness that can't be faked. Christ, he really loves her.

I scan the room for Vi but come up empty-handed. Gareth is sitting next to Benji and what look like the rest of Leslie's coworkers from Nikon. He scowls at me angrily, and I just shake my head. I refuse to let him intimidate me. I don't care how many bloody goals he's stopped.

I chug down some water at the head table as Theo and Leslie cut the cake. Jaci no K snaps her fingers and two busboys fumble in to roll the cake away. Leslie looks over at me as the music for their first dance begins. I grin happily and stride over, pulling a face at Marisa as I approach. She flails her arms happily when I scoop her into my arms.

We retreat to a safe distance as Theo pulls Leslie against him. "Mummy and Daddy loved you enough to include you in the ceremony, but some things are just better for two people," I whisper into Marisa's ear. She lets out a mighty giggle as I nuzzle her neck with my chin. Leslie and Theo look over at me and smile as I sway her along with the notes of Ingrid Michaelson's "Can't Help Falling in Love." The candlelight twinkles on the two of them moving together to the music, and I can't help but think back to the night I asked Vi to dance with me in her living room. My heart sinks.

"Hey," a voice says from behind me, interrupting my wayward thoughts.

I turn to find Rey standing behind me, looking a little sheepish in a black floor-length gown.

"Hiya," I say cautiously, recalling our last encounter not going so well.

Glancing down at Marisa, she smiles and reaches her hand out to her in a greeting. "Look, I just want to apologise for the night at Frank's. I don't know what I was thinking." She looks back up at me and pushes a hand through her long dark hair. "I guess I still feel protective of you. I'm having a harder time letting you go than I thought I would."

I frown and shift Marisa into my other arm. "There's no need for you to worry about me anymore, Rey. I'm doing fine. I have a solid support network around me."

"I know," she says with a sigh. "I see that, and I guess I'm just a little jealous."

My brows lift. "Jealous?"

"You and I were codependent on each other, Hayden. For a long time, you were my crutch and I was yours. Just because I started going to therapy and you went to rehab doesn't erase all of our history."

"I know, Rey. But things are different now. I'm working on my own kind of happy."

"Liam says you're not seeing Vi anymore," she states brazenly.

My jaw clenches. Reyna never was one to mince words. "Liam doesn't know what he's talking about."

"Don't get defensive, Hayden," she retorts. "Tell me what happened."

"It's complicated, Rey." I pull Marisa up to my neck and tuck my head on top of her.

"Well, Hayden, I have a feeling you and I are cut from the same cloth when it comes to relationships and letting people in. And if you're going through what I did last year, I don't envy you."

"Thanks for the pep talk, coach," I reply dryly.

She giggles. "You'll figure it out. If she's worth it, you'll figure it out."

She turns to walk away, but before she gets too far, I call out, "Got any advice?"

She turns her head and purses her lips to the side for a moment. Finally, she replies, "Don't waste another moment. Wasted moments are hard to overcome." She smiles knowingly as she retreats, leaving me here holding the only woman in the world who has never doubted my level of devotion to her for a second.

After the dance, dinner is served. I can barely stand watching Vi from across the room. Ethan slithers over at one point while Gareth is at the bar, and I nearly crawl out of my skin with rage. Thankfully, he got distracted by a properly pissed Julie who, out of nowhere, leapt on his back. I haven't seen them since.

Inspiration strikes when I see Gareth up at the bar nursing a beer. Maybe if I can get through to him, I can get through to Vi. I stride over to him, wishing like fuck I wasn't wearing braces right now. Hip or not, waltzing up to a professional footballer in a three piece suit while I'm dressed like Stephan Fry isn't exactly a confidence booster.

"What the hell do you want?" Gareth drawls and slides his phone back into his pocket.

"I want to talk to you," I state seriously.

"You're barking up the wrong tree."

He moves to walk away, so I place a firm hand on his shoulder to stop him. "The way I see it, you're the one obstacle between me and Vi, so you're exactly the tree I need to pee on."

He roars with laughter and lifts his brows at my hand on his shoulder. It's a silent warning. I move my hand. "Hayden. You're underestimating my sister. I'm not the one you should be troubling over. She has it in her head that you don't care for her, and that shit is an issue for her. A big one. You're lucky I'm not wringing your fucking neck for causing her so much pain."

"Well, why aren't you then?" I ask in a weak moment of flippant defensiveness. I'm tired of the empty threats. The drive-bys. The brooding glowers. Fuck! I've had enough.

He closes his eyes for a moment before opening them and glaring at me. "Look, Hayden. I don't have a mum anymore. All I have is her." He points back at the table where Vi is laughing at something Benji said. "That's the single most important woman in my life, so you'll forgive me and my brothers for being a bit protective. We liked you mate. You were in, and that's not a fucking easy feat with Harris Brothers. In fact, it's unprecedented. But you trashed it. You spit on it. On us. On her. You're not getting through to her again."

I slice my hands through my hair in frustration. "Don't you get that is exactly why I'm fucking staying away from her?" I growl angrily. "Caring for people is what got me into trouble in the first place.

So protect her all you want, mate. That's all I was trying to do, too. And last week, I thought protecting her involved me leaving her. But that was before."

"Before what?"

"Before I got a clue. Before I had the wake-up call of my life." I clench my jaw and eye him seriously adding, "Before I realised I didn't just like your sister."

His eyes flash knowingly, but he's still not convinced. "You should have known that long before now, mate." He moves to walk away again, and I jerk him back…again.

Through desperate, clenched teeth, I add, "This isn't a flippant kind of feeling for me, Gareth. It's something I've never felt before. With anyone." He huffs out a laugh, but I continue. "It's the kind of love we all bore witness to in that chapel today."

Gareth's amusement drops and his jaw clenches, an angry muscle in it ticks ominously. My big mouth refuses to take a hint.

"Your sister is mine, Gareth. She's tied to my heart whether you accept it or not."

"Is that right?" He squints in challenge.

"She's my forever," I add seriously, surprising even myself with that statement.

His glower drops, and he leans closer to me. "Then what the fuck are you waiting for?"

Ruined

Vi

"ALL MEN ARE FUCKING WANKERS," JULIE SNAPS, PLOPPING down into the open seat beside me. Her posture and scowling expression are at complete odds with her gorgeous little black dress and perfect hair and makeup. She begins ripping hair grips out of her updo and tossing them into the centre of the table. "Stupid, spiteful, ball-less wankers. They all shave their balls now because one person got it in their head that it makes their cocks look bigger. All it does is make them look like pussies. The lot of them."

I bite back the urge to laugh because Julie is obviously not in a joking mood. "Everything okay, Julie?"

She looks at me like I have three heads. "No! It's not okay! Christ! My life is so far from okay that the word should start with an *F* and end with *UCKED*." She rips the final hair grip out with a mighty tug, and her thick black hair cascades down to her shoulders. She leans into me with a deathly serious look. "Let me give you a piece of advice, Vi. You think women's lib has evolved our species. It hasn't. And if you ever get the fucking stupid idea that you want to drop down on one knee and start your happily ever after, then you've just kissed a three-year relationship goodbye."

My eyes turn wide. "You proposed to Mitch?"

Pure rage seethes in the blacks of her eyes as she stands up and musses her hair wildly. She turns to leave but pauses and leans down to add, "Mitch buggered off faster than I could stand back up. If you're on your knees and you don't have a cock in your mouth, then you've dug your own grave, my girl."

She strides off toward the bar and whacks shoulders with Gareth as he comes back toward the table.

"Care to dance?" a male voice utters in my ear. I glance up and take in Ethan's blue eyes that contrast stunningly against his latte skin. He really is a striking specimen of a man.

"She's taken," Gareth booms from behind me.

I frown at his widened stance. "And she can speak for herself," I snap. I look back at Ethan. "I'm not taken, but I'm also not interested. Thanks anyway."

"Suit yourself. Jules will come back anyway," he grins naughtily. "They always do."

I blanch at the blatant innuendo and my eyes catch sight of Hayden storming this way.

Knowing I'd really rather not be in front of all of my coworkers when Hayden's caveman comes out, I hop to my feet. "I'm just running to the toilet," I murmur, holding down the light chiffon fabric that flows a bit too easily as I make haste.

I swerve between the tables and out into the narrow stone-covered hallway that's barely illuminated by a few flickering candle sconces on the wall. Feeling Hayden's presence approaching as if I'm a psychic channelling into his energy, I tuck into a tiny dark alcove that houses row after row of dusty bottles of wine.

"Seriously, you're hiding from me now?" Hayden barks as he comes to a stop in the shallow arched entryway.

"Not hiding. Just curious about this bottle here," I state pragmatically while dusting off a bottle of wine. "Wow, 1821. Think it was a good year?"

He ducks his head to enter the small space, and my heart

instantly seizes. His scent, his aura, his presence. It's overwhelming.

He grasps the bottle in my hand and our fingers brush. A sharp intake of air on my part doesn't go unnoticed by him. His pupils glitter within the grey depths of his eyes as he watches me for a few seconds.

"Vi, please hear me out," he states softly while carefully returning the bottle to its shelf.

"It's really not necessary, Hayden." I swallow hard, attempting not to let his tortured, beautifully broken face pull me in. "You said a lot to me that day in Notting Hill. Things that I won't be forgetting."

He blinks as if in pain. "Vi, what that lady said scared the shit out of me. Surely you can see why."

I shrug my shoulders, doing my best not to look like I've just been punched in the gut again. "I get it, Hayden. I don't need you rubbing salt in the open wound."

"That's not what I meant," he warns, his eyes narrowing to slits.

I shake my head, not allowing him out of this one. "Just say it, Hayden. I know it's me. I'm unlovable, or unspecial, or something that makes you not want to jump in with me. Your first impression of me should have been a warning sign that I really was nothing more than a simple distraction. I mean, look. You loved Reyna so easily. You told me you fell in love with her, and that was after you told me you two know nothing about each other! How do you think that makes me feel after we've shared so much?"

"I had years with Reyna, Vi," he snaps, raking his hands through his hair in the dim lighting. "Years of time for me to build her up to be more than she ever was."

"Stop. This is rubbish. You loved her. You said she broke your heart when you said those words to her. I've never said those words to any man, Hayden. Only you! Now my heart is broken more than I ever thought possible." My voice rises with a maniacal giggle. "And, Christ, I'm such a loser thinking I had found someone who could actually love me back."

"I was lying, Vi!" he shouts, rattling the bottles around us and leaning down to capture my gaze with his. "I was lying to myself most of all. I've been lying to myself since the second I first laid eyes on you at The White Swan Pub."

He grips my face firmly in his hands, and every part of his body trembles with fear as he utters, "Vi, just as you've always feared you're unlovable, I fear that I can't love you. I am fucking terrified when I look into your eyes and tell you things because I feel like I am being understood. Possibly for the first time in my entire life. But if I can't love you the way you deserve, what would it do to you? I'm trying to protect you! Don't you see that? My past...Christ! I just wish my past wouldn't—"

"Oh, stop wishing away your past, Hayden!" I snap, pulling my face from his grasp. "Start wishing to make the most of your future for a change. You don't get it. I would have given myself to you. Completely. I would have been yours and let you shove and manhandle any bloke who came within miles of me because, by you doing that, it would mean you're mine as well." I brush back a piece of his hair that's sticking up. The sensation is a punishing stroke on my broken heart.

He closes his eyes at my betraying caress. "Vi, just listen. You are in my heart. You're like a thread tied around it. It hurts and it's uncomfortable, but it's embedded so deep that it's a part of me now. I can see a life with you. A forever life. A place where I will want to be sad, angry, happy, delirious. The past few years have been riddled with lows for me. But the past six weeks, all of my highs have included you."

"Hayden, stop." Tears fall down my cheeks as my façade of dismissiveness begins cracking.

"Love me still. Please," he begs, his hands trembling against my cheeks.

I shake my head, refusing to accept the pain on his face. The pain that he caused me now reflecting back. "I can't, Hayden. It's too late," my voice cracks. I turn to hide my tears and, without warning, he moves into me and yanks my face to his.

Pain…

Lust…

Punishment…

And love.

All of it overcomes me as the familiar stroke of his lips on mine crushes every remaining shred of strength I had. My hands bite into his biceps as his tongue enters my mouth, demanding its welcome. Demanding its acceptance. Demanding what else, I'm not entirely sure.

He presses me up against the bottles and grabs the back of my thigh, pulling it up to his hip. Closing the distance between us, he touches himself against my warm centre as his tongue tangles with mine. The ache I feel to connect with him—to pull him inside of me and hold him there—brings tears to my eyes as the absolute truth of the moment cascades over me.

This kiss is ruining me forever.

I won't live through this.

Because the idea of ever kissing another man—a man who's not Hayden—is a death sentence for my fragile heart.

Tears invade our mouths. Hayden breaks away from me, panting heavily against my face. The tortured look in his glossy gaze is pleading. "This isn't fucking over, Vi." His voice stutters with uncertainty, recognising what I've always known to be true. "You're mine." He pushes himself off the wall and storms out of the alcove.

And possibly out of my heart for good.

Last 11:11

Hayden

"STOP WISHING AWAY YOUR PAST, HAYDEN. START WISHING TO make the most of your future."

Vi's words are a strike to my heart as I glance down at my watch to see 11:11 approaching. "Fuck," I mumble, cupping my head in my hands at the head table.

How I thought I could ever survive a world without Vi is beyond me. Kissing her is like breathing. Necessary and rudiment for survival. In the short time I've known her, she's brought so much out in me. I hate myself for not seeing it sooner.

Leslie bustles over in her huge gown, her happy eyes widening as she takes in my pained expression. "What happened?" she asks as she slides into a chair beside me.

"I love her, Leslie. I *love*, love her," my voice croaks as I exhale a painful sigh over the fear that it might not be enough. "But I think I've ruined it."

"Nonsense," she says, yanking my hands away from my head. "You didn't ruin anything. Hayden, do you have any idea how much it took for me to fall for your brother? He chased me all through London because my outlook on love was terrible. My past saw to that. But look at me right now. Do you see anything in me besides one hundred percent certainty in my feelings for Theo?"

I shake my head incredulously. "You guys make it look easy."

"Love is never easy. But when it's right, it's number one above everything." She touches my wrist gently, and my brows crumple in silent pain. "If she's the one, Hayden, you have to show her that you will put her first…above your past."

"I've spent years wishing away my past," I reply, staring down at her hand cupping my wrist, my eyes nervously flashing to the time on my watch.

"Then start there. Prove it to her somehow. Hell, make a splash, Hayden!" she exclaims and grabs the wireless mic from the table.

I stare at it in horror. "No. Not here. Not now."

"There's no better time, baby bro. I don't know if you noticed, but Theo and I are kind of on your side and stuff." She winks playfully and offers me a saccharinely sweet smile. "And we want Marisa to have a cousin sooner rather than later."

I roll my eyes, but the corner of my mouth lifts. I glance down at my watch again. Only a few minutes to go. Out of the corner of my eye, I see Vi striding back to her table. Gareth stands and she gestures to her jacket. He looks confused but hands it to her.

No! She can't leave. Before I even make a conscious decision to do what I'm about to do, my fingers wrap around the mic. "Just remember you fucking asked for this."

Leslie giggles with excitement. "Oh my God, this is going to be awesome. Do it to it!"

"I'm doing it," I growl as I flick the mic on halfway through my sentence. A loud crack and hiss of feedback halts everyone's conversations. "Uh, sorry. Hiya. Um." I suck in my cheeks and bite down to stop myself from cursing. "I'm Hayden Clarke, Theo's brother."

"And mine," Leslie chirps quietly from beside me. The crowd looks up at me excitedly. Except Vi.

"I know speeches happened already, but there's one more speech I need to make." The background music suddenly cuts off, and I see

Jaci no K press through the frozen couples on the dance floor. She is staring at me in horror over messing with her perfectly mapped itinerary. My nerves roll in like a dust storm as I add, "And I'm sorry, but it has nothing to do with the bride and groom."

I tear my watchful eyes from a furious Jaci and glance pointedly at Vi. Her jaw hangs open as she remains unmoving by the table. She looks so fucking gorgeous, even with her gobsmacked mouth.

"Vi," I start, looking down awkwardly. "You told me once that I don't get to keep forever to myself, and I'd like to repeat those words back to you right now."

A few gasps echo in the room, and I look up to see her bring a hand to her mouth in shock. "Your forever is mine, Vi. Your forever belongs to me whether you're ready to accept it or not.

"I was afraid there was too much that time could not erase for me." I peek down at my watch and see there are still two minutes to go. "But when I hold you in my arms, time doesn't even exist anymore. I feel brand new. I feel happy and healthy. I was so determined to get there on my own that I couldn't accept all that you were giving me. You listened to every horrid moment of my life and not one of them scared you away."

My head drops. The feeling in my chest that started as a trickle the first moment I saw her now bursting inside of me like a gushing pipe.

"Vi Harris, falling for you has been a series of single, solitary important moments. That moment I first saw your tears as we sat together in the dog park. That moment Bruce knocked you over on your porch and you just giggled. God that giggle." I close my eyes against the tears. "That moment when I watched you holding my niece," I croak and then open my eyes to meet her glossy gaze again. "That moment you kissed my scars.

"Vi, you're afraid that you're unlovable? Bunny, I fell in love with you the day we ran in the rain outside your flat. There was a moment when you looked at me and saw into my soul. Christ, Vi, I love you. I've never felt more alive than right this moment, loving you."

A sob erupts from Leslie, but I refuse to look down. I refuse to break my blurred, tunnelled, suspended view of the woman I love.

"It's 11:11, Vi. And my final wish—my final request to the universe—is that I will save all my wishes for you. Every one of them. Belongs to you."

Her face crumples as she cups her mouth to hide her sobs. Gareth motions with his head for her to come to me, and my grasp instantly releases the mic. I rush around the table and slip between the couples still frozen in shock on the dance floor. She bustles over to me, her blonde hair and red dress flowing freely behind her.

Just as we connect in the middle…

Just as my trembling hands take hers in mine…

Just before she presses her lips to my mouth…

…I look into her glittering blue eyes and realise that all of those wishes I made before trying to change my past would have kept me from this beautiful reality standing in my arms.

"I love you, Vi. I've loved you for so many moments, and I don't want to waste any more time not telling you."

She silences me with her lips. Her perfect fucking lips that kiss me harder than I've ever been kissed in my entire life. Or maybe it's just a normal, everyday kiss but feels different now that everything's changed.

She pulls away, reverently wiping away the tears falling freely down my face. "You could have just said all that earlier, you know. Who knew My Hayden had such a flare for the dramatics?" she giggles.

God, she fucking giggles.

She kisses me once more before pulling back and whispering in my ear the words that I'm finally ready to hear. The words that have the ability to bring me to my knees and raise me right back up.

"I love you, too," she says with a sigh.

I smirk.

She loves me, too.

Barca or Bust

Vi

Hayden's voice is loud and demanding. "You are out of your fucking mind if you think you're going to Barcelona with Vi. I mean it, Booker. This isn't even up for discussion."

"Who the bloody hell do you think you are coming into my house and barking orders around like you're the boss? You're right lucky I'm not skinning you alive, you fucking wanker," Booker snaps aggressively.

"Wanker?! Real mature." Hayden looks at me, his grey eyes going wide like he's asking me to step in and help.

I just continue hiding my smile.

"Yes, Hayden, you're a fucking wanker. An old fucking wanker, and you're not going to Barcelona with my sister," Booker barks again.

"Booker, you would tread very carefully if you knew what was good for you." Hayden's tone is low and menacing.

"You think I'm afraid of you? What a laugh. Oi, are you going to thump me with your calculator? You fucking nerdling."

"Oh, go kick a fucking ball. I'm taking Vi to Barcelona!"

"Think I should break this up?" I murmur under my breath to Gareth all the while attempting to hide my giggles.

His eyes alight with amusement. "Hell no! This is the best fare-well I've had so far! Let's see who draws blood first!"

We're seated at the end of the long wooden table in our dad's kitchen, our chins propped on our hands as Hayden and Booker stand nose-to-nose at the opposite end. They are in the middle of an epic battle of wills for who gets to go with me to Barcelona. I silently cast my vote for Hayden because I feel badly about inviting Booker originally. And damn if I wouldn't love a proper holiday with Hayden. It's been three weeks since Theo and Leslie's wedding, and I am more smitten with him now than I was before. There's just something about a man uttering the words "I love you" while he swats your arse lov-ingly that makes everything inside of you get all warm and gooey.

"This is actually my house," Dad finally interjects after he's nearly licked the plate of Swedish pancakes I made special for Hayden's visit today.

I hop up when I hear Bruce barking at the door. I let him in from his trot outside. He's panting ferociously with huge strings of slobber hanging from his mouth.

"Good dog," I say as he nosedives for his water bowl. I squat down beside him and whisper in his ear, "What do you think of him, Bruce? Do you approve of my bulldozing bruiser of a boyfriend?"

Hayden's heated gaze glances over at me, clearly no longer listen-ing to my brother who's still chirping away. He watches me with that possessive sense of ownership that he gets every time he hears me call him my boyfriend. It would be quite funny, actually, if it wasn't so bloody sexy.

Bruce suddenly laps at my face happily, soaking my entire cheek.

"I'll take that as a yes," I cringe and give him a hearty pet. Then I stride over to the sink to rinse my face, feeling Hayden's eyes still on me.

"Vi, are there any more?" Tanner asks, carrying his plate over to the counter and picking around the dishes that are scattered everywhere.

"They're going with Gareth to Manchester. Sorry, Tan."

He frowns. "Gareth gets everything."

"Because he's a bloody suck up," Camden mumbles as he washes his hands in the sink next to me.

This makes me smile. Today was Hayden's first proper Harris Sunday dinner. Gareth definitely helped clear the path for his re-entry into the Harris Brothers' good graces. Whatever Hayden said to him at Leslie's wedding must have won him over because I've never seen him react to a boyfriend this well. Although, after this Barcelona battle, I'm quite certain Hayden will be on Booker's shit list for quite some time.

"Oi!" I finally interrupt after having listened to this dreary argument for nearly twenty minutes. "Enough. I've brought presents for everyone, and I'd like to hand them out now if you'd all shut your gobs."

Hayden and Booker's heads both swerve to me. Booker's expression looks positively psychotic. Hayden's face is flushed red with anger, but his eyes heat with a different kind of fire when they land on mine. God, he's beautiful. And he loves me.

I bite my lip to conceal my happy smile and stand to grab the large bag I brought over with me. Everyone settles into their chairs, Booker still mumbling obscenities under his breath.

"So," I start as Hayden takes the heavy bag from me and sets it on the table. I grin at him as he subtly pats my bottom behind the table. "This is something kind of special that took some organising for me to get it all perfect. As you all know, I went through Mum's cookbooks and basically claimed that entire box as my own. But what you don't know is that there weren't only cookbooks in there."

I pull out a wooden keepsake box from the bag. My fingers smooth over the glossy wood and I smile recalling the night I helped Hayden stain them. I sit down on my stool and eye all of my brothers meaningfully.

"There was a special book inside the box that wasn't full of recipes. It was full of poems. Poems that Mum wrote. I couldn't read them for the longest time because most of them were written in Swedish, and it took some time for me to get them all translated. That's what I've done here.

"They vary in topics, but the majority of them are the feelings she had during motherhood. There are also several poems about you, Dad." I look at my dad, whose eyes are rimmed as he stares at the box in my hands.

"I'm not sure I can read them," he croaks and turns away, a faraway look in his eyes. Gareth eyes me seriously, speaking straight to my soul with unspoken words about the guilt our father must still carry with him.

Grabbing the box, I walk over to him and touch his shoulder. He shudders with emotion, and Tanner and Camden's eyes go wide in confusion.

"You must read these, Dad. The way Mum spoke of you…" My voice cracks. "We should all be so lucky to find what you two had."

Dad looks up at me, his dark blue eyes glistening with unshed tears as his chin betrays him with a mighty wobble. "I should have done better."

I smile sadly. "You did what you could. Mum saw that, and she loved you fiercely. Even in the end. You'll see." I push the box toward him.

"Oh, Vi," he croaks and pulls me down into a fearsome hug. "Thank you, my darling."

"You're welcome, Dad. I love you."

"I love you, too." He releases me and I see Camden's eyes red around the edges.

"Chin up, men. Let me pass all these out. I have specific boxes for each of you because Mum also saved some crafts that we made for her as kids. Booker, your craft is quite awful, really. You were only one and clearly untalented."

Camden and Tanner howl with laughter. Dad places a reassuring hand on Booker's shoulder all the while his belly is shaking with silent laughs. Booker frowns in annoyance. "That's just cruel, Vi."

I giggle and wink at him while peeking inside each box and handing them out appropriately. I carry Gareth's over to him and notice that he's been eerily silent this entire time.

"There's a special one about friendship in there," I say quietly to Gareth. "It's called 'Friendship Has No Age,' and I'm pretty certain it's entirely about you."

Gareth's jaw clenches and he nods woodenly. They all open their boxes and begin shuffling through the poems that I had printed on special paper.

"Dad, I put the Swedish originals in your box."

"These boxes are beautiful," Booker says, rubbing his fingers over the underside of the lid where Hayden burned an inscription on the interior:

Vilma Nyström Harris ~ Wife, Mother, Friend
An original soul always in our hearts.

"Hayden made them, actually. All of them. And he did the inscription."

Booker's eyes lift to mine and then flash over to Hayden. He frowns and croaks seriously, "Thank you."

"Don't mention it," Hayden replies and they exchange subtle nods. A peace offering, perhaps?

"You're still not going to Barcelona," Booker grumbles and everyone bursts into a mix of annoyed groans and laughs.

I smile at my dad and four brothers, who really aren't all that dissimilar to Hayden in the end. Perhaps that's how he was able to somewhat win them over. The whole lot of them are all brooding, protective, over-bearing, but completely devoted men, who care for you absolutely once you've breached their hardened hearts. I hope someday my brothers can all have their own love stories.

And Hayden has breached my heart for good. My soul sings as I stare at the crinkles around his eyes as he laughs along with the other important men in my life. Those crinkles are the sexiest road map to his happy place. A happy place that includes me.

It's dark outside by the time Hayden and I leave my dad's. We head straight to my flat where we've been spending most of our nights. We do hang out with Theo, Leslie, and Marisa some, but the majority of our time is spent here. I think Theo and Leslie have been appreciating their alone time, especially since Marisa seems to be growing out of her fussy stage.

"Your brothers aren't as tough as they seem," Hayden says as we flop onto the wicker sunbed in my rooftop garden. The Chinese lanterns glow down on us, casting a warm, cosy ambience in the dark London night. "They're all bark, no bite. Booker is lucky that I was feeling generous today."

I grin as he tucks into my back and spoons me in that delicious way that turns him into the cosiest Hayden blanket. "Booker gets Barca, you get South of France," I say with a comfortable sigh.

"Mmm, you could have told me you have some time off before I got in a huge battle with your brother, you know," he moans and nips my neck playfully. "But I forgive you because I get to see you in a bikini."

Cupping his head to my neck, I reply while he nuzzles, "Actually, I was thinking we could try one of those nude beaches."

His nibbling halts instantly. "Like fucking hell we will."

I bite my lip to stop my giggle. "It's all the rage there, and I do hate tan lines."

"Look at me." Hayden yanks my shoulder back so I'm lying on my back and he's holding himself over me. All good humour completely evaporates from his face. "I can't tell if you're joking."

My eyes twinkle with mirth. "It's a bucket list thing I've always wanted to try."

"You're out of your mind, Vi, if you think I'm going to allow my girlfriend to traipse around a beach bloody naked for all of France to ogle. Christ, I'm actually getting fucking pissed off just thinking about it." He runs a hand through his hair as my heart does little summersaults over his girlfriend title for me.

It never gets old.

I clasp his face in my hands. "Maybe we can work out an alternative."

"What is that?" he groans, his grey eyes watching me in agony. "I swear you like to torture me."

I lift my brows. "Rooftop sex is also a bucket list item for me."

His eyes instantly heat with desire. The possessive side of him has to look around first, clearly noting that we're the tallest building for miles and there's no way anyone can see us.

"Or, we could always go back to the cinema." He shoots me a salacious grin. "I know my Bunny loves the movies."

His head drops down to my neck, and he places kisses down every square inch, all the way to the tops of my breasts. He bites down on my tank top strap and pulls it down my shoulder. His breath stutters with excitement when he sees I've ditched my bra for the night.

"Fuck...Kissing you will never get old."

"You know what never gets old for me?" I ask and my breath catches as he cups the weight of my breast in his warm, rough hand.

"Hmm?" he asks as his lips continue their assault along my collarbone.

"Hearing you call me your girlfriend."

"Mmm, you like that do you?" he asks, thumbing my hardened nipple. "I got one better for you."

"What's that?" I suck in a quick breath and let out a sudden moan as his lips wrap around my nipple and he bites down softly.

"Future wife." His head pops up to watch my reaction.

My hooded eyes turn wide. My expression drops in shock.

"I…I…" I stammer.

"I'm not asking yet, Bunny. Believe me. When I ask, you'll know. But I want you to know that's where I see this going with us. I told you I wasn't going to waste any more moments with you, so that's why I'm telling you now." His face is deathly serious. His grey eyes warm pools of open sincerity.

"Okay then," I croak in a lame reply.

The corner of his mouth tilts up proudly. "So eloquent with words." His wicked laughter vibrates against my chest as he touches his lips to mine in a sweet, final gesture.

I wrap my legs around him and inspiration strikes. I blurt against his mouth, "Maybe you should move in here?" He pulls back and looks down at me with a distinct twinkle in his eyes. "Bruce and I have discussed it already, and we both think it's a good idea. I'll have to warn you about Bruce Hugs, though. They can be rather intense. But it'd be nice to have you around to fix things, take him for a walkies, water the plants."

"Water the plants?" he asks, pursing his lips to conceal a laugh.

"Yes. I think you'd do a proper job," I state with a deadpan expression. "Vincent is such a flirt, you know."

"Vincent *is* a flirt," he grumbles. "I think I can water your plants. And I can take care of your dog. And I can take care of these precious assets," he purrs, squeezing my bum. "It's time for more."

I touch the crinkles around his eyes affectionately all the while knowing that 11:11 has come and gone and he's stayed right here with me…in the moment…in the present…talking about our future.

"That's exactly what I had in mind."

$\mathcal{V}i$

A Few Weeks Later

"These floor-to-ceiling windows won't do, Bunny." Hayden harrumphs as he drops a moving box down inside my en suite bathroom and ruffles his dirty blonde hair.

"What do you mean?" I ask, crossing my arms and leaning against the doorframe to ogle my man in his worn jeans and a fitted white T-shirt and making my thighs clench like a sex addict.

My eyes shift to his hands as he adjusts the brown leather cuffs on his wrists. I suddenly forget about his physical beauty and see the inner beauty that drew me to him in the first place. Hayden wears the cuffs to hide his past from the world, but he'll take them off when he's with me. He'll expose his scars, let them breathe, give them light because, when we're together, there is no darkness anymore.

Hayden gestures to the huge, sweeping window beside my large claw-foot bathtub. "I don't need all of bloody London constantly seeing you naked, Vi. Now that we're living together, I think I deserve to have you all to myself." His grey eyes pierce me with a possessive glower that doesn't intimidate me.

It excites me.

"Correct me if I'm wrong, but didn't you fill a bubble bath for me at one point in time?"

His face remains firm. "That was different."

"Different how?" I ask with a laugh.

"I was wooing you." He looks away, clearly embarrassing himself with his response.

I burst into a full-on belly laugh at his expression and shake my head. "Relax, Hayden. We're in the tallest building around for miles."

He gives me a pouty look. "I don't care."

I have mercy on him. "It has a reflective exterior."

"What do you mean?" His voice is different now. So are his eyes.

I bite my lip and then nervously reply, "I mean London only sees London out there." I gesture toward the matching windows in my bedroom behind me. "What we see in here is only for us."

Hayden's possessive glower turns into molten lava as he strides toward me.

I inhale sharply. "Don't we have more boxes to bring up?" I nearly pant. God, I'm pathetic. I'm a pathetic, wanton floozy, but it's My Hayden…and he loves me.

"Stuff the boxes. They can wait," he murmurs, seizing my mouth with his and anchoring one arm tightly behind my back as he walks me across my bedroom until I'm pressed up against the smooth, cold glass.

The contrast of his warm lips working magic against mine is heady, and I cry out when his hand firmly squeezes my arse. Without hesitation, he spins me around to look out the window.

Oh, God, I really hope he…

Slap.

That.

The Ripple Effect

Hayden
One Year Later

Standing outside of BOLT FROM THE BLUE CAKES AND looking at Vi's excited eyes as she awaits our mystery cake box delivery is an experience in and of itself. I don't think I ever fully realised how much she loved this place the first time she brought me here. Her blue eyes are bright and twinkling. Her feet won't stop shifting in anticipation. And she keeps beaming back at me like this is the best day of her life.

I grin.

Bunny has no clue what's coming.

That's my new favourite thing about her.

Life with Vi isn't perfect. Far from it. But with her beside me, I don't feel broken. I feel whole. I feel loved, and I feel fucking fantastic because she makes me strong enough to know I *can* feel. Being angry, or sad, or upset doesn't feel like the end when you have that one person in your life who wants to love you through it, no questions asked. She fucking loves me. Any ripple in our relationship is a wave we ride together. Our ripples make us, *us*. Loving her doesn't make me weak. In fact, I've never felt stronger than when I hold her in my arms.

Vi Harris makes me desperate to continue moving forward. She stirs the ripples.

And now it's time to make a fucking splash.

The man behind the window returns with a very different type of box from the normal cardboard ones the mystery cupcakes usually come in. I imagine Vi is frowning in confusion, but I can't see her expression…

…because I'm kneeling behind her.

She grabs the box and turns around with a puzzled look as she finds me on the ground.

"Hayden?" she croaks, her mouth a strange mixture between an O and a smile.

"Vi," I start with a sneaky smirk. "Open the box."

She purses her lips together and, with trembling hands, she strokes the lid that I've spent months hand-carving to make utterly perfect. It's a baroque-style design, espresso-stained, wooden keepsake box. I carved in a round clock face with the time 11:11 engraved on the lid. Right next to it, there's a tiny ornate genie lamp representing a wish. She swallows hard and opens the lid.

Inside are two cupcakes with a ring box nestled in between.

She smiles.

She cries.

She giggles.

She makes me the happiest fucking man on Earth and I haven't even asked her the question yet.

"Vilma Harris, will you marry me?"

My words are simple because I've spent the last year of our life together never wasting a single moment. If she looks beautiful, I tell her. If I love something she makes, I tell her. If she makes me spitting mad, I tell her. And then we fight. Hard.

And then we make up. Harder.

God, do we make up.

Vi makes me feel everything all the time. But mostly, she makes me feel *alive*.

"Yes," she answers with a squealing sigh. "God, Hayden, yes! I will so marry you!"

She falls down on top of me, knocking me off balance and taking us both down as she goes. She giggles and smashes her lips to mine while clutching the box awkwardly between us. The corner digs into my chest. The pain is noticeable, but it's also perfect because it's not perfect. It's exactly how life ought to be.

"Happy birthday, Bunny," I murmur against her eager lips.

"I officially love my birthday." She grins and kisses me sweetly once more.

I smile at her and reply, "It's about time."

36

A Perfect Moment

Vi

"**B**UGGER. BUGGER. BUGGER!"

My hands tremble as I watch the pee creep over the white box. First, one pink line shows up, then a second.

"I thought these were supposed to take a minute," I murmur to myself as two pink lines glare back at me.

I shakily replace the cap over the pee stick and double-check the instructions. Two lines mean "pregnant," so this means it's *positive*?

I put the stick down on the counter and stand to pull up my knickers. I smooth down my black sequined party dress and pause as panic takes over me.

I'm pregnant.

We just got engaged!

Tonight's our engagement party.

This was not part of the plan.

As I wash my hands, I glance at the stick again to be sure my mind isn't playing tricks on me. There are still two taunting pink lines in the little box. Two glaringly obvious streaks having a laugh at the irony of this situation.

I stare at myself in the mirror. My blonde curls are perfectly loose. My makeup light and flawless. My blue eyes bright and vibrant.

But for some reason, I look different now. I no longer look like the responsible one. I can barely see the twenty-six-year-old daughter whom my father still leans on for support, or the girl who sets an example for her man-whorish brothers. Even though they are all grown men, they still need someone to guide them. To be their rock. Their one constant.

The person looking back at me with a baby inside of her isn't the Vi Harris I've strived so hard to be.

And what about Hayden? I couldn't even believe he proposed to me two weeks ago. Sure, we'd been living together for a year, but Hayden is…Hayden. It took everything he had just to tell me he loves me. We had a rocky go of it and he spooks so easily. This could mess everything up.

Twirling on my Louboutin heel, I march over to the large floor-to-ceiling window in my bathroom and stare out over East London. I shiver as I recall the day that Hayden drew me a bath and dangled sex in front of me like a cupcake. Why didn't we practice abstinence? Why did I have to be so horny around him *all the time*?

A knock on the bathroom door makes my heart leap into my throat. I grab the pregnancy test, swivelling my head around frantically for a place to stash it. I decide my cleavage is safest, so I shove it down the front of my dress and reply with a forcibly cool voice, "Who is it?"

"It's Booker."

I exhale with relief that it's not Hayden or worse, one of my other overbearing, loudmouth, pushy brothers whom I can't seem to get shot of. Booker will take it easy on me. It's Booker.

I open the door.

Booker's brow is furrowed. "Hayden sent me in to see what's taking you so long. He's running Bruce downstairs to the neighbour's flat and said the guests will be here any minute."

"Come in. Quickly." I yank him inside, pressing my back against the closed door. "I really mucked it up this time, Book."

He pulls a face. "You? Vi, you're perfect. You're the only perfect one in our mess of a family."

I smile at his naivety. Then I want to cry as shame casts over me. I've prided myself on setting a good example for all four of my brothers. It wasn't a choice I made. It was a reflex. I've always been their moral compass and their voice of reason. Now that their careers are taking off, it's my job to ensure they don't turn into self-important arseholes. That is my job in life. They need me to be the stable one!

Now I've screwed everything up and got it all horribly out of order. I'm a hypocrite. An irresponsible imposter.

Booker's face falls when my chin begins to wobble. "Vi, what is it? What have you done?"

Just when I begin to pull the pregnancy test out from my cleavage, I'm shoved forward by the door and topple over into Booker's arms.

"Oi, you bloody twats! You nearly knocked Vi over." Booker helps right me, and I turn to see our eldest brother, Gareth, towering over us with his dark, intimidating glower. Shoving each other playfully behind him are Camden and Tanner.

"What's wrong?" Gareth's deep voice demands as he takes in my face that's probably starting to turn red and blotchy by now.

"Nothing!" I reply quickly and force a smile.

Camden shoves past Gareth and marches right up to me. "It's not nothing, Vi. What's happened? Did Hayden call off the engagement?"

"On the night of your fucking engagement party? I'll kill him!" Tanner shouts and turns to storm out of the doorway only to be fishhooked under the arm by Gareth.

"Let's give Vi a chance to tell us what's going on before we go thump her fiancé." Gareth turns and, as if on cue, my brothers file in, close the door behind them, and line up next to each other. I could laugh when they all cross their arms over their chests, awaiting my response, but I'm too busy trying not to cry.

"I think I'm going to be sick," I rasp, clutching my belly and turning away from the Harris Brother Death Stare. "I don't want to tell you guys yet."

"Just tell us, Vi," Booker adds gently, giving me a soft look that he probably means to be calming, but it only sets me off further.

"We're not leaving until you do," Camden adds with a firm tone.

"Why can't I have a moment of peace?" I exclaim completely irrationally. "Why can't I have one tiny thought to myself? A secret even! I'm a grown-up. Hayden and I are living together. Why do you four think you can bulldoze your way in here and bark orders?" I place my hands on my hips and stamp my foot in a familiar, scolding fashion that I've used so frequently throughout our lives.

"You're our sister, Vi," Tanner replies, scratching his blonde beard like he's completely confused that I'd even question this situation. "We want you to be happy. It's more important than pretty much anything."

I blink and tears slide down my face.

"That looks like the opposite of happy," Tanner adds flatly.

I burst out with a garbled laugh and swipe at my cheeks.

"What is it?" Booker asks again.

"Out with it," Gareth adds.

I exhale and decide to stare at the floor while I say it. "I'm pregnant."

I'm met with silence, so I look up to see their reactions.

Camden's face looks contorted. "With whose baby?"

"Hayden's!" I bellow. "Who else's would it be?"

His shoulders drop as he runs a hand through his hair. "Well, fuck! I don't know. You're crying, so I thought maybe you were up the duff with another bloke's kid and that's what has you all emotional."

"No," I groan.

"Then why are you crying?" Booker asks.

I drop down onto the edge of the tub with my head in my hands, unable to look at them. "I'm supposed to be setting a good example for you four. You'd all be the biggest sluts in football if I didn't thump you from time to time. Now I'm being a hypocrite and getting things horribly out of order. This isn't the way things are supposed to be."

"Vi," they all reply in unison.

I look up when Gareth approaches me. He's got his big brother face on again. The one that almost always makes me cry. His dark-rimmed hazel eyes pierce through me with so much emotion, I feel my knees begin to tremble.

He sits down beside me. "We weren't supposed to lose our mum before you guys started primary school either, but we did."

The entire room freezes with Gareth's change of subject.

Gareth doesn't talk about Mum.

He did with me after Hayden and I broke up, but never again.

He wraps his arm around my shoulders and adds, "Life is full of things that aren't supposed to be, Vi. We weren't supposed to watch Dad spiral into a deep depression for years after Mum passed, but we did. I wasn't supposed to sign with Dad's old team, but I did. If things happened the way they were supposed to, life would be pretty boring. Doesn't mean it can't turn out great in the end."

"Just look at how great the two of us are," Tanner adds, throwing his arm around Camden that ripple effects into Cam shoving Tanner into Booker.

An amused glint in all of their eyes as they playfully shove each other brings a genuine smile to my face, and even to Mr. Serious, Gareth.

"Yeah, you guys aren't all bad I guess," I reply and Gareth nudges me with his shoulder.

"I know you're going to make a wonderful mum," he says softly.

My happy smile falters. "How do you know?"

"Because you were wonderful to all of us."

"I'm going to puke," Tanner bellows, smashing the moment to smithereens. "This is way too much emotion. I survived for about two minutes, but I've reached my quota. Can I leave? There's a guest out there with my name on her." I roll my eyes and he adds, "No, literally, she has the name Tanner tattooed on her wrist. It has to be destiny."

Camden shoves Tanner out the door, and Booker comes over to give me a gentle hug. He whispers, "Congratulations," before following in the twins' wake.

"Can I give you one piece of advice?" Gareth asks from the doorway while I stand by the sink touching up my makeup. "Tell Hayden tonight. I have a feeling it'll only make this evening all the more special for him."

He shoots me a wink and departs, leaving me alone with nerves swirling in my belly. I have the perfect time in mind.

I feel a moment of guilt when I stride out of my bedroom to see that the party is in full swing already. I say my hellos to some friends from work and accept their hugs of congratulations, but I can feel Hayden's eyes on me the entire time. It's like a warm heat blowing against my skin. I look over my shoulder and we connect eyes. He tries to have a silent conversation with me from across the room, but my father is doing his best to keep Hayden's attention focused on him. Our eye contact breaks when the lift dings and I look over to see Frank, Theo, Leslie, and a newly-walking Baby Marisa stride in.

"Vi!" Leslie shouts from across the room and releases Marisa's hand to run over to me. Her auburn hair accents her yellow jumpsuit perfectly—a look only an artist like Leslie can pull off.

Dating brothers has really brought us closer, and I'm chuffed at the idea of calling her my sister.

"You look gorgeous! You're practically glowing!"

"Thanks, you too!" My eyes drop to Theo and Marisa slowly walking toward us. I instantly crouch down as Marisa clumsily runs into my arms. I hug her, wondering if Hayden and I will be welcoming a baby before our wedding, too.

She begins babbling something in my ear, so I pull back to look into her gorgeous green eyes.

"You want to see Uncle Hay?" I ask and her smile grows.

"Right behind you, Squirt." I look up from my crouched position with her to see Hayden smiling down at us. The crinkles around his eyes are utter perfection as he scoops Marisa up off the floor and begins buzzing her cheeks with his lips to her gleeful delight.

He looks every bit the image of hot daddy perfection. Smart, grey suit, perfectly styled blonde locks, and grey eyes that exude complete love and adoration.

Watching him hold Marissa, my hands develop a mind of their own.I find myself clutching my small belly. There's not even physical evidence of the pregnancy yet, but I feel it. I feel our baby inside of me. And I feel it when I watch him. It's an amazing sensation to have something bigger than myself happening right here.

Hayden's smile falls as he looks at me. "Bunny, what is it? What's the matter?"

It's then that I realise tears are falling down my face. "Nothing. I'm fine. I'm just...I'm just..."

Hayden passes Marisa over to Theo and cups my face in his hands. "What's going on? And don't tell me it's nothing. All four of your brothers are looking at me like they want to hug me or kill me, which isn't that unusual. But on a night like tonight, it seems off-putting."

I feel everyone's eyes on me when I look at Hayden with a wobbly smile. "I have something to tell you."

"What is it?" He strokes his fingers down my cheeks and tucks a strand of hair behind my ear.

I glance over at the clock. "Not yet. It's too early. I'll tell you soon, though. I promise."

"Bunny," he mock scolds.

I lick my lips and grab his lapels, yanking him down to my

mouth and kissing him with all the goodness I feel inside of me as an act of reassurance. He responds in earnest, his hands letting go of my face as he wraps his arms around me and crushes me against his body.

"If this is what you have to tell me, perhaps we should go to the roof," he murmurs against my lips. "I'd be all yours up there."

"Meet me up there at eleven," I rasp, my voice betraying my level of control. "No matter who you're talking to, break away and meet me up there."

He smiles. "Anything for you, Bunny."

The rest of the night is a blur of engagement congratulations, happy hugs, bubbling cocktails, and one hilarious ginger entertaining us all.

"All right you footie boys, listen up." I have to cover my mouth as Frank stands in front of my four brothers and addresses them with all the flourishes that make Frank, Frank.

"My name is Frank McElroy. Not Frankenstein, not Carrot Top, not Cock-Block, and most definitely not Frank and Beans." Frank pauses to shoot Leslie and Finley a menacing glower. "You boys are beautiful and so are Finny and Lezzie, so it's not your fault you listened to them. You were likely thinking with the wrong heads." He points down at their groins, and they all shift uncomfortably. "So I'll let it pass this time. But if you fuck with me again, I'll have to show you how a real man scores a goal."

My brothers burst out laughing, and Tanner throws his arm around Frank's narrow shoulders. "You're bloody fantastic, Frank. You have to go clubbing with us sometime."

Frank's brow arches. "Would you consider a gay club?"

Tanner strokes his beard and nods. "If it means more laughs with you, I'd give it a go."

Frank's eyes alight as he exclaims, "This is the best night of my life!"

My laughs are interrupted by two hands that snake around

my waist from behind. Hayden's voice whispers in my ear, "It's not quite eleven yet, but I can't go another second without touching you, Bunny. Let's go up to the garden. Please. They won't even know we're gone."

"From our own engagement party?"

He nips at my ear. "Our party. Our rules."

He twines his fingers with mine and pulls me through the flat and out onto the large balcony. A couple of our friends are standing out here with cocktails, but they must read between the lines because they smile politely and head inside.

"Coast is clear. Let's go." Hayden nods toward the ladder that leads up to the roof. After my ascent up the ladder, I stretch out on the lounger, kicking my shoes off and wiggling my scrunched toes. Hayden finishes his climb and looks at me with a dark heat in his eyes as he slips off his suit coat.

"Did I tell you, you look absolutely beautiful tonight?" he asks, slowly walking toward me. He deposits his jacket on a nearby chair and begins unbuttoning the snaps around his wrists.

"I don't think you got around to it."

He shakes his head, standing at my feet now. "A moment lost. Allow me to make up for it." He shoots me a dirty smirk, making his sentiments known.

Instead of replying, I squint at the watch on his wrist.

"Why are you so concerned about the time, Vi?" Hayden asks. His sleeves are rolled up on his forearms and he's popped a couple of buttons on his chest already. "Did you hire a plane to fly by with an 'I want to shag Hayden Clarke' banner? Because I don't need a sign to grant you that wish."

I giggle and shake my head, leaning back and propping myself on my elbows. "You are a cheeky sod, you know that?"

He smiles and nods proudly while slowly uncrossing my feet and spreading my legs. I gasp as he begins crawling up the length of my body, my dress hitching up the closer he gets. We've had sexy time on this sun lounger more times than I can remember. My reactions are a reflex at this point.

Hayden kisses me sweetly on my shoulder. "I'm your cheeky sod. We're just moments away from making it official." He begins nibbling my neck and sending goosebumps all over my body.

"It's going to take more than a few moments to plan a wedding, Hayden," I reply breathlessly as I squeeze my legs around his hips.

"You know what I mean." He pauses to look me in the eyes. "This is it, Vi. We're engaged. This is our life. Together. Just the two of us and nothing else." His gaze falls to my lips before he closes the space between us and kisses me, pressing his tongue into my mouth so deeply that I forget all common sense for a moment.

He moves his hand from my waist and reaches between us, slowly stroking up my inner thigh. When he slides past the band on my knickers and pushes one finger inside of me, I swear I could come within seconds from the combination of his words and his touch.

He breaks our kiss and presses his forehead to mine. "And when times get tough—when I feel myself slipping—we come up here. A place no one can touch us. No one can bother us. No one can tell us that we aren't enough for each other."

His breath is heavy, and he kisses me with a sudden sense of desperation, mimicking the motion with his fingers between my legs. I reach for his belt buckle, brushing over his hard bulge and frantically tearing away at his clothes, aching to feel his words inside of me. He grabs the centre of my knickers and pulls until they split open. Within seconds, he's thrust so deep inside of me, I don't know where Hayden ends and I begin.

Because we are one.

We are each other's landing point and catching ground, moving together in a perfect synchronisation that feels as if we were truly made for each other. As he rocks inside of me and kisses me savagely, I squeeze his face with all my might and kiss him so hard, I swear I'll be leaving a permanent love bite behind.

"Hayden." I cry out his name as my climax comes much too soon. I don't want this to be over. I want to stay lost in this world with him inside of me. Where there are no problems around us, no sudden changes coming. I don't want to think about the time on his watch or what I need to tell him. I just want to stay us. "I love you."

He pulls his face back so he can look at me. His grey eyes are wide and wonderful. "I love you, too, Bunny. You are all I'll ever need in this life. As long as I have you, I'll always have a reason to live. I can't wait to make you my wife."

His words are brutal and beautiful. They hold so much meaning because of his past. Because of what he's been through. Because of what he almost gave up. My Hayden.

Tears well in my eyes and I pull him close, kissing him with everything I have left inside of me, riding out the aftershocks of my orgasm until he comes himself.

When we're finished, he pulls out and drops onto his side, rolling me over to face him. I press my forehead to his and stare at his mouth because I'm sure if I look at his eyes, he'll see. He'll see it all.

I grab his hand and pull it up between us, glancing at the time. As if the universe is having a laugh right now, the time ticks over to 11:11. I say with a sigh, "I'm pregnant."

Hayden goes still. His breathing stops. His arms grow tense. I swear, even the world stops spinning.

This is what I feared. This kind of change would spook him. And after all the beautiful words he said about just the two of us up here, an ominous feeling creeps over me.

The time 11:11 became something wonderful we've shared over the past year. We'd catch 11:11 on a clock and make a wish about our life together. Of course we still remember the loved ones we lost. But instead of wishing for the past to change like he used to, we wish for them to continue inspiring our future.

"Hayden," I say, looking up into his expressionless eyes. "Say something."

His face continues to remain frozen.

"Was that a wish or a fact?" he asks, finally breaking the silence.

I bite my lip and sit up, pulling away from his stiffness. "What do you want it to be?"

He sits up, too, his pants pulled backed up but his buckle still undone. His hand reaches toward my chest, and he pulls the white plastic stick out from between my cleavage. It must have worked its way up. I'd completely forgotten it was there.

He holds it in his hand, examining the test window carefully. The corner of his mouth creeps up into something resembling a smile.

"You know how we always make a wish together at 11:11?" he asks.

"Yes," I whisper, terrified of what might come next.

"This was one of my wishes."

"It was?" I gasp and he nods. "But you never said. Everything we've talked about up here has always been about us alone. Travelling, seeing the world, maybe opening up our own business, buying a house. We've never talked about kids, Hayden."

He swallows. "I didn't want to spook you."

"Spook me?" I bark. "I thought this would spook you!"

"Look, Vi." He shifts closer to me and holds my hand in his, pulling it up to his mouth to kiss it softly. "I have a fucked-up past. That's very well known. But I don't want you to be afraid of what kind of dad I'll be. I'll always be here for you and our baby. You were all the reason I needed to live before. Now, that fact has been doubled. Maybe tripled. Twins are hereditary, right?"

He glances up and his grey eyes look so wide and innocent, I can't wrap my head around what he's saying.

"Bunny, say something."

I shake my head.

"You don't have to be scared."

I start laughing. "I'm not scared, Hayden. I'm bloody thrilled." I throw myself into his arms, and he falls backwards on the lounger, holding me to him as I drop thousands of kisses all over his cheeks and lips. I giggle. "This is the best engagement party ever."

"This right here really is a perfect moment." He chuckles softly against my lips right before kissing me fiercely.

I inwardly sigh as I realise that all of my wishes are actually coming true.

EPILOGUE
That's a NO to Tannerita

Hayden

"TANNERITA HAS A NICE RING TO IT, HAYDEN!" TANNER STATES loudly before he wraps his lips around a pink balloon and blows into it with all his might. He yanks it out of his mouth and begins knotting it, refusing to take his eyes off of me. "You think I'm joking, but I'm not. My niece deserves a name that is going to make her stand out in a crowd."

I shake my head as I lay out the charcuterie board on the coffee table in the sitting room.

Gareth's deep voice cuts in next. "Tannerita is a name that will get our niece thumped in primary school. It's bad enough she's related to you by blood, Tanner. Let's give the girl a chance to survive with a normal name."

Camden chortles at Tanner's crestfallen face. "Broseph, you truly are a righteous idiot."

Tanner is completely undeterred. "You just aren't a big picture thinker like me, Cam. But it's not your fault I took all the brainpower in the womb."

"Brainpower?" Booker interjects with a twisted look of judgement on his face. "That's the word you're going to use when bragging about your intelligence?"

Tanner releases an unknotted balloon that sputters around the room as he darts for Booker. In a flash, Tanner has Booker on the floor in some sort of human pretzel-looking thing that has his arse pressed right against Booker's horrified face.

It's not pretty.

Bruce pounces over top of them, barking up a storm while we all watch in gleeful delight. At the same moment, the lift door pings open with a seven-month pregnant Vi standing inside.

We all freeze in shock as she takes in the scene. "What in the—"

"You're early," I stammer, dropping the box of crackers and rushing toward her like I can somehow conceal the surprise baby shower we're setting up behind us. "You weren't supposed to be home until five."

She places her hand on my shoulder and looks around me to take in our flat that basically looks like a messy pink explosion went off all over. "What is this?"

"A baby shower," Gareth replies with a prideful smile. Normally, Gareth is very stoic and unfeeling, but I've noticed that he's been different these last few months. Almost as if he's softening a bit. With him living in Manchester, I often wonder what goes on in his life up there that none of us ever see.

Camden adds, "Hayden said you are having one with your mates, but it's just a girls' thing. We think that's rubbish, so we told him we were having one for you as well."

I shake my head, my eyes warming affectionally on my surprised fiancée. "I couldn't talk them out of it. Your brothers are pushy sods."

My words are said in jest, but in reality, I love the annoying arseholes nearly as much as I love their sister. The Harris Brothers are difficult not to love. They are unapologetically themselves all of the time. And, even though they are in each other's business and constantly rowing about something because they are all so uniquely different, they listen to each other and care about what the other thinks. There's a tremendous amount of honour and respect between these four men. And they have welcomed me into the fold despite my background and my rocky moments with their sister. Now, I'm able to thoroughly enjoy watching the antics they get themselves into on a regular basis and give them a knowing smile that says, "I told you so."

"This is incredible," Vi says, her face lighting up as she takes in the enormous baby banners taped to the windows that overlook the balcony. There are a few game stations set up and pink balloons strewn about the floor that Bruce is constantly nipping at like they are his own personal dog toys. And of course, a special display of cupcakes from her favourite shop.

Finally, Tanner releases Booker from his grip, and Booker stands up while sheepishly adding, "Are you pleased, Vi?"

Vi lets out a garbled laugh, tears I hadn't even seen forming spilling out of her eyes as she ruffles Booker's hair. "I'm completely overcome."

"That's good, right?" Tanner stupidly asks.

Vi nods. "Yes. It's very good, Tan."

The next couple of hours include lots of laughs, lots of happy tears, and some ridiculous baby games that Tanner and Camden found on Google—one of which includes sampling various un-marked jars of baby food and identifying the flavours, and scoring each other to see how many we get correct. Tanner makes our stom-achs churn when he greedily polishes off the remaining jars of food like he hasn't eaten in weeks.

"What?" he baulks from his seat bedside Gareth, who's staring daggers at him. "These mashed peas are healthy!"

"God, you're embarrassing," Camden says running his hand through his hair as he bows his head in shame.

"Who am I embarrassing you in front of?" Tanner mumbles around a tiny baby spoon in his mouth. "It's just us here!"

"Your soul should be embarrassed of you," Booker replies, his nose wrinkled in disgust.

Tanner simply shrugs and grabs another jar while Vi laughs and laughs. It's a beautiful sight. But it's her brothers who laugh the hard-est when Vi decides to claim her cupcake in the middle of some baby quiz we're all taking.

Without a word, Vi sets down her quiz, leans forward from her spot on the sofa, and grabs a pink frosted cupcake from the tray. She brings it to her mouth and delicately swipes her tongue across the top, careful not to actually eat any of the frosting. She sets it back in its place on the coffee table and resumes her quiz.

We all stare at her in confused silence.

She finally looks up. "What?"

Camden is the first to reply. "Mind telling us what that was all about?" he asks, gesturing to the recently saliva'd cupcake.

She shrugs her shoulders and replies, "Bacon Sandwich Rule. I licked it, so it's mine."

Her brothers burst into laughter while I quizzically watch them all high-five their sister. It appears to be a student-surpassed-the-teacher moment that I certainly don't need the details of to enjoy the show of them all laughing together.

After her brothers leave, I sit at the kitchen island drinking in my beautiful fiancée who's currently standing at the kitchen sink, barefoot and pregnant. Call me barbaric, but there's something really fucking perfect about the image in front of me, and I'm not ashamed to admit it.

"Are you ready for your final surprise?" I ask, interrupting Vi as she hums a tune to herself.

"There's more?" she asks, drying her hands and turning to look at me.

I nod and lift up a white scarf of hers with a waggle of my brows. Her eyes darken because this is the same scarf that we've used in the bedroom.

"Head out of the gutter, Bunny," I state, my voice deep and warning.

"That's impossible around you, Hayden." She smiles and rubs her belly. "These pregnancy hormones don't help matters."

I shake my head and walk over to her. "I really hope those don't go away after the baby is born because I quite like my horny fiancée."

She giggles and takes the scarf from my hand as her eyes drop down to my groin. I hurry to blindfold her before I forget about the surprise and end up taking her to bed instead.

Carefully, I walk her toward the balcony doorway that we concealed behind a giant banner so she wouldn't see the surprise until after her brothers left. I pull down the obnoxious "It's a Girl" sign and slide open the door, gently helping her walk over the threshold and into the night air.

"Stay right here," I whisper, leaving her to hustle around Bruce and over to the outlets to plug in all the lighting.

"What are you doing?" Vi asks, her head turning into the new lighting shining through the scarf.

"Patience, Bunny. Patience."

She harrumphs with annoyance. "If you're drawing me a bubble bath with the intention of leaving me to relax by myself, I'm going to be a very rude rabbit."

I chuckle at her tone. "It'd be hard to draw you a bath on the balcony."

"Semantics," she murmurs, crossing her arms over her chest.

Once I am certain that everything is perfect, I stride over to stand behind her. My hands wrap around her waist, stroking her swollen belly. The belly that I've loved watching grow these last several months.

Vi's head falls back onto my chest, her hands wrapping around mine as I feel our daughter kicking inside of her. It's still as miraculous today as it was the first time I felt her move. Since then, there hasn't been a single day that's gone by that I don't touch the life we created together.

I rest my chin on Vi's shoulder and inhale the scent of her hair while murmuring in her ear, "I know you've hated not being able to climb the ladder to sit up on our rooftop garden lately, so I had Vincent help me bring your oasis down here."

I untie the scarf and step aside to watch her take in the newly decorated balcony that went from a simple slab with a few lounge chairs to a stunning secret garden. Vincent brought in some small trees in planters that are elaborately decorated with twinkle lights. There are loads of colourful pots overflowing with blooms that are situated around the lounge chairs. In the corners are large leafy arrangements that have a tropical feel to them. On the ground, he added some fuzzy rugs and throw pillows that bring more colour and cosiness to the entire area.

"This is my baby present to you, Vi," I state as her jaw remains dropped and her eyes wide.

"I thought you hate Vincent," she says with disbelief in her voice.

I smile and shrug. "The bloke knows what he's doing."

She giggles and shakes her head. "I've been trying to tell you that."

She walks into the space, rubbing her belly as she takes everything in with wide, sparkling eyes. Off in the corner is a smaller version of the round sofa bed she has on the roof with a small running water fountain beside it.

She turns on her heel and places her hands on her hips. "Get over here, Hayden," she says with a sternness to her voice that I quite like.

I quirk my brow and do as I'm told because there's not much that can keep me away from her these days. I slide my hands around her waist as she twines her fingers behind my neck and presses her firm belly against me.

She pulls my forehead down to hers and says with a happy sigh, "You never cease to amaze me."

"Are you joking?" I reply with a haughty tone. "You're the one doing all the work." I rub the sides of her belly affectionately, impressed by how she manages it all the way she does.

"It's not work to love you, Hayden," she replies, her voice trembling with emotion. "It's like breathing."

My heart thunders inside my chest because surly she can see that she's given me my life back. Surely she knows that having her with me makes life worth living.

"Marry me, Vi." I repeat the words I said to her several months ago.

She laughs. "You know I will, Hayden."

"Marry me now," I urge.

"Who will officiate?"

"Bruce."

"He does have a way with words." She giggles and then cups my cheeks to look into my eyes. "Marrying you will be the happiest day of my life, Hayden. But not now. We're having a baby and life is so wonderful. We are perfect right now. Let's just enjoy it and worry about the wedding business later."

I purse my lips together and drop a chaste kiss on her forehead. "As long as your forever is mine, Bunny."

She looks up at me with a smile. "Always, My Hayden. Always."

The End…

…but not really, because the Harris Brothers Series is now live and complete! Dive into the first brother's book, *Challenge*, or read on for a sneak peek!

Bonus Epilogue Alert!

If you've read the Harris Brothers Series, you may be interested in a bonus Hayden and Vi epilogue available to all of my newsletter subscribers. This epilogue has never been published before, so before you sign up, be warned there may be some Harris Brothers spoilers.

Sign up here and we'll email you the link!
www.subscribepage.com/StrengthBonusEpilogue
Prepare for some swoons!!!

MORE BOOKS BY AMY DAWS

The London Lovers:
Becoming Us: Finley's Story Part 1
A Broken Us: Finley's Story Part 2
London Bound: Leslie's Story
Not the One: Reyna's Story

A London Lovers/Harris Brothers Crossover Novel:
Strength: Vi Harris & Hayden's Story

The Harris Brothers Series:
A spin-off series featuring the football-playing Harris Brothers!
Challenge: Camden's Story
Endurance: Tanner's Story
Keeper: Booker's Story
Surrender & Dominate: Gareth's Duet

Wait With Me: A Tire Shop Rom Com

Pointe of Breaking: A College Dance Standalone by Amy Daws &
Sarah J. Pepper

Chasing Hope: A Mother's True Story of Loss, Heartbreak,
and the Miracle of Hope

For all retailer purchase links, visit:
www.amydawsauthor.com

ACKNOWLEDGEMENTS

First and foremost, I need to acknowledge those who suffer from depression and suicidal tendencies every day and continue to get up and live life and feel all the damn feels. Living in Hayden's world for this book was an extremely eye-opening experience, and I was honoured to tell his story. I felt every word I wrote, and he became a real person to me in so many ways. Please continue to feel, continue to screw up, continue to be mad, happy, sad…everything! Feeling anything, good or bad, is living. And know that despite what your depression tells you, there's always someone who loves you. Let yourself feel that!

A huge, tremendous thanks to my editor, Stephanie Rose. We made a splash together, girl! Seriously, you've been there for me since the creation of Hayden in *London Bound* and I twittered-stalked you into submission. Let's keep rippling books together.

My London Lovers Fan Group. You ladies have been calling Hayden yours for ages, and I hope I did him justice for you. Thanks for the constant network of cheerleading and support and for tolerating all the times I want to puke from anxiety or make out with you from excitement. You guys embrace my crazy and make this job freaking fun as hell.

I had a great team of beta readers early on with this book whom I can't begin to thank enough. Hayden upped the stakes and I needed you all. Jaci no K, thanks for the early chapter reading/cheerleading. My favourite British perv, Belinda, for your countless replies to my British queries. Your dirty mind speaks to my soul. To my PA, Julia for doing everything I ask…I can't wait to ask you to strip sometime just to see if you'll do it. To my timeline-keeper-extraordinaire, Kelly.

To Sayjil, Erin, Abby, Nikki Groom, and Kirsty for sharing their very personal thoughts and feelings on this story with me. Thank you! And thanks to my proofers, Mercedes, Becca, Jen, Donna, and Teresa!

Hubby, you tolerate me and my emotions and my multiple neurosis like a champ. Thanks for holding down the home front and making the yummy lasagna.

To my mini-me, Lolo. You were fussy Baby Marisa, honey, and I loved you through every colicky minute of it. Let's keep wearing our shades when we walk into school every day. We look cool doing it, and I love seeing your carefree personality shine brighter than the sun. All my wishes are yours, baby.

To my six sky babies. Thank you for existing. It was a dark and horrid time when I was losing you all, but I was alive. I made it through, and now my good days outnumber my bad. I hope you all can see that. I hope I make you proud, because all of you make me proud every day.

MORE ABOUT THE AUTHOR

Amy Daws is an Amazon Top 25 bestselling author of sexy, contemporary romance novels. She enjoys writing love stories that take place in America, as well as across the pond in England; especially about those footy-playing Harris Brothers of hers. When Amy is not writing in a tire shop waiting room, she's watching Gilmore Girls, or singing karaoke in the living room with her daughter while Daddy smiles awkwardly from a distance.

For more of Amy's work, visit: www.amydawsauthor.com or check out the links below.

www.facebook.com/amydawsauthor
www.twitter.com/amydawsauthor
instagram.com/amydawsauthor

44947251R00197

Printed in Poland
by Amazon Fulfillment
Poland Sp. z o.o., Wrocław